Amerikana

AMERIKANA

a Novel

DANIEL HRYHORCZUK

GOLDEN BOUGH

Golden Bough, LLC
33 N. Dearborn Street, Suite 504
Chicago, Illinois 60602-3958
goldenboughpress@gmail.com

This is a work of fiction. All of the characters, organizations, and events portrayed in this novel are either products of the author's imagination or are used fictionally.

ISBN: 978-1-7352400-0-8
LCCN: 2020911086

Cover and interior design by Alan Pranke

I dedicate this novel
to my parents, Dmytro and Natalia,
and to America, which welcomed them

CHAPTER 1

Duck Key

The image seared his retinas like a solar eclipse. She was facing him, wet and naked, on the blacktop of the Overseas Highway, her lissome body illuminated by the dawn. With the ocean behind her, she looked like Aphrodite rising from the sea. Mark slammed the brakes on his Trans Am and screeched to a stop just inches from her hips. Surprisingly, she made no effort to step away. *She must be in a trance or tripping or just plain crazy,* he figured.

The young woman leaned over his car. Her wet, golden hair draped her breasts. Drops of salt water dripped from her hair and evaporated on his hot red hood. Mark stiffened. She stared right through him with her belladonna eyes to the expanse of blue water and white bridges that stretched behind him toward Key West. Her naked innocence disarmed him. The crescendo of an outboard motor sent a flock of terns flying across the ribbon of highway from the ocean to the flats. The startled birds splattered his windshield. The ruckus snapped her out of her trance. Mark looked to the east and saw a high-speed inflatable dinghy racing toward the shore. A sleek white yacht was anchored a mile offshore. The driver of a LandShark beer truck bound for Key West slowed his 18-wheeler and lowered his window to ask if they needed help. Before Mark could reply, the woman opened his passenger-side door and jumped into the bucket seat.

"Drive!" she pleaded. "Just drive!"

Mark floored the pedal of his vintage 403 V-8. He had bought the car on eBay from the estate of the Road Kill drummer, who had recently died of a heroin overdose. The band's name was still on the trunk in fire-orange paint. He had picked up the car in Key West the day before, partied at Sloppy Joe's till closing, and slept in the car for a few hours before hitting the road. As the rpms climbed, he saw a man from the dinghy jump ashore and recede in his rearview mirror. *Christ! What am I doing? Saving her or kidnapping her?*

"Who are you?" he asked when they had passed mile marker 64.

No answer.

He turned his head and saw her forehead pressed against the dashboard. She had a trident tattoo on the back of her shoulder. He nudged her thigh, but no response. Her knees were scraped from climbing out of the water onto the rocky shore. A red-eyed screwworm buzzed down from behind the visor and landed on her raw wound. Mark squashed the stowaway with the back of his hand. His slap elicited only a groan from his ungrateful passenger. He grabbed a beach towel from the back seat and covered her naked torso. *Damned invasive species.*

He continued driving north toward Islamorada.

* * * *

Senator Julian Rich Jr. pulled the Egyptian cotton sheets over his eyes to block the first rays of sunlight, which were streaming through the porthole. A trophy head of a wild boar stared back at him from across the room. The rhythmic swaying of the waves, rather than rocking him back to sleep, was making him nauseous. The overnight cruise aboard the 256-foot yacht *Kalinka* had been everything his host had promised.

He was still dreaming of the temptress that Victor Ivanovich had solicited for him last night. They had discussed art and politics over iced vodka and caviar long after the midnight fishing charters had passed the *Kalinka* on their return to the Duck Key Marina. The aspiring young sculptress from Ukraine had flipped through her portfolio on her cell phone, allowing him to edge closer and invade her personal space. Her work was transformative. She could turn any base metal into art.

During dinner she had been flirtatious yet coy, and she withdrew whenever he tried to touch her leg under the table. Victor Ivanovich had said things to her in Russian that had made her blush, but she simply laughed them off. As a nightcap, Ivanovich and Rich toasted to raising Cain. She had disengaged from the conversation and stared blindly into space, as if her soul had left her body to float over the dark, open sea. She no longer flinched when the senator ran his hand up her thigh. *The vodka has finally numbed her inhibitions*, he reasoned. When the conversation turned to evangelism, the host had tapped on his Sky Moon wristwatch, indicating that it was time for bed.

The senator led her by the wrist into his stateroom. She offered no resistance as he undressed her and laid her spread-eagle on the bed. *Men succumb to beauty, and women succumb to power*, he convinced himself as he ravished her. When he withdrew, she suddenly awoke like a child with night terrors. Her demeanor changed from docile to feral. She screamed, scratched, and pummeled him with her fists. He vaguely recalled trying to enter her again before blacking out.

Rebreathing the air beneath the sheets was making him even more nauseous. He turned his head over the side of the bed and vomited the remains of the evening into the silver ice bucket. Bits of regurgitated caviar floated in the melted ice. He looked at himself in the ceiling mirror and pinched his love handles. *Not too bad for a thirty-eight-year-old man.* He pressed the call button on the side of the bed.

A steward in a crisp white nautical uniform stepped into the stateroom. A cord spiraled into his ear. "Good morning, Senator. Shall I bring you your breakfast in bed?"

"Bring me the girl that I had last night," the senator demanded. "Invite her to join me for a *petit déjeuner.*"

"I'm afraid that won't be possible," the steward replied. "She disembarked before daybreak."

"Left the boat?" The senator sat up in bed. "I may have been a bit rough with her, but I could tell that she wanted it." Her evening dress and underwear were crumpled on the floor. "Have the dinghy bring her back. Tell her that I'll find a place for her sculpture on Meridian Hill."

"You'll need to speak with Victor Ivanovich directly. May I suggest that you join him on the upper deck for breakfast?"

The senator stepped out of the soiled bed onto the teak floor. He staggered toward the head, blaming his lack of balance on the vodka and rocking caused by the waves. The bathroom fixtures, including the toilet, were plated in gold. His teeth ached as he probed them with his toothbrush. He looked in the mirror and admired the scratch marks on his torso. *Quite a night,* he complimented himself. *A wildcat like that needs to be tamed.* He donned a blue polo shirt and white skipper shorts for a JFK nautical look and twirled the lock on his forehead that had made him the heartthrob of housewives throughout small-town America. *I think I might be able to stomach a Bloody Mary for breakfast. The hair of the dog is the surest cure for a Saint Patrick's Day hangover.*

* * * *

Victor Ivanovich sipped his double espresso and paged through the runaway's passport. Tanya Bereza was well traveled for the age of twenty-four: entry and exit stamps from Paris, Venice, Prague, Munich . . . and an O-1 visa for entry into the United States. He had sponsored her visit to the United States through his nongovernmental organization in Prague. She had won the Most Promising Young Artist award at the Biennale Arte in Venice with her pièce de résistance, a kinetic sculpture of the Heavenly Hundred, the heroes who had given their lives during Ukraine's Revolution of Dignity five years before. The metal sculpture was comprised of a five-meter-high spiral of a hundred doves that were ascending to heaven from a circle of burning barricades. The birds were torch-cut from titanium and were held together with tensile wire. The sculpture vibrated harmonically with the slightest breeze and gave the illusion of birds in flight.

He took another sip of his espresso and wondered whether the young sculptress realized whom she was dealing with. Among the mafia bosses in *vor v zakone*, "thieves-in-law," Ivanovich was regarded as first among equals. Given his origins in Krasnoyarsk, his bloody rise to power in the Siberian underworld, and his bravado in slaying the Amur tiger that had killed his godson, his thieves-in-law had given him the nickname Sayan. In Siberian legend, Sayan was a mythical warrior whom the ancient gods made the Lord of the Taiga. Still, even he was not above taking orders from the Kremlin. The Kremlin's pact with the oligarchs was simple: obey and feast from the public trough or defy them and die. The Main Directorate asked only two things of him: to help them rewrite history and to enable them to manipulate the word of God.

The US Senate had recently passed a bipartisan resolution commemorating the fifth anniversary of Ukraine's Revolution of Dignity and honoring the memory of the protestors who were killed. The US chapter of the International Association of Art invited Bereza to display her work in the nation's capital. The Kremlin seized the opportunity to reopen the debate about the legitimacy of the popular uprising that had ousted Ukraine's pro-Russian government. It instructed Ivanovich to sponsor her way with a travel grant from his Institute for Democratic Progress. The public display of her controversial sculpture would expose the fault lines in congressional support for Ukraine. Those congressmen who were still on the fence would be targeted for lobbying and soft-power intervention.

His institute funded a reception for her at the Ukrainian embassy in Georgetown and invited friends and foes alike. At the reception, Ivanovich introduced her to Senator Julian Rich Jr. The senator was as captivated by her beauty as he was by her art. After his third glass of champagne, he decided he had to have her. He even promised to use his influence to see whether her sculpture might be displayed at a park in the nation's capital. Ivanovich had suggested that they discuss the details during an overnight cruise on his yacht in the Keys.

The cruise had embarked as planned, but Victor Ivanovich quickly concluded that she was not as promiscuous as he had been led to believe. Despite plying her with vodka, there had been no chemistry between her and the senator. To complete his *kompromat*, Victor Ivanovich had been forced to spike her drink with devil's breath. Dmitri, his young chief of security, had mastered the clandestine use of poisons during his training at the *Federalnaya Sluzhba Bezopasnosti* (FSB) *Kamera* laboratory. He kept an assortment of exotic vials of liquids and powders locked in his ostrich-leather briefcase. Most were undetectable during routine toxicology studies. Most of the toxicants in his briefcase could only be analyzed by a handful of specialized laboratories in the world, and then they needed to know what they were looking for.

Victor Ivanovich tucked Bereza's passport and cell phone into his pocket and scanned the horizon with his binoculars. He surveyed the marina—nothing but captains and mates provisioning their fishing boats for the morning charters. He refocused on the Overseas Highway and squinted. He spotted her getting into a red car at the point where the bridge entered Duck Key. From this distance he couldn't make out the plates. He was able to read *LandShark* on the side of a beer truck that had stopped in the southbound lane just before the car sped away in the direction of Islamorada. A minute more and Dmitri would have caught her. He was returning to the yacht without their captive. He wondered how, after being drugged with devil's breath, she could have managed to elude his guards, swim to shore, and hail a random car. He would need to study the footage on the security cameras, especially the one hidden in the mirror over the senator's bed.

Victor Ivanovich finished his espresso as the dinghy pulled up to the stern. Dmitri scampered up the ladder to deliver the bad news.

"She jumped into a car before I could catch her," Dmitri said in Russian.

"Were you able to identify the car?" the boss asked.

"An old model American car, red with a black emblem on the hood."

"Plates?"

"Florida, but it was too far away to read the details," Dmitri replied.

"There was an inscription on the trunk, but I couldn't make it out."

"Get back to the marina. Send one car north and you take another car south. I saw them converse with the driver of a LandShark beer truck. It should be easy to locate. Perhaps the driver can give us some information about the getaway car."

Dmitri jumped back into the dinghy and sped away just as Senator Rich ascended to the upper deck.

Victor Ivanovich stood up from the table and kissed his VIP guest thrice on the cheeks. "Good morning, Julian. I trust you had an entertaining night?" Ivanovich was dressed in a French blue-and-white sailor jersey that had been custom-tailored to his muscular frame. His salt-and-pepper beard was meticulously groomed. An Orthodox cross pendant hung from his neck on a thick, gold chain. His gunmetal-gray eyes remained trained on his guest.

Senator Rich pulled down the neck of his polo shirt to reveal the scratches on his chest. "Wilder than you can imagine. Your man said she left the boat before daybreak."

A large shadow crossed the wake of the speeding dinghy and disappeared beneath the yacht.

"What was that?" the senator asked.

"Either a shark or a manatee," Victor Ivanovich surmised. "How far do you think it is to shore?" he asked his guest.

"I don't know. A mile?"

"Do you think you could swim it?"

"Why? Are you going to make me walk the plank?" the senator joked halfheartedly.

"I'm afraid our sculptress is quite the *rusalka*," Victor Ivanovich replied. "Our water nymph has swum to shore. I spotted her through my binoculars as she jumped into a northbound car."

The blood left the senator's face. "She's absconded? No one can know that I was on your boat! I'm supposed to be staying with my wife and daughter at Hawks Cay. You have to find her. You have to make sure she stays quiet."

Victor Ivanovich showed no sign of concern. "Dmitri is already on it. I wonder why she felt the need to flee. What did you do to her last night?"

"Nothing. We made love. That's all."

"Perhaps we should study the video together," Victor Ivanovich suggested.

"Video? You filmed me? You son of a bitch! If you try and blackmail me, I'll destroy you."

"Now, now, Julian. The film is simply my insurance policy. I want nothing more than for us to remain good friends and business partners. In addition to my thirty-percent stake in your development in Key Largo, my bank in Cyprus is ready to offer you a fifty-million-dollar no-interest loan. More importantly, let's get back to the business of saving souls."

* * * *

Mark pulled into the entrance of Bud and Mary's Marina and parked his car by the farthermost dock. The early bird pelicans were perched on their posts, waiting for scraps of fish heads and entrails. The landlubbers were starting to gather around their party boats, awaiting the captains' permission to come aboard with their coolers and beer. The first-timers were pacing back and forth, waiting for their Dramamine to kick in. Mark overhead a captain yell, "No bananas on the boat!" Mates in rubber overalls were loading the private charters with buckets of sand and chum and debating whether the offshore winds were favorable for kingfish.

Mark walked past the fiberglass replica of a 417-pound shark that was hung by its tail and went into the tackle shop to ask for help. The staff behind the counter included a grizzled old salt with an ulcer on his nose and a teenager who, given his attempt at a mustache, looked like he was still struggling through puberty. The old salt wore a cap with *Captain* spelled across it. The teenager had a green four-leaf clover left over on his cheek from the night before. At twenty-eight, Mark figured he couldn't relate to either, so he took a chance on the captain. The creases in his face made him look like he'd heard it all.

"Good morning," Mark greeted him.

"You the fella who called about the bone fishing?" the captain asked.

"No, but I could use some advice." Mark tried not to stare at the ulcer on the man's nose. "I have a young lady passed out in my car. I think she's on drugs or something. I want to get her to a doctor."

"OD'd?" The captain picked up a landline phone. "Want me to dial 911?"

Mark wavered. "How far to the nearest emergency room?"

"Mariners Hospital up in Tavernier. About ten miles up the road."

"She seems to be breathing OK. I'll just drive her straight there. I also need to get her some clothes."

The captain eyed him suspiciously. "Back aisle, behind the rods."

Mark nodded and rifled through the back rack.

The captain's attention turned to a father and his two daughters who were booking a half-day trip to the flats. The younger daughter's cell phone was blaring "Cheeseburger in Paradise." She was tugging on her father's pants and demanding a cheeseburger for breakfast.

Mark grabbed a pair of white sweatpants, some flip-flops, and a Bud and Mary's T-shirt that he thought would fit. He pulled out a credit card but then decided to pay with cash. He also ordered two cups of coffee from Kev's Café in the back, black with no sugar.

As Mark returned to his car, he saw the party boat pull away. The mate who had untied the mooring ropes grinned, pointed to his Trans Am, and gave him a thumbs-up. Mark balanced the clothes and coffee against his chest as he struggled to open the driver-side door. It was locked from within. The key was still in the ignition. He looked through the window and saw her curled in the front seat with her knees pressed against her chest. He walked over to the passenger side and knocked on the window.

"Relax," he tried to comfort her. "I'm not going to hurt you. My name's Mark Rider. You jumped into my car back by Duck Key. I brought you some clothes and some coffee."

The young woman studied him for a several seconds before rolling the window halfway down. She grabbed the clothes and motioned for him to turn around. He counted the cars heading north on Highway 1 while she slipped on the sweatpants and T-shirt. After two trucks, a bus, a motorcycle, and eight passenger cars, he turned around and offered her the coffee. She warily took the cup as if suspecting it were poisoned. Her pupils had contracted to reveal irises of cerulean blue.

"Do you need help? A doctor? Can I call someone for you? The police?" he asked.

"No police!"

"Who are you? What's your name?"

"Tanya. Can I use your phone?"

Mark handed her his phone.

She secured the hot coffee between her thighs. She punched in some numbers and waited through the rings as the phone kicked into voice mail. "Mirana, it's me, Tanya. I'm calling from some stranger's phone. I'm coming up to Miami to see you. Don't tell anyone I called."

"Who were you leaving a message for?"

"A friend. In Miami."

"Bear one another's burdens, and so you will fulfill the law of Christ," he remembered from Bible study.

When she handed him his phone, he said, "I overheard you saying you want to go to Miami. I'm heading that way, and I can give you a lift. I just have to make a few short stops on the way."

Tanya nodded and unlocked the doors. Mark eased into the driver's seat.

"You don't have to tell me what happened back there in Duck Key unless you want to," he said.

She cupped the coffee with both hands and took a long sip.

"I'm a journalism student," Mark said. "I'm doing a blog on Americana."

Tanya pulled down the visor to shield her eyes from the morning sun. Her eyes were the color of the sea. "Americana?" she asked.

"I'm trying to find the *real* America. You know, all the uniquely American things—the landmarks, customs, and folklore—that make us who we are. Think of it as cultural heritage. In this age of globalization, we've lost our sense of what it means to be American. The artifacts are all around us, yet most people zoom by without realizing that they're even there. I'll show you an example. One's coming up in just a mile or two: the National Hurricane Monument. We'll just pull in for a few minutes to check it out, if it's OK with you."

Tanya was staring out the side window. She was massaging her temples to soothe a pounding headache. "We can't stop. We need to keep moving. They're going to come after me."

Mark looked in the rearview mirror. "There's no one following us. The only person who saw you jump in my car was the LandShark truck driver, and he was going the other way. The dinghy was too far off to make us out."

"They won't stop till they catch us."

Mark didn't like the sound of *us*. "I just need to stop in for a few minutes to take some photos for a class that I'm taking. I'll stay on the Old Highway as far as she'll take us. I'll park in the back where no one will see us."

Tanya curled up in her seat.

Mark rolled down the window. "We're a nation on speed. Always rushing from one place to another without appreciating what's in between. Life is what happens while we're getting there. High-speed turnpikes, drive-throughs, instant messaging . . . It wasn't always like that. People used to have a sense of place and time. I'm trying to get us to slow down, to appreciate what we have before it's gone. You're . . . you're not from here, are you? I don't want to pry, but I noticed your accent."

"I'm from Ukraine," Tanya replied. "From Ternopil."

"Ukraine? Small world. I live in the Ukrainian Village neighborhood in Chicago. I'm American—I mean Norwegian American—by background; my family's been here for several generations. I see expressions of your culture everywhere in my neighborhood: Byzantine-style churches, Ukrainian museums, bakeries . . . You can even hear Ukrainian spoken on the street. I've learned a little bit about your country from the Ukes who hang out at the local bars like Tuman's and Tryzub."

Mark turned right on Johnston Road onto the Old Highway. "There it is," he pointed out. "The Florida Keys Memorial. Come take a look." He parked his car and opened the passenger-side door for his reluctant tourist.

The monument was composed of native keystone with a frieze that depicted coconut palm trees bending before the force of hurricane winds while the sea lapped at the bottom of their trunks.

"It's also called the Hurricane Monument," Mark said. "It commemorates the Labor Day Hurricane of 1935 that wiped out Islamorada. It had two-hundred-mile-per-hour winds and a twenty-foot storm surge. The cremated remains of about three hundred victims are buried in the crypt in front of the monument. Many were destitute veterans who were building the Overseas Highway. Ernest Hemingway remarked that the wealthy stayed away from the Keys during hurricane season while allowing the veterans to stay. I don't know if he really said that or not. I read it on the internet. Most people drive by without even knowing that this memorial is here."

"How is it that *you* know?" Tanya asked.

"I studied American history at Wheaton College as an undergrad. I then entered the divinity program at the Garrett-Evangelical Theological Seminary at Northwestern."

"You're a minister?"

"No, no, the seminary was my parents' idea. From the day I was born they had me pegged to be a minister. I've read the Bible so many times that I know much of it by heart. But after two semesters in divinity school, I realized I didn't have the calling. I even started to question my faith. My parents begged me to crush my inner rebel, but I wanted to free him. I decided to focus on this world rather than the kingdom of God. I transferred to the master's in journalism program at Medill."

"I take it your parents disapproved."

"They're both ministers, so it was difficult for them, especially for my mom. So now I'm the prodigal son."

"You're lucky to have parents who love you."

Mark thought of Revelation 3:19: "As many as I love, I rebuke and chasten." Their disapproval had hurt him deeply. He had not considered that it might be an expression of love. Still, he had made the decision to break away, and he needed to move on.

Tanya was tracing her fingers along the bent palms and surging waves of the Hurricane Monument.

"I need to blaze my own trail and not just follow in my parents' footsteps," Mark continued. "I'm taking the spring semester off to write my blog on Americana. I actually get a few credit hours in a personal journey elective while I figure out what I want to do with my life. I figured I'd start out in Key West and blog my way across mainland America. I bought this car on eBay. I figure I'll make it as far as Seattle, then sell the car and fly back home."

"Who pays for your blog?"

"Crowdfunding. It brings in enough to cover my gas. Maybe I'll turn it into an app, make a million bucks, and pay off my student loans. I've got about two hundred followers. Most of them are foreigners who are planning to visit the states. Americans just take our country for granted. I'd like to give it some depth, some history, but then again most people don't read past the headlines anymore."

"How did you develop this passion for digging up the past?" Tanya asked.

Mark was surprised that this enigmatic beauty was taking an interest in his personal journey. She was looking at him rather than at the monument. "I was just born curious, I guess. One summer when I was ten, my friend Mary and I found a half-buried wagon wheel in a dried out creek bed behind my parents' farm. We spent most of the summer digging up all kinds of artifacts: an iron axle, bottles of all shapes and sizes, a finger bone with a silver ring." He smiled.

"You seem to remember it fondly," Tanya said.

"I'm recalling that sense of childhood wonder; you know, when the whole world is new and innocent and beguiling."

"Whose do you think it was?" Tanya asked.

"What?"

"The silver ring."

"We never figured it out for sure, so we made up our own stories about whose it was and what had happened. Mary imagined that two lovers had eloped because their parents disapproved of their romance. I said it belonged to a skeleton man who was escaping from the circus. Whoever it was, they didn't make it."

"Neither did they," Tanya said, standing over the crypt that held the cremated remains of the hurricane victims.

They took a moment of silence to commemorate the victims of the Labor Day Hurricane. The monument hid the two from the road. As they stared at the frieze, a black SUV with tinted windows sped north on Highway 1 in pursuit of a vintage red American car.

* * * *

The LandShark beer truck was parked in the lot of the Tarpon Bar and Grill and was easily visible from Highway 1. Dmitri pulled over in his BMW SUV and approached the driver as he was unloading stacked cases of beer. The driver was wearing a Marlins baseball cap.

Dmitri tested his Sunny Isles accent. "Hey, buddy. Was that you talking to some guy who picked up a girl back there in Duck Key?"

"Why? What's it to you?"

"She's my boss's daughter," Dmitri lied. He pulled out a roll of bills. "He's a rich man. He's worried sick about her. Did you stop to talk to them?"

The driver eyed the cash. "Maybe I did, and maybe I didn't."

Dmitri counted out two hundred-dollar bills.

The driver righted his dolly. "Yeah, it was the craziest thing. I saw this naked chick jump into this Trans Am Firebird like her ass was on fire."

"How do you know it was a Firebird?"

"Hell, it's a kick-ass car. It had the black Firebird emblem right there on the hood. Plain as day."

"Did they say where they were going?"

The driver grabbed the cash. "Nope."

"Did you get a look at the plates?

"Florida plates. Probably registered in Key West."

"How do you know?"

"It had Road Kill spray-painted on the trunk. It's a local band."

"What did the guy look like?" Dmitri asked.

The driver put out his hand for another bill.

Dmitri handed him another hundred. "For your baseball cap," he said.

The driver eyed the hundred, then handed over his cap. "Late twenties. Sandy hair. He was wearing a Steve Earle Copperhead Road T-shirt."

"Steve Earle?"

"You don't know Steve Earle? Where you from, man, another planet?"

Dmitri put on the cap and made a mental note of Steve Earle. He then called the driver of the black SUV that was racing north and told him to look for *Road Kill*.

* * * *

"It's been over an hour and still no sign of her," Senator Rich bitched as he paced the upper deck. The sun was starting to burn. "I thought you said your men are professionals. If there's no news by noon, I'll turn it over to my security detail."

"Patience," Victor Ivanovich said. "You don't want to escalate this unnecessarily. Your secret service will want to know everything about her, including why she was on my yacht last night. I don't want them probing into our *business* relationships."

A hundred yards from starboard, a hammerhead shark was thrashing with a manta ray. The churning water was turning red. Smaller fish and sea birds were circling the fray. Victor Ivanovich watched the struggle with detached amusement. A call on his phone interrupted the spectacle.

"I see," he spoke into his phone. "Good work. It almost makes up for your carelessness in letting her escape."

"Well? What is it?" Senator Rich asked.

"Dmitri spoke with the driver of a truck who had seen her get into a car and head north. She's in a red Trans Am Firebird with Florida plates."

"Who's the driver?"

"Still a mystery," Victor Ivanovich replied. "A man in his late twenties with light hair. A Steve Earle fan."

"I can have the local police put out an APB."

Ivanovich bristled at his guest's naivete. "We don't want her talking to the police," he repeated. "Let Dmitri handle it."

Victor Ivanovich called an encrypted overseas number on his cell phone. "Sophia, we have a situation. One of our exchange fellows has slipped away—Tanya Bereza. Dmitri is after her. I have her cell phone, but it's password protected. Tell Gennady to hack into her electronic accounts—email, social media, phone records, bank accounts, medical records. I need to know anything and everything about her. Call me back when you have some usable information. Start with any contacts within two hundred miles of Key West. Once you find them, hack them as well. This rusalka is resourceful. We'll need to cast a wide net to catch her as quickly as possible."

Senator Rich was biting the inside of his cheek imagining the worse scenarios. "You need to find both of them before she talks," he said. "If whoever picked her up knows too much, then do whatever you have to do. Just keep me out of it." He then joined Victor Ivanovich in watching the death throes of the manta ray.

* * * *

Once he reached Key Largo, Mark opted to take the scenic route to the mainland. Rather than continue on Highway 1, he headed north on 905 toward Sound Card Road. The route took them through a habitat of tropical hammock, poisonwood, and gumbo-limbo trees interspersed among mangrove swamps and brackish inlets. A sign on the road read CROCODILE CROSSING.

"We're driving through the Crocodile Lake Wildlife Refuge. One of the few nesting spots in the Keys for the American crocodile. They're a threatened species. Like many other off-the-road spots, this place has an interesting backstory."

"What story is that?" Tanya asked.

He had finally succeeded in piquing her curiosity. "It used to be a missile site during the Cold War. Nuclear-tipped Hercules missiles were stationed here to shoot down Soviet bombers. We came this close to the apocalypse during the Cuban Missile Crisis. It's now been abandoned to the crocodiles and Burmese pythons. I haven't explored it myself, but I've read that it's a creepy place to visit. You need a permit to enter anywhere beyond the butterfly garden. I want to include it in my blog. We can sneak in for peek at the abandoned missile silos. OK if we stop to explore?"

"No!" she replied. "We could get arrested. I have no documentation.

I need to get to Miami."

"OK," Mark sighed. "I'll just save it for another day. How about lunch? There's a little place up the road called Alabama Jack's that's a favorite with the locals." He took her silence as a yes.

He paid the dollar to cross the Monroe County Toll Bridge and pulled over for lunch. Alabama Jack's was built on pilings over a waterway with wobbly floating docks. The sides of the building were painted sky blue with decorative white clouds. Motorcycles were parked in front, and yachts from as far away as Boca Raton were moored on the waterway in back. Mark asked the waitress for an outside table overlooking the mangroves. The waitress was a sun-wrinkled, white-haired woman in an Alabama Jack's tank top who looked like she'd lived through the Hurricane of '35. On their way to the outdoor patio they passed the raw bar that was marked with a rustic sign that portrayed a naked woman covering herself with a towel. They sat down at a wobbly table set with plastic lawn chairs.

"Something to drink?" the waitress asked.

Mark looked at Tanya, but her eyes were busy surveying the clientele.

"I'll have a Kalik beer, and bring the lady an iced tea."

"Know what you want to eat?" the waitress asked.

"We haven't had a chance to look at the menu, but what do you recommend?" he asked her.

"Conch fritters and crab cakes. Sides?"

"What are the favorites?"

"Hopping John rice and sweet potato fries."

Tanya got up from the table to look for a toilet. A gang of middle-aged bikers ogled her as she maneuvered through their tables on her way to the restroom. From the way she rebuffed them with a disinterested glance and swing of her hips, Mark could see she knew how to handle men. He opened his wallet and counted his cash. Before embarking on his extended road trip, he had bought the used car on eBay with some of his student loan money, switched to electronic bill paying, and stopped his mail. He wanted to ramble cross-country unencumbered by his past. His last girlfriend had been a nightmare, and he needed to move on. The waitress brought over a tall glass of iced tea and a cold bottle of beer.

"Mind if I ask you something?" Mark asked.

"Looks like you already got a date, honey," the waitress quipped.

"I'm writing a blog on Americana. I want my followers to know what makes a place authentic. How it got to be the way it is."

"You mean Alabama Jack's? I've been working here close to forty years. Used to be one of four places to eat and drink here on Card Sound back in the sixties—along with Smitty's, Bob and Lou's, and Fred's place. That's until the county started to run us off."

"Why the county?"

"Card Sound used to be a quiet little fishing village. Mostly nice folks lived here, though we had a few who were running from the law and looking for a new start. Back in '75 the county said that anyone who couldn't produce documentation of a valid lease had to leave. They said we were destroying the ecosystem. Now, Alabama Jack's is pretty much all that's left. Check out that sign over there." She pointed to a rusty sign that read DOWNTOWN CARD SOUND. "If you want my opinion, the politicians wanted the land for themselves. They're crooks and thieves, every last one of them. Folks here filed a lawsuit against the county with the help of the University of Florida Conservation Clinic that's been dragging on for years."

Mark watched a great white heron glide over the waterway and settle on a mangrove root on the opposite bank. It stood motionless, waiting for an unsuspecting fish to swim within striking distance. A forty-foot yacht ignored the No WAKE signs as it sped down the waterway. Its radio was blasting Russian techno music. The waves lapped against the pilings and rocked the floating docks. The heron flew off in search of calmer waters.

When Tanya returned from the restroom, the crab cakes and conch fritters were already on the table. She had braided her saltwater-tangled hair into a single long braid. Mark could see the fresh bruises on her arms and neck.

"I wasn't sure which basket you wanted."

Tanya opted for the crab cakes and the sweet potato fries. Mark doused his conch fritters with Alabama Jack's hot sauce. They ate without conversing, and Tanya finished her lunch with a simple "thank you." When the waitress brought the check, Mark gave her thirty dollars even and thanked her for the history lesson.

On their way to the car, they passed the gang of bikers as they were donning their helmets and revving their engines to ride south. Mark had often dreamed about what it would be like to cruise down an open road on a Harley with the wind blowing in his face, the engine rumbling in his ears, and the bike becoming one with the road. Bikers were the diehards who were still focused on the road rather than on the destination.

The bikers were staring at his car. "Kick-ass car," remarked a biker who was wearing a leather jacket lettered with The Insane Unknowns. His red beard reached his belly and looked like it had snared a hundred bugs on the road. "Damned good band too."

"I just picked it up," Mark said. "It used to belong to the drummer."

The biker nodded and spit a wad of Red Man into a Coke can. "Your lady looks mighty fine in that Bud and Mary's T-shirt," he continued. "I used to go party boating at Bud and Mary's with my dad when I was a kid."

Mark found it hard to imagine that this grizzled road warrior was once a child.

"I don't know if the fish were that big or if I was so small, but I thought that my dad and I had found fishing paradise. I think we might stop in there on our way to Key West. See what the afternoon fishing boats bring in."

"Check out the Hurricane Memorial on the Old Highway," Mark suggested. "It's at mile marker 81 just about a mile before Bud and Mary's. It commemorates the hurricane that wiped out Islamorada back in '35."

The biker nodded. "Yeah, I heard of it. Any other tips?"

"Watch out for the screwworms down in Pine Key. They're wiping out the Key deer. Don't let them lay their eggs in any open cuts. The hatching larva will eat you alive."

Tanya sank back into the bucket seat of the Trans Am and stared out the passenger-side window. Mark turned on the radio to fill the silence. Jimmy Buffet was singing something about it being his own damn fault.

About a mile north of Alabama Jack's, a weathered billboard spoiled the landscape. It read FUTURE SITE OF LITTLE CARD SOUND ESTATES. It pictured a man in a blue suit, white shirt, and red tie who was pointing at a future paradise of oceanfront luxury homes. He had the engaging smile of a man who wanted to sell you a Florida swamp. The credits read RICH ENTERPRISES: REBUILDING THE SOUTH, ONE DEVELOPMENT AT A TIME.

Tanya gasped when she saw the sign.

"Sucks, doesn't it?" Mark joined in. "The county evicts the fishermen to save the ecosystem so this asshole can build weekend retreats for millionaires."

Tanya had the same wild stare that she'd had on the highway back in Duck Key.

"Are you OK?" Mark asked. "You look like you've seen a ghost."

"I know that man," Tanya said.

"Who?"

"The man on the billboard."

"How do you know him?" Mark asked.

"He raped me," Tanya replied.

Mark continued driving north toward Florida City without saying a word. The magnitude of her accusation was difficult to fathom. The journalist in him wanted to ask more, but she was clearly in a state of shock.

Senator Julian Rich Jr. was always in the news, if not on the front page then on the second. He was a rising star in the Republican Party. He was the chair of the Foreign Relations Committee. Many had him slated to be a future pick for secretary of state or even vice president. The pundits had predicted that he would easily defeat Mary Walsh, the Tennessee state attorney general and war hero, in the upcoming Republican primary. Walsh's campaign was based on ridding the system of corruption. Julian Rich Jr. was the scion of a respected Tennessee family and future heir of his father's Christian media empire. Before running for office, Rich Jr. had dragged the family business into speculative real estate developments that Walsh alleged were funded by black cash. His murky investors and international holdings posed countless potential conflicts of interest. She demanded that he release his tax returns and make his financial dealings public. He responded by calling her allegations fake news. Tanya's accusation, if true, would create a storm in the American political system greater than the Labor Day Hurricane.

CHAPTER 2

Wynwood

Dmitri completed his ritual FSB workout by the aft deck pool. The aft deck on the *Kalinka* was usually reserved for VIPs. Dmitri wanted the crew to know that he was not only Ivanovich's chief of security but also the second in command. In his turquoise Vilebrequin trunks with the sea turtle logo and the bull tattoo on his chest, he looked the part. The sweat rolled off his lithe body as he finished his last set of one-arm push-ups. He dove into the pool and emerged refreshed and ready for the chase. A steward handed him a towel and a glass of lemon water. Dmitri reclined in a deck chair and fired up his laptop while he waited for Gennady's call.

Dmitri had graduated first in his class from the FSB Academy in 2016. A major general who had seen him perform the role of Trofimov in Chekhov's *The Cherry Orchard* had recruited him from the Satyricon Theatre. With his penetrating eyes and winsome smile, Dmitri could convince you that he was your half brother from your mother's fling with a Russian ambassador. He was the bastard son of the cultural attaché at the Russian embassy in Havana and had spent his formative years in the company of actors, ballet dancers, and *son* musicians before returning to Saint Petersburg for his higher education. He prided himself on mastering not only languages but also phonetics of regional accents within a language. He could switch from *cot* to *caught* in midsentence. His instructors at the academy had nicknamed him the chameleon for his uncanny ability to impersonate. His greatest role was convincing his superiors that he was straight.

Ivanovich's previous chief of security had been killed in a car bombing in Kyiv. Ivanovich blamed the assassination on a rival oligarch. The Ukrainian press blamed the *Glavnoje Razvedyvatel'noje Upravlenije* (GRU), the Russian Main Intelligence Directorate. The rival oligarch alleged that Ivanovich himself had ordered the hit. After several days, the explosion had become old news, and Ivanovich had gone about the business of hiring a new chief of security. The young Dmitri had been rapidly ascending the ranks of the FSB and was up for promotion to colonel. From there he could be assigned to a political post and partake in the trough of the trillions of rubles being siphoned from the public to the private sector.

Ivanovich had lured him away from a career in the FSB with the offer of a faster track to the lavish lifestyle of the Russian oligarchs. Ivanovich had promised Dmitri access to his black-cash investments with their triple-digit returns. More important, he had promised to induct Dmitri into the *vor v zakone* once he proved his worth. While Dmitri's net worth was growing by millions per year, Ivanovich kept him on a short leash lest he become overly ambitious. Ivanovich tossed him handfuls of shares like scraps off the table. Dmitri set up an LLC in Nevis to hide the shares like a dog buries bones.

Reclining poolside and enjoying the sun's warmth, Dmitri checked the balance in his offshore accounts. His net worth was just under €10 million. In the world of oligarchs it was, as the Americans put it, chump change. He realized that at this rate it would take several lifetimes to earn a leading role on the oligarch stage. He coveted the Patek Philippe Sky Moon Tourbillon watch Victor Ivanovich so nonchalantly flashed in his face, and fantasized about removing it from his dead wrist. He knew he was smarter than his superiors. For now he bided his time as an understudy and watched how his boss coerced loyalty from his business associates through a masterful combination of rewards and threats. Those who refused to cooperate would, as Macbeth had said, "fret their hour upon the stage and then be heard no more."

The ring of his phone indicated that Gennady had succeeded in hacking into the water nymph's contacts.

"Yes, Gennady, I'm listening."

"The most likely contact for Bereza is Mirana Garcia on Indian Creek Island in Miami Beach. They were together in Venice last summer. From their texts, they may have been more than just colleagues. I'll text you her contact information. She's currently painting murals in Wynwood. You can google her. She's a celebrity. She has over a million hits."

"You've done well. Now see if you can identify the driver of the car: a red vintage Firebird with Florida plates registered in Key West. Possibly connected to a band called Road Kill."

"I'm on it."

The ping on Dmitri's phone signaled an incoming text with Mirana Garcia's contact information. He entered her into his contacts and googled her name. As Gennady had said, her life story was a matter of public record. Scores of newspaper and magazine articles chronicled her rags-to-riches rise from asylum seeker to prominent Miami artist. She had been born in Santiago, Cuba, and fled to the United States with her dissident parents on an overcrowded fishing boat that capsized off the Florida Keys. The coast guard rescued the sole survivor, an unidentified fifteen-year-old girl who was suffering from posttraumatic amnesia. A Latin recording artist named Luz became her guardian and took her to live in her mansion on Indian Creek Island. One day after returning from a South American tour, Luz discovered that her ward had painted a mural labeled *Medusas* on her patio wall. She took the photo of the disturbing mural and texted it to a *santero* in Little Havana. After viewing the photo, the healer recommended that the child undergo a ritual purging. He also recognized that the mural, with its unusual elongation of the drowning figures, was reminiscent of the work of a child prodigy who had received international acclaim for her UNESCO

Art Miles mural and who had gone missing just a few months before. With the help of Luz's *santero*, Mirana was able to let go of her survivor guilt and regain her memory and identity.

Luz continued to support her ward through high school and college. Mirana dropped out of the University of Miami in her junior year to pursue the exciting underground art scene at Wynwood. Graffiti artists from all over the world were flocking to this urban wasteland to transform the bare warehouse walls into kaleidoscopes of color and social commentary. Mirana's talent soon led to celebrity, and her murals were viewed by over a million people each year. Her Facebook friends included many up-and-coming artists, including the Ukrainian sculptress Tanya Bereza.

Too easy, Dmitri thought. He had hoped for more of a challenge. He went to his cabin and packed his clothes, theater makeup kit, and poisons. He took $10,000 in crisp hundreds from his safe. The dinghy took him to the Duck Key dock, where a black SUV was gassed up and waiting. Dmitri put Mirana's current location into his GPS. He tuned his radio to a Cuban American station in Miami and took the fastest route to Wynwood. A ping on his phone indicated a second incoming text message. It read Car registered to Mark Rider, Chicago, Illinois.

* * * *

Mark drove to Miami up the Dixie Highway rather than the turnpike. Parts of the highway that once connected Chicago to Miami were on the National Register of Historic Places. Al Capone used to take this road back in the Roaring Twenties. The longer drive gave Mark time to reflect.

His only hookup since he had left home had been a nightmare. He had met Lili at the Rainbo Club in Chicago's Ukrainian Village. She asked him if he was with the band when she served him his beer. He was intrigued by the tattoo on her forearm: the face of a winged spirit with a headdress of a black moon. She said her name was short for Lilith, the night demon, and she embraced the image of being a bad girl. He hoped that she would unleash his inner spirit, but she immured him instead. She was a demon that fed on his dreams and sucked the life out of them.

She fed on his infatuation with Americana, and then ridiculed his obsession with abandoned theme parks, historical trivia, and forgotten legends. In the few months they lived together, they drifted further apart until one day their relationship ended not with a bang but with a whimper. The real reason, he admitted to himself, was that they lost what little chemistry they'd had between them. She emasculated him when she accused him of being no better than a missionary in bed. He felt like he no longer excited her. He blamed his lack of prowess on his evangelical upbringing, where if a boy so much as looks at woman, he has already sinned.

His passenger was fast asleep. As they entered Miami, the South Dixie Highway became Biscayne Boulevard. The glass-and-steel skyscrapers of downtown loomed in the distance. It was as if a tectonic shift had raised them out of the art deco landscape of the Magic City. He stopped to admire the blue-and-white ceramics on the facade of the iconic Bacardi Building. The Bacardi Corporation had moved, and the building was now occupied by the YoungArts Foundation. He gently rubbed Tanya's forearm until she opened her eyes.

"We've arrived in Miami. You said that your friend lives in Wynwood. Do you have an address where we might find her?"

"No," Tanya replied. "We'll find Mirana through her art."

Mark had been to Wynwood only once before as a sophomore in college. His dorm mates convinced him to take a jaunt to South Beach for spring break. After three days of beer and bikinis, he'd eschewed the beach and the bars to explore the city. He had strolled down Calle Ocho in the heart of Little Havana with its cigar shops, *cafecitos*, and conga lines. He'd laughed at a Spanish comedy at the Tower Theater and listened to Afro-Cuban jazz at Hoy Como Ayer. The next day, while his buddies were sleeping off their hangovers, he grabbed a taxi to Wynwood to view the graffiti that had transformed the warehouse walls into works of art. He stood and admired Aiko's *The Goddess of Wynwood* while troves of tourists snapped their selfies and rushed to the next point of interest on their tourist map.

Mark figured that the best place to start searching for Mirana was at the Wynwood Walls. He parked the car by the Wynwood Brewing

Company, and they delved down the rabbit hole into the kaleidoscopic world of bubble letters, wild murals, and celebrity tags. The utility posts were pasted with signs that warned about the danger of mosquitoes and the Zika virus. Cryptic messages were inscribed on the sidewalks. He paused at one that read "We swallowed the chaos because we knew we didn't want to be ordinary." *Today is anything but ordinary*, he thought. *I need to swallow the chaos.*

They stopped at a stall peddling posters. The woman behind the counter wore a pink tank top and white shorts that barely concealed a Daliesque full-body tattoo that began at her neck and extended to her ankles. Her back depicted a falling angel. Her chest showed a woman enticing a man with an apple in a lush Garden of Eden. *A graphic retelling of* Paradise Lost, Mark thought. *It must have taken weeks, if not months, to transform this woman into a living canvas. The artist and the woman had become one through the act of creating.* As Mark ogled the tattoo, Tanya came straight to the point.

"Please, can you help me?" she asked. "I am looking for a friend, an artist by the name of Mirana Garcia."

The woman threw a look at Mark as if to ask "why the hell are you staring at me?" She turned to Tanya and said, "Mirana? Sure, everyone knows Mirana. I think she's working on a new mural on Thirtieth Street near First Avenue."

They walked north on Second, past the restaurants, clothing stores, and galleries, and turned the corner on Thirtieth Street. They passed a black SUV with tinted windows that was parked across the street from a makeshift scaffold that abutted a warehouse wall. A woman atop the scaffold was spray-painting a scene of a naked emperor delivering a speech to a crowd of smiley-face zombies who were holding up their cell phones in salute. A small American flag covered the emperor's crotch like a fig leaf.

"Mirana?" Tanya yelled out.

The graffiti artist was wearing headphones. She did not turn around. Tanya climbed up the scaffold. Mark waited at the footing.

"Mirana, it's me, Tanya." Mirana took off her headphones, embraced her, and gave her a kiss on lips.

"Did you get my message that I was coming?" Tanya asked.

"No, I make it a habit of turning off my phone when I'm working," Mirana replied. "What in the world are you doing in Miami? Last time I saw you, we were at the Biennale in Venice."

"We were celebrating my award at that little bar close to Marco Polo's house," Tanya replied. "The bartender and I had to carry you back to the Gritti Palace."

Mirana laughed. "Rum I can handle. Grappa is another story."

"Who's your companion?" Mirana asked, looking down at Mark.

"A kind stranger. We just met this morning. I jumped into his car in Duck Key."

Mirana looked at her quizzically.

Tanya's eyes went dark, as if a storm cloud had blotted out the sun. "I was running away. I was on the yacht of a Russian oligarch—Victor Ivanovich. I . . ."

Mirana knew the look of being lost at sea. "The Russian mobster? Did he hurt you? You can trust me. Tell me what happened."

Tanya retold her story up to the night on the yacht. She stopped midsentence to compose herself.

"Go on."

"During dinner my mind started to wander. It was as if I was drifting over the sea. When I awoke in bed, the senator was on top of me. I must have been drugged. I forced him off me and fled."

"Which senator?" Mirana asked.

"Rich—the one who's on all the billboards. I needed to flee. I have no money, no passport . . ." Tanya began to cry.

Mirana hugged her. "Come home with me. I'll give you some money and some clothes. We'll figure out what to do. What about your friend?"

Tanya looked at the young man who was pacing the brown field like a puppy looking for a place to pee. He stopped for a moment to talk to a man in a Marlins baseball cap.

"He rescued me," Tanya said, "and brought me to you. I need to find some way to repay him."

"I'll invite him over as well," Mirana said. "I'm still staying with my friend Luz on Indian Creek Island. She's away on tour. You can tell me everything over a mojito."

"Not grappa?" Tanya asked.

"No, not grappa," Mirana replied. But this time she wasn't smiling.

* * * *

Mark followed Mirana's Vespa down Biscayne Boulevard and east on the Broad Causeway toward Bal Harbour. They turned right on Harding, then right on Ninety-First Street toward Indian Creek Island. Tanya chose to ride on the motorcycle with Mirana. He already missed her electrifying presence. He recalled the inscription on the sidewalk: *We swallowed the chaos because we knew we didn't want to be ordinary.* He had only known her for a few hours, and what little he knew seemed too fantastic to believe. Oligarchs, senators, street artists . . . there was more happening in the here and now than in all his exhumations of America's past. The dead had lived their lives; it was now time for him to live his. Mirana had been kind enough to invite him over for dinner. He hoped this was just the beginning of his journey and not the end. He was too lost in his thoughts to notice the black SUV that had been tailing them ever since they left Wynwood.

Mirana stopped her Vespa at the guardhouse and motioned to Mark to follow her in. The guards recorded his license and his plates. Most of the thirty-three mansions on the island stood vacant as their owners jet-setted around the globe. Luz's mansion was on the west shore of the island. Eight of the ten bedrooms were vacant. Mirana took Tanya to her room and instructed Mark to have a seat on the patio below her infamous mural. Mark viewed the nightmarish scene of a young girl clinging to an upended boat that was being swallowed by violent waves. Scores of lost souls thrashed in vain amid the whitecaps. Purple jellyfish tentacles clung to their bare, elongated flesh. Mark turned his gaze to the green iguanas with yellow eyes that were staring back at him from the palmettos. A runaway blue macaw looked down from a papaya tree. Mirana brought over a tray with three tall mojitos. She sat down across from him at the wrought iron patio table and offered him the refreshing concoction of crushed mint, muddled limes, sugar, soda, and rum.

Tanya was still in the house, trying on clothes.

"Tanya told me that you rescued her this morning. How much do you know about her?"

"Almost nothing," Mark replied. "I was driving north from Key West, and she was standing naked in the middle of Highway 1. She jumped into my car. She was out of it, as if she was hallucinating." He turned red. "I covered her up with a beach towel and got her some clothes. I bought her lunch. She's much better now."

"Did she tell you what happened to her?"

Mark shifted in his chair. He didn't know how much to share.

"Did she tell you she was assaulted?"

"Yes," Marked admitted. "She said she was drugged and raped . . . by a senator, no less. I offered to call the police, but she refused. She wanted to come see you instead. I hope you can talk her into getting some help."

"What do you know about the man who owns the yacht?"

"Nothing. I did see a yacht anchored about a mile offshore where she got out of the water. A dinghy was racing toward us."

"The yacht belongs to a Russian oligarch by the name of Victor Ivanovich," Mirana said. "He's Russian mafia. He started his career as a petty thief in Krasnoyarsk and worked his way up through the Siberian underworld. When the Soviet Union collapsed, he made his fortune during the fire sale of state assets. He bought and sold oil and gas companies. He then diversified into trafficking women, drugs, and weapons. He's rumored to be selling Soviet-era arms to African nations—everything from AK-47s to attack helicopters. That's just the tip of the iceberg. He's now one of the fifty wealthiest men in the world."

"How is it that you know so much about him?"

"My friend Reya has dealings with his brigadiers in South Florida. They like to brag about their boss after they've had their second hundred grams of vodka."

"So why would Senator Rich risk associating with a Russian oligarch?"

"Ivanovich, like your US robber barons, bought his respectability. He's expanded into legitimate global businesses and donates huge sums of money to charitable foundations and nongovernmental organizations. He even participates in the Davos Economic Forum."

A sleek sports-fishing boat planed around the bend from Indian Creek Lake and came within twenty-five yards of Luz's dock. The wake splashed against the seawall. Mirana breathed a sigh of relief when she saw a gaggle of rowdy teenagers on the stern.

She turned her attention back to Mark. "Who was that man you were talking to in Wynwood? The one with the baseball cap?"

"No one. Just some guy asking me if I knew where he could buy some Steve Earle records."

"Old, young?"

"He looked about my age. Fit. Fancy Rolex."

Mirana called the guardhouse and gave the man's description to security.

"Don't trust strangers. Ivanovich has a long reach. You need to get her as far away from here as possible."

"Me?" Mark asked incredulously.

"She trusts you," Mirana said. "You came into her life randomly. I'll attract too much attention. I'm constantly stalked by the press."

"But where can we go?" Mark protested. "She's afraid of the American authorities. From what you've told me, the Russian mafia is everywhere."

Mirana took a long sip of her mojito. "I told you about my friend Reya. She has insight into the Russian underworld. I suggest that we go see her first thing in the morning. She'll know what to do. Tonight you can stay in our home. Luz is on tour in South America. I'll text her to let her know that you're here."

* * * *

Dmitri followed the Trans Am until it stopped at the guardhouse that stood at the entrance to the bridge that led into Indian Creek Island. He turned right on Bay Drive and pulled out his Nikon with the telephoto lens. He counted two security guards. He could eliminate them easily. More worrisome were the video cameras that recorded the plates and face of every driver that passed through. He checked his location on Google Maps and saw that there was no other entrance onto the island. Several boats were moored on the private docks in Surfside that he could easily highjack. He figured it would be too risky. The multimillion-dollar mansions no doubt had their own security systems. He decided to call his boss.

"Victor Ivanovich, I've located them in Miami. They're staying on Indian Creek Island with a Cuban artist by the name of Mirana Garcia. I've also been able to identify the driver of the Trans Am. The car was bought on eBay a few days ago from the estate of a drummer in a local rock band. It's now registered to a Mark Rider, twenty-eight years old, from Chicago, Illinois. I pulled up his driver's license photo and he's a match. I await your instructions."

Victor Ivanovich paced the deck of the *Kalinka* and mulled over his options. "Have they had any contact with the police?" he asked.

"Not as far as I can tell," Dmitri replied. "I have Gennady monitoring their communications."

"If possible, bring her back alive. She can be a useful bargaining chip in my dealings with the senator."

"And the others?"

"If she's talked to them about me, then liquidate them."

"As you wish, but it may be a difficult kill. There are guards and security cameras everywhere."

"They can't hide there forever," Victor Ivanovich said. "Stake them out. Continue to monitor their communications. Find out everything you can about the driver."

The sun was setting to the west behind Indian Creek. The white bridge leading onto the island was illuminated with floodlights. Dmitri reparked his SUV on Bay Drive next to a pink stucco house that had a FOR RENT sign in the front yard. It offered an unobstructed view of the vehicles that entered and exited over the bridge. He googled "Mark Rider, Chicago, Illinois." The first result that popped up in his search was a blog on Americana. He studied the "About Me" page and then began his virtual tour through America's forgotten past.

* * * *

The Firebird Trans Am exited over the Indian Creek Island Bridge at six in the morning. A cacophony of birds stirred the hot, humid air. Mirana had hoped to slip out of their refuge undetected. The streets were empty except for a lone SUV that flicked its wipers to clear the dew as they passed. Mirana watched the SUV from the back seat as Mark drove away toward Coconut Grove. Fortunately, it remained parked as they sped down Bay Drive toward the Broad Causeway.

Reya's home in Coconut Grove was so overgrown with lush foliage that it was barely visible from the street. The plants exuded allomones. The scent reminded Mark of his first date with Lili at the Lincoln Park Conservatory when they meandered through an Alice in Wonderland world of exotic plants and disappearing Cheshire cats.

Reya opened the door. She invited them to breakfast in her garden. "Espresso? Cappuccino?" she asked.

Mark immediately noticed something odd about her. She was an elegant woman in her fifties who looked like she had spent the early morning hours making sure that her makeup was perfect. Despite her blue mascara and long eyelashes, her chiseled jaw and narrow hips made him unsure of her gender. The two women seemed unfazed by her appearance.

Reya had laid out her Amazon-motif china that was decorated with brilliant blue butterflies. Four fluffy croissants rested on a serving dish in the center of a round patio table that was inlaid with rain-forest quartzite. The croissants were meant to look as if they were casually placed, though Mark could tell that Reya had labored to make them look just so. Sliced papaya, mango, and kiwi were ornamentally arranged on a plate in the shape of a flower. Mark grabbed a croissant and smeared it with orange marmalade as Reya played the role of barista. When she handed him his cappuccino, he thought he saw a heart etched into the milk froth. He gulped it down to make the heart disappear.

The tropical canopy in the garden was so thick that it blocked out the morning sun. Mark felt as if the tendrils of the trees were creeping up on him behind his back. Orchids peeked out of every nook of the garden like fairies. One group of pink orchids in particular caught Mark's attention. Large bees appeared to be feeding on their nectar, yet the bees were completely motionless. Mark walked over to take a closer look.

"I see that you're admiring my bee orchids," Reya observed in a husky voice. She placed her hand on his shoulder. "Lurid, aren't they? The bees, as you can see, are part of the flower. The plant attracts male bees with the promise of love. When the bees attempt to mate, they're naturally frustrated. The pollen is transferred during the act of self-copulation. Unfortunately in this part of the world, we don't have the right species of bees. The orchids must self-pollinate."

Mark forced a smile. "A strange sex life indeed," he said and sat back down at the table. Tanya and Mirana had been whispering something to each other during his awkward exchange with Reya. Mirana turned to Reya. "Thank you for agreeing to see us. We apologize for the early hour, but as I mentioned on the phone, our visit requires us to take certain precautions."

Reya nodded and cocked her head flamboyantly.

"Tanya had an unfortunate . . . encounter . . . on Victor Ivanovich's yacht."

Reya looked at Tanya with apprehension.

"I was *raped*," Tanya interjected. "By an American senator. I panicked and fled."

"Have you contacted the police?" Reya asked.

"No. I was afraid," Tanya replied. "In my country the police work for the politicians."

Reya wiped a bead of sweat off her brow that threatened to run her mascara. She frowned when she saw that Mark had slurped down her creation like an uncouth client. "Another cappuccino?"

"Yes, please," Mark replied. Reya picked up his cup with two fingers and walked back to the kitchen, one foot in front of the other, as if she were walking down a modeling runway.

"Are you sure this is a good idea?" Mark asked Marina and Tanya. "There's something very odd about her."

"Reya has her quirks, but I trust her," Marina replied. "She has an understanding of the Russian underworld. She's what you would call a madam. She provides them with specific types of escorts for clients whose tastes run somewhat outside the ordinary. She owes me a favor. One of her girls, an undocumented Cuban, was beaten half to death and tossed out of a moving car in Wynwood. Luz and I sheltered her on Indian Creek Island until she was healthy enough to flee Miami.

Unfortunately, a few weeks later she was found dead of a heroin overdose in Orlando."

Tanya grimaced at the ending to Mirana's story. Mark couldn't tell if she was angry or afraid. After a moment she took a deep breath and recounted her own story.

"There is a park in my hometown of Ternopil with an exhibit of nameless, life-size silhouettes. They stand faceless, like ghosts warning you to not follow their path into the underworld. Each tells the story of a young person, boys and girls, who left Ukraine for the promise of a better life elsewhere. They obtain illicit visas with the help of human traffickers. Each such visa costs at least ten thousand dollars, depending on where you want to go. When they arrive at their destinations, the traffickers seize their passports and their money. They force them to work as prostitutes. Two of the silhouettes in the park were my classmates. When I learned what happened, I tried to rescue them, but they had simply disappeared. I'm now one of those nameless silhouettes."

"Not yet," Mark said. "You have friends. We'll help you find a way out."

Before Tanya could reply, Reya reappeared with Mark's cappuccino. She had donned a wide-brimmed hat with a plumed feather to shield herself from the scattered rays of the morning sun that were peeking through the leaf canopy. She sat down between Tanya and Mark, gripped their wrists, and drew their faces into the center of the table as if to share a dark secret.

"You were right to come to me," she said. "As Mirana well knows, many of my clients are pigs. They drink vodka for hours, copulate for ten minutes, and then blurt out secrets in their drunken stupor to show my escorts how important they are. The man you mentioned, Victor Ivanovich, controls the Russian Mafia in South Florida. One of his accountants, Yuri Turchin, fled Russia when he realized that all of his predecessors had taken his ledgers to their graves. He sought asylum in the United States and was given a new identity under the FBI's witness protection program. He's rumored to be cooperating with the US Treasury Department in unraveling Ivanovich's worldwide money laundering operations. He might be able to help you."

"I heard of a Yuri Turchin from my chess tutor in Ternopil," Tanya said. "He was a child prodigy in chess. Many had him destined to be a grand master, but he ran afoul of the Communist Party. Then he disappeared from public view. Do you think it could be the same Yuri Turchin?"

Reya raised the brim of her hat and arched an eyebrow. "Based on what I am about to tell you, it very well could be."

"How will we find him if he's in witness . . ." Mark stopped talking.

"What is it?" Reya asked.

At first Mark wasn't certain, but he thought he spied a figure lurking in the dense foliage. The figure was motionless, like the bees on the orchids. His nose and mouth were covered with a bandana. Protective goggles covered his eyes. His hands held a machete. Reya and Mirana were eyeing the intruder as well. When he realized he was discovered, the intruder began to hack the lower fronds of a nearby palmetto tree. With a few brisk strokes, the dead fronds crashed into the undergrowth. He picked up the fronds and pretended to be inspecting them. Reya pressed down on Mark's shoulder to prevent him from displaying any bravado. Instead, she and Mirana walked over to confront the man with the machete. They spoke with him out of earshot then returned to the table. The man dropped the fronds and exited the property.

"Who was that?" Mark asked.

"Just one of my landscapers," Reya replied.

"At this hour of the morning?"

"He said he's inspecting the property for puss caterpillars. There's an infestation in our neighborhood. They look like furry little kittens, but their spines are highly toxic. I've been stung more than once."

"You're sure he wasn't one of Ivanovich's men?" Tanya asked.

"Positive," Mirana replied. "His Cuban was perfect. I haven't heard such a pure dialect since I left Santiago."

Reya scanned her garden to make sure the man was gone. She leaned over to Tanya and whispered a destination in her ear.

* * * *

Dmitri discarded the goggles and bandana that he had stolen from a landscaping truck that was parked a block away. His quarry was cornered. He could easily take her alive. The only question was how many of the others he would need to kill. Each additional victim would complicate the police investigation exponentially. He considered his options and then decided on the mundane. He could kill them quickly with carfentanil and then return to the scene to plant the paraphernalia. The police would likely write it off as just another statistic in the opioid epidemic. He called his boss for permission to proceed. Ivanovich had been up since five.

"If you kill them now, it won't solve the riddle of their rendezvous," Ivanovich responded after listening to Dmitri's plan. "I understand why our rusalka turned to the Cuban. I can see that she's inveigled the driver . . . but why would they turn to this deviant, the queen of the garden of earthly delights?"

"I overheard the queen mention a name," Dmitri replied. "Yuri Turchin."

Dmitri heard a deep sigh on the other end of the line. "I've been searching for him for a long time. He's been hiding where the devil says good night."

Dmitri had heard Ivanovich use that phrase only once before, in an interview that Ivanovich had given to *Russia Today*. The interview was filmed in his dacha in Crimea. Ivanovich sat on a leather chair in his study beneath the trophy heads of endangered species. The interview centered on the ill-fated hunt that had taken the life of Oleg Skylarov, Ivanovich's godson. The young man had asked his godfather to take him on a big game hunt for his twenty-first birthday. A local governor gave them a permit to track and kill an Amur tiger on the taiga. Ivanovich described how against his better judgment, he agreed to take the novice on the hunt for the biggest cat in the world. But the hunters became the hunted. The tiger ambushed the young man in a blizzard and dragged away his body to feed her cubs. Ivanovich followed the tracks to her lair and shot her cubs in front of her eyes. He then killed her, skinned her, and presented the head and skin to his *kum*, a fellow oligarch who had now risen to the post of deputy minister of the interior. When asked by the interviewer for the location of the tiger's lair, Ivanovich had replied, "Where the devil says good night."

"Who is Yuri Turchin?" Dmitri asked.

"Turchin was one of my accountants. He betrayed me. He's a potential witness in an investigation against me. He sought asylum in the United States and is living under an alias. Well, well," he laughed. "We cast a net for a rusalka and catch a talking fish instead."

"What would you have me do?" Dmitri asked.

"If you are given something, take it. Turchin is a bigger threat to me than the rusalka. Follow her until she leads us to him. I've had a one-million-euro open contract on his head. Needless to say, if you're successful, the money is yours."

"And the others?"

"Tell Gennady to keep them under surveillance. First take care of Turchin. Then bring back Bereza. The others will just have to wait their turn."

CHAPTER 3

Beech Mountain

The secret destination that Reya had whispered in Tanya's ear was the Chess Pavilion at North Avenue Beach in Chicago. Yuri Turchin's Achilles' heel was his passion for chess. Brezhnev had awarded him the Medal for Distinguished Labor for winning the World Junior Chess Championship in Birmingham at the age of seventeen. He fell out of favor with the party when he challenged the requirements for obligatory classes on Marxist-Leninist ideology at Moscow State University. He was expelled from the party when he protested the Soviet invasion of Czechoslovakia, and his future as a chess master came to an abrupt end.

After the fall of the Soviet Union, Turchin tried to resurrect his career in chess but never regained the brilliance that he had displayed in his youth. He applied his analytic mind to numbers and became a bookkeeper in the murky underworld of high finance. His photographic memory proved to be a liability rather than an asset to his employers. When Ivanovich realized that Turchin carried all of his accounts in his head, Ivanovich thought it expedient to simply remove the head. Turchin disappeared before the order could be carried out.

He was thought to be living under an alias in the United States as an informant to the Treasury Department. One of Reya's escorts had overheard the rumor of a man with a Russian accent who played chess with the locals on North Avenue Beach. He was said to be unbeaten. The few times he had played to a draw were the results of bungled moves that were so out of character that they were deemed to be intentional.

Mark offered to drive Tanya to Chicago on the condition that they head north through North Carolina rather than take the shorter route through Atlanta and Nashville. He needed to stop and see his aunt and cousin in Beech Mountain on the way. He assured her it would only add a day to their journey. Reya's lead was at best a long shot, and his family needed him now.

His uncle had passed away from the gray death a few weeks before, and Mark had been unable to attend the funeral. Mark's parents, who were both evangelical ministers, had presided over the service on a cold, wet February morning. They had driven down from Wisconsin with Aunt Sarah's son, Otto, and his wife, Mary. His father told Mark on the phone that his aunt had shown up at the service drunk and that his cousin Dana had shaved her head. Mark preferred to remember the happier days, when his family would drive down from Baraboo in their station wagon to visit their kin and vacation in the Blue Ridge Mountains. He and his cousins had hiked and fished and hunted for black bear with play bows and arrows. What he remembered most, however, was the magical theme park atop Beech Mountain called the Land of Oz.

The drive from Miami to the highest town east of the Mississippi would take about eleven hours. Had he been on his own, he would have stopped at several points of interest—Cape Canaveral, Saint Augustine, Savannah, and Columbia, to name but a few. The temperatures fell as they headed north. The palm trees and orange groves of Florida gave way to the red soil and rolling pine forests of Georgia and South Carolina. Tanya passed the hours staring out the window and rarely spoke except for polite chat during their obligatory stops at gas stations and rest areas. They passed billboard after billboard of Christ warning of his return. She asked about the recipe for Papa Joe's pork chops during their lunch stop at the Waffle House. Mirana had given her a wad of money, and Tanya insisted on contributing for gas and paying for her own food. The drive up Highway 181 was more of a climb. Patches of snow were clinging to the ruts in the fallow fields and resisting the late-March melt. Trucks barreling down from the north would downshift and send sheets of ice flying from their roofs into the windshields of the cars that were too afraid to pass them on the winding two-lane road.

Dusk crept into the mountains early this time of year, and Mark was worried that they might not reach their destination by nightfall. His father had warned him that the final stretch of road leading up to the peak was intermittently closed depending on the ice. The pitch was such that a car without snow tires or chains could easily backslide off the road into a steep ditch or ravine. Mark's uncle had made his living fitting cars with chains and snow tires at his Tire Works shop in Banner Elk, at the base of Beech Mountain. In warmer seasons he had supplemented his meager income by welding odds and ends.

The silence in the car, which had been awkward at first, had become easier with time. Tanya's body language was more relaxed, and she seemed to marvel at every church steeple, weathered barn, and general store that they passed along the way. They were sharing the same space in his Trans Am, breathing the same air, and listening to the same country songs and static that he could pick up on his AM radio. Still, he was relieved when his headlights finally began to illuminate the roadside signs for the Beech Mountain ski resort and vacation paradise.

"We're almost there," he told his passenger.

"America . . . it's beautiful," Tanya replied. "These mountains remind me of the Carpathians in my homeland."

"I used to vacation here with my parents," Mark said, happy to have found a resonant theme. "The Blue Ridge Mountains are especially beautiful in the summer. There's a highway not far from here, the Blue Ridge Parkway, that's one of the most scenic roads in the United States. Perhaps I can show it to you while we're here."

Tanya did not reply. She continued to gaze into the now dark alpine forest that was encroaching on the mountain road.

Fortunately, the road up to the apex of Beech Mountain was open. Mark decided it was best to stay in the Alpen Inn rather than in his aunt's house. Given what his father had told him about his kin, he did not want to put Tanya in the middle of some family drama. He pulled his Trans Am into the empty parking lot of the Alpen Inn at eight in the evening. The door was open, and the light in the reception area was on. A handwritten note taped to the counter instructed customers to call Hans on his cell phone number after hours.

"How many?" Hans asked over the phone.

"Two," Mark replied.

"King bed or two doubles?"

"Two rooms . . ." Mark began. Before he could finish, Tanya grabbed his cell phone and interjected, "One room, two beds."

"I'll be there in fifteen minutes," Hans replied. "You might want to get a bite to eat at Bullwinkle's. They close at nine. It's the only place on Beech Mountain that's open late this time of year. The ski resort closed in February. Damned global warning."

Mark looked at Tanya quizzically as he shut off his phone. "I could have paid for your room," he said.

"It's not the money," Tanya replied. "I can't register on my own. I have no identification. We need to look like we're traveling together."

"Share a room? Are you sure?" he asked. "We just met two days ago."

"Are you afraid of me?" she asked.

Mark hesitated for half a second. "No."

"Good, because after all that's happened, I'm afraid to be alone."

The Alpen Inn had the decor of most ski resorts: exposed beams, comfortable couches, and worn carpeting to cushion the thump of ski boots. Hans had provided them with the best mountain-view suite in the inn, as they were the only customers. The cost was an even hundred dollars. Tanya threw the duffel bag that Marina had given her on one of the quilt-covered beds and went to freshen up in the bathroom. Mark decided to give her privacy and waited for her in the lobby. Bullwinkle's Bar and Grill was a five-minute walk away. Hans had warned them to stay clear of any black bears that might be rummaging through the garbage.

Bullwinkle's cavernous hall could easily accommodate a hundred patrons, which was common at the height of the season. This evening there was a lone customer drinking beer and watching March Madness highlights at the bar. With his silver-blond hair and surfer physique, he looked strangely out of place on a mountain summit. The bartender was a sallow-faced young man with a wispy goatee who seemed annoyed at the entry of the late-night customers. He had already inverted the chairs in the dining area and had filled a bucket of water to mop up the floor.

"Kitchen's closed," he informed them, "but you can still get a drink at the bar."

"The young travelers look hungry," the silver surfer interjected. "At least make them some cheese bread." He motioned for Tanya and Mark to take a seat at the bar. "Best cheese bread in the world."

The bartender put down his mop and lumbered over behind the bar. "Lenny, two Beech Blondes for my friends here, and an order of cheese bread, on me." He pointed at the huge moose head mounted on the wall. "And a marker for Bullwinkle."

"Thank you," Tanya replied before Mark could find a way to dissuade her from befriending strangers in bars. The surfer's smile and booming voice were disarming, and they soon found comfort in this chance encounter of strangers from random points of the compass on the summit of the highest peak east of the Mississippi River. The cold beer and bubbly cheese bread hit the spot after the long and winding drive up the mountain.

The surfer downed his beer and ordered another round for all. "Not many people pass through this time of year," he said. "Ski resort is closed. Oz won't open till the summer. Mind if I ask what brings you to Beech Mountain in the off season?"

"My uncle died a few weeks ago," Mark replied. "Maybe you knew him—Joe McBride. He ran the Tire Works down in Banner Elk. Just dropping by to pay my respects."

"I know the place, but I can't say I knew your uncle. People from down there just don't come up the mountain. It's like an invisible divide between the rich and the poor. Real people can't afford to live up here."

"So why are you here?" Tanya asked.

The surfer laughed. "I'll take that as a compliment. Just a year ago I was the king of the beach. Then one day I realized that life was passing me by. My friends were married with kids and collecting lifeguard pensions. I was just drinking beer and fishing. Nothing left in the ocean except grunt. I needed a fresh start."

"Now he thinks he's the king of Beech Mountain," the bartender butted in.

"But what's so magical about Beech Mountain?" Tanya asked.

"Why it's the Land of Oz," the surfer replied. "The place where the American Dream turns into the American fairy tale. For me, though, it's much more personal. My mom and dad used to take me up here for vacation. They recently passed away. I'm trying to find my way home."

"So are we," Mark said, grateful for the kindness of strangers in the hall of the mountain king.

* * * *

Tire Works was little more than a Quonset hut and junkyard that were tucked into a creek flat on the side of Balm Highway. The Shawneehaw Creek in back of the property was overflowing from the spring melt, and from afar the hut looked like a beer can half-buried in mud. A pickup truck stacked with handmade wooden birdhouses was parked at the side of the hut.

Tanya was immediately drawn to the birdhouses that were haphazardly stacked in the bed. Each birdhouse was different and assembled from combinations of natural and synthetic materials. Roofs were fashioned from flattened oilcans, portals from the base of Coke bottles, and framing from the beechwood for which the mountain was famous. "Whoever made these is a gifted artist," she said. "They may look primitive, but there's a sophistication in the geometry and choice of colors and materials."

"I think they were made by my cousin Dana. She was always making stuff when we were kids. My aunt told me she'd dropped out of Lees-McRae College when her father stopped working. Maybe she's trying to support the family by making these birdhouses."

The McBride family home tilted precariously on the other side of the Shawneehaw Creek and was reachable by an iron footbridge that Mark's uncle had welded together from sundry junkyard parts. The turbulent current of the creek threatened to wash away the makeshift bridge. The guardrail had rusted through and had been replaced with a yellow nylon cord that was fastened to the support posts with pioneer knots. Tanya held on to the back of Mark's belt as he led her across the bridge.

The front yard was littered with empty beer cans and pizza boxes. The siding on the ramshackle home was in disrepair, and one of the windows was boarded over. The wooden porch supported a cooler and two rocking chairs. A Confederate flag was draped over the railing. They climbed the rickety porch stairs and knocked on the door. A young woman in jeans and a "Make America Great Again" T-shirt opened the door. Her hair was clipped like a boot camp's recruit. A swastika was tattooed on her shoulder. The sparkling green eyes that Mark remembered as a child were now as murky as the meltwaters of Shawneehaw Creek.

Mark gave her a warm hug. "Dana, it's been too long. I'm so sorry about your dad. I should have come sooner."

Dana gave Tanya a cold stare.

"Oh, and this is my . . . friend Tanya," Mark said. "She's just hitching a ride with me up north."

Tanya unexpectedly kissed Dana thrice on her cheeks. "So nice to meet you. Are those your birdhouses?"

Dana nodded.

"They're exquisite. I'm a sculptress myself. I can see the artistry in your work. Perhaps you can show me your studio?"

"My studio? Oh, you mean where I make them. Sure. It's in the Tire Works. Let me wake up Mom, and then I'll take you over there. Wait here. The place is a mess."

Mark and Tanya waited on the porch as Dana fetched her mom. They could hear some shouting and clinking of plates and pans. After several minutes, Dana reopened the door. Mark's aunt Sarah was sitting at the kitchen table smoking a cigarette and sipping a beer. She was still in her robe. Her ratted hair looked like old pink cotton candy. The hand holding the cigarette was shaking.

"I'll let you and Mom catch up," Dana said to Mark. "Tanya, come and see my . . . studio."

Mark walked over and gave his aunt a kiss on the cheek. He thought for a moment about kissing her thrice but let it go.

"Don't give me no grief about how I look," Sarah said. "I had a hard night."

"I'm sorry I couldn't make Uncle Joe's funeral," Mark said. "I had exams."

"In some ways it's better that he's gone," Sarah said. "Do you want a beer?"

Mark opened the fridge and grabbed a beer. Other than some buttermilk, there was little else to drink.

"How's it better?" Mark asked.

"It's never been the same since Joe hurt his back two years ago. He went on disability and stopped working. The doctor gave him some kind of pain pills that stopped helping after a while. Joe kept demanding something stronger for his pain, but the doctor wouldn't give it to him. He then took to buying OxyContin from some college kids in town. Then he started buying pain patches from one of the orderlies who was stealing them from the hospital. One day I found him on the floor all blue and still. I dialed 911, but by the time they got here he was gone. They said it was the gray death." Sarah wiggled her beer can. "Be a good nephew and fetch me another beer."

Mark remembered his uncle as a boisterous, hardworking man who loved his family and loved the outdoors. He would take Dana and him on long hikes through the foot trails that had been blazed through the lush forests and lost coves of the Blue Ridge Mountains. Mark would dress as a cowboy and Dana as an Indian. When they encountered a deer or black bear, Mark would shoot with his cap pistol and Dana would launch a suction cup arrow, all under the watchful eye of Uncle Joe. He found it hard to believe that anything could break the man, especially the demon of addiction that seemed to prey on the weak-willed.

"So what will you do now?" Mark asked.

"I ain't like a woman that got no choices," Sarah replied. "When me and Joe first met in the Land of Oz, I was working the concessions, and he was playing the Cowardly Lion. I even subbed for Dorothy when she got the chicken pox. Joe didn't know it, but before we got hitched the Tin Man was also sweet on me. He now owns a bar down on Main Street. He's been paying me an awful lot of attention since Joe's passed."

"How's Dana?" Mark asked.

Sarah took a long swig of her beer. "Stupid girl's lost her mind. She and Joe were close. She quit school and spends her days in the Tire Works making birdhouses. We got no more disability checks coming in, so she's got to do something. She sells enough to get by, but it's no kind of living. When she's in the house, she just sits on her computer. She's got no real friends. She's always chatting with someone on her screen who calls himself Robert E. Lee."

"The Confederate flag on the porch?"

"He told her to put it up. Told her to shave her head too. When we do talk, which isn't often, she's always bringing up some bullshit about white supremacy and oppression by the Jews and all sorts of nonsense. She's even got a swastika tattooed on her arm. See if you can talk some sense into her."

Mark walked over to the glass case that housed his uncle's cherished gun collection. The rifles were still under lock and key, but the Ruger Redhawk revolver was gone.

"Did you sell Uncle Joe's handgun?" Mark asked. "I remember that was one of his favorites."

"Is it missing? Dana must have taken it out. We got feral pigs trying to eat us out of house and home. She clipped one the other day, but it ran off into the woods. Bears probably finished it off."

Mark felt sorry that his aunt's American Dream had ended in a nightmare of empty pill bottles, beer cans, and feral pigs. He felt guilty that he had not done more to save his cousin from the same fate. He remembered that when they were on vacation and had stayed with his aunt and uncle, Uncle Joe had done most of the cooking. Mark rummaged through the cupboard and found a box of pancake mix. He whipped up a batter with the buttermilk and cooked up some flapjacks. He poured some honey over a stack and served his aunt her first real breakfast since his uncle had died. He told her about school, about his blog, and how he had met this strange woman on his way back from Key West. Aunt Sarah listened with vicarious enjoyment of a housewife who escapes from her daily grind to watch her favorite soap opera. She especially enjoyed the subplot of the mysterious stranger.

"Tanya and I will stop by Uncle Joe's grave to pay our respects," Mark said, "before we continue our drive north."

"You won't be staying?" Sarah asked.

"Tanya has some urgent business up in Chicago," Mark replied. "I promised her we'd stop at Beech Mountain just for the day."

"Make sure you say bye to Dana," Sarah said. "She looks up to you. Tell her to find a real-life boyfriend and get a steady job. The girl's got some looks, just like her mother."

"You're as pretty as ever," Mark said. "Good luck with the Tin Man. I'll try and get back soon." Mark left his aunt with her beer and went looking for Dana and Tanya in the Tire Works.

The door to the Quonset hut was open. The hut was strewn with piles of used tires, racks of metal blocks and rods, and canisters of acetylene gas. The women were working on something in the back. Their heads were covered with welding masks. The flash of an acetylene torch cast phantasmagoric shadows on the roof of the hut. As he neared he saw that they were working on a metal sculpture of a bird in flight.

Dana lifted the visor of her mask. There was a twinkle in her eye that he hadn't seen since she was a tomboy frolicking with him through the pristine wonderland of Beech Mountain. "I call it *Free Bird*," Dana called out when she saw him. "Tanya's teaching me how to weld."

"You have the artistic vision," Tanya said. "You have the tools and raw materials in your studio. Now you have the basic skills."

The *Free Bird* sculpture was only partly constructed, but Mark could envision the finished work. Dana had welded her sculpture from scrap metal parts that she and Tanya had scavenged from the racks in Uncle Joe's Tire Works. The sculpture was primitive but sophisticated in its combination of sundry junk parts for the wings, body, head, and tail. He was amazed at how his cousin had learned to transform junk into art.

"Text Mark a photo when you're finished," Tanya said, "and I'll see if I can find a buyer. I know some people who might be interested in a joint work by Ukrainian and American sculptors."

Aunt Sarah had wanted Mark to lecture Dana about her life choices, but Tanya had found a way to connect with her through art. He wanted to stay and reminisce about their shared childhood experiences. He wanted to talk to her about the poor choices he'd made and how he was searching for himself through his travels. He knew it would take more time than he had. Tanya was in more desperate straits than his cousin. He now had even more reason to help her.

"Dana, Tanya and I need to be on our way. We'll stay connected electronically. I have a blog that you might be interested in."

"I know," Dana replied. "I'm one of your followers."

* * * *

Mark and Tanya stood over his uncle's grave in Banner Elk Cemetery. The site was marked with a wooden cross that Dana had carved from beechwood. An inscription was burned into a plaque at the base of the cross: "In loving memory of my dad, Joseph McBride." Tanya crossed herself three times and whispered an Our Father in Ukrainian. Mark felt obliged to say a few words:

> Uncle Joe, for me you're as much a part of this place as the mountain we're standing on. I remember you laughing at your own jokes, scaring us with tall tales of flying monkeys that would snatch young kids who ventured into the lost coves alone, and how Dana and I hung on to your legs when we came across our first black bear that was rummaging through the garbage dump in the back of your property. I don't know if I ever told you I loved you, but I'm pretty sure you knew. I know how proud you were of your stint as the Cowardly Lion in the Land of Oz, and how you fell head over heels over Aunt Sarah. She may not have been all that you hoped for, but she misses you. Dana misses you. I know you're up there somewhere, so I promise to do my best to help out my cousin. May you rest in peace.

Mark could feel a lump in his throat as he said the words *rest in peace*. The finality disturbed him. Here he was, breathing the crisp mountain air, hearing the first songbirds as they returned to nest in the alpine forest, and feeling the cold breeze that blew down from the summit, while his uncle lay still in a pine box in the black earth beneath his feet. He felt angry at the system that had failed his uncle, from the bankers who sank the economy to the insurance companies who had duped him with policies that covered opiates but not the rehabilitation that his uncle had needed. A proud, hardworking man had been broken, pill by pill, patch by patch, until he succumbed to the gray death.

Tanya touched his hand. "I can see that you loved your uncle very much."

"It's just not fair," Mark replied. "The rich get richer while honest men like my uncle don't live to realize their humble dreams. It's what's wrong with America today."

"I heard you say that your uncle was the Cowardly Lion in the Land of Oz. What did you mean by that?"

"I meant it as a compliment. It was more than a decade before I was even born. The Land of Oz is a theme park on the summit of Beech Mountain. It's just a few minutes away from here. Would you care to see it?"

"If it will bring back some happy memories of your uncle."

"Thank you, it would. It's closed now, but I'm sure we can sneak in. It's a shell of what it used to be. They still have Journeys with Dorothy on Fridays in June and an Autumn at Oz festival, but not like the heyday when my uncle and aunt worked there. My uncle said that after the owner passed away and after the fire in 1975, it never regained its original attraction. Let's take a walk into the past down the yellow brick road."

Tanya still held his hand as they walked back to his car. He didn't know what to make of it. Perhaps she just wanted to console him. Whatever the reason, he figured that Uncle Joe's spirit had a hand in it.

They took the back road up the mountain to view the alpine mansions that were occupied by the rich folk during Christmas break and for a week or two in the summer. Rivulets of snowmelt were running down the mountain. The rhododendrons and azaleas would soon carpet the mountain with their pink and purple blooms. Deer stared back at them from behind firs and brambles. A cloud had settled on the peak and immersed the Land of Oz in a fog-machine haze.

The gates to the Land of Oz were chained closed, but Mark and Tanya found a break in the fence that had been mowed down by snowmobilers. The yellow brick road wound its way across the summit. What remained of the attractions, like Dorothy's house in Kansas, appeared in the haze like archaeological remnants of a long-lost civilization. Tanya was like a schoolgirl in this American wonderland. She ran ahead to search for the Emerald City.

"Slow down, you'll get lost," Mark called out. "The flying monkeys will carry you away."

Tanya turned around. It was the first time he had seen her smile. "I need to find the Wizard so he can help me get back home."

"The Wizard was a charlatan," Mark replied.

"Then I need to find some magic slippers. I'll just tap them and wake up from this feverish dream."

"If you're Dorothy, then who am I?"

Tanya stopped her prance down the yellow brick road and put her finger to her mouth. "Let's see . . . you have courage, you joined me in my search for the Wizard. You have a heart, I could see that you care for your cousin, so that makes you . . ."

"The scarecrow?"

"Who else would pick up a naked stranger on a highway?"

Mark had no ready answer to her question. He remembered how, when he was seven, he had chased his cousin Dana down this same yellow brick road. She, too, had longed to be Dorothy and find happiness somewhere over the rainbow. Instead of helping her escape, he had left the Land of Oz, and she had stayed. She was trapped in a world of poverty, bigotry, and addiction. He had not come back to save her. He had not even gone to his uncle's funeral.

The steel framework of the Wizard's balloon rose up from the mist. It was a skeleton of its former self. Mark imagined how years before he was born his uncle and aunt entertained throngs of visitors who then descended from Beech Mountain to grow old and live their ordinary lives. They would eventually realize that their American dreams were no more real than the Land of Oz.

* * * *

Dmitri climbed through the break in the fence. He followed the sound of their voices through the mist until he came upon the yellow brick road. It seemed unlikely that Turchin would be hiding in a shuttered amusement park, but he needed to be sure. The Tire Works was more likely, but he had only spied Mark and Tanya talking to a teenage girl. He had texted the coordinates to Gennady and was waiting for a reply. Dmitri moved through the mist like a wraith. He needed to stay close enough to hear their conversation. The wind that was blowing over the summit could disperse the mist at any minute. If discovered, he would play the role of a watchman. His phone vibrated in his pocket. He ducked behind a replica of a Kansas home to check the message: *Tire Works is registered to Rider's deceased uncle, Joseph McBride. Survivors include wife, Sarah, and daughter, Dana. Daughter in GRU database. Details to follow.* Gennady had come through as always. Before becoming the director of information technology for Ivanovich's Institute for Democratic Progress, Gennady had worked at the Internet Research Agency in Saint Petersburg, where he still maintained contacts. Dmitri suspected that Gennady was actually an FSB plant to monitor Ivanovich, but the relationship between the state security apparatus and the criminal mafias had become symbiotic. As long as everyone received "what's mine," then all was well.

Dmitri tried to put the pieces of the puzzle together. *A seemingly random stranger rescues the rusalka in the middle of the Florida Keys. They meet with a Cuban street artist who leads them to a madam who's done business with Ivanovich. They rendezvous with Rider's cousin who's being recruited by the GRU. They are purportedly leading him to a mafia informant with a million-dollar contract on his head.* Dmitri did not believe in coincidences. *What was Ivanovich not telling him?* To play his part effectively, he needed to read the entire script and not just his bit role in one of the scenes. Who was the playwright? Ivanovich? The FSB?

The GRU? He felt like he was being played.

His boss, like all oligarchs, had a working relationship with the Russian intelligence agencies, but he was as expendable as Nemtsov. Dmitri knew that his boss was conspiring with the American senator. He had overheard them talking about a Last Awakening that somehow involved American evangelicals and Russian Orthodoxy. He also knew from his days in the FSB that the Kremlin was running multiple simultaneous operations to influence American politics with and without the help of the oligarchs.

At the troll factories, apparatchiks were divided by floors and by projects and only interacted in the cafeteria and elevators. Only a select group of strategists was aware of the grand plan, so individual departments often ran the risk of tripping over their coworkers' operations. The individual trolls were mostly university students who were well paid to make up shit, toss it against the wall, and see what sticks. It was surprising how much of it stuck. Every now and then some American journalist would put together the pieces and spark a congressional inquiry. The trolls would simply make up more fake news and pit the Republicans and Democrats against each other until the public tired of both. If the Americans got too close to the truth, the Russians would officially deny the operation, and the GRU would eliminate any loose ends. Dmitri did not want to risk becoming one of those loose ends.

His immediate assignments were clear: track the rusalka till she leads him to Turchin, liquidate Turchin, and return her to Ivanovich, preferably alive. She, like most everyone that his boss did business with, could probably be bribed. The only question was whether her silence was worth the price. If she chose her virtue over money, then her fall from grace would be much worse. The trolls could rewrite her history. She could be portrayed as a high-priced prostitute who assaulted a US senator while in a drug-crazed state. It would be easy enough to addict her to heroin and put her to work on the streets of Miami as had happened to so many women before her. Her contacts with Reya would support this variant. The only question was how many of her other contacts would need to be liquidated. By now she had most likely confided in Rider. The more people she spoke to, the messier it would become. Ivanovich would have to pay him considerably more than the million-dollar bounty on Turchin's head. Turchin could be anywhere in the country. The assignment could take weeks rather than days.

The cold mountain wind numbed his hands and face. He would need warmer clothes and provisions to continue to track his prey. He backtracked to his SUV and googled the closest Walmart. He located a supercenter in Watauga Hills about twenty miles away with an ETA of forty-three minutes. He checked the locator on Mark's phone and saw that they were still meandering through the Land of Oz.

He drove down Highway 184 past Sugar Mountain Resort, turned east on 105, and passed through the town of Seven Devils. As he pulled into the Walmart parking lot, he heard a ping on his phone. Gennady had tracked down the dossier on Dana McBride with help from his friends at the Internet Research Agency.

The dossier revealed that Dana was one of several hundred young white supremacists who had been recruited through a GRU-operated website called Confederate Blood and Soil. The intent was to stoke the fire of the alt-right movement. The Confederate Blood and Soil website was run out of the troll factory in Saint Petersburg. Dana had been recruited and engaged through a Russian handler with the alias Robert E. Lee. Robert E. Lee was a female undergraduate student at Saint Petersburg University who was working evenings in the lowest tier department at the Internet Research Agency. Dana's file made reference to an operation called Saving Dixie, though details of the operation had been redacted. Dmitri perused the entire file, including the online conversations. For his own security he needed to know more. He called Gennady on his encrypted phone.

"Gennady Vassiliyevich, I have a favor to ask of you."

"You received the information that I provided?"

"I did. Tell me more about Saving Dixie."

"All I know," Gennady replied, "is what's in the file. It's been heavily redacted. I no longer have that kind of security clearance."

"But you know people who do."

There was a long pause on the other end of the line.

"I'll take that as a yes," Dmitri said. "One more question. I have access to Rider's messages, emails, photos, and GPS on his phone. Can you get me real-time access to the phone's camera and microphone?"

"He would have to download the Saving Dixie app," Gennady replied. "Then you can watch and listen to his every move."

"How do I convince him to download this app? Can you push ads on his phone?"

"His cousin, Dana McBride, has already downloaded the app on her phone and computer. Perhaps she can persuade him."

Dmitri ended the call. He needed the right disguise for so delicate a deception. He spent several minutes observing the garb and mannerisms of the shoppers at Walmart. There was no consistency to their appearance. Some looked as if they had landed from another planet. He rifled through the racks of men's clothing and selected a white polo shirt, khakis, and a camouflage hunting jacket. He bought an electric clipper and went into the men's room where he buzzed his hair and changed into his new outfit. He paid for his purchases in cash.

On his way back to Banner Elk, he tuned into a local talk radio station. The host was raging about the rainbow radicals who were desecrating statues of Confederate war heroes. He checked the locator on Rider's phone and saw that his quarry had not moved off the summit of Beech Mountain. He turned off Highway 194 to Main Street and pulled up to Tire Works. The door to the Quonset hut was open. Dana was in the back, welding a wing onto her *Free Bird* sculpture.

"Looks like the South rising from the ashes," Dmitri called out in a High Country accent.

"We're closed for business," Dana replied.

"I'm not here looking for tires," Dmitri replied. "I came looking for you."

"And who might you be?" Dana asked.

"A friend. My name is Robert E. Lee."

CHAPTER 4

Williamstown

The sun burned the mist off the summit of Beech Mountain. Mark drove his Trans Am down the South Beech Mountain Parkway toward the Blue Ridge Parkway. They had passed the turnoff on their way up the mountain the previous evening, but it had been too dark to appreciate the vista of the Blue Ridge Mountains as they rose to meet the clouds that had settled in the deep-green glens. He pulled over to a scenic overlook so that Tanya could experience the beauty with all her senses. For all of his fascination with Americana, the real marvel was America herself in all her natural glory.

Tanya took a deep breath and gazed at the mountain ridge that stretched as far as the eye could see. Her eyes reflected the blue hue of the mountains. A hawk circled in the updrafts, hunting for its prey in the deep reaches below. The wind carried the scent of evergreens. Songbirds cooed to lure their mates. Mark took out his phone and snapped a picture of Tanya as she was taking in this iconic American scene. She caught the movement out of the corner of her eye.

"No photos," she protested.

"I took it from in back," he replied. "You can't see your face. I just wanted to capture the moment. This place holds a lot of memories for me."

Tanya took his phone from his hand and scrutinized the photo. Her windswept blonde hair obscured her profile in the photo. With the Blue Ridge Mountains in the background, it could pass as a postcard. She scrolled through the other pictures on his phone to make sure he hadn't captured her unawares. There were only photos of the Hurricane Memorial, Crocodile Lake, and Card Sound.

"You have a good eye for photography," she said.

"I take a lot of pictures for my blog. A hundred people can look at the same scene, and yet each can perceive it differently. I want my readers to see the world through my eyes. This parkway stretches for hundreds of miles. There are lots of scenic points. We can drive down a little farther and then double back."

"I need to get to Chicago," Tanya said.

Mark nodded, disappointed that they were rushing toward their destination. As they drove toward Johnson City, Tanya savored the beauty of the Cherokee National Forest. Every nascent nook and cranny was bursting with buds and blossoms and green shoots pushing up through the forest floor.

"I want to thank you for helping my cousin Dana," Mark said. "It meant a lot to her. It meant a lot to me."

"She's at a difficult age," Tanya said. "She needs someone she trusts to guide her."

"I'll come back once you're safe and this is all behind us."

"You don't need to see this through to the end. You've done enough already."

"You probably think of me as just some random blogger who prefers to see the world as it was rather than how it is now. Truth is, I'm a journalist, and a pretty good one at that. I can help you figure this out if you let me."

Tanya looked at the intent young man who was gripping the steering wheel as he navigated the twists and turns of the mountain road.

"Why would you risk your life for me?"

Mark took a long time to answer. "God must have brought you into my life for a reason. I've failed everyone else in my life—my parents, my girlfriends, my cousin . . . He's giving me a chance to redeem myself."

"Your family needs you."

"I'm estranged from my family."

"Dana needs you."

Mark didn't answer. Tanya saw that she had struck a nerve. "I can't drag you any further into this," she said.

"But I'm already into this."

Tanya realized that Mark was right. He already knew too much. Sooner or later, Ivanovich would start eliminating loose ends. "Then you'll need to trust me."

"I do," Mark replied.

"I mean *really* trust me. You'll uncover things you wish you didn't know."

"Jesus said that the truth will set us free. Let's start at the beginning. Why was an American senator on the yacht of a Russian oligarch?"

Tanya tried to recollect the conversation. "At first it seemed to be a purely social visit. The only business discussed during dinner was the unveiling of my statue of the Heavenly Hundred. Then my mind began to wander. It was as if I was there and not there at the same time. I heard them talking about the Bible and saving souls."

"Evangelism?"

"It was odd. They talked about controlling what people think and do by citing the Bible."

"People do look to the Bible for answers. I could see how it could be a powerful political tool in the wrong hands. There's a place on our way to Chicago that might give us some insights. OK if we check it out?"

"Only if you think it will help."

"The place I'm thinking of is called Noah's Ark."

Mark plotted the route to Williamstown, Kentucky, on his Google Maps. The route he selected meandered west through the Cherokee National Forest and Smoky Mountains toward Johnson City, Tennessee, and then north into Kentucky. The time to their destination was about six hours. The route took them down from the summit of the High Country into a landscape of rolling hills and millennial valleys. Farmland had been wrested from the wilderness with axes and plows. Most towns they passed through had no stoplights. White wooden churches were at the heart of every town with announcement boards that gave the day and time of services. They posted Bible verses or cryptic sayings like "God favors the fortunate." There was little in the way of businesses, other than the occasional gas station and general store. Even McDonald's had forsaken this part of the country.

"These are like our villages in Ukraine," Tanya observed. "They're populated by the poor and the faithful. They're oblivious to the outside world, yet they remain the bastions of our culture. They protect our language, our traditions, our music, and our beliefs. They embody what it means to be Ukrainian."

"The folk who live in these parts embody what it means to be white, Protestant American," Mark replied. "They're the descendants of the pioneers who built this country. Like Christ said on the Sermon of the Mount: they're the 'salt of the earth.' I once believed that you had to be a white, God-fearing Christian to be a real American, but now I'm not so sure. Northwestern opened my eyes to a whole new world. My classmates are as diverse as the peoples in the Bible. I used to think that God made this land just for us Christians, but now I think it's big enough for all of us."

"But why focus just on Americana? It's so . . . *provincial*. It's a big world out there."

"Because it's my home. I want to understand it. When I'm on the road, I try to stop at every historic marker I come across to find the real America. They're like pieces of a puzzle. I want to figure out the big picture."

Each turn in the road revealed a new face of Americana: a hillside graveyard dating back to the Civil War, a rusted Studebaker with a FOR SALE sign, a barn with a smoking Camel painted on its side. There were few people to be seen. The ground was not yet ready for planting. Mark wondered how anyone could eke out a living in these forsaken towns, devoid of the energy of city life. No one came through these towns anymore, other than the occasional traveler who had gotten lost while searching for some long-lost relative.

The roads gradually widened until they finally veered onto the ramp for Interstate 75. Cars and trucks were barreling down the interstate way over the speed limit. Most had no appreciation of the land they were racing through. Billboards for motels, fireworks, and adult stores marked upcoming exits. They flashed past a three-story-high cross on a hill overlooking the interstate. Before Mark could turn his head to discover its significance, it was gone. Only the occasional glimpse of blue grass and horses hinted at what lay beyond the guardrails. *They have no sense of place*, he thought. *No sense of history.* The interstate looked identical whether it was North Carolina or Tennessee. *Tanya is different. She's seeing America with wide-open eyes. I wish I could show her everything that I've seen, every curiosity, every point of interest, every artifact of Americana.*

Toward evening they pulled off the interstate in Lexington to find a place to eat. Mark did a quick Google search on his phone and decided on Middle Fork Kitchen Bar. It was situated in the old James E. Pepper Bourbon Distillery and boasted a list of close to ninety bourbons. Mark abhorred chain restaurants, and if he couldn't find the old and authentic, he looked for the new and original. They were seated at a high wooden table with a view of the open kitchen and bar. The plates were designed for sharing. Mark ordered a Basil Hayden's on the rocks. Tanya asked for just water.

"So why did you stop for me on that highway?"

"You gave me no choice. You practically jumped into my car."

"You could have left me at that marina."

"I was raised to be kind to strangers. Jesus said, 'For I was hungry and you gave me something to eat, I was thirsty and you gave me something to drink, I was a stranger and you invited me in.'"

"Do you always quote the Bible for your answers?"

Mark blushed. "No . . . not always. Sometimes. I just think in Scripture. The verses just pop into my head. It's easier than thinking for myself."

Tanya put her hand on his. "Thank you for being a Good Samaritan."

AMERIKANA

The clientele at the Middle Fork Kitchen Bar were mostly hipsters. The waitress was a buxom coed in a University of Kentucky sweatshirt. She brought Mark his Basil Hayden's in a glass with a single large cube of ice. "Have you decided what'd you like?" she asked. "The plates are big enough to share."

"I changed my mind," Tanya said. "I will try a bourbon, the same as my . . . companion. Then I'll have the green tomatoes and shiitake bowl."

"Hog and oats," Mark added.

When the waitress brought her the bourbon, Tanya pretended to know what she was doing. She picked up the glass to note the rich caramel color. She lifted it to her nose. "Smells like plums and cinnamon." She took a sip. "It tastes like roasted pears, walnuts, and apples."

Mark laughed. "You have extraordinarily keen senses." He lifted his glass and took a sip. "It reminds me of Christmas," he said. He clinked her glass. "Here's to our great adventure. Fuck Rich and Ivanovich."

He immediately realized his gaffe.

Tanya put down her glass. Her levity disappeared. "Men like Rich and Ivanovich are worse than evil—they're amoral. The only code they live by is power and greed. In my country, they do whatever they want and get away with it. There is no justice. I thought Americans would be different."

"We *are* different. We have rules of law. What these men did to you— they need to be prosecuted and punished. Rich may be one of the most powerful men in the Senate, but he won't get away with it."

"You're being naive," Tanya said.

"I know," Mark said, "that power corrupts. But America's different. I believe in our Constitution. I believe in our system of government. We have a system of checks and balances—the legislative, judicial, and executive branches—that prevents abuses of power."

"What if your system becomes corrupted? What if it fails you?"

Mark downed his bourbon. "What are you advocating? Revolution?"

"America was founded through a revolution. You fought a civil war to preserve your union."

"I have faith in our democracy. We live in a rules-based world. Revolutions are a thing of the past."

Tanya sighed. "In my country, to restore the rule of law, we had to take power in our own hands."

"I know," Mark said. "The Revolution of Dignity. The whole world was watching. Did your revolution succeed in changing things for the better?"

"Yes and no. We realized that we have the power to change things. We discovered civil society. We became a nation."

"Then why do you say that things haven't changed?"

"Because at the highest levels, those who were in power remain in power. In the West, countries have mafias. In my part of the world, the mafia has countries. Once it sucks its own country dry, it survives by spreading. It corrupts. It foments frozen conflicts to paralyze the countries it wants to control. Think of Abkhazia, Ossetia, Nagorno-Karabakh, Transnistria, Crimea, Donetsk, and Luhansk."

"Most Americans have never heard of these places."

"Because all they care about is themselves."

Mark stared down into his empty glass.

Tanya put her hand under his chin and forced him to look up. "Look, I'm sorry. I didn't mean to imply that you're one of them. But I'm frustrated with America. People my age are dying every day on both sides of the front. We thought the West would help us, yet from what I see, your politicians like Rich are colluding with the Russians and leaving us to fight our battles alone."

"We have our own problems to deal with."

"What you don't realize is that it won't end in Ukraine," Tanya said. "The Russians will undermine your society and turn you against each other. Brothers will turn on each other like Cain and Abel. You'll lose faith in your press. You'll lose faith in your government. You'll cry out for some strong man to save you, and you'll abandon your principles. I know that unless we stop them, what's happening in my country will happen in yours."

Mark thought of his parents, of Mary and Otto and Dana and how their way of life was under attack from an unseen enemy, a mafia with nuclear weapons that could start Armageddon. It was not a war of nations. It was a war of the powerful against the meek. Christ had said "the meek shall inherit the earth." But when? After the Tribulation? He thought of the nuclear-tipped Hercules missiles at Crocodile Lake and how close they had come to being launched. Perhaps the End Time was nearer than he thought.

Mark received a ping on his phone. It was a message from Dana: *Check out this awesome app: Saving Dixie.*

"Who's texting you?" Tanya asked.

"My cousin Dana. She wants me to download some app about Dixie. She's passionate about preserving our Confederate heritage. I don't agree with her views, but it might be a way for me to keep an eye on her and what she's into."

"May I see your phone?" Tanya looked at the animation of the Confederate flag waving in an electronic wind and inviting the user to click and download. "Can I ask you for a favor?" she asked.

"Sure."

"Please don't download or upload anything until we part."

Mark was momentarily taken aback by her talk of parting. "But what about my blog?"

"Take your notes and take your photos, but don't post them until we find Turchin and finish this."

Mark liked her choice of pronoun. *Yes, until "we" finish this,* he thought. *But let's relish the journey.* He looked at the beautiful runaway who had jumped in his car and into his life on the Overseas Highway. She had ensnared him in a quest that wasn't his, yet here they were, sipping bourbon in a refurbished distillery in Kentucky. *It might be her quest, but this is my country. Perhaps we can discover America together, but then again, I just might be whistling Dixie.*

* * * *

The ark was visible from five miles away. It was much larger than Mark had imagined. The wooden structure was over four stories high and longer than three space shuttles. He bought a combo ticket for the Ark Encounter and the Creation Museum at the ticket counter. The people around them were homogeneous—white, lower- and middle-class Christians who had traveled here on a pilgrimage from throughout the country. A young father in front of Mark was holding a child with erupting chicken pox. There were as many baby strollers as motorized wheelchairs.

Mark and Tanya boarded one of the many buses that shuttled them to the ark complex with its outdoor restaurants, topiaries of elephants and camels, and souvenir shops. The landscaped walk to the ark took them past cuneiform tablets that depicted the creation of man, the fall of man, punishment and promise, Cain murders Abel, wickedness fills the earth, and Noah and the ark. The reproduction of Noah's ark was built according to the dimensions specified in the Bible. A placard informed visitors that Noah was able to rescue his family and sixty-eight hundred animals in pairs, including dinosaurs, before the Great Flood wiped out all terrestrial life on Earth.

As they entered the ark through a long ramp, music reminiscent of a Cecil B. DeMille movie resonated in the cavernous hold. The preflood-world exhibit was divided into the *Perfect Creation* and the *Fall up to the Flood*. In the perfect world, there was no death or suffering. People and dinosaurs coexisted in harmony. A film clip of *Genesis: Paradise Lost* dazzled the viewers with the latest in 3D technology. The second half of the exhibit depicted a sinful world of violence, decadence, and divine retribution. The ground was cursed because Adam and Eve ate the fruit from the tree of knowledge of good and evil. People were forced to toil the earth, smelt metals, and develop civilization. A series of lurid dioramas portrayed onlookers cheering as victims were being slaughtered by a giant and a carnivorous dinosaur in a coliseum; pagans climbing the stairs of a temple to sacrifice their children to a golden snake god; and the wicked, who deserved to be judged, drowning in the Great Deluge.

One exhibit outlined the shortcomings of evolutionary theory. The idea that life spontaneously formed from nonliving matter through chance chemical reactions had never been proven or replicated in a lab. Moreover, the foundation of naturalistic thinking is materialistic and ignores the nonphysical such as logic and morality. The worst of both worlds is the attempt by some to combine aspects of biblical creation with evolution over millions of years. According to the Bible, Romans

5:12, "Wherefore, as by one man sin entered into the world, and death by sin; and so death passed upon all men, for that all have sinned." In essence, there had been no death, and therefore no evolution, until Adam sinned.

While Mark was reading the fine print on every exhibit, Tanya was admiring the craftsmanship of the ark's construction and the detail of the countless cages that simulated a floating zoo. Many of the cages were filled with facsimiles of living and extinct animals, including dinosaurs and primitive mammals from which the millions of current species apparently descended. A cacophony of animal sounds emanated from these cages. Smaller jugs purportedly held insects with diagrams describing how they were kept alive for the 150 days before the ark rested on Mount Arafat.

Wide-eyed children marveled at how the biblical story of Noah's Ark had come to life before their very eyes. Parents explained the finer points of Scripture, and how it was possible for people and dinosaurs to coexist. God had created all creatures on the sixth day. Not all animals survived to the present day, which explains the dinosaur fossils that are excavated around the world.

The largest exhibit, *Why the Bible Is True*, was on the bow's end of the ark on the third floor. It was designed as a walk-through graphic novel meant to appeal to the millennial generation. As Mark and Tanya were entering the exhibit, Mark felt someone tug on the back of his shirt. He turned around to see a woman in her fifties sporting a Team Nazarene T-shirt. She was pushing a disabled young woman in a wheelchair. The young woman's head was cocked to the side.

"Excuse me, but you young people look to be about my daughter's age. I was wondering if you would be kind enough to take her through this exhibit. It's meant for young people. It would mean the world to her to experience it with people her own age."

The young woman in the wheelchair stared vacantly into space. She looked to be in her twenties. Her muscles were wasted, and her shoulder bones protruded in her "Believe" T-shirt. Before Mark could answer, Tanya said, "Of course we will." She took the handles of the chair from the young woman's mother. "What's your daughter's name?"

"Sharon."

"Come with me, Sharon," Tanya said. "My friend Mark studied the Bible. He'll be our guide."

"God Bless you," the mother said. "I'll wait for you by the exit to the exhibit."

Walking through the exhibit was like walking through the pages of a comic book. Beautifully illustrated panels with dialogue in bubbles told the story of three college students who seek answers to their questions about life and the truth of the Bible, including why there is death and suffering. Tanya positioned the chair in front of each panel as Mark told the story.

"Three friends, Gabriela, Ryo, and Andre, are in college together. Andre is a believer. Gabriela walked away from the church, and Ryo believes that everyone finds his own truth in life. They attend a lecture in a class on comparative religions taught by a professor who's an atheist. The professor says that the Bible is full of contradictions and is written by people who have no knowledge of science. He scoffs at the idea that the world is only six thousand years old. Gabriela and Ryo ask Andre how he can believe in this stuff. He answers, 'Because it's the word of God.'"

The eleven scenes in the exhibit follow Gabriela and Ryo's path to belief and salvation.

"In this scene," Mark said, "Gabriela questions why a loving God would allow her father to suffer a painful death. Ryo questions how a loving God would drown all humans on Earth except for Noah and his family."

Sharon raised her head to Mark and uttered a single word in a voice that sounded like she hadn't spoken in years: "Why?"

Mark searched for an answer. "Because . . . because God created the perfect world, and we're the ones who wrecked it."

Sharon tried to lift her head and rested it back on her shoulder. Mark could see that his answer had not eased her pain. The authors of the novella had anticipated this low point in the arc of their story. Tanya wheeled Sharon to the next set of panels, illustrating the doors of the Bible.

"Let's listen to what Andre has to say as he shares the gospel with his friends," Mark told Sharon. "Here he shows us the animals walking through the doors of the ark. A thousand years later, the Jews are marking their doors with lamb's blood. Here we see Jesus as the shepherd guarding the gate to the pen—the sheep cannot go in and out without going through him. Here we see Christ resurrected walking out of his tomb."

The final panel of the *Doors of the Bible* series showed a wide gate that leads to destruction and a narrow gate that leads to life. "We are all guilty of sinning against our Holy Creator," the panel said, though Mark wondered what sin Sharon was guilty of. "There is only one door that can save us from eternal judgment. Jesus Christ is that door."

Sharon's mother was waiting at the exit with a bag of Oreo churros. She put a piece into her daughter's mouth and offered a churro to Mark and Tanya.

Tanya knelt so she would be face-to-face with Sharon. "God loves you," she assured her.

"Have a blessed day," the mother said and took her daughter to view the living quarters aboard the ark.

The population inside the ark was beginning to swell. Mark and Tanya had been among the first few thousand visitors of the day, but as lunchtime was approaching, the waiting lines for the exhibits grew ever longer.

"This place is unbelievable," Tanya said.

"Or believable," Mark said, "depending on your faith. I think you can now appreciate the profound effect that the Bible has in the life of a lot of Americans. Here, take a look at this exhibit, *The True History of the World.*"

The intricate timeline was mapped on a scroll that stretched dozens of feet across a wooden wall of the ark. Biblical events were interwoven with historical facts. The world, according to the scroll, was created in 4004 BC.

Tanya looked at Mark quizzically. "You grew up with the Bible. Do you really believe that the world was created six thousand years ago and that people lived with dinosaurs?"

"I'm a modernist. I believe that you don't need to interpret the Bible literally to understand its meaning," Mark replied. "Take Genesis 1: 'In the beginning God created the heaven and the earth, and the earth was without form, and void; and darkness was upon the face of the deep. And the Spirit of God moved upon the face of the waters. And God said, let there be light: and there was light. And God saw the light, and it was good: and God divided the light from the darkness.' To me that passage simply means that God created the universe. He could have done it with the big bang. The days could have been billions of years. You can believe in science and also believe in God."

* * * *

The slogan for the Creation Museum was Prepare to Believe. As Mark and Tanya pulled into the parking lot, a light rain began to fall. They didn't notice the black SUV that had followed them from the Ark Encounter. They presented their combo tickets at the entrance and followed the path to the museum, which meandered through a lush botanical garden reminiscent of the Garden of Eden. Hidden sprinklers effused an ethereal mist.

Dmitri checked his disguise in the rearview mirror before stepping out of the black SUV. Today he was a Bible salesman from North Carolina with a goatee and a "Make America Great Again" baseball cap. His wrinkle-free polyester pants were a bit too long and occasionally snagged the heels of his white leather shoes. He considered wearing a crucifix, but his inspection of the visitors at the Ark Encounter quickly revealed that this was not common practice among evangelicals.

He had tracked his quarry in the Ark Encounter, always only a few steps behind, without detection. He had watched them view the dioramas, wheel a disabled woman through a graphic novel, and study the true history of the world. They had ignored him just as they had ignored the multitudes of God-fearing folk who politely traipsed from exhibit to exhibit enthralled by the animatronic reenactment of Bible stories. Dmitri felt unappreciated, like an actor in a supporting role whose brilliant performance is wasted on his audience. He decided he wanted to play a more leading role.

The Creation Museum was a sleek, modern structure nestled in a lush botanical garden with waterfalls, bridges, and a bog with carnivorous plants. An open-space portico with an indoor waterfall welcomed visitors to begin their historical tour of Genesis. The Stargazer Planetarium awed the viewers with the vastness of the universe. A Grand Canyon exhibit featured two men examining the same fossil evidence, one a creationist and the other an evolutionist. It prodded the viewer to answer the question: "God's truth or man's reason—which will you choose?"

"I choose reason," Tanya whispered in Mark's ear.

"I think the right answer is God's truth."

In the Biblical Authority room, great men of God—Moses, David, Isaiah, the Apostle Paul, and Martin Luther—attested to the truthfulness of the Bible. A replica of Guttenberg's press demonstrated how the word of God was distributed to the masses. The Scopes Trial exhibit highlighted how in 1925, Christians compromised their faith and now suffer the consequences of abandoning creationism. A passage through a dark alley defaced with graffiti and video vignettes showed how modern evils like abortion, drugs, and pornography were the consequence of the church's compromise on creationism. A time tunnel led them into the main attraction: a walk-through Genesis.

The one-way passage snaked through the first eleven chapters, from Creation to the Deluge. The extravagant, life-size exhibits were shielded from the viewers by glass. Adam, in a resplendent Garden of Eden, names the animals that were cocreated on the sixth day. Adam and Eve rejoice in each other's company as a dinosaur looks on. A tree of life with thirty-one thousand leaves anchors the known universe. A red serpent tempts Eve with fruit from the tree of the knowledge of good and evil . . . Mark mused for a moment on what it would be like to be paired with Tanya in Paradise. *Would we live idyllically in Paradise or would she offer me the fruit from the tree of knowledge of good and evil? Would I taste of the fruit and choose her over God?*

Dmitri had been one step behind them since the Wonders of Creation room. He had the keen sense of smell that was essential to a predator. When he escorted Tanya onto the *Kalinka*, he had imprinted her scent in his brain. She was Slavic, yet refined by her travels—the forests of the Carpathians, the lavender of Paris, the wet stone of Venice. He prided himself in being able to recognize a target in the dark. Her companion was too obsessed with the exhibits to notice the Bible salesman who had come within inches of the nape of his neck. Rider, Dmitri decided, smelled of earth and hay and sweaty leather. He smelled like the pages of a pocket Bible. The scent excited him.

The impressive life-size exhibits portrayed Adam and Eve being banished from Paradise for their sin. They now had to toil the earth. The animals, which had once lived in harmony, began to devour one another. An angry God demanded blood sacrifice. The wickedness continued as Cain murdered Abel. Mark and Tanya walked from scene to scene with Dmitri only a few steps behind. An animatronic Methuselah greeted them as they entered the *Noah's Ark* exhibit. In the Voyage room, an animatronic Noah explained how he was able to construct the ark and save his family and thousands of animals from God's terrible vengeance.

Dmitri approached them at the tower of Babel. He tapped Mark on the shoulder. "Zachary Hopewell, Ashville, North Carolina. I can tell that you're a believer like myself."

Mark turned around to see a middle-aged man with a "Make America Great Again" cap and a goatee.

"Quite a museum," Mark answered. "It brings the Bible to life."

"Speaking of Bibles, I can get you any Bible you want: King James, Scoffield, New International. I distribute them throughout the southeast, from Florida to Virginia and west to Mississippi and Tennessee. I can get them in any language you want. I couldn't help but overhear that your companion's got an accent. Let me guess—Russian?"

Mark looked for Tanya but she had moved on to the Geology Room. "Ukrainian," he said.

The Bible salesman shook Mark's hand. "I *knew* it," he said. "I was thinking eastern European, Russian, Bulgarian, Polish, but Ukrainian, yeah, I can see it."

"I don't think we need any Bible just yet," Mark said.

"Hell, it's on me," the Bible salesman said. "Spread the word of the Lord, that's why I'm in the business. Just give me an address where I can send it to, and I'll have it to you in a couple of days."

"Thanks, but don't bother. We'll still be traveling for a while."

"Where to?"

Mark was becoming uncomfortable with his new friend. "No place in particular. I'm a blogger. I write about Americana. We go wherever the road takes us. You can check me out on the web."

Dmitri nodded. He relished the torment. As a child, he liked to pull the wings off flies. Dmitri brought up Mark's blog on his phone in less time than it would take to search. "Well, Bless the Lord, here you are. *Americana* by Mark Rider. You must be some kind of famous. All kinds of interesting stuff here: the Hurricane Monument, Crocodile Island, the Land of Oz. You just got yourself another follower. Are you going to blog about the Creation Museum? Noah's Ark?"

While Mark intended to share his insights with the world, this "fan" made him feel violated, as if he'd invited an unwanted stranger into his home. "I'm on vacation," Mark lied. "I'm taking a break from blogging. I won't have any new entries for a while."

"Well then have a blessed day," the Bible salesman said. "Perhaps our paths will cross again."

Mark caught up to Tanya at the Last Adam theater. The trek through the Creation Museum had led them through the seven Cs of history: creation, corruption, catastrophe, confusion, Christ, cross, and consummation. The climax of the Creation Museum focused on humanity's need for a savior: Jesus Christ. Christ was the second Adam, except that he obeyed God in everything, unlike the first.

"Where were you?" Tanya asked. "I thought you were right behind me, and when I turned around you were gone."

"Some Bible salesman from North Carolina latched on to me," Mark said. "He was pushy—he wanted to know where I live, where we were traveling. He claimed he wanted to send us a free Bible."

"What did he look like?" Tanya asked.

"Like no one in particular. He was pushy."

"Did you tell him where we were going?"

"No."

"Is he still behind us?"

Mark looked at the visitors that were waiting in line for the next viewing of the exhibit called *The Second Adam*. "I don't see him behind us."

"I'm feeling claustrophobic," Tanya said. "Is it OK if we go?"

"Sure. I think I we've seen enough for today."

On their way out of the Creation Museum they opted to skip the Dragon Theater, which explained why ancient legends about dragons were true—the mythical creatures were actually dinosaurs that God had created together with man on the sixth day of creation. The Bible salesman stepped out of the Dragon Theater, licked his hand to refresh Rider's scent, and followed them out into the bog.

CHAPTER 5

Nashville

Mark and Tanya set out from Williamstown in the early morning. Tanya had barely slept through the night and was napping in the car. Mark had tossed and turned as well. The encounter with the Bible salesman had unnerved him. If a stranger could know so much about him by reading his blog, then Ivanovich would know that and more. Tanya had insisted that they not contact the authorities, but they were in the United States, not Ukraine. If there were one person whom Ivanovich or Rich could not reach, it would be Mary Lou Jackson, the attorney general of Tennessee and Rich's rival in the upcoming primaries. While Tanya was sleeping, Mark pulled off the expressway at an interchange and reversed course toward Nashville.

Tanya awoke to the sight of steep cliffs and ravines rather than the rolling hills and plains of Ohio. "Where are we?" she asked.

"Tennessee. I decided to detour through Nashville rather than head through Cincinnati and Indianapolis."

"Nashville? Why?"

"I just want to cover all of our bases before we confront Turchin. Nashville is known as the Protestant Vatican. It's the world's largest producer of Bibles. If someone is trying to politicize the Bible, they would have heard about it Nashville. I know some biblical scholars there that I can talk to. It's also Rich's hometown."

"You're taking me *to* him?" Tanya reached for the door handle as if she were going to jump out of the moving car. Mark grabbed her by the wrist. A log carrier blasted its horn, swerved, and nearly ran them off the road.

"I'm not taking you to him. I'm just trying to figure out what this is all about before we're in over our heads."

Tanya stared out the window, uncertain whether to believe her unreliable ride.

"Look, I'm sorry," Mark said. "I should have woken you and asked you. We're just a few hours away. We'll just stay one night, no longer."

"How is that you know these biblical scholars?"

"When I was a divinity student at Northwestern, I accompanied my father to an evangelical convention that was held there. My father introduced me to them. He was giving a lecture on the timing of the Tribulation. There was quite a lot of debate."

"The Tribulation?" Tanya asked.

Mark was happy to divert Tanya's questioning to biblical prophecy rather than the real reason he had headed for Nashville. "Are you familiar with the End Time? Mark 24, Mark 13, Luke 21, or the book of Revelation?"

"I confess I haven't read much of the Bible, but I got a good sense of it yesterday."

"The Creation Museum and the Ark Encounter focus mainly on how the world *began*. These passages that I cited tell us how it will *end*. We believe that the End Time is as certain as death and taxes."

"We?"

"My parents, my cousins . . ."

"But what do *you* believe?"

Mark thought about the countless hours he had spent studying and memorizing the passages in the Bible. He knew it was the path to salvation, but for him it hadn't been enough. "I wanted to believe what they believe," he said, "but I didn't live up to their expectations. I guess that all men fall short of the glory of God. I don't blame them; I blame myself."

"Do you still consider yourself to be a Christian?"

"I'm still hoping to be born again."

"What if it never happens?" Tanya asked.

A billboard on Interstate 65 read HEAVEN OR HELL? PREPARE TO MEET THY GOD. JESUS IS COMING SOON.

"I think there could be more than just one path to salvation," Mark replied.

"Tell me more about the End Time."

"The Bible foretells a series of events leading up to the End Time. Hopefully we'll be raptured before it all begins."

"Raptured?"

"According to 1 Thessalonians 4:16, Christ will come in the clouds and those who believe in him will be taken bodily up to heaven. Some think this will happen before the Tribulation begins. Others believe that the Rapture will occur during the Tribulation but before the seven bowls of the wrath of God."

"What happens to those of us who aren't raptured?" Tanya asked.

Mark hesitated to answer. He couldn't imagine that Tanya would not be among the raptured.

"Then we're left behind to suffer through the Tribulation. During the seven years of the Tribulation, those who remain will experience worldwide hardships, disasters, war, pain, and suffering before the Second Coming of Christ."

"This is all foretold in the Bible?" Tanya asked.

"Yes, if you piece it together from the various books. They foretell that a man empowered by Satan will gain control of the world with promises of peace. A false prophet will establish a new religion to worship this Antichrist. In the first part of the Tribulation, a great army from the north attacks Israel and is defeated by divine intervention. At the midpoint of the Tribulation, the Antichrist breaks his covenant with Israel and reveals his true colors. During this abomination of desolation, a great persecution breaks out against all who believe in Christ. At the end of the Tribulation, Jesus returns with the armies of heaven, and in the Battle of Armageddon saves Jerusalem and defeats the Antichrist. The Antichrist and the false prophet are thrown into the lake of fire. Christ will then judge the survivors of the Tribulation. The righteous will enter the Millennial Kingdom; the wicked will be cast into hell."

"So the suffering during the Tribulation is the result of this world—I mean heavenly—war?"

"God's wrath on the wicked is much worse than just war," Mark replied. "God's judgments are enacted through the seven seals, the seven trumpets, and the seven bowls. These judgments get increasingly worse as the End Time progresses. The seven seals include the appearance of the Antichrist, war, famine, plague, the martyrdom of believers in Christ, a terrible earthquake, and astronomical upheaval. Those who survive the seven seals will be subject to the seven trumpets. The trumpets include hail and fire that destroy much of plant life on Earth, the death of much of the world's aquatic life, the darkening of the sun and moon, a plague of demonic locusts, and a demonic army that kills a third of humanity. And if that's not enough, the seventh trumpet calls forth seven angels who carry the seven bowls of God's wrath."

"What's in these bowls?" Tanya asked.

Mark took his eyes off the road for a moment to look at Tanya. He felt he was preaching, but her blue eyes looked curious rather than bored.

"I didn't realize my year in divinity school would come in handy," he said and smiled. "The seven bowls are actually pretty frightening. They're from Revelation 16, the vision of the revelation of Jesus Christ by John of Patmos. Seven angels are given seven bowls of God's wrath to pour out on the wicked after the sounding of the seven trumpets. When the first bowl is poured out, painful sores appear on those bearing the mark of the beast. With the second bowl, the seas and the oceans turn to blood and everything in them dies. The third bowl turns the rivers to blood. The fourth bowl causes a heat wave to scorch the planet. The fifth bowl pours darkness over the kingdom of the beast. When the sixth bowl is poured out, three unclean spirits come out of the mouths of the dragon, the beast, and the false prophet to gather the nations of the world to battle against the forces of good in the Battle of Armageddon. When the seventh bowl is poured out, a global earthquake causes cities to collapse and mountains and islands to vanish from their foundations."

Tanya cracked open her window to let in some air. The air smelled of diesel exhaust. "Given the cataclysmic events in the world today, with emerging diseases, mass extinctions, global warming, hurricanes, and earthquakes, you might think that the Tribulation has already begun. I never imagined that the world might end in our lifetime."

"It doesn't end after the Battle of Armageddon," Mark continued. "After Christ wins the Battle of Armageddon, Satan will be bound and thrown into a bottomless pit for a thousand years. During this millennium, Jesus will rule the world, and Jerusalem will be His capital. After a thousand years, Satan will be released from his prison and start a rebellion that will again be defeated. All the wicked from history will be resurrected to stand before God in a Last Judgment, and all the sinners will be cast into a lake of fire. God will then remake the heavens and the earth and there will be no more pain, death, or suffering."

"I can see why you would want to be born again and raptured before the End Time," Tanya said. "Does the Bible tell us when these horrors will begin?"

"Many think that it will happen in our lifetimes."

"What do *you* think?"

"Hell, I don't know. I hope not."

"It sounds to me like you can interpret Bible prophecy any way you want."

"You need to read it for yourself."

"I think I will," Tanya said. "Our Orthodox faith is much more rigid. Our priests interpret the Bible for you."

"In Protestant churches, there is no single authority for interpreting Scripture. If you want to delve into the various denominations of Protestantism, then Nashville's the place."

As they neared the city limits, a large billboard obscured the skyline. It read TENNESSEE FIRST and pictured a smiling visage of Tennessee's favorite native son, Senator Julian Rich Jr. in his bid for reelection. As they crossed the city limits, a second billboard caught Mark's attention.

It portrayed a resolute young woman in an air force uniform standing in front of an Apache helicopter. It read ATTORNEY GENERAL MARY LOU JACKSON FOR SENATE. FIGHTING FOR TENNESSEE. *This may be the sign from heaven*, he thought. *If anyone can help Tanya, it's Mary Lou Jackson.*

* * * *

The Reverend Dr. Mathias Kane sat at the reserved table in the Oak Bar of the Hermitage Hotel sipping a Tennessee waltz. He had preached against the evils of liquor on his televised homilies yet believed that to preach against temptation, you had to first experience it yourself. As a young man, he had been reborn in the summer of 1968, but it had not been the ecstatic lifting of the spirit to Jesus that most of his brethren had experienced. He had stolen the centerfold from a *Playboy* magazine at the local barbershop and taken it to Devil's Hole Cave near his home in Self, Arkansas. The cave was rumored to be the lair of a mythical beast called a *gowrow*. After succumbing to temptation, he threw the crumpled page into the mouth of the cave. A thundercloud blotted out the sun and cast the opening of the cave into near total darkness. He heard a hissing sound come from the mouth of the cave, followed by a deep growl that emanated from the belly of an unseen beast. Mathias's blood ran cold. He saw four great beasts emerge from the cave: a lion, a bear, a leopard, and a horrific beast with iron teeth and ten horns. The last beast spoke to him and blasphemed God. Mathias regained his nerve, ran home, and told his mother what he had seen. Rather than whipping him, she opened a Bible and with wide-open eyes read him the passages from the book of Revelation and book of Daniel that described the events of the End Time. She told him that he had been chosen by God to be a preacher and to convert as many souls as he could because the Tribulation would soon be upon us.

When Mathias's mother passed, his uncle, Reverend Anderson, took him under his care. He arranged to have Mathias attend the Baptist Bible College in Springfield, Missouri. Mathias Kane proved to be a charismatic preacher. He founded a fundamentalist church in a shuttered movie theater in Self and then expanded his congregation through door-to-door visitations, mailings, radio, and television. His message was simple: the Bible is inerrant and the End Time is near. People traveled from surrounding towns to hear him preach. The theater in Self soon proved to be too small to hold all who needed to be saved, so with the donations of believers, he began taping his Sunday service. Thousands watched as the crippled regained their strength and cast away their crutches. Demons were cast out. Simple folk spoke in tongues. With support from a few business-minded brethren, he formed an organization to channel the donations to save even more souls. One of his patrons, Julian Rich Sr., signed him to radio and television contracts in his Christian media empire. The Reverend Dr. Mathias Kane rose to become one of the top televangelists in the land with several million followers. His ministry opened Facebook and Twitter accounts to reach the young. Dr. Mathias Kane's call for a Last Awakening had gone viral. Even the president, to placate his base, frequently referred to Dr. Kane as his spiritual advisor.

"Shall I bring you another Tennessee waltz?" the bartender asked.

"Nothing like great American rye," Dr. Kane replied. "The key is to enjoy the spirit without succumbing to the temptation of the flesh. All is best in moderation. You can bring me another when the senator arrives."

Dr. Kane had requested the table in the alcove of the bar so even the bartender could not eavesdrop on their conversation. It was ten in the morning, and the Oak Bar would not officially open for another hour. Senator Julian Rich had called the hotel manager to request the facility for a private meeting. Dr. Kane settled into the plush leather chair and checked his schedule on his phone. He was booked solid starting at noon, and it was already ten past ten. Senator Rich had requested the meeting to discuss the Family Values March to the White House on the Fourth of July that he hoped would attract a million marchers. Only a handful of televangelists had that kind of reach, and the Reverend Dr. Mathias Kane was one of them. The liberal media had labeled it as the white march, and Senator Rich insisted that some diversity was essential, if not of race, then at least of religion. The Russian Orthodox, he said, were willing to join in the effort to save Christianity.

Senator Rich descended the stairs into the Oak Bar followed by a steely-eyed man in a sable-collared coat. The senator greeted the reverend with his trademark handshake—a firm grasp of the hand followed by a yank that drew the reverend into his bosom.

"Dr. Kane, always a pleasure. Allow me to introduce my business associate, Mr. Victor Ivanovich, director of the Institute for Democratic Progress."

Ivanovich shook the reverend's hand and offered a slight bow of deference that Dr. Kane took as a sign of respect. "You are, of course," he asked Ivanovich, "a Christian?"

"Russian Orthodox but Christian nonetheless," Ivanovich replied. "May we sit?"

"Yes, forgive my manners," Dr. Kane said. "It's just that I thought I would be meeting with the senator in private."

"I can vouch for my colleague," Senator Rich replied. "We were just at a meeting in Washington at the Ukrainian embassy when the topic of our Family Values March came up. Victor argued that the cause is universal and should be promoted as such. Perhaps I should let him explain."

The waiter offered them the specialty drinks menu.

"I know it by heart," Senator Rich said. "Please bring the reverend another Tennessee waltz and I'll have the same. My colleague would prefer something with vodka. Perhaps . . ."

"Just straight vodka, no ice," Ivanovich said. "A Tito's. Corn-based, I believe. Everything in America is somehow based on corn. Even your gasoline."

"It's God's bounty," the reverend said.

"Reverend," Ivanovich began, but Dr. Kane shifted in his seat. "Shall I address you as Reverend?" Ivanovich asked.

"You may call me Dr. Kane."

"Dr. Kane, as the esteemed senator had mentioned, we began a discussion of the importance of family values at our recent meeting at the Ukrainian embassy. Your idea of holding a march for family values on Independence Day was inspirational. Families come together on holidays. What better day to convince the politicians that you are, indeed, one nation under God, and not just any god but Jesus Christ?"

"I didn't quite get where you're from?" Dr. Kane asked.

"I'm a citizen of the world. My Institute for Democratic Progress is based in Prague. I'm an ethnic Russian but with extensive business interests throughout Eastern Europe. The important point is that I'm a Christian, which is where I believe we may share a common cause."

The waiter brought two more Tennessee waltzes and an old-fashioned glass half-full with vodka. Ivanovich eyed the glass as if something was amiss, downed it in one gulp, and tapped the glass for another.

"Dr. Kane," Ivanovich continued, "since we overthrew the godless communists, Russia has seen a rebirth of Orthodox Christianity. Yet our faith is under constant threat."

"From radical Islam," Dr. Kane stated.

"Yes, but even more dangerously from the West. Western civilization is becoming godless, secular, and radical. This decadence is infecting our youth like a venereal disease. Today, abortions, broken marriages, gays, lesbians, transgenders, and all manner of perversions threaten to be the new norm. Where do you see these condoned in the Bible? We Orthodox have made a choice to reassert ourselves as a Christian nation. God, not the tsar or the president, is our highest authority."

Dr. Kane looked to the senator as a touchstone.

Senator Rich was nodding in agreement. The senator quoted Billy Graham: "'Let us tell the whole world that we Americans believe in God and that we are morally and spiritually strong.' I agree with Victor that this diversity of religion, race, and sexual preference has gone much too far. We're not alone in this struggle. Russia has had the courage to address these issues head on, without bowing to political correctness. I know we have our political differences, but they pale in comparison to our messianic mission of saving Christianity. 'Let us tell the world that we are united and ready to march under the banner of Almighty God. Let us take as our slogan that which is stamped on our coins: In God We Trust.'"

The waiter brought Ivanovich a second glass of vodka.

"You're suggesting some form of alliance?" Dr. Kane asked.

Ivanovich had anticipated this point in the conversation. His theological consultants had pored over Kane's publications and televised speeches. They had mined the text of his sermons and reduced them to sets of likely points and counterpoints. "Nothing formal," Ivanovich said. "Simply an acknowledgment that we share the same values. I am not a religious scholar, but I know that we share much of the same doctrine."

"We differ with the Orthodox on several major points," Dr. Kane countered. "Do you believe in the inerrancy of Scripture?"

"We believe that Scripture is inerrant, but our understanding of it is not always so."

"Do you believe that sound teaching can only be based on the words in the Bible?" Dr. Kane asked.

"We believe that the Bible is God's word. But we disagree in that the church, not the individual, provides the overall sense and meaning of the Scriptures under God's guidance and inspiration."

"Do you believe, as Jesus told Nicodemus, that 'no one can see the Kingdom of God unless he is born again?'"

"We Orthodox believe in justification by faith, but we expand it to the concept of theosis, which is the working out of holiness in the life of the believer. Yes, the believer is saved, but he is also being saved. Orthodox Christians believe the church can help to achieve salvation, much like Noah's Ark."

"You keep emphasizing the role of the church," Dr. Kane countered. "There is no true or perfect church. If one claims to be, then don't join it. Any gathering of two or more Christians is a church."

"It is precisely on this point, Dr. Kane, that I agree with you and not with my Orthodox brethren. They would label my belief as heresy because it undermines their power. A Russian Orthodox monk in the Pochayiv Monastery in Ukraine, Brother Alexiy, preaches that we need a reformation of Orthodoxy as has occurred centuries ago in the West. He is a mystic and can see into the future. He has seen the End Time, and the Last Days are nearer than we think. I think the two of you would have much in common. He, too, sees the need for a Last Awakening. He says we are in the midst of a famine—a famine for the words of our Lord. Let us unite. Let us save mankind together."

"A prophet in the wilderness," Dr. Kane said, recognizing the citation.

"But what of Ezekiel 38:2 and the prince of Rosh?"

Ivanovich had anticipated Kane's counterpoint that a tyrant from Russia would lead the alliance of nations that would invade Jerusalem and precipitate the End Time. "Brother Alexiy foresees that God will use an enormous army led by Russia and China to punish the Western nations for their sins. This fighting will lead to the Tribulation. Our role is not to stop God's plan for the Second Coming; our role is to save as many souls as we can."

"So your Brother Alexiy believes that we should be God's instruments in precipitating Armageddon?

"God has already decided our roles. You are the prophet of the Last Awakening."

Dr. Kane fiddled with the Luxardo cherry in his Tennessee waltz. "I would need to pray on this. I'm already the most successful televangelist in America."

"Forgive me for my presumptuousness," Ivanovich said. "My people have done some research prior to our meeting. You are the third most successful televangelist in terms of followers and fourth in terms of income."

Dr. Kane rose from the table in response to this brazen falsehood, but Senator Rich eased him back into the chair. "Mathias, there are different ways of looking at these numbers—figures lie and liars figure. The important point is that we can make you number one. Allow Mr. Ivanovich to present his proposal."

"We have given this considerable thought," Ivanovich continued, "and we believe that the best approach would be a three-pronged strategy. First, we'll begin with public displays of unity, like the March for Family Values in Washington. Second, we'll expand your Christian messaging to Russian-speaking populations through our own media networks. And third, we'll help you significantly expand your social media presence to reach the millennials."

"Why specifically millennials?" Dr. Kane asked.

"In 2019 they will surpass the baby boomers in terms of numbers of eligible voters."

"Voters?" Dr. Kane asked.

"A euphemism for adulthood, simply a statistic from your own Pew Research's Religious Landscape Study. The point is you need to connect to the younger generation."

"I already have a Facebook page with over a million followers, and a Twitter account as well," Dr. Kane responded.

"Yes, but you're connecting with them passively. We're advocating a more active approach."

"In what way?"

"Millennials don't read books anymore, let alone the Bible, so we need to bring Scripture to them in a form they understand. With the help of a professor from Oxford, we've developed a new Bible app that you can download onto your phone. It uses the latest advances in artificial intelligence. It seamlessly syncs with your other apps, including your browser, GPS, Facebook, camera, and contacts to develop an evolving profile of the user. The more you use it, the more it learns about you. It even listens to the tone and tempo of your voice to determine how you're feeling at that particular moment. The AI software proactively develops and continually updates your personalized salvation plan in real time by pushing verses from the Bible. Let's say that a person has an addiction to pornography. Our algorithms would push Matthew 5:28, 1 Corinthians 6:18-20, and 1 John 2:16. If a man is a compulsive liar, our program would push Colossians 3:9 and Exodus 23:1. If the GPS says you're in Las Vegas, it will push Hebrews 13:5 or Ecclesiastes 5:10. If you're feeling sad, it will push Psalm 40, lift you out of the slimy pit, and set your feet back on a rock. You get the picture. Think of it as your virtual guardian angel."

Senator Rich chimed in. "Our marketing research tells us that people *want* to be told what to do. We're simply letting Scripture be their guide."

"How would I benefit from this new app of yours?"

"It needs a *brand*," Ivanovich replied. "There are dozens of Bible apps, but none that stand out above the others. If we added your name and endorsement, we could distribute millions. We estimate that you would triple your number of followers in less than a year. The app would be free, but it would continually solicit donations, especially when the user has sinned."

Dr. Kane took a long sip of his Tennessee waltz as he pondered this offer. He speared the Luxardo cherry that was wedged beneath the oversize ice cube in his old-fashioned glass. "And this monk . . . Brother Alexiy?"

"He's a mystic. He speaks in riddles," Ivanovich said. "We need a communicator. We need someone who can connect with the common man. You project confidence. You project faith. Senator Rich has assured me that you are the prophet of the Last Awakening. We believe that God has chosen *you* to deliver His message."

Dr. Kane popped the cherry into his mouth. "Do you, sir, believe in the prosperity gospel?"

Ivanovich smiled. "Financial blessings are the will of God."

"Then perhaps we can work something out," he said. "Send over a business plan. If your offer looks good, we can market this new app at the International Christian Media Forum in Las Vegas in May. As for the march, I'll extend an invitation to your Brother Alexiy. We'll make it interdenominational. Your offer to go global with my message is enticing. I'll let you know my intentions before tonight's radio gospel hour."

Ivanovich reached in his pocket and pulled out a piece of paper with a handwritten note. "I've taken the liberty of suggesting a topic that you might touch on in tonight's sermon, but only if you concur, of course. It will be a sign that you're seriously considering our offer."

Dr. Kane read the note. "Amos 8:11–12 and the Holodomor. Stalin's famine of 1932 and 1933?"

"An unfortunate, albeit temporary, sacrifice in the process of collectivization," Ivanovich replied. "The kulaks revolted against having their property taken over by the state, and they suffered the consequences. Reactionary forces refer to the famine as murder by hunger, or Holodomor. Can you imagine, your own US Congress called it genocide against our Ukrainian brothers? We are simply trying to correct historical misconceptions."

Kane looked at Senator Rich for guidance, but Rich failed to meet his glance.

"Whatever happened was God's will," Kane surmised. "The unfortunate souls must have done something to incur His wrath." He kept reading the note until he came to a name. "And who is this Bereza?"

"A whore who spreads lies like a venereal disease."

"Like the whore of Babylon," Kane replied. He put the note in his pocket. "Just make sure your spreadsheets are in dollars, and not rubles."

The guttural laughter burst out of the Oak Bar like the growl of a gowrow from the mouth of Devil's Hole Cave.

* * * *

Attorney General Mary Lou Jackson looked at the photo on her desk that she had used for her election billboard. It pictured her in pilot gear in front of her Apache helicopter at an air base in Afghanistan. She still had both of her legs. It had taken her years to overcome her posttraumatic stress, and the rigors of the primary campaign were triggering flashbacks. She vividly remembered swooping into the mountain gorge at sunset to support the evacuation of army rangers who had stumbled upon a Taliban stronghold during a reconnaissance mission. Her chain gun and rockets had given the accompanying Black Hawk enough time to complete the evacuation. In the chaos she had missed the cave to her flank until it was too late. A rocket-propelled grenade shot out of the mouth of the cave like a spitting cobra. The Apache reeled from the blast as it lost its rear rotor. She had been able to pull out of the gorge and careen out of the mountains as a plume of burning fuel traced her zigzag course through the night sky. She crash-landed her Apache on a plateau about ten miles from the gorge. The next thing she remembered was waking up in a hospital bed to the stone face of her commanding officer who informed her that she was a true American hero. It was then that she realized that her right leg was gone.

During her primary campaign for the Senate, the internet trolls began to challenge the official version of her story. Anonymous survivors of the firefight claimed that they had never seen her Apache descend into the gorge. The online chat rooms were abuzz with debates about whether women should serve in combat roles, especially as pilots of attack helicopters that cost over $35.5 million each. That money came out of the pockets of hardworking Americans. No one could challenge her missing leg, yet some speculated that she crash-landed during a training mission. Campaign surveys showed that in her home state only 40 percent of men and 62 percent of women believed her story. Her public relations advisors told her that challenging the fake news only added fuel to the fire.

Doubts were ricocheting in her brain like machine gun fire.

Her secretary opened her door after the attorney general did not respond to her vigorous knocking. "I apologize for the intrusion," the secretary said, "but there's a young man here who insists on seeing you. He won't give his name. He claims to have some information about Senator Rich. Shall I tell him to schedule an appointment?"

The attorney general looked at her watch: half past seven. "What kind of information?"

"He says it's highly confidential. He'll only speak to you."

Mary Lou Jackson was trailing badly in the polls. The Republican primary was still months away, but her campaign had failed to gain traction. She had spent years trying to indict Julian Rich Jr. on a growing list of charges, including tax evasion, money laundering, and perjury. Her cadre of recent law school graduates was no match for his father's army of Ivy League lawyers. Each case was hopelessly stalled in a quagmire of motions and counter motions. The *Tennessean* had received an anonymous tip that one of her assistant attorneys was a Muslim. That sparked a rumor that she had converted to Islam while in Afghanistan and, if elected, would impose Sharia law in the heart of the Bible Belt. The story was fanned by Rich's Christian media stations. The Reverend Dr. Mathias Kane had implored her on national television to take Jesus into her heart.

The attorney general considered her options. "Send him in," she said.

Mark Rider walked into her office unsure as to how to address the attorney general of the state of Tennessee. "Ms. Jackson . . ."

"Madam Attorney General," she corrected him. "You have five minutes. Why are you here?"

Mark didn't know whether to sit or stand. He decided to stand. "I'm a journalism student. I saw your billboard driving into Nashville, and

I have some information about your opponent. I could also use your professional advice."

Mary Lou Jackson studied the young man. He reminded her of her fellow pilots in Afghanistan. It took balls to barge into the office of an attorney general.

"It's about Senator Rich Jr.," Mark continued. "I believe he committed a crime."

"He's committed countless crimes," the attorney general retorted. "Come to the point."

"Three days ago I picked up a hitchhiker on Highway 1 in the Florida Keys. A foreigner. A Ukrainian. She claims that Senator Rich Jr. sexually assaulted her."

Mary Lou Jackson sighed. "Do you know how many women have filed sexual harassment charges against the senator?" she asked. "Too many to count. She'll need to get in line."

"I didn't say sexually harassed. She says she was raped."

"Was she medically examined? Any DNA samples?"

"She refused to seek medical attention."

"Where is she now?"

"She's at a hotel here in Nashville."

"Where did the rape occur?"

"Around Duck Key."

"The State of Florida has jurisdiction over rape cases in their state," the attorney general informed him. "She'll need to file charges there."

"She's afraid of the police."

"Then I'm afraid there's nothing I can do. Try and convince her to change her mind."

Mark nodded and turned toward the door. "There's one more thing," he said.

"What's that?"

"The rape occurred on the yacht of a Russian oligarch."

The attorney general sat up in her chair. "In international waters?"

"I don't know."

"What flag was it flying?"

"I don't know."

"Do you remember his name or the name of the yacht?"

"Ivanovich, something or other," Mark replied.

The attorney general stood up. "Tell your friend I need to talk to her. Anywhere where she feels safe. She's involved with some very dangerous people. Here's my card. I'll write my personal cell phone number on the back. Call me from a public phone. Don't use your cell phone. What did you say your name was again?"

"I didn't say."

"Listen. You look like an intelligent young man, but you're in over your head. Don't get entrapped in a Russian mafia war. This runaway may just be using you."

Mark took the card and put it in the pocket of his jeans. Her change in demeanor when she heard Ivanovich's name rattled him. As he was leaving the attorney general's office, the secretary stopped him. "He said he couldn't wait," she said.

"Who?"

"The young man who came in behind you."

"You must be mistaken. I came here alone."

"He asked if you had gone in to see the attorney general. I just assumed he was with you."

Mark felt like his heart stopped.

"Are you all right?" the secretary asked. "You look like you've seen a ghost."

Mark left without answering. As he ran down the stairs, his heart started pounding. *I left Tanya alone! I need to get to her before he does.* When he exited the John Sevier building, he scanned the plaza for his pursuer. People were simply going about their business. *It could be any one of them.* He zigzagged through side streets and alleys on his way back to the DoubleTree. When he returned to their room, Tanya was gone. Her clothes were scattered on the bed. The minibar was open. Two empty mini bottles of Jack Daniels were on the dresser. A note was scribbled on the bathroom mirror in lipstick: GONE OUT. He rushed downstairs to ask the doorman if he had seen her leave.

"That fine lady you came in with? Sure, I couldn't miss her."

"Was she alone?"

"As far as I can tell."

"Did she say where she was going?"

"She was asking for directions to Broadway She wanted some recommendations for country music bars."

"What did you recommend?" Mark asked.

"Tootsies. Everybody goes to Tootsies."

* * * *

Tootsie Bess, a singer with Big Jeff & The Radio Playboys, bought Mom's in 1970. One day she came in to find that a painter had painted the place orchid, hence the name The Orchid Lounge. Mark knew the place simply as Tootsie's. Of all the honky-tonk and dive bars on Broadway, Tootsies was his favorite. Legends like Willie Nelson, Waylon Jennings, and Kris Kristofferson had played on the cramped stage. Mark had not heard tonight's group, Jeff Mustang and the Pickups, before, but he knew they had to be good. Everyone who performed at Tootsies had a shot at the big time.

Tootsie's was packed with patrons. The bouncer at the door checked IDs and let people in as others exited. Mark waited patiently in line as hordes of revelers ambled down Broadway in their jeans, boots, and cowboy hats, all trying to be "country." Drunk college boys were bouncing into tourists as they chased gaggles of girls from bar to bar. Mark squeezed in when a raucous bachelorette party spilled out of the bar. He saw Tanya sitting at the far end of the bar with a shot and a beer.

"What the hell do you think you're doing?" Mark shouted over the music.

"Getting away from you," she retorted. "You brought me to Nashville without even discussing it with me. I'm not your girl. I decided that if I'm in Music Town, I might as well have some fun."

"It's too dangerous."

"Then why did you bring me here?"

A comely bartender in a tight Tootsie's T-shirt asked for his order.

"Two Bud Lights and two shots of bourbon," Tanya called out.

"You don't think you've had enough? We need to get out of here."

"I'm not leaving. I need an escape, even if it's just for one night." She started moving her shoulders to the beat of the Pickups. Jeff Mustang was thrusting his hips and singing about a small-town boy who fell in love with a big-city girl. The drums and bass guitar reverberated through the floor. Patrons were rocking in front of the stage. Those who weren't dancing were singing along whether they knew the words or not.

"I want to dance," Tanya said before Mark could object. He gulped his beer and followed her to the stage.

Tanya wiggled through the packed bar toward the band. She began to undulate her hips to the beat. Jeff Mustang tossed a band T-shirt into the crowd and Tanya caught it in midair. It was black with white letters that read "Got a Truck?" She pulled it over her own, and Jeff Mustang yanked her atop the stage to the delight of the crowd. He put the mike to her mouth. She playacted the lyrics and joined him in the refrain: "What's it gonna be boy, me or country?" Her voice was surprisingly good with just a hint of an accent. Patrons passed them shots of whiskey and beer chasers, half of them shouting, "stay country" and other half, "take the girl." Mark could see how her flirtatiousness would attract any hot-blooded boy, especially one who'd had too much to drink. He began to wonder what really happened on Ivanovich's yacht. *I bring her here to protect her, and she's singing and dancing on the stage.*

Mark felt someone lick the back of his neck. When he spun around, he saw the grinning face of a redneck with a scruffy beard and a Predators sweatshirt.

"Ain't you the guy who writes that Americana blog," the man asked, licking his lips. "I'm a real fan."

Mark wasn't sure how to react. He wiped the spit off his neck with his hand. He tried to step back but was cramped in by the dancers. "I'm with the young lady who's on the stage," he blurted out.

"Mighty fine girl if I say so myself. You got a truck?"

Mark coaxed Tanya off the stage as soon as the song was over.

Jeff Mustang pointed his mike at her. "Let's all give a hand to"—Tanya looked up but did not offer her name—"our city girl. Come up after the show. I'll show you what a real country boy is made of." Other women stood up on their tables and wiggled their boobs hoping for a similar invitation. Jeff Mustang, however, kept his mike aimed at the mysterious city girl who could dazzle an audience with the best of them.

"You're attracting too much attention," Mark said. "We need to move on."

"But I love American country music. It's so *real*." The shots she had on stage were going to her head.

"Some asshole just licked the back of my neck," he said. He pulled her back to the bar and took a long swig of his full bottle of beer. It was ice-cold and refreshing. He suddenly realized that the beer wasn't his. He had left his half-finished when they had gone to dance.

"I didn't order this beer," Mark told the bartender.

"Some Predators fan bought you a second round," the bartender replied.

Tanya was facing the stage, still trucking to the music.

"Tanya, did you see the guy who bought me this beer? He was standing next to me when you were up on the stage. Do you recognize him?" Mark had seen those eyes before, but where?

Her head was spinning. The bar was hopping. It was dark except for the illuminated bar bottles and the lights on the stage. "I don't know who you mean."

Mark tried to find him in the crowd but the man was gone. Paranoia crept up his spine.

"We need to leave," he said. "I'm pretty sure we're being followed."

Tanya's face went from giddy to stone sober.

"Let's head toward the back," Mark said. "There has to be another way out of here."

The exit to the alley was up the stairs through a second-story bar with more live music. Mark took Tanya by the hand and elbowed his way toward the exit. As the patrons looked to see who was pushing through, Mark said, "I'm going to be sick. I need to get some fresh air."

An EXIT sign shone over a metal door that opened into stairs to the alley outside. The cool night air greeted them in the alleyway, a welcome relief from the exhaled breath of stalkers and strangers. They startled a mongrel dog that was rummaging through the garbage. *Must be Jeff Mustang's hound dog,* Mark hunched over and vomited. There were flecks of fresh blood in the vomit. *Was I poisoned?* He knelt in the alley and forced himself to vomit until he could vomit no more. Tanya helped him to his feet. They staggered out of the alleyway and disappeared into the throngs of bar hoppers who were merrymaking their way down America's Honky-Tonk Highway.

Dmitri stepped into the alleyway and shut the door behind him to silence the alarm. There was no point in chasing after his poisoned prey. He could locate them at any moment through Rider's cell phone. Rider had made a fatal mistake. He had spoken to the attorney general of Tennessee. Dmitri looked at his watch. He was curious as to the kinetics of the three drops of hemolytic toxin that he had added to Rider's beer. The poison was a mycotoxin responsible for outbreaks of sago hemolytic disease in Papua New Guinea. The purified toxicant was previously tested on prisoners but had never been used under actual field conditions. Dmitri studied the pool of vomit on the alley floor. Rider must have forced himself to vomit. The dose was now unpredictable. He could live or he could die. If he hadn't purged enough of the poison, then the rusalka would just have to find herself another ride.

* * * *

Mark and Tanya left the hotel before midnight without checking out. The roads would be empty at this hour except for long-haul truckers, and he wanted to reach the safety of his apartment in Chicago by daybreak. He felt exhausted, and he figured that they had swallowed enough chaos over the past three days. His pulse was racing, and he seemed to be breathing faster than usual. Tanya was fast asleep in the passenger seat. At three in the morning, he stopped for gas and a Mountain Dew at Crazy D's. It felt like the temperature had dropped by ten degrees. When he went to pee, he noticed that his urine was the color of Coca-Cola. He jumped back in his car and sped toward home.

The staccato white highway lines were hypnotizing. He felt like he was being hunted. *What have I gotten myself into? Who's following us?* Perhaps the Predators fan had licked his neck as a joke. Still, the encounter felt more deliberate than a prank, as if some drunken roughneck was goading him into a fight.

Mark turned on the radio to stay awake. He happened on a Christian radio station that was rebroadcasting Dr. Kane's Gospel Hour. The good reverend was quoting Amos 8:11–12:

> Behold, the days are coming, declares the Lord God, when I will send a famine on the land—not a famine for bread, nor a thirst for water, but of hearing the words of the Lord. They shall wander from sea to sea, and from north to east; they shall run to-and-fro, to seek the word of the Lord, but they shall not find it.

Dr. Kane preached how famines were the just result of God's wrath on the wicked. He used the historical example of the Holodomor, and how millions of sinners had died for resisting authority that was granted to Stalin by God. He cited Romans 13:1:

> Let every person be subject to the governing authorities. For there is no authority except from God, and those that exist have been instituted by God. Therefore whoever resists the authorities resists what God has appointed, and those who resist will incur judgment.

He warned his listeners that the Last Days were upon them and that he had seen the whore of Babylon riding upon her scarlet seven-headed beast. She was already among us spreading her blasphemous lies. He used the example of a Ukrainian prostitute by the name of Tanya Bereza who kept the company of transvestites, and how she was spreading lies about God-fearing politicians whose authority was granted to them by God. He beseeched her to come to him to seek forgiveness. He finished his sermon with the words: "Even whores can be born again."

The white median stripes were blurring into gray. Tanya was awake and staring at the radio in disbelief. The last thing Mark saw before blacking out was a black billboard on the side of the road with three monosyllabic words written in white: HELL IS REAL.

CHAPTER 6

Chicago

Mark dreamed of Gog, the king of the North, and the army of two hundred million assembled to plunder the land of the Jews. He dreamed of the Rapture, the abomination of desolation, Armageddon, and the End Time. He dreamed of a nuclear holocaust. The bells of Saint Nicholas Cathedral rang eight times before he opened his eyes. He awoke shaking in his own bed, unsure of how he had gotten there. The last thing he remembered was an ominous warning on a billboard in the black Indiana night.

The sun streamed through the leaded glass windows of his vintage apartment on Walton Street. Mark had chosen to live in the Ukrainian Village for its authenticity and proximity to the Loop. Chicago, he had discovered, was a patchwork of ethnic neighborhoods. Some had withstood the changing times and retained their character, and others had not. The Ukrainian Village had seen four waves of Ukrainian immigrants since the 1880s that had come to find work in the City of Big Shoulders. The village was also home to Poles, Italians, and Puerto

Ricans. There was a bar on every block. In addition to the local dives that catered to ethnic regulars, some watering holes, such as the Rainbo Club, changed with the times and evolved from a Prohibition speakeasy to a polka club to a hangout for the likes of Nelson Algren and Liz Phair.

Mark lay naked in his bed. He was covered with an extra blanket, and his clothes were laundered and folded on the side of the bed. His bedsheets smelled of sweat. A dozen strange glass cups were neatly arranged on the nightstand next to his phone. There was a voice mail message from Dana asking if he'd made it home safely. When he checked the date on his phone, he realized that he'd lost an entire day.

The oak floor creaked when he stood up out of bed. He pulled on his briefs and stumbled over to the bathroom to empty his bladder. His urine was still dark. When he looked in the blackened mirror, he barely recognized himself. His face had aged ten years. His skin was sallow. Even the whites of his eyes had turned the color of piss. He turned on the light and gasped—his torso was covered with a dozen perfectly round bruises. He splashed his face with cold water and rubbed the crust out of his eyes. He found Tanya asleep on the couch in the living room. She had covered herself with the quilt that Lili had given him last Christmas.

His laptop was on the coffee table next to the couch. It was open to a conspiracy website in which most of the text was capitalized, underlined, or in italics. Yellow sticky notes with scribbles in Cyrillic were arranged on the glass tabletop in some indiscernible connect-the-dots pattern. He sat down on the edge of the couch and scrolled through the search history on his browser. At first the links appeared to be only tangentially connected:

"Little Card Sound development funded by laundered Russian money"

"Senator Rich supports repeal of Magnitsky Act"

"Mystery 'whore of Babylon' identified as missing Ukrainian sculptress"

"Bloomberg reports on global Christian media merger"

"Mathias Kane to launch new Last Awakening app"

Tanya touched him on his knee as he was following her clues. "You're up. I was worried about you." She was wearing his Northwestern

Wildcats T-shirt as a pajama.

"It looks like you've been browsing all night," he said.

"I'm making progress."

A black veil fell over Mark's eyes. He grabbed the edge of the coffee table to keep from collapsing. Tanya put her hand around his waist to brace him and eased him back onto the couch.

"You need to eat something," she said. "You look like you've just risen from the dead. I made some borscht while you were asleep."

"How did we make it home?"

"You were weaving. I made you pull over, and I drove the rest of the way."

"How did you know where to go?" Mark asked.

"Your address is on your driver's license, and your keys were in your pants."

"How . . . how did I make it up the stairs?"

"You were delirious but still able to walk. We climbed one step at a time."

"You undressed me?"

She looked at him like a teacher looks at a schoolboy who's afraid to raise his hand to go the bathroom. The late morning sun streamed through the single-pane windows, revealing the polka-dot bruises on his torso.

"What . . ." he began to ask.

"Cupping," she replied. "When I couldn't wake you, I realized there was something terribly wrong. I went looking for a pharmacy. I found one on Chicago Avenue that sells homeopathic remedies. The pharmacist said the cups would suck out any bad blood and make you better. It's a common folk remedy in my country. They used them on me in the internat."

"Internat?"

"It's an orphanage, except that most of children who are placed there aren't orphans."

"How is that possible?"

"We were abandoned by our parents. We're social orphans. The state took care of us."

Mark was surprised that someone as accomplished and cosmopolitan as Tanya had grown up in an orphanage. There were depths to her that he still couldn't fathom. At least she hadn't tried leeches.

Tanya helped him to his feet and walked him to the kitchen. She sat him down at the table and heated up a pot of borscht. He held on to the table to steady himself. She ladled the blood-red borscht into two bowls and sat down across from him.

"I've been having terrible nightmares," Mark said. "The last thing I remember was driving down Interstate 65 listening to some televangelist and seeing a sign that said Hell Is Real."

"He was real," Tanya said. "The sign was real." She grabbed his hand. "That preacher—he called me out by *name*!"

His apartment with its deadbolt locks in the low-crime Ukrainian Village neighborhood no longer seemed safe.

"This televangelist . . ."

"Kane. Mathias Kane," Tanya said.

"I recognize the name. My parents have been listening to him for years. But how could he possibly be connected to Rich and Ivanovich?"

Tanya took a sip of the steaming borscht. "I still haven't been able to fit together all of the pieces. The web is rife with conspiracy theories about Russian collusion. Several links name Rich specifically, but the allegations have never been proven. His father runs a Christian media empire. Kane is his marquee televangelist. I told you I overheard Rich and Ivanovich plotting something about saving souls when I was aboard the *Kalinka*."

"You also said you were drugged. It's hard to believe that a Russian oligarch and American senator would be conspiring to save souls. I've been bombarding you with arcane biblical prophecies since I took you to Noah's Ark. Are you sure you didn't imagine it?"

"Like your sudden illness?"

Mark sickened at the thought of the tongue licking his neck. *Hell is real.* He put his hand on Tanya's. "I think I was poisoned. If I hadn't forced myself to vomit, I could have died. Thank you for taking care of me."

"You took care of me when I needed you," Tanya replied.

"I think we're in way over our heads," Mark said. "We need to ask for help." He reached in his pocket but came up empty.

"Is this what you're looking for?" Tanya asked as she handed him the business card of the attorney general of Tennessee. I found it in your pocket when I was looking for your keys."

"I . . . I can explain," Mark stuttered. "Mary Lou Jackson is Rich's political opponent. I thought she could help us. I went to see her, and she's offered to help. She recognized Ivanovich. She said we're dealing with very dangerous people. She asked that you call her from a public phone."

"You lied to me. You said you were going to consult some friends of your father."

"I'm so sorry. I won't lie to you again. The lie almost killed me."

"Did you tell her my name?"

"No. Not even my own."

Tanya put the card in her pocket. "You're naive," she said. "Don't trust anyone in power. Today they're political opponents. Tomorrow they're business associates. People like you and me, we're their marionettes. When the performance is over, they just stuff us back in a box."

"America's different," Mark said.

"Your Senator Rich is American. How is he different?"

Mark couldn't offer a rationalization. "OK," he said. "We'll do it your way."

Tanya turned her attention back to her sticky notes. "I still don't understand why Kane singled me out by *name*? And why did he call me the whore of Babylon?"

"The whore of Babylon is a biblical persona that rides on the beast before the End Time. No one's quite sure what she represents. Some people think she's the Catholic Church. Others believe she represents the fallen Protestant churches. Those who read the Bible literally believe that she's a real entity. Her arrival presages the Tribulation."

"If they're demonizing me, then they're afraid of me. It means that I'm no longer just a victim. They're afraid I'm going to expose their conspiracy."

Mark felt proud of her. She was no longer the frightened runaway that he had picked up on Highway 1. She seemed determined to turn the tables on her antagonists. He looked at the notes that she had scattered over the table. "How do we begin?"

"First we follow Reya's lead and find Turchin. I'm sure he knows where all the bodies are buried."

* * * *

Lincoln Park has its buried secrets. The southern end was once a small public cemetery, where victims of smallpox and cholera were buried in lakeside graves. The standing water in the graves flowed into Lake Michigan, threatening the young city's water supply. During the late 1800s, after citizens protested, many of the bodies were exhumed and transferred to other cemeteries. Some historians maintain that thousands of bodies had been left behind. As the dead turned to dust, generation after generation of dreamers and developers transformed the park into what it is today, the second-most-visited park in the United States with twenty million visitors a year. Lincoln Park now contains a zoo, a conservatory, a theater, a historical museum, a rowing canal, as well as beaches and playing fields. As in Edgar Allan Poe's purloined letter, perhaps the best place to hide something of value is in the most conspicuous place.

Mark and Tanya parked in the North Avenue Beach lot on the east side of Lake Shore Drive and walked toward the beach before turning south toward the chess pavilion. An early spring had awakened the dormant earth: the grass was turning green, and daffodils, crocuses, and snowdrops were in full bloom. Bikers and skateboarders were cruising down the lakefront path in shorts and T-shirts. The modernistic open-air chess pavilion was constructed of concrete and Indiana limestone. The chessboards were sheltered by a winglike overhang and decorated with bas-relief components, incised carvings, and sculptural elements depicting chess pieces. Players were at the chessboards, some playing for fun and others hustling for money. Mark and Tanya studied the players, trying to spot the incognito Russian.

An elderly black man was hustling the novices: "Five bucks for five minutes with the bishop; the free tables are by the kiddie zoo."

A disgruntled tourist tipped his king after a fool's mate and freed a place at the table. Tanya took his spot.

"You sure you ready to play the bishop?"

Tanya placed five dollars on the table.

The bishop smiled, took a five-dollar bill from his roll and placed it on top of hers. He picked up a black pawn and a white pawn and asked, "Which hand?" The third finger of his right hand was adorned with a white gold episcopal ring. It was mounted with a large ruby surrounded by diamonds. The band was engraved with crosses on both sides.

"I choose the right hand," Tanya said.

He opened his right fist to reveal the black pawn. "The ring gets them every time," he gloated. He opened with the queen's gambit and hit the timer.

"Are you really a bishop?" she asked as she played the Albin countergambit.

The bishop laughed. "Hell, no. I won the ring from a real bishop in a chess game. From then on, people started calling me the bishop. This pavilion is my cathedral."

Twelve moves later, the bishop conceded.

"Two out of three," the bishop demanded. He reached into his billfold and pulled out another five-dollar bill. Curious onlookers, including some whom he had recently hustled, gathered around the board to see if the bishop had finally met his match. Tanya opened with the king's pawn. The bishop countered with the Caro–Kann defense. Fifteen moves later he again conceded.

"Best of five," he said.

"I can keep playing until I win the ring," Tanya replied.

The bishop considered for moment and then picked up his pieces. "Damn, woman. I just got hustled. Where did you learn to play like that?"

"I was a junior chess champion in Ukraine. You opted for the Caro–Kann defense so I countered with the Panov–Botvinnik attack. Have I beaten the best player on North Avenue Beach?"

"You have to beat the king to claim that title."

"How do I get to play the king?"

"You got to work your way up to play the king."

"Didn't I just beat the *second* best player on the beach? If so, can you arrange it, or do I have to play someone else for the privilege?"

"Maybe I can, maybe I can't. Come back here Saturday morning. Junior chess champion of Ukraine, huh? I'll still bet my money on the king."

Mark and Tanya walked over to the edge of the water. A cool wind blew in off the lake. The Chicago skyline, illuminated by the late morning sun, gleamed like a city of gold. Lake Shore Drive arced in a crescent from the Gold Coast to the tip of Navy Pier. Mark named the landmarks that rose out of the lakefront and reached for the sky.

"The architecture," Tanya said, "reflects the character of your city, bold and progressive—many different styles, many different ethnicities, but a vibrant, congruent whole."

Mark took a deep breath of the fresh April air. "Your play was pretty impressive. Were you really a champion, or was the bishop not as good as he thought he was?"

"He's an excellent player," Tanya said, "but he relies more on instinct than on theory. He didn't expect me to be so disciplined. There are infinite permutations in chess, but the opening moves and their counters and gambits have been played, studied, and perfected for centuries. And no, while I did win a few tournaments in my youth, I was never the national champion."

"Then where did you learn to play like that?"

"The matron's husband at the internat was a Master of Sport in chess before vodka got the better of him. He took a fancy to me"—she hesitated for a moment—"and taught me how to play. He would tell me stories of the grand masters and their greatest victories and defeats. He schooled me in strategy and made me play and replay countless permutations of the same move. If I made the same mistake twice, he would punish me."

"Punish you how?"

Tanya turned sullen. "I don't want to talk about it. The important thing is I learned how to beat him."

Mark knew better than to press her. "Hopefully Turchin will be curious enough to accept your challenge. Saturday is still five days away. In the meantime, let's see if we can track down some of these other leads. One of my professors at Medill, Bo Johnson, is an expert on religious media. Perhaps he can tell us something about the global Christian media merger and our mysterious Dr. Kane."

Tanya smiled. "Divine Providence."

* * * *

Medill's downtown campus was located on the sixteenth floor of a Gotham City skyscraper on East Wacker Drive. The windows overlooked the Tribune Tower and Chicago River as it flowed into Lake Michigan through the Chicago Harbor Lock. They were fortunate to find Professor Bo Johnson still at his desk during spring break. Between grading exams, he played blues riffs on the B. B. King guitar that he'd bought at a charity auction for Health in the Arts. A half-eaten Gold Coast Dog lay on his desk between piles of student papers. The walls of the office were plastered with signed posters of big-name artists and photos of him performing with lesser-known talents. He motioned with the headstock of his guitar for Mark and Tanya to take a seat while he worked out the opening to "Three O'Clock Blues." Bo Johnson was a large black man who was as comfortable performing at local clubs as he was lecturing to a packed hall of graduate students. Once he figured out the riff, he put down his pick and reached out his hand.

"Bo Johnson, pleased to meet you. I'm guessing you're not here to listen to me play."

"I'm Tanya Bereza, a friend of Mark's—and you're quite an accomplished musician. Do you play professionally?"

"I did a stint as a blues musician in my youth. My folks wisely told me to get a day job. Now and then I'll back up a friend or two at one of the local blues bars. As B. B. King once said, 'Blues is a tonic for whatever ails you.' How about you, do you play?"

"I'm a visual artist," she replied. "I sculpt. You would make a fascinating subject."

Mark was embarrassed by her forwardness, but after Nashville he had come to expect it.

"Very happy to meet a fellow artist," the professor replied as he stood up to shake her hand. "Mark, good to see you too. How's your blog? You had some great stuff on the Hurricane Monument, and I loved the entry on the Land of Oz, but then you clammed up. I thought you'd be spending this semester on the road. Looks like the road got the better of you. What's up?"

"I took a detour," Mark explained. "I met Tanya in Florida; we ran into a bit of trouble."

"What kind of trouble did the two of you get into?"

"I jumped into his car," Tanya said, "and trouble followed. I came to the United States two weeks ago to display my sculpture of the Heavenly Hundred. My sponsors tried to take advantage of me." She lowered her eyes to the floor.

"The Revolution of Dignity," the professor said. "I watched it unfold on social media."

Tanya looked up at Professor Johnson in earnest. "I understand that men can be pigs. What I can't understand is why an American preacher would single me out by name and attack me in one of his radio sermons. He's also spreading lies about the Holodomor. Mark said you're an expert on religious media. We're hoping you can give us some insights into why."

Professor Johnson put down his guitar. "What minister?"

"The Reverend Dr. Mathias Kane," Mark interjected.

"A real celebrity. Did he cite any specific chapter and verse?"

"Yes, Amos 8:11–12," Mark said.

Professor Johnson took a King James Bible off his bookshelf and found the passage. "Hmmm . . . 'a famine of hearing the words of the Lord.' Interesting that he would link it to the Holodomor."

"What more can you tell us about Dr. Kane?" Mark asked.

"Only that he's one of the most popular televangelists in the country," Professor Johnson replied. "He's the voice of the Last Awakening."

"What's the Last Awakening?" Tanya asked.

Professor Johnson plucked the E string on his B. B. King guitar, which lay across his desk, as a prelude to his discourse. "The word *evangelical* comes from the Greek word 'evangel,' meaning the 'good news' or the gospel. Evangelicals became the common name for the spiritual revivals that swept the English-speaking world during the eighteenth and early nineteenth centuries. The First Great Awakening swept through the American colonies in the 1730s and 1740s. People dissociated themselves from established approaches to worship and instead turned to great fervor and emotion in prayer. Some historians believe that the First Great Awakening, with its rejection of religious authority, was an important precursor to the American Revolution. The Second Great Awakening broke out in camp meetings in Kentucky and Tennessee at the turn of the nineteenth century. Prayer and conversion became intensely social public events. During these revivals, people were affected with all sorts of bodily agitations. The Second Great Awakening made evangelical Protestantism the dominant religion in the country."

"So where does Dr. Kane come in?" Mark asked.

"There have been other revivals since the Second Great Awakening and other charismatic preachers, such as Billy Graham," Professor Johnson said. "But these revivals mainly drew people who were already members of Protestant congregations. Dr. Kane figured out that the best way to draw new converts is to threaten them with the message that the end is near. He believes that the Rapture, the Tribulation, and the End Time will occur during our lifetimes. The Last Awakening is your last chance to come to Jesus before these biblical prophecies come to pass. Sort of like the last gas station before entering Death Valley."

"What's his relation to Senator Rich?" Tanya asked.

"Rich is reading from President Reagan's playbook. Kane's message is resonating with evangelicals and helping the senator consolidate his base. The Riches are marketing him as the prophet of the Last Awakening and giving him top billing in their media empire. It's stunning how many Americans rely on Christian media for their information. About two-thirds of weekly churchgoers and evangelicals tune in to Christian radio and television on a regular basis. About a third of Americans read Christian books, and forty percent have seen a Christian movie in the last year. The real growth is online. About twenty-five percent watch or listen to Christian programming on their computers every week. That comes to about sixty million adult Americans every week."

"But why would Kane bring up the Holodomor? And why mention me?"

"That's what doesn't make sense," Professor Johnson replied. "Kane's message is directed at Christians who are hoping to be saved. It's all about what's going to happen in their lifetimes and not about what happened back in the 1930s, especially in a country that most Americans can't locate on a map. He's preaching to an 'America first' following that couldn't give a damn about what's happening on the other side of the world. The Holodomor message is more appropriately directed at a Russian-speaking audience."

"Perhaps that was their intention," Tanya replied.

"What do you mean?" Professor Johnson asked.

"Think about it. A prominent American evangelist denying that the Holodomor was a man-made famine would be picked up and spread by Russian media," Tanya said. "There's a war being waged in my country, instigated and denied by Russia. It's fought on multiple fronts: on battlefields, on the airwaves, and on social media. This is exactly the kind of disinformation that they use as cannon fodder for their fake news stories."

"But what's in it for Kane?" the professor asked.

"The Kremlin is fueling the fire of Russian nationalism. They're resurrecting imperialism and glorifying their Soviet past. Kane's denial of the Holodomor would give him credibility with Russia's radical right. It would give him millions of new listeners. That's probably what Senator Rich and Ivanovich were talking about on the *Kalinka*."

"The *Kalinka*?" Professor Johnson asked.

"Victor Ivanovich's yacht in the Florida Keys. Ivanovich is a Russian oligarch and mafia boss."

"How do you know this?" Professor Johnson asked.

"I was there," she replied.

"So *that's* how you fit in," Professor Johnson said. He looked out his window at the Tribune Tower on the other side of the river. For over one hundred years, the venerable, neo-Gothic building had stood for the best in Chicago journalism. The *Tribune* had self-styled itself as the world's greatest newspaper. He turned his attention to Mark. "If I was the editor of the breaking news desk at the *Tribune,* I would tell you that you might be onto something and to use your investigative talents to get to the bottom of it. Senator Julian Rich Jr. is the rising star of the Republican Party. He's the chair of the Foreign Relations Committee and is slated to be a candidate for either vice president or secretary of state. He's up for reelection next year. Simply associating with a Russian businessman is not a crime. If you can find evidence that he and this Ivanovich are colluding to influence Rich's upcoming Senate campaign, then that's a breach of the Bipartisan Campaign Reform Act. You need to, as they say, 'Follow the money.'"

"We have a potential source," Mark said.

"You're dancing with the devil," Professor Johnson said. "Have you ever heard of Robert Johnson?"

"I can't say that I have," Mark replied.

"Delta blues artist. Best there ever was. I have all twenty-nine songs that he recorded for the American Record Company before he died in 1938 at the age of twenty-seven. I never knew my own daddy, so when I was young, I made up a story of how Robert Johnson and my grandma had a fling after one of his gigs in a Mississippi blues bar, and that's how I got the name Johnson." The professor added a wink. "That way, I would have inherited the gift. Anyway, my favorite song of his is 'The Crossroad Blues.' It's about a young man who finds himself at a crossroad and has to decide which way to go. The professor picked up his B. B. King guitar, played a riff, and transitioned into the chords. "Goes something like this." He sang the last stanza in a raspy barroom voice that seemed tempered with smoke and whiskey.

"Cream." Mark recognized the song.

"Yeah, they did the rock version. The point is, you're at a crossroads. You need to decide which road you're going to take."

Tanya put her hand on Mark's hand. "Whatever road we decide, we'll take it together."

Professor Johnson smiled. "Bob Johnson wished that he had a sweet woman to save him."

"To save him from what?" Tanya asked.

"From selling his soul to the devil. At least that's the legend."

"We sell our souls if we choose to do nothing," Mark said.

Professor Johnson put down his guitar. "Then there are two ways I can help you."

"We're listening," Tanya said.

"The Chicago-Kyiv Sister Cities program is hosting a delegation of journalists from the National University of Kyiv-Mohyla Academy. We met with them here at Medill just the other day. I was very impressed with these young journalists. They pioneered the debunking of Russian fake news reports with their StopFake project back in 2014. They started out as a fact-checking website then expanded to produce a weekly TV show and podcasts. This Friday evening, they'll be giving a presentation on the Russian disinformation campaign at the Ukrainian Institute of Modern Art. They have their fingers on the pulse of Russian media. I don't know why Dr. Kane is targeting you, but if your theory about Kane's motivation is correct, then his broadcast on the Holodomor should be spreading through Russian media like wildfire."

"And the other way?" Tanya asked.

"One of my good friends is the editor of the breaking news desk at the *Tribune*. If you find evidence of collusion, then he might help you spring the story. But be careful. Potential witnesses in these Russian collusion investigations tend to disappear."

* * * *

Chicago architect Stanley Tigerman designed the sleek curved facade of the Ukrainian Institute of Modern Art. The building stands in marked contrast to the Depression-era brick buildings on Chicago Avenue. Someone claiming to represent the KKK had once threatened to destroy the building in order to keep immigrants from securing a foothold in the neighborhood. The institute is triangulated by three architectural pillars of the Ukrainian community: Saint Nicholas Ukrainian Catholic Cathedral, built by the first wave of immigrants in 1913 and modeled after Saint Sophia in Kyiv; the newly constructed Selfreliance Federal Credit Union, established by post–World War II immigrants who had been active in Ukraine's cooperative movement; and the golden-domed Saints Volodymyr and Olha Ukrainian Catholic Church, built in 1968 during the calendar war that split Chicago's Ukrainian Catholics into those who followed the Julian calendar and those who followed the old-world Gregorian calendar.

Like many of Chicago's ethnic neighborhoods, the Ukrainian Village had been at risk of losing its residents and heritage during the white flight of the 1970s and 1980s. The most recent wave of Ukrainian immigrants, however, had revitalized the community. Their numbers included choir directors, semiprofessional soccer players, opera singers, and lawyers who worked as tradesmen and caregivers during the day and pursued their passions on evenings and weekends. The institute was one of the places in the Village where old met new. The permanent collection showcased pieces by renowned artists such as Urban, Hnizdovsky, and Milonadis, while the rotating collection featured avant-garde works by Ukrainian artists. One such work, Daria Marchenko and Daniel Green's portrait of Putin called *Face of War*, was assembled from five thousand spent cartridges from the war in Donbas. The institute was also a forum for authors and political scientists.

The speakers for Friday's event were three faculty members from the School of Journalism at the National University of Kyiv-Mohyla Academy. Mark had been at the institute only once before to hear Anne Applebaum speak about her latest book, *Red Famine*. Mark put ten dollars into the voluntary donation box and led Tanya into the Strutynsky gallery. All of the 120 folding chairs were occupied, so they had to stand against the wall with several other latecomers. Mark and Tanya did not notice the elderly Orthodox priest who walked in just as the consul general of Ukraine was concluding her introductory remarks. The consul general highlighted the critical role that the StopFake program had played in exposing the Russian disinformation campaign during the Revolution of Dignity, the annexation of Crimea, and the war in the east. When the Ukrainian journalists were introduced, Mark was surprised to see that they looked to be about his age or younger.

The first speaker, Vadim Nakonechny, opened with the revelation that fake news travels six times faster than truth on the web and that fake news stories were 70 percent more likely to be retweeted than true stories. He discussed how Ukraine had been Russia's laboratory for modern disinformation warfare since the Maidan Revolution. The underlying concepts and techniques had been developed by the Soviet Union decades ago and were now being calibrated and applied to new media platforms. The underlying theory relies on what the Russians call reflexive control.

Reflexive control causes a stronger adversary to voluntarily choose the actions most advantageous to Russian objectives by shaping the adversary's perceptions of reality. Russia takes advantage of preexisting dispositions among its enemies to choose its preferred course of action. In Ukraine, for example, Russia's primary objective has been to persuade the West to do what the West's leaders wanted to do in the first place, namely remain on the sidelines as Russia dismantled Ukraine. Key components to the strategy include concealing Moscow's goals and intentions, denial and deception, retaining superficially plausible legality, threatening the West with exaggerated claims of its military power, and deploying a vast and complex global effort to shape the narrative about Ukraine through traditional and social media.

The second speaker, Svitlana Nalyvayna, spoke about the most nefarious case of disinformation warfare: the Russian troll campaign that followed the downing of Malaysia flight MH17. Within the first two days after the civilian airliner was shot down, Russian trolls posted at least sixty-five thousand tweets trying to blame Ukraine for the disaster. A multinational investigation supported by painstaking research clearly established the source, path, and timeline of the Buk antiaircraft missile that downed the commercial airliner on July 17, 2014, killing all 298 people aboard. Despite mounting evidence that Russia supplied the Buk antiaircraft missile system that downed the plane, Russia continued to offer alternative theories. One included the tale of a mysterious Spanish air traffic controller named Carlos who had been working with Ukrainian aviation at the time of the attack and who claimed to have spotted two fighter jets near MH17. His interview on a Spanish Russian-language station was widely broadcast. In 2018, Radio Free Europe/Radio Liberty provided proof that the individual was not named Carlos, and he was not an air traffic controller. Other false flag operations included doctored satellite images, dubious ballistic experiments, and alleged Ukrainian confessions. Ms. Nalyvayna concluded that the overall disinformation strategy was to confuse rather than convince and that future historians would view Russia's response to the downing of MH17 as a key case study in twenty-first-century disinformation warfare.

The last speaker brought the threat home to the American audience. He made the point that while Ukraine was a testing ground for Russian disinformation warfare, the United States and its allies were equally vulnerable. Anyone who uses social media is susceptible to manipulation. Antin Derkach cited a *New York Times* report about how the Russians attempted to influence the last US presidential campaign using American technology platforms. Russian agents had disseminated inflammatory posts that reached 126 million users on Facebook, published more than 131,000 messages on Twitter, and uploaded over 1,000 videos to YouTube. The Internet Research Agency linked to the Kremlin had posted approximately 80,000 pieces of divisive content on Facebook that reached about 29 million people. Those posts were then liked, shared, and followed by others, spreading messages to tens of millions more people. In addition, Facebook had found and deleted more than 170 accounts on Instagram that had posted about 120,000 pieces of Russia-linked content. Twitter suspended more than 3,800 accounts that were associated with the Internet Research Agency. One pretended to be the unofficial feed of the Tennessee Republicans, which had more than 140,000 followers. While the impact on the results of the election was debatable, the Russians had achieved their goal of dividing and polarizing American voters.

Mark wondered how much of the divisive messaging that he had viewed on social media during the last presidential campaign was generated by these fake accounts. He had paid them little attention other than being disgusted by the ignorance and hate contained in many of the posts. The nation, it seemed, was breaking apart along the fault lines of race, religion, and social class.

The wine-and-cheese social that followed the talks gave the attendees an opportunity to mingle with the visiting journalists.

"I'll be in the adjacent gallery," Tanya told Mark. "Let me know when the consul general leaves the institute."

"You don't want to ask her about getting a new passport?"

"I don't want to take a chance. She'll make inquiries. It could get us killed."

Mark tried to swallow the chaos. He still felt the lingering effects of the poison. He felt like he'd been embalmed. The thought of the Predators fan licking the back of his neck made his hairs stand on end. He knew that if something happened to Tanya, he was a material witness. He now knew as much about her conspiracy theory as she did. Professor Johnson had warned him that witnesses in Russian collusion investigations tend to disappear.

He shadowed the consul general as the dignitary mingled with the president of the institute and the chair of the Chicago-Kyiv Sister Cities program. After twenty minutes the consul general had her fill of wine and canapés and left for the consulate on Erie Street.

Mark found Tanya in the adjacent gallery admiring a Milonadis mobile sculpture. "The consul general has left," he said. "The journalists are still here."

The crowd in the Strutynsky gallery had thinned along with the hors d'oeuvres. "I need to speak to one of them alone," she said. "If anyone tries to interrupt our conversation, make up some excuse to pull them away."

Tanya walked up to Svitlana Nalyvayna as she was hovering over the last canapé. Before Tanya could think of a greeting, Svitlana blurted out in Ukrainian, "Tanya Bereza! I love your work! What an honor to meet you here in Chicago. Will you be having an exhibit here at the institute?"

Tanya was taken aback at being recognized so quickly by a Ukrainian journalist. "How did you know who I am?" she asked.

Svitlana turned red. "I'm sorry if I'm being too forward. You were all over the news in Kyiv before we left for the states."

"What were they saying about me?"

"They said you came to the United States to display your Heavenly Hundred statue in Washington, DC."

"Is that all?"

"I'm afraid the rest isn't very flattering," Svitlana said. "Some sculptor from Luhansk is claiming that you copied his work from a sketch that he emailed you. He presented your email correspondence on television as evidence."

"What else did they say?"

"One of the television channels did an exposé about your life story. They said your parents abandoned you and placed you in an internat. They say the matron's husband taught you to play chess. He was . . ."

"An aspiring master."

"They interviewed his wife. She said you seduced her husband and broke up their marriage."

Tanya did not reply.

"They also said you ran away from the internat and walked the streets until you fell in with some decadent artists."

Tanya neither confirmed nor denied the allegation.

"What is the American press saying?"

"Nothing yet, but you know it's only a matter of time before some conservative news-show hosts start parroting the Kremlin narrative. Why are they targeting you?"

"I pose a threat to them," Tanya replied. "You mustn't tell anyone we met—for your own safety. The truth will come out soon enough. If something"—Tanya couldn't find the word—"*happens* to me, then tell my friends in Ukraine that the story about me stealing someone else's work is a lie."

Svitlana nodded.

"One more thing," Tanya said. "Have you heard anything about an American evangelist disputing the Holodomor?"

"Dr. Mathias Kane? He's all over the Russian-language stations."

An elderly Orthodox priest helped himself to the last canapé within earshot of their conversation. He gulped it down in one swallow and hastened to the exit with the gait of a twenty-five-year-old man.

* * * *

It rained on Holy Saturday. The weather discouraged all but the diehards from competing in the Chess Pavilion in Lincoln Park. The bishop was nowhere to be seen. Mark and Tanya waited under the pavilion for the king to appear. A disheveled man with a grizzled beard sat on a bench in the rain and watched them from a distance. He was sipping hot chai from a thermos. After the last two players left, he stood up and ambled over toward Tanya.

"Are you the Ukrainian champion?" he asked in Russian.

"Yes," she replied.

"We play alone."

Tanya nodded. "Wait for me by the car," she told Mark.

"It's not safe—" he began.

She cut him off with a look that meant there would be no discussion. She and Turchin took their seats across the board.

Mark walked toward the car but took shelter under a tree from where he could see anyone who entered or left the pavilion.

"It's rare for me to play a worthy challenger," the king said in Russian. He looked at her with suspicion. "You are a worthy challenger, aren't you?"

"I'll do my best not to disappoint you," she said. "Five, ten, or thirty minutes?" she asked.

"Ten," he replied. "You may take white."

Tanya opened with e4.

The king took a sip of his tea from the open thermos. He pondered his move for a moment then countered with the Sicilian defense.

"I know who you are," Tanya whispered. She moved her knight to f3.

Turchin paused with his pawn in his hand before placing it on d6. "Did you come here to kill me?"

"I came to ask for your help," Tanya said. "I, too, know secrets that could get me killed. I can run and hide, or I can confront my enemy. Help me confront him."

The next several moves and taps on the timer went in staccato succession.

"They are a family of dragons," Turchin replied. "You need to kill them all if you want to be free."

"Then help me to destroy them all."

Turchin hit the timer. "Your move. Move or forfeit."

Tanya moved her pawn to b5 and hit the timer. Turchin captured it with his knight. "You're losing your concentration," he said. "You'll be checkmated in six moves."

Tanya moved her bishop to f3 and tapped the timer.

Turchin considered capturing the bishop with his rook, then paused. As he studied the board, the look on his face changed from consternation to resignation, and finally to satisfaction. "I underestimated you. Where did you learn that counterattack?" he asked.

"From you. My chess tutor at the internat called it Turchin's ploy. It's used when your strategy is to play a stronger opponent to a draw. You sacrifice pieces intentionally and give your opponent a seemingly easy path to checkmate. You trap them with their hubris. By moving your bishop to f3, you turn the tables and force a draw. My tutor said you used it against Mechnikoff at a tournament in Yalta three years before he became a grand master. It's legendary for its brazenness."

"That was decades ago. I didn't think anyone would remember."

"It's become chess lore. You lure your opponent into thinking they've won the game, when you've been in command the whole time."

Turchin smiled. "I *was* the best player of my generation. And by the way, I won that game."

"But how? The history books say it was a draw and that Mechnikoff went on to win the match."

"The Soviets rewrote history."

"Why?"

"Because I wouldn't buy into their system. I *dissented*."

"I heard you refused to compromise," Tanya said, "and the system tried to destroy you. The sad thing is that when the Soviet Union collapsed, the system survived. The communists became capitalists. The KGB operatives became politicians. The same powerbrokers that tried to destroy you are now cruising the Caribbean in their luxury yachts. Let me be your avenging angel."

Turchin knew his next move. Before touching his piece he leaned across the board and whispered something in her ear.

"Thank you," she said. "Thank you."

"Go now," he said.

"But we're not finished," Tanya said. "I want to see how you beat Mechnikoff."

"You'll need to figure it out yourself," he replied. "Now if you'll excuse me, there's someone else waiting to play."

Tanya looked behind her and saw an old Orthodox priest in a monastic robe emerge from the shadows. She saw Mark running toward the pavilion. The priest did not give Mark so much as a glance.

"Tell your friend to not be a hero," Turchin said. "Then flee as far away as you can. Death is over your shoulder."

Tanya got up slowly and turned to face the old priest. In his hooded robe he looked like Death. His gaze was fixed on Turchin. Tanya ran out of the pavilion into Mark's arms. "We need to get away from here as fast as we can," she said. "Death is over our shoulders."

The hooded priest sat down in Tanya's place. Turchin turned his head to see if Tanya had heeded his warning. He looked back at his assassin. "Can we at least finish the game?" he asked. "It looks like you have the advantage."

Dmitri studied the board.

Turchin's queen was his for the taking. He captured it with his bishop. As he picked the piece up off the board, his sleeve clumsily knocked over Turchin's king.

Turchin righted his king and took a long sip of his Russian tea as if to savor the homeland for the very last time. He moved his knight to g6. "Check."

Dmitri considered his moves. His situation was hopeless.

"Do you concede?" Turchin asked.

"But I've already won," Dmitri replied. He pressed the clock. "In five minutes you will knock down your king."

Turchin looked at his tea. "Cyanide?"

"Heartbreak grass," Dmitri replied.

"What's the price on my head?"

"One million euros."

Turchin shook his head. "Is that all? The price has come down. Is that why Ivanovich sent a novice?"

Dmitri bristled at the insult.

"Your eyes betray you," Turchin pointed out. "You have the eyes of a young man, and the guise of an old man."

Dmitri lowered his eyes. His right hand was still hiding the vial of Gelsemium toxicant.

"You're a pawn in Ivanovich's game," Turchin continued. "Like so many before you. What did he promise you? To join the club of billionaires? Induction into *vor v zakone*?"

"What did you whisper to the woman?" Dmitri asked.

"I told her where to find the Flame of God," Turchin replied. "I will have my revenge."

Turchin felt his extremities twitch and his heart wriggle like a bag of worms. As the darkness descended, he smiled knowing that he had at least won his last game.

* * * *

In two hours the streets of the Ukrainian Village would be teeming with parishioners carrying their baskets to the 5:00 a.m. Easter Service at Saint Nicholas Cathedral. Walton Street was still silent. The light from the sodium-vapor lamps cast twisted shadows through the dormant trees. Dmitri had studied the three-story apartment and determined that the easiest access was through the covered wooden porch in the back. A sign on the front entry read NEIGHBORHOOD WATCH, but at this hour only dogs would sense him coming.

He sneaked through the gangway to the backyard and easily picked the flimsy latch on the rear porch door. He climbed the wooden stairs one creak at a time. The lock to Rider's back door was refitted with a deadbolt. The transom above the door, however, could be pried open with a knife. It dated back to the days before air-conditioning, and the building's owners had simply painted it over with layers of paint. Dmitri crawled through the transom and landed on his feet like a cat.

The intrusion he decided would look like a bungled burglary. He would bludgeon Rider with a blunt object, then make it look like the woman was assaulted before she was strangled. He would need to extract Turchin's secret through any means necessary. He was not fond of torture; he preferred the elegance of undetectable poisons. Turchin's last words, however, gave him no choice. The secret behind the woman's lips could kill him.

Dmitri spotted a marble wine chiller on the kitchen table and picked it up with his gloved hand. He peeked into the bedroom by the kitchen and saw only a desk and a makeshift bookcase. The linoleum floor of the kitchen ended at the corridor. The floor in the rest of the apartment was original oak. He stepped toe first onto the wooden floor, then gently eased his weight onto his heel. In six steps he was at the door to the master bedroom. He turned the brass knob on the oak door and looked in: it was empty. He walked to the bedroom that overlooked Walton Street—also empty. The locator on Rider's phone had gone dead. On instinct he looked into the microwave in the kitchen: Rider had fried his phone and his laptop.

He called Gennady on his encrypted phone. "My marks are on the run," he said. "They know they're being hunted. Any digital trail before the phone and computer went dead?"

"There was a text to Mirana from a burner phone at 3:00 a.m. It just said 'Found T. Will keep in contact.'"

"Can you locate it?"

"I'll have to triangulate. Right now it's about hundred and fifty miles due west of Chicago. Somewhere in eastern Iowa."

"Let me know when you have the exact coordinates. Also get me the names of anyone they could turn to west of the Mississippi. I should be able to catch up to them in a few hours."

Dmitri's next call was to Ivanovich.

"Why the hell are you calling me at this hour?"

"Your accountant is dead," Dmitri answered.

"I'll wire your bonus to your account in Nevis after my morning coffee. And our rusalka?"

Dmitri hesitated to answer. "I'm still on their trail," he finally said and hung up the phone.

CHAPTER 7

Baraboo

Mark and Tanya pulled into the parking lot of the white wooden church at daybreak. The small lot was full. Mark parked his Trans Am in the adjacent graveyard between a beat-up Oldsmobile and a weathered headstone. He turned off the motor and lowered the window to take in the fresh country air. His strength was slowly returning. His urine had become paler. The smell of earth and manure from the surrounding fields reminded him of his childhood.

Tanya had not spoken a word during the four-hour drive to Baraboo. They had taken the back roads as a precaution in case their pursuer had hacked into the tollway computers. Mark figured that Ivanovich's hit man would try to track them through their recent contacts. On their way out of Chicago, he had bought a burner phone at a twenty-four-hour Walmart in Johnsburg and sent a single text to Mirana. He hid the phone in the cab of an 18-wheeler with Colorado plates that was parked in the loading dock.

"Do you want to attend the service or wait in the car?" he asked.

Tanya had tears in her eyes. "I led them to him," she said.

"It's not your fault. It's mine. They must have ID'd my car back in Duck Key. They connected it to my name. Then they tracked us on my cell phone."

"The gardener at Mirana's . . ."

"I had a hunch that something was off," Mark continued. "And the Bible salesman in Williamstown, the Predators fan at Tootsie's, the priest at the institute—they all had the same eyes. Whoever he is, he was playing with us like a cat that plays with a mouse before he kills it. Christ . . ."

"What is it?" Tanya asked.

"He must have followed us to Beech Mountain. That means he knows about Aunt Sarah and Dana."

"They're no threat to him. It's us he's after."

"It's just a matter of time before he tracks us here. He'll soon figure out we sent him on a wild goose chase with that burner phone. We need to ditch this car. I'll ask my father to lend me some money. I'll also ask him what he knows about Kane. I just don't know where we're going to go."

"But I do," Tanya said. "We're going to Death Valley to find the Flame of God."

Mark didn't ask Tanya why. He knew she'd tell him when she was ready. Death Valley was two thousand miles away. Logistically the journey would be difficult: no tickets, no credit cards, cash only. And they needed a car. He knew he could count on his father, but his mother could be unreasonable. As a teenager, he had rebelled against her strict rules of no drinking, no smoking, and no dancing. He had broken her heart when he dropped out of divinity school. She had never forgiven him when he shortened his name from Riderson to Rider.

"I think we should go in and pray," he said.

When Mark and Tanya opened the door of the church, Minister Riderson paused his sermon. He was a gaunt, ruggedly handsome man in his early sixties. His blond hair and blue eyes reflected his Norwegian stock. Generations of his family had ministered to the Norwegians who had immigrated to the heartland in the mid-1800s. Members of the congregation, many of whom Mark recognized, turned to see the return of the prodigal son. The folks in the last pew slid over to give them a seat. When their eyes met, Mark's father looked joyous rather than angry. *My parents,* Mark thought, *have always preached that while salvation is entirely of God, so are the good works that follow salvation. Perhaps God always intended that I help Tanya.*

Minister Riderson continued his sermon about how Jesus, through His death and resurrection, is the only source of salvation and forgiveness of sins. His voice carried a joyousness that Mark had not heard since his father spoke about the Rapture in Nashville. The morning service among a congregation of friends and neighbors brought back happy memories of his childhood. In Sunday school he had listened to the Bible stories with fascination and awe. He recalled church picnics at Devil's Lake, jumping into the haystack on his parents' farm, and biking with his friends on County O. He recalled fishing on the Wisconsin River, sneaking away with Otto and Mary to see Fort Dells, and his first beer at Brothers. He recalled his parents taking him and his cousins to Circus World to ride on the elephants.

Tanya placed her hand on his. "I want to receive Holy Communion," she said.

"The body and blood of Christ," Reverend Riderson said. A plate of crackers and a tray of tiny cups with grape juice were passed among the congregation while Reverend Riderson recited Scripture. Tanya ate the "bread" and "wine" and crossed herself from right to left in the Orthodox tradition. Mark took communion and prayed in silence.

After the final amen, Mark waited in the back of the church until the last of the congregants had departed to celebrate Easter with their families at home. He met his father in the center of the church. Before he could bring himself to say I'm sorry, his father embraced him.

"Christ has blessed us with your presence. Your mother will be so happy to see you. Thank you for joining us for the Easter celebration."

"I know I've been a neglectful son," Mark said. "I'm sorry I missed Uncle Joe's funeral. I visited Aunt Sarah and Dana in Beech Mountain a few days ago."

"Your aunt Sarah called to let us know. But introduce me to your friend. I'm glad you brought her. From the way she made the sign of the cross, I would guess she's Greek Orthodox."

"Ukrainian," Mark replied. He motioned to Tanya to come up. "Tanya, I'd like to introduce you to my father, Dr. Timothy Riderson."

"Tanya Bereza," she said offering her hand. "It's an honor to meet you. Mark has said such nice things about you."

The minister laughed. "I'm sure he has. Now we should hurry home. Mark's mother should be done with her dawn Easter service by now, and—"

Mark cut in. "My mother's congregation is located about twenty miles north of here, between Wisconsin Dells and Portage. We had a dairy farm there before moving to Baraboo. We lived there until my parents gave the farm to my cousin Otto. My mother continues to minister to that congregation."

Minister Riderson locked up the church and hopped into his rusted Ford pickup. He had taught Mark to drive a stick shift on the back roads that wound up and down through the Baraboo hills. It was one of Mark's fondest memories. "She's still running," he assured Mark. "Follow me."

Their farmhouse was less than a quarter mile away. The fields that yielded corn and soybeans were still not plowed. Scattered weeds had sprung up between the rows of stubble. A collie came barking up to the car as Mark followed his father's pickup into their gravel driveway. She looked older than Mark remembered but was still spritely for her age. Greta jumped on Mark when he got out of the car. Her pupils were obscured by cataracts. She licked his face, then ran around the car to Tanya.

"Careful, she might bite," Mark called out, but Greta greeted Tanya as if she were a member of the family.

He saw his mother's white Chevy Impala parked by the barn. The others waited in the yard as Mark went into the barn to greet her. She was breaking a bale of hay with a pitchfork to feed their lone dairy cow. Her gray hair was tied in a bun.

"Mother," he said.

She looked at him for what seemed like eternity before responding. "I'm glad you decided to finally come home," she said. She looked behind him through the open barn door. "I see you've brought someone. Are you married?"

"No, no," Mark replied. "Tanya's just a friend."

Tanya walked up and offered her hand. "Hello, I'm Tanya Bereza. I'm very pleased to meet you."

"The sculptress?" his mother asked.

"Why . . . yes," Tanya replied and wondered how she knew.

Mark's mother held on to the pitchfork without shaking Tanya's hand.

"Will you be staying for Easter lunch? Your cousin Otto invited us to share their table. He and Mary would be pleased to see you. Sarah said you stopped by to see her on your way back from . . . ?"

"Key West. I bought a used car there and drove it back home. It eats too much gas. I think I'll trade it for something more practical."

"I'll call Mary and tell her to add two more places."

Mark couldn't tell from her countenance if she was happy to see him or not. She had always been sparse with her affection. He knew she loved Jesus more than she loved him. Their mother-son bond began to fray when he reached puberty. He had drawn a sketch of Mary as Eve in a Garden of Eden and hid it under his pillow. That same evening his mother barged into his bedroom and caught him red-handed. He pulled the sheet up to his neck in panic. She yanked off the sheet and exposed his sinful erection. She grabbed the sketch from his hand, crumpled it in disgust, and stood over him until he shrank to his boyhood innocence. She accused him of being the devil's spawn. She made him believe that what came naturally was unnatural, that sex was sin, and that seeking independence from your parents was the same as forsaking God.

Mark was her only natural child, but he knew in his heart that she favored his cousin Otto. Otto never questioned her authority. She had raised him after her sister, Sarah, got pregnant out of wedlock. Otto didn't speak until the age of five, and the burden of raising him had proved too much for Sarah. She moved to North Carolina to work in the Land of Oz, where she met and married Joe McBride. Otto had stayed behind with his aunt and uncle.

Mark remembered how in the summer before leaving for college he had taken Otto's future wife to the Winnebago Drive-In Theater in the Dells. Mary had worn lipstick. Mark enticed her to smoke some cigarettes that he had pilfered from his uncle in Beech Mountain. She had held his hand and tried to place it on her knee. Before he could kiss her, she had turned green from the nicotine and vomited in his lap. When he returned home after midnight, his mother was waiting for him on their unlit porch. He had not even kissed Mary, yet his mother accused him of being a sinner and trying to ruin his cousin's life. She had said: "'Then when lust has conceived, it gives birth to sin; and when sin is accomplished, it brings forth death.'"

His mother's stern voice brought him back to the present. "The electric fence is down after last week's thunderstorms. I'd ask you to help your father fix it, but it's Easter Sunday."

"I'd be happy to look at it," Mark said.

"One more thing," his mother said. She looked at Tanya and whispered into her son's ear: "How *dare* you bring that harlot into our home. Do not lust in your heart after her beauty or let her captivate you with her eyes."

* * * *

Mathias Kane sat back in the hand-stitched leather seat of his Gulfstream V private jet as it climbed above the clouds on its way to Washington, DC. As the sun broke in the east, the color of the clouds brightened from livid to shimmering white. He reviewed his notes for his annual Easter Day address to the nation. With the help of Senator Rich and his Russian partner, his upcoming sermon from the First Evangelical Church would now be televised all over the world. He looked over the suggested script that Ivanovich's director of media relations had emailed him. The topics seemed innocuous enough: the decline of family values; the menace of European secularism; and the threat of radical Islam. They aligned with Kane's agenda but were more global in reach. The director had made the point that to reach a Russian audience, one needed to address issues that were relevant to everyday Russians. It might also benefit Americans, he added, to learn more about the threats to Christianity beyond their own borders.

Dr. Kane paged through his worn King James Bible to find supporting passages from Scripture. He had learned through his years of evangelizing that while some might disagree with his interpretations, they could not disagree with the literal word of God. He found it best to begin and end his sermons citing chapter and verse. For family values he turned to Colossians 3:18–21:

> Wives, submit yourselves unto your own husbands, as it is fit in the Lord. Husbands, love your wives, and be not bitter against them. Children obey your parents in all things: for this is well pleasing unto the Lord. Fathers, provoke not your children to anger, lest they be discouraged.

For the menace of secularism he decided to use 1 John 2:15–17:

> Love not the world, neither the things that are in the world. If any man love the world, the love of the Father is not in him. For all that is in the world, the lust of the flesh, and the lust of eyes, and the pride of life, is not of the Father, but is of the world. And the world passeth away, and the lust thereof: but he that doeth the will of God abideth for ever.

Finding a passage for the threat of radical Islam was more challenging, since Islam came into being over five hundred years after the Bible was completed. He decided instead to raise the looming threat of Islamic world dominancy in the context of its possible role in the End Time prophecy. Who is the Antichrist? Who is the false prophet? What is the Mystery Babylon One-World Religion? Ivanovich's director of media relations suggested that he conclude his sermon with a call for the Christians of the world to unite. He had even asked to review the sermon before it aired, but Dr. Kane refused. He resented being told what to preach. God was speaking through him, and who were the Russians to question the word of God?

Ivanovich's business plan projected millions of new dollars in offshore donations to Kane's ministry in the first year alone. Kane's lawyers had wanted more time to research the tax implications of these offshore donations, but Ivanovich assured him that his own lawyers in London could create financial structures in Cyprus, the Cayman Islands, and Nevis that would never appear on Kane's US financial statements. If corporations could be multinational, then why couldn't the ministry of the Last Awakening? The more prosperous he became, Dr. Kane convinced himself, the more his work was pleasing to God.

* * * *

Otto's farm lay on the east bank of the Wisconsin River about ten miles south of the Wisconsin Dells Dam. The Riderson family had worked the land for generations. About half of the property was pasture; the rest was riverine forest that was mostly flooded in the spring. But in the summer, fall, and winter, it turned into a wondrous natural playground. The dairy cows had free range in the forest and pasture, and the two cousins were constantly inspecting the age and consistency of cow pies. They would fish the river in the early mornings for redhorse, bass, and walleye, as well as the occasional sturgeon and snapping turtle. Their favorite pastime, however, was going around the farm on their bikes on the circular route of County O, barreling down the hill that they called the point of no return and visiting the abandoned house that they called Creep Joint.

Otto had grown into a Paul Bunyan of a man. He had a good heart and a simple mind. Otto had been homeschooled, and his aunt and uncle had taught him how to farm. His stepfather had taught him how to fix cars during the family's summer visits to Beech Mountain. Rusted wrecks and broken tractors were strewn behind the barn in a makeshift junkyard.

Mary was as buxom and pretty as Mark remembered her. She had the healthy glow of a farm girl who drinks fresh milk from a pail. When Mark and Otto reunited at the doorstep of the centuries-old farmhouse, Otto gave him a hug that squeezed the air out of his lungs. Mary simply offered her hand. Their two German shepherds, Thor and Loki, ran up to lick his face.

"Mark, Mark, so happy to see you!" Otto said. "Your friend is beautiful. She has kind eyes. Is she really from Babylon?"

Mary elbowed her husband in the ribs. "Don't mind him," she said. "I'm sure he meant it as a compliment."

"Hello, I'm Tanya. I'm from Ukraine." Otto shook her hand. Mary smiled politely.

"May I use your bathroom?" Tanya asked.

"Yes, of course," Mary replied. She led her to the lone bathroom with a window that overlooked the pasture.

Mark's ancestral home was as he remembered it. The simple utensils, pots, and quilts looked as if they had come from an antique store. The long Shaker table was covered with a yellow tablecloth and porcelain china. A glazed Easter ham lay in the center surrounded by mashed potatoes, green beans, garden salad, and hot cross buns. Each salad plate held several colored Easter eggs that Mary had painted herself using natural dyes.

When Mark's parents arrived, the family sat down at the table and waited for Tanya to come out of the bathroom before saying grace. She emerged beaming and sat down next to Mark.

"You seem relieved," he said.

"I'm not pregnant," she whispered audibly in his ear.

Mark's mother turned livid.

Tanya examined one of Mary's Easter eggs. "A beautiful color."

"Purple cabbage," Mary replied.

"Easter eggs are very popular in my country," Tanya said. "We call them *pysanky*. We inscribed them in the orphanage where I grew up. We used an ancient artistic technique. We inscribed a design over a colored egg using a stylus filled with melted beeswax. We then dipped the egg in a darker color and again inscribed it with wax. We kept repeating the process with different colors until the design was finished. Afterward, we melted off the wax and created a multicolored Easter egg. I can teach you how to do it if you'd like."

"I'd like to learn," Mary said.

"What kinds of designs do you inscribe?" Mark's father asked.

"Mostly symbols. Many are Trypillian, dating back thousands of years. The custom predated Christianity in my country."

"Pagan symbols on Easter eggs?" Mark's mother asked.

Mark terminated the discussion before it spiraled. "We learned in divinity school that the custom of painting eggs during Easter is at least seven thousand years old. The word *Easter* comes from "Eostre," an early German-Anglo-Saxon goddess of the dawn-rebirth of the year. Her symbol was a rabbit that laid eggs. As Tanya was saying, egg symbolism dates back to the Neolithic civilizations of Eastern Europe."

"Is that what they teach in school these days?" his mother asked. "Next they'll be saying we descended from monkeys."

"Perhaps we should say grace," Mark's father said. He opened his Bible and handed it to Mark. "Would you please read us the story of the Resurrection, as has been the custom in our family for generations?"

Mark took the Bible from his father and read out loud:

> In the end of the Sabbath, as it began to dawn toward the first day of the week, came Mary Magdalene and the other Mary to see the sepulchre. And behold, there was a great earthquake: for the angel of the Lord descended from heaven, and came and rolled back the stone from the door, and sat upon it. His countenance was like lightning, and his raiment white as snow. And for fear of him the keepers did shake, and became as dead men. And the angel answered and said unto the women, Fear not ye: for I know that ye seek, Jesus, which was crucified. He is not here: for is risen, as he said.

Mark's father then offered grace: "Let us pray. Lord God, you bless us with all we need—food, clothing, home, family, work, friends, joy, and peace. We thank you for the many ways you bless us in this life. Because of Jesus's death and resurrection, you have also blessed us with the gift of everlasting life. We are grateful for those who are gathered around this table with us. We also remember those we love who are not with us today, and those who now rest from their labors. Please bless this food we eat. May it remind us of the joyous heavenly banquet we will one day share with you and those we love. Amen. Alleluia, Christ is risen!"

Mark's mother, Otto, and Mary then responded in unison: "He is risen indeed. Alleluia!"

Mark and Tanya had not eaten since they fled Chicago the night before. Tanya speared a piece of the ham with her fork. "This ham looks delicious," she said.

"I smoked it myself," Mary replied. "Farmer Anderson butchered his hog last week and gave us one of the hams. Otto had helped him fix his tractor."

"We understand you're a sculptress," Mark's father said.

"Yes, how did you know?"

"Dana told us. She said you taught her how to weld."

"She's a talented artist," Tanya replied. "She was working mainly with wood, building these beautiful birdhouses. I saw all of this metal and equipment in her father's shop and just showed her how to use it."

"What sorts of things do you sculpt?" Mark's mother asked her.

"People, life, feelings."

"What sorts of feelings?" Mark's mother asked.

"Love, hope, forgiveness."

"Tanya is a world-famous sculptress," Mark said. "Her friend Mirana told me that Tanya had won the Most Promising Young Artist award at an international competition in Venice."

Mark's mother looked at her watch when they were done with the main course. "I think it's time for Reverend Kane's address to the nation," she said. She glowered at Tanya. "We *always* listen to Dr. Kane. We can have our dessert afterward. Mary, would you be so kind as to turn on the television?"

The Zenith television had stood in the same place in the living room since Mark was a child. The only difference was the addition of a converter box.

The Reverend Dr. Mathias Kane had already begun his Easter address to the nation. The angle of the camera made him look bigger than he was. He raised the Bible and thumped it on the pulpit. Minister Riderson rolled his eyes at Kane's fire-and-brimstone theatrics.

"You don't agree?" Mark asked his father.

"Dr. Kane preaches a message of fear. I preach a message of love."

Kane ranted about the decline of family values, the rise of European secularism, and the threat of radical Islam. He spoke of the Antichrist, the whore of Babylon, and the End Days. A running ticker at the bottom of the screen repeated the address of a post office box where the faithful could mail their donations and a toll-free number for those who would rather use their credit cards. Anyone donating a hundred dollars or more would receive a prosperity cloth in return. In contrast to previous sermons, the post office box address ended with the United States of America.

"How can I learn more about Dr. Kane?" Mark asked. "I'm writing a paper on televangelists for school. Dr. Kane seems like a good subject."

"He's an extreme fundamentalist," Mark's father replied. "I would suggest you start with his roots and branch out from there. He was born again near his birthplace in Self, Arkansas. He was orphaned as a teenager. Reverend Anderson was his mentor until they had a falling out several years ago. You might want to interview him as well. He now ministers to Native Americans in Pawhuska, Oklahoma."

Mark planned their route in his head: *Wisconsin, Arkansas, Oklahoma, California*. He decided to mesh Tanya's search for the Flame of God with his own quest for Americana. *We'll take Route 66.*

After Kane's sermon, the family returned to the dining table for Easter cake, oranges, and chocolate.

"How long will you be staying?" Mark's father asked.

"Just a day or two," Mark replied.

"Then I insist that you stay with us," Mary chimed in. "We have a lot to catch up on. I'll prepare the guest room for Tanya. You can sleep on the couch in the living room."

"Thank you for sharing your meal and your home," Mark said. "I have one more favor to ask of all of you. Please don't let anyone, especially strangers, know that we're here."

* * * *

Dmitri caught up to the cell phone signal at the World's Largest Truck Stop on I-80 in Iowa. Rider's car was not in the lot, so Dmitri figured they must have dumped the car and hitched a ride in one of the trucks. The trucks were parked in a dense array for the night. He began checking them one by one.

A trucker returning from the bathroom caught him peering into the cab windows. Dmitri felt a rough hand on the back of his neck.

"Fucking pervert!"

Dmitri spun around like a cat and punched the assailant in the throat. The trucker fell to the ground gasping for air. His fellow truckers began to turn on their lights to see what the ruckus was all about. Dmitri disappeared into the night and retreated to his car till daybreak. He would have to wait for the convoy to break up on I-80 the next morning to hone in on the cell phone signal. He spent the witching hours thinking of all the things he would do to Rider before he killed him.

* * * *

Tanya awoke to the crowing of a rooster. Mary was already in the kitchen baking muffins and brewing tea. Otto was in the barn checking on a heifer that was calving. Mark was fast asleep on the couch.

"Whatever you're baking smells delicious," Tanya said.

"Just some corn bread muffins," Mary replied. "Have a seat. I'll fix you some bacon and eggs."

"Thanks, I'll just wait for Mark."

"Have you two been together long?" Mary asked.

"We just met . . . accidentally. I got into some trouble, and he's being a Good Samaritan."

Mary pulled the muffins out of the oven and poured Tanya some hot water for tea. "Anything we can help with?" Mary asked.

"No, you and Otto have been so kind. We can't impose on you any more than we have."

"It's not imposing," Mary replied. "Mark's family." Mary was fidgeting in the kitchen, making herself look busier than she really was. Tanya realized that in Mary's eyes, the only thing wrong with this Norman Rockwell family reunion was the "whore of Babylon" that Mark had picked up in Florida.

"Mark told me that you assist Mrs. Riderson with her congregation. He said you help her teach Bible School."

"The Ridersons gave us their farm," Mary replied. "It's the least I could do."

"Was Mark's mother always as *severe* as she is now?"

"Mrs. Riderson is a good, kind-hearted woman. She took care of Otto when his mother ran off to North Carolina. She raised him as her son. She raised Mark to be in upstanding young man. Then he just turned his back on all of us. He gave up on divinity school. He gave up—" Mary stopped her sentence.

"He gave up on you?" Tanya asked.

Mary did not reply.

"When you teach the children in Bible School, do you tell them any stories about forgiveness?"

"I teach them how Christ poured out his blood for the forgiveness of sins. I use the example of the pelican."

"Why a pelican?"

"You don't know?" Mary was proud to show off her knowledge of not only Scripture but also world literature. The Baraboo library had every book that was worth reading. "The pelican is a symbol of the passion of Christ. The image of a pelican piercing its own breast to feed its young with its blood is engrained in our faith. Dante and Shakespeare allude to it. Mary went to her room and brought back a book of hymns. "This is from 'Adoro te Devote' by Thomas Aquinas." She read aloud:

Like what tender tales tell of the Pelican
Bathe me, Jesus Lord, in what Thy Bosom ran
Blood that but one drop of has the power to win
All the world forgiveness of its world of sin.

"I'm surprised that you read Thomas Aquinas," Tanya said.

"Why? Because I'm just a country girl?"

"No," Tanya replied. "Because he believed that man was essentially good rather than depraved. He was quite controversial in his time."

Mary smiled. "I like to think of him as a medieval Protestant."

"You're a remarkable woman," Tanya said. "I can see that you're very fond of Mark. It must have been hard for all of you when he left to find himself. From what little I know, he's still searching. Give him time. Sooner or later he'll find his way home."

"Have you found what you're looking for?" Mary asked.

"I found myself *within*. I express myself through art. I also believe that art can heal. Do you think Otto would mind if I worked on a sculpture in your barn?"

"No, not at all," Mary replied. "He loves Mark like a brother. He would do anything for him and for Mark's friends."

On Easter Monday Mark helped Otto with the chores around the farm, including birthing a calf, while Tanya tinkered in Otto's barn. Otto had converted a back section of the barn to resemble his stepfather's workshop in Beech Mountain. The cows seemed oblivious to the welding and clatter. When asked what she was working on, Tanya replied, "A bird."

Mark asked Mary to inquire whether any of their neighbors might be interested in trading one of their cars for an American classic. The widow Erickson expressed interest. Her husband's El Camino had been collecting dust in the barn ever since he passed away two years ago. Most of the local farmers needed heavy-duty pickups, and she found it hard to sell a vehicle that was neither car nor truck. A vintage Trans Am, on the other hand, might appeal to widowers who were nostalgic for the vintage muscle cars of the 1970s. Mark convinced Mrs. Erickson that he would need to take the El Camino on a road trip before completing the trade. There was no need to change license plates or title. She could keep his Trans Am as collateral until he returned.

The following afternoon, as Tanya was rusting the patina of her sculpture with vinegar, hydrogen peroxide, and salt to create the illusion of feathers, she heard a stern voice behind her.

"Is this another one of your pagan symbols?"

Tanya put down the spray bottle and took off her goggles and gloves. Despite her intent to intimidate, Mrs. Riderson looked like a mother who had lost her son.

"Quite the opposite," Tanya replied. "It's deeply Christian. I asked

Mary to think of a Christian symbol for forgiveness, and she told me the story of the pelican."

The abstract piece was a tangle of old auto, tractor, and motorcycle parts, cut and welded into an image of a pelican piercing its breast. The neck was an exhaust pipe folded upon itself and the beak was cut from an oil pan. The belly was a motorcycle gas tank.

"So now you presume to create art in the name of Christ?"

"I create it for those whom He left behind."

Mrs. Riderson ran her hand along the edge of the rusted oil pan that was hammered into the shape of a pelican's beak. "What do you intend to do with it?"

"I made it for you," Tanya replied.

Mrs. Riderson stood dumbfounded. "For me? Why in the world would you make it for me?"

"Because you need to forgive. You need to forgive your sister, Sarah. And most of all, you need to forgive your son."

The mother let go of the beak. "My son? Let him repent and return to God so that his sins can be wiped out!"

Tanya saw Mark standing in the entry to the barn. His mother turned to him with hurt in her eyes. "Your friend has pierced me in the chest."

Mark ran up to her to make sure she was speaking figuratively. "I know I've disappointed you," he said, "for all the things I've done and not done, and you have a right to be angry. But I need to find my own way. You taught me that 'love bears all things, believes all things, hopes all things, endures all things.'" He opened his arms.

"God closed my womb after I gave birth to you. You must return to Him before you return to me."

Mark hoped for an embrace that didn't come. His mother took one last look at Tanya's sculpture and went out into the fields to pray.

As she was walking away, Mark bit his tongue and thought of Lamentations 4:3, "Even the sea monsters draw out the breast, they give suck to their young ones."

* * * *

Dmitri caught up to the burner phone in Lincoln. He found it tucked under the passenger seat cushion of a Walmart truck. He scrolled through the records and found a single text to Mirana. There were no incoming or outgoing calls. The driver, a young Bulgarian, had no idea how it had gotten there. Dmitri considered venting his frustration on the trucker but decided to channel his anger instead. He had underestimated his prey. He wondered whose idea it was, the rusalka's or Rider's? He knew the rusalka was clever, but he had thought that Rider was just some hapless boy whom she was manipulating. Using a burner phone to send a terse text message to Mirana was a subtle twist. The ruse had cost him two precious days. Turchin was dead, so the two of them were simply running for their lives.

He called Gennady to see if he had uncovered any new leads. There were still no digital tracks to follow—no emails, no messages, no phone calls—not a single stray electron. Whoever was sheltering them was either highly skilled at encryption technology or a Luddite with no digital footprint. Rider's license plates had not popped up on any tollway or red light cameras. Gennady had assured him that no one could stay invisible for long, but Dmitri was getting impatient.

Lili was now his most promising prospect. Her emails and texts to friends revealed that she and Rider had broken up on Christmas Day the year before. She had given him a Wiccan quilt as a Christmas present, and he had given her a Bible. They had not communicated since. She had been sexting with a new fling since Thanksgiving while she was still sharing Mark's apartment on Walton Street. Her new paramour had fantasized about making love to her at the open-air opera in Verona while watching a performance of *Aida* replete with camels and elephants.

Dmitri studied her Facebook and Tinder profiles and decided that she was most likely to "match" with a troubled soul with money who needed to take a walk on the wild side. He decided to play the role of a Harvard-educated lawyer who was on retainer to an Italian shipping magnate and who had just broken up with his girlfriend in Florence.

Dmitri "bumped" into Lili at the juice bar at the Midtown Athletic Club and asked her if she was Italian because she reminded him of Federica Ridolfi. The following evening they were dining at A Tavola.

After sharing a bottle of amarone, she opened up about her failed relationship with a Northwestern grad student who had no ambitions other than to exhume American artifacts.

"You can't imagine how *boring* it was to live with someone who goes *on* and *on* about the most trivial things. I mean I take him to see *Fifty Shades of Gray* and all he can talk about is the Iroquois Theatre fire back in nineteen-o-something."

"Your ex sounds like an artist that I once dated in Florence," Dmitri said. "She was working on restoring frescoes in the Palazzo Medici Riccardi. She was infatuated with Catherine de' Medici and her penchant for poisons. Murder by poisoned gloves? Ingenious! Your ex wasn't Italian by any chance?"

"Italian? Oh, I wish. He was a simple boy from Baraboo, Wisconsin. Both his parents were evangelical ministers. Can you believe it? Well I can. He was as straight as an arrow. He had more hang-ups in bed than a missionary. You'd think his mother was in the bedroom staring at us from her rocking chair! He even did a year of divinity school before going into journalism. He gave me a Bible as a Christmas present. Can you imagine? A *Bible*. How romantic is that?"

"What attracted you to him in the first place?" Dmitri asked.

"He was a lost soul who wandered into the Rainbo Club. He was handsome, in a wholesome kind of way. You know, the kind who blushes when you ask him if he has a hard-on."

Dmitri inhaled deeply through his nostrils and took a sip of his amarone.

"I thought I could bring out the devil in him," Lili continued, "but I couldn't even convince him to get a tattoo."

"Let me guess. His name had to be something biblical. John? Matthew? Luke?"

"Shut up!" Lili said. "He was named after an evangelist. Mark. Mark Rider. It was actually Riderson, but he had it shortened to distance himself from his parents."

"He changed his *name*?"

"Yeah, when he quit divinity school. He said he wanted a complete break from them. They wouldn't let him think for himself. Imagine, *two*

Bible-thumping, fire-and-brimstone parents. He couldn't drink, dance, or even play pinochle for pennies. Rather than play baseball like normal kids, he attended Bible school. Everything he was taught came from the Bible. I tried to get him to loosen up, you know, show him the ways of the world, but he just couldn't let go of his faith. I mean, what kind of fun is that?"

As Lili was speaking, Dmitri was texting to Gennady. "He must have hated his family," Dmitri said.

"I wouldn't say he *hated* them. Resented is more like it. He was sweet on his cousin in North Carolina. And get this—he had a crush on his cousin's wife up in Baraboo. That may have been one of the reasons he stayed away."

After another half hour of banter, Dmitri understood why Rider had broken up with her. At first Dmitri had expected her to be intriguing, hopefully even malevolent. The demon spirit that she inked on her forearm represented chaos, seduction, and ungodliness. But her "badness" turned out be as superficial as her tattoo. She reminded him of the baroness at Harry's Bar in Venice who always took the same table and monopolized the conversation, except that she was far less interesting than she thought she was. Perhaps it was the novelty of dating a city girl. Perhaps Rider was captivated by the idea of being seduced by a demon.

"I need to freshen up," she said after her third glass of amarone. "When I return, you need to tell me all about yourself. I want to know every dream, every fantasy, every desire."

When she returned from the bathroom, she found her table empty. The waiter explained that her date had taken care of the check but had been called away on an urgent international call—something about a socialite who had choked on an olive at a bar in Venice while dining with one of his clients.

Dmitri walked across the street to the Tryzub bar and ordered a Hetman vodka and Lvivske beer chaser. He decided to corroborate the information that he had just gleaned from Lili. He stepped out of the bar and dialed a cell phone number in North Carolina.

"Hi, Dana, it's me, Robert E. Lee." Their conversation began with the usual slurs about fascist democrats, illegal immigrants, and gays, then flowed into their plans to attend the Preserve our Heritage Rally at the Jefferson Davis Monument in June and the March for Family Values in Washington, DC, on Independence Day. Dmitri asked if she had any family members who shared their views. Other than her mother, her aunt and uncle were evangelical ministers who opposed violence, even for righteous causes. Her half brother Otto was slow-witted and had no political views to speak of. His wife, Mary, was a Bible school teacher. Their only contact with the outside world was a dumb TV, a landline, and *Christianity Today*. She had just spoken to Mary by phone on Easter Sunday, and Mary had seemed cheerier than ever, though she wouldn't tell her why. Two addresses popped up in his messages. Dmitri thanked Dana for her patriotism and programmed the map directions in his phone for Baraboo.

* * * *

Widow Erickson's El Camino was the perfect car for a cross-country road trip. The coupe utility vehicle was a cross between a station wagon and a pickup truck. Like many things American, it was innovative in its time but was now just another rusted hulk in the junk heap of Americana. "See the USA in your Chevrolet," the widow Erickson had told him when she was sealing the deal.

Otto had given the car a thorough going over. He had replaced the starter and water pump with parts that he found at a junkyard in Portage. Otto had stuck a penny into the tire tread grooves and told Mark that he was good for at least another seven to ten thousand miles. Otto put a four-inch plastic Jesus on the dashboard for safe travels.

"Let's take her out for a test drive," Mark said. "Anyone want to come along?"

Tanya hopped in to ride shotgun.

"Mary, Otto, how about you?" Mark asked.

"No," Mary replied. "Maybe later. Otto and I still have chores to do. Show Tanya a bit of the countryside. Take a drive up to Devil's Lake and show her the view from Wawanissee Point."

Mark turned red. When he, Mary, and Otto were in high school, Wawanissee Point was where young lovers took the leap from puppy love to true romance. A sudden thunderclap startled the cows. Black clouds billowed in from the west.

"I don't think we want to hike the bluffs in the rain," Mark said.

"Then take Tanya to see Circus World. That's where Mark developed his passion for bygone America."

"I'd love to see that," Tanya said.

When Mark started the El Camino, it belched black smoke from the exhaust until it found its timing and the engine started to hum. Otto gave him a thumbs-up, and Mark and Tanya set off down County O toward the Dells. The country road meandered through forests and farmlands. The scent of impending rain was in the air. It was still too early to plant. Dairy cows were grazing on the tender grasses. A barking dog bolted out of a driveway and chased them for a quarter mile. They took Highway 16 into Wisconsin Dells, then followed Highway 12 into Baraboo. He parked the El Camino on Water Street across from the entrance to Circus World. His was the only car on the street.

"So this is where your curiosity in Americana began?" Tanya asked.

"It began with the exploration of the creek bed on my parents' farm, but this is where it evolved. Circus World opened my eyes to a whole new world outside my own. As you saw for yourself, I had a very strict upbringing. My family and the Bible were my entire existence. The one exception was Circus World. For some reason, both of my parents loved coming to this place."

"I, too, loved the circus when I was a little girl."

"Baraboo," Mark said, "was the home of the Ringling Brothers Circus. They began their first tour back in 1884. This was their wintering ground until 1918. The Circus World Museum opened here in 1959. My parents used to bring us here at least twice a year. We would ride elephants, climb on the railroad cars, and watch circus acts. They have a fantastic collection of circus memorabilia. Last year the Ringling Brothers performed their final show at Nassau Coliseum in Long Island. This and a few other museums are all that's left of the circus in America."

"Can we go in?" Tanya asked.

"Sure. They're open year-round, though we might be their only customers this time of year."

For less than a ten-dollar ticket fee, the Circus World Museum was a treasure trove of Americana. It spanned sixty-four acres on both sides of the Baraboo River. The main entrance and exhibition hall were located on the east bank along with the overwintering quarters for elephants, camels, and baggage horses. A red bridge crossed the river to the west bank, where the circus wagon pavilion, circus train, and hippodrome were housed and open only during the summer season. Mark and Tanya, together with a father and son, were the only visitors.

The Irving Feld Visitor Center housed a fabulous collection of life-size circus posters that advertised human oddities such as the conjoined twins, the bearded lady, and Tom Thumb. Parade floats with heroes and dragons recalled the glory days of the Great Circus Parades in Milwaukee, Chicago, and Baraboo. Professor William Fricke's Imperial Flea Circus, which once featured three hundred genuine European human fleas, displayed its artifacts of miniature cars, cannons, and a high wire. A mobile steel cage held a replica of Gargantua the Great, the most famous circus gorilla of the twentieth century. A booth illuminated with ultraviolet light invited visitors to enter and see a man transformed into a monster.

"I can see why you were fascinated with this place when you were a boy," Tanya said. "It's so *different* than your American Gothic."

"For over two centuries the circus would pull into American towns that were mostly white, homogenous, and rural," Mark said. "It brought exotic creatures, magnificent acts, sideshows, and cheap thrills. It was the 'greatest show on Earth.'"

"Then why did it end?"

"Many reasons. The most immediate were the protests of animal rights activists. They claimed circus animals were subjected to unconscionable cruelty. Yet according to Genesis 1:26, God said: 'Let us make man in our image, after our likeness: and let them have dominion over the fish of the sea, and over the fowl of the air, and over the cattle, and over all the earth, and over every creeping thing that creepeth upon the earth.'

Personally, I think that the animal rights activists overdid it. They're denying us our right to appreciate God's creations."

"So you think that God gave us the right to put hats on elephants and parade them under the big top?"

"Sure," Mark replied, not knowing where she was going with this.

"Does this sense of divine entitlement extend to wiping out all living things on Earth except those that we can eat?"

"Well, no. We should be stewards of what God has given us."

"Have you heard about the Club of Rome?" she asked.

"No, I can't say that I have."

"They were a group of scientists and policymakers who met in Rome in the 1970s. They predicted that the world as we know it will experience cataclysmic changes beginning in 2035."

"The Tribulation?"

"Call it what you want. Their arguments are scientific, not religious."

"What did they say?"

"They said that we humans are destroying the earth. Our overconsumption of resources and our skyrocketing population are not sustainable. It's all going to come crashing down on us like some wrath of God."

"But we've been good stewards," Mark protested. "Just look around you. I think we're doing pretty well."

Tanya looked at the posters of elephants and camels parading down the streets of Milwaukee. "What would you say if I told you that we humans make up less than one percent of all life on Earth but have destroyed over eighty percent of the wildlife? If you exclude our pets and the animals we eat, there are currently *half* as many vertebrate animals today as there were back in 1970. We're precipitating a mass extinction through habitat destruction, global warming, and pollution. Soon the only wild animals left will be confined to circuses and zoos."

The wheeled cage of Gargantua the Great stood empty as it had since 1949.

"I still find that hard to believe," Mark said. "Just take a look at Otto and Mary's farm. In addition to the cows, there are birds, squirrels, grasshoppers, rabbits, foxes, and deer. I can't imagine they're going to disappear. The farm's stayed unchanged for a hundred years. It will stay the same for a hundred more."

"That's exactly the problem," Tanya said. "You can't *imagine*. We live in the age of the Anthropocene, where those of us who were made in the image of God have overrun the planet to the detriment of all other living things. The end is closer than you think. We're changing our climate and destroying the ecosystems that sustain us. The only things that emerge from the habitats that we destroy are new infectious diseases. The Club of Rome predicted that the world as we know it will come to a catastrophic end in *our* lifetimes. As our population skyrockets, we're going to surpass the earth's ability to sustain us. We're going to run out of food and fresh water. The disparities between the haves and have-nots will result in mass migrations and global conflict. Our leaders, rather than address these issues, are building walls and hoarding resources with the mottos of making their countries first. The rule of power is trumping the rule of law. I'm afraid that this idyllic American life that your family is enjoying will come to a cataclysmic end, whether they're aware of these threats or not."

"The End Time."

"Exactly, and we're bringing it upon ourselves. It will begin in those parts of the world where the population is increasing and the resources are dwindling: the Middle East, sub-Saharan Africa, Southeast Asia, and Latin America. It will then spill over into the developed world. It's convenient to believe that you'll be raptured before the Great Tribulation begins. But not everyone on Earth believes in your great escape. People are coming to America to save themselves and their families from violence, poverty, and starvation."

"How is it that you know so much about these things?"

"Because I'm a citizen of the *world*," Tanya replied. "I care what happens to *all* of us."

As they were crossing the red pedestrian bridge to view the exhibits on the west bank, Mark heard Mary call his name. He turned around to see her running up to him on the bridge.

"Someone came to the farm asking about you," she said as she tried to catch her breath. "He said he was a classmate from divinity school.

When I asked him what Bible he preferred, Saint James or Scofield, he said he preferred the Saint James version because he thought the translation of the New Testament from Greek to English was more accurate! I asked him to complete Genesis 12:3, 'I bless them . . .' and he couldn't! He was pushy—he tried to force his way into the barn. Otto had to bring out the shotgun to chase him away."

"You didn't tell him . . ."

"No! Of course not! We said we hadn't seen you in years. I called your parents to let them know he might be coming their way."

"Are you sure you weren't followed?"

"Positive," Mary replied. "He had this fancy black SUV. I came down County O and A. He would have taken 16 and 12 to go to your folk's place."

"We can't go back to your farm," Mark said. "We'd put you in danger. I just wish we'd brought our things."

"I figured you might need to move on," Mary said, "so I brought your bags. I also brought what little cash we have."

Mark gave her a hug that made her smile from ear to ear. "Thank you," he said. "Thank Otto and my parents. Tell them I'll be back when this is all over."

"You can't tell me what *this* is, can you?"

"No," he said. "If we're successful, you'll read about it in *Christianity Today*."

CHAPTER 8

Self

The road to Self runs through the heart of the country. Beginning in Chicago, Route 66 runs through Illinois, Missouri, Kansas, Oklahoma, Texas, New Mexico, and Arizona before reaching the END OF THE TRAIL sign in Santa Monica, California. Mark had always wanted to travel down the Main Street of America for his Americana blog, and now it was leading him and Tanya to Death Valley to find the Flame of God.

Mrs. Erickson's Chevy El Camino was a practical way to see the USA. A hatch-style tonneau cover fit over the bed, and the AM/FM radio still worked. The fathom-green exterior had faded to pea. It fit into the places they would be visiting like a Meramec Caverns sticker on a chrome bumper.

Mark found an old Rand McNally atlas of the USA in the glove compartment. He figured the drive from Baraboo to Self, Arkansas, would take about ten hours. He planned to stop past Saint Louis, then make it to Self by noon the next day. For the sake of time, he took I-94 to I-55, bypassing the historic places along old Route 66 that could have populated his Americana blog for days: the Odell gas station, the J. H. Hawes Grain Elevator Museum in Atlanta, the Railsplitter Covered Wagon in Lincoln, the Ramsey Barn in Glenarm. He at least convinced Tanya to sample "the world's greatest chicken" at the White Fence Farm in Romeoville.

Mark's father had recommended that the best way to dig into Reverend Kane's past was to start with his roots. He agreed that Kane's new interest in Soviet history was odd. The man, to his knowledge, had never traveled abroad. When Mark asked his father if he frowned upon their digging into Reverend Kane's past, his father replied by quoting Teddy Roosevelt: "the men with muck-rakes are often indispensable to the well-being of society, but only if they know when to stop raking the muck."

"I learned more from my father than from any professor in school," Mark confided to Tanya as they sped down I-55 past Funks Grove.

"Your parents are both good and caring people," Tanya said. "I believe your mother will come around in time. She loves you so much, she can't let you go. I'm glad I had the opportunity to meet them."

"A little narrow-minded?" he asked.

"They're firm in their beliefs. They live by God's word."

"But what about our words?" Mark asked. "I've read books that have opened my eyes to a much broader and much more complex view of the world. Philosophers, historians, writers . . ."

"Artists?" Tanya asked.

"Yes, and artists. Art expresses things that words alone can't. It transforms. It can heal. I saw it in Mirana's mural. I see it in your sculptures."

The farther south they drove, the closer they came to the Bible Belt. Farmland stretched as far as the eye could see. *The heart of the heart of the country*, Mark thought. *The people are tied to the land, the seasons, and their Christian communities. Many towns retained their Native American names. Others were named after the first settlers who had driven out the Native Americans. Still others were named after the cities from where the residents had emigrated.*

In the two weeks they had been together, he had shown Tanya more of America then many American-born residents had seen in their lifetimes. There was so much he wanted to show her, so much he wanted to share, but for now he was content to just share the same space. She was as beautiful as the first time he saw her. He knew that God had brought them together for some higher purpose, and though he didn't know how it would end, he was grateful for the journey. They were together in a moment of eternity. *Perhaps time is illusion,* he thought. *Perhaps there is only Now.*

The Gateway Arch welcomed them as they crossed the Mississippi River into Missouri. Barges laden with grain and lumber navigated the shoals on their way to New Orleans. The lights of Saint Louis illuminated the night sky and washed out the stars.

They stopped for the night at a Motel 6 in Eureka. Mark tried to be respectful by ordering two rooms, but Tanya said she would feel safer with just one. The room smelled of mold and air freshener. Tanya took her time in the bathroom. When she emerged, her hair was wet and her skin was steaming from the hot shower. Her torso was loosely wrapped in a towel. She moved as gracefully as a dancer, aware of her body in space and time. No wonder her sculptures were so evocative. The image of Aphrodite rising from the sea was forever etched in his brain. The myth was pagan, but to him it was existential. His mother's warning ran through his head: *"Do not lust in your heart after her beauty or let her captivate you with her eyes."*

She combed the water out of her wet, blonde hair. When she saw Mark staring at her she smiled. "I left it open for you."

His heart skipped a beat.

"The bathroom," Tanya said. "I can dry my hair here."

Mark grabbed his wash kit and locked the door to the bathroom. He undressed, turned on the shower, and stepped in. He was rock hard. He closed his eyes and let the pagan goddess enter his inner sanctum. As the water pulsed, he stroked, at first reluctantly, then rhythmically, then furiously. He was in a time and place where idols were worshipped and men spilled blood to appease their gods. Every muscle tensed, and he shed his seed in vain. He scrubbed himself clean until his skin was almost raw. He knew he was evil in the sight of the Lord but didn't care. He stepped out of the shower and looked at himself in the mirror. He wondered if Tanya found him attractive or not. Mary had thought him handsome. So had Lili. He resembled his father in his height and Nordic features. Until now he had never dwelled on his looks. Vanity, his mother had told him, was like pride, one of the seven deadly sins. When he came out of the bathroom, Tanya was fast asleep. He crawled into his bed and tried to clear his mind of the guilt and proverbs that were racing through his head.

* * * *

Self was not on Mrs. Erickson's Rand McNally atlas. It was nestled in the Ozarks somewhere near Omaha, Arkansas. Mark pulled off US 14 and asked for directions at a roadside café. The waitress, a gray-haired woman in a pink uniform, drew him a map on the back of a napkin. The ten-mile drive to Self took them down Old Highway 65 and wound through a series of mountain roads. The Ozarks were steeped in superstition. In the light of day, the woods were resplendent with wildflowers and redbuds in bloom. In the dark of night, the Howler roamed the woods. As they entered the hamlet of Self on Dubuque Road, Mark noticed a "National Register of Historic Places" plaque on a Craftsman-style building that was finished in a rubblestone veneer.

"This might be a good place to begin," he told Tanya. An elderly woman was letting her spotted pointer finish its business on the lawn. "She looks like she's lived here for a while. Maybe she knows something about Dr. Kane." When they got out of the car, the woman whistled the dog back to her side. It was not happy to have its private time interrupted. It bared its teeth.

"Excuse me, ma'am," Mark said. "We were just driving through—"

"No one just drives through Self," she said. "You looking for the Devil's Hole? That's about the only reason people come here."

"We heard about Devil's Hole," Tanya said. "Isn't that where Reverend Kane was born again?"

"Our most famous native son," the woman replied. "Are you friends or kin?"

"I'm a divinity student," Mark said. "At least I was. I guess the Lord told me to come here. I hope to follow in Dr. Kane's footsteps. Did you know him?"

The pointer stopped baring its teeth. It was now sniffing Tanya. It started humping her leg before the woman yanked it back by its collar. The dog growled and went sniffing for a new place to poop.

"Sure did. I knew his mom. We sat in the same row right there in Cottonwood School back in the thirties."

"Is that where Dr. Kane went to school?"

"The Cottonwood School shut down in forty-nine. He went to school in Prosperity."

"Is his mom still alive?" Mark asked.

"Oh no, poor thing. She passed when Mathias was still a teen. She struggled with depression until the good Lord took her. I blame it on her no-good husband. I never knew a meaner man. He would beat her senseless. He drank away what little money she had and got himself killed. Left her penniless. The Kane family pretty much lived on charity and welfare. She never did get to hear Mathias preach. Reverend Anderson took him under his wing when she passed, God bless him. Made him the man he is."

"Reverend Anderson in Pawhuska?" Tanya asked.

"Somewhere in Oklahoma," the woman replied. "He guided Mathias to the highest pulpit in the land, then left to minister to a bunch of Indians. I guess it was God's will."

"Are there any public records of Dr. Kane's childhood in Self?"

The woman laughed. "Public records? We don't even have a post office. You might want to check in Harrison, the county seat."

"How about church records?" Mark asked.

"Closest would be New Hope. Only records here are the tombstones in the old graveyard."

"Does Reverend Kane have any family left in Self?" Mark asked.

"None that aren't buried," the woman replied.

"Thanks, you've been very helpful," Mark said. "We would like to see the Devil's Hole. Can you tell us the way?"

"Sure can," the woman replied. "Just don't let the gowrow get you."

* * * *

Dmitri knew that Mary had lied to him. He was trained at the academy to detect the subtle physical signs of lying: the hesitancy in voice, the blinking, the touching of the mouth. Even the most accomplished liars had a "tell," and Mary was no accomplished liar. He realized that she had tested him with her questions about the Bible and regretted that he had chosen the role of a divinity student without adequate preparation. He had cased the parents' home but saw no signs of his quarry. He returned to Mary's farm after nightfall. He shut off his headlights and drove the last half mile down County O by moonlight. As he pulled up to the entrance, the two German shepherds ran to his car barking and snarling. He opened the car window and tossed out several pieces of meat laced with strychnine. The dogs snatched up the bait and within minutes were convulsing in the ditch on the side of the road. Dmitri waited to see if the barking alerted the owners, but the door to the farmhouse stayed closed. The only sounds were the chirping of the spring crickets and occasional moos from the barn.

He sneaked up to the farmhouse and peered through the window. Mary was washing and putting away the dishes. He counted only two settings. Her husband was sitting at the dining room table oiling his shotgun. Dmitri studied the various size footprints that led from the house to the barn: three men and three women. The barn door was open. He lit a path using the flashlight on his phone. The cows shifted nervously in their pens. A tangle of metal in the back of the barn caught his eye. Scraps of metal had been welded into the shape of a pelican with its head buried in its chest. He had seen a similar style piece at the Tire Works in Beech Mountain.

The Trans Am was nowhere to be found. Dmitri figured that Mary must have warned them. He considered extracting information from her through sodium pentothal but decided it wasn't worth the risk. Rider was not foolish enough to endanger his family by telling them where he and the rusalka were headed. Her husband was a giant of a man and armed with a shotgun. Dmitri would have had to kill them both. The murders would spook Dana, and she was still a valuable asset. Gennady was monitoring her phone and internet accounts. The Trans

Am couldn't avoid traffic and tollway cameras forever. Sooner or later Rider would feel safe enough to reestablish contact. The demonstration at the Jefferson Davis monument was planned for June 1. If there was no contact from Rider before then, then Gennady's people would need to bot Dana's face all over social media until it went viral. She would become the public face of the alt-right, and Rider would have to return to save her from herself.

* * * *

The opening of Devil's Hole Cave was a mile walk from the gravel road where they had parked their car. The footpath wound through a white oak glade. The path was overgrown with switch grass and brush. Many of the tall oaks that formed the canopy were dead, and their grotesque branches cast eerie shadows over the glade. Gnats swarmed around their faces and tried to fly into their eyes. They passed a ramshackle hut that was barely visible from the path. It was constructed of plywood and covered with a blue tarp. Open tin cans were scattered about. The old woman had warned that though the property was private, lost souls were rumored to be squatting on the land. The locals forbade their children from going anywhere near Devil's Hole Cave.

The entrance to the cave was a fissure in the cliff face. The sun was still visible but would soon set over the hills. Mark lit a road flare that they had found in the hatch of the El Camino.

"What do you think we'll find?" Tanya asked.

"I'm not sure," Mark replied. "The actual hole must be inside the cave. This is the place where Reverend Kane had his vision of the End Time. It's how he was born again. Maybe there is some power in this place, good or evil, that can show us the way to heaven."

"Or hell," Tanya added.

They stepped through the crevice and entered the darkness. The flare cast a reddish light that lit up the cave ten feet ahead of them. They treaded carefully, step by step. The ground turned from rough soil to rock. The roof of the cave was about eight feet high. Tanya was the first to see the abyss. It was a black hole in the floor of the cave that could easily swallow a person. Pieces of trash and chicken bones were scattered about. The initials "EJR, 1887" were scratched into the wall of the cave. Other visitors had followed suit and scratched their own names and dates onto the walls. The most recent was "JS, 1955."

Mark put the flare over the mouth of the hole. It illuminated the upper rim, but the pit itself seemed bottomless. He picked up a stone and tossed it into the hole. After four seconds, he heard the rock thump once, then silence. It sounded like it had hit a ledge, bounced, then continued falling farther down the hole. Reverend Kane had confessed to his followers how as a teenager he had crawled into this very cave, succumbed to temptation, and thrown the crumpled pornography into the hole. His story gained new details with each telling. He had described how he heard a hissing sound and had fled the cave. He hid by the entrance and watched as a terrible beast emerged from its lair. When questioned about his embellishments, he would reply that even if he occasionally erred on the details, his conversion story was "truer than true."

Tanya grabbed Mark's forearm. "Do you hear that?" she asked.

Mark knelt and put his ear to the abyss. He, too, thought he heard a hiss coming out of the darkness. The blackness of the hole drew him in. Fear crept up his spine. "Disquieting thoughts from the visions of the night," he said.

"Visions?" Tanya asked.

"It's a phrase from the book of Job. I think I'm beginning to understand the meaning. We fear the unknown. Imaginary beasts emerge from our subconscious. Maybe we create myths and religions to mitigate these fears."

"But what if they're not imaginary? Baudelaire said that 'the finest trick of the devil is to convince you he doesn't exist.'"

Mark stared into the abyss. "It's frightening to think that the devil exists, and it's even more frightening to think that he doesn't. If we believe every word of the Bible, then it's easy to make sense of the chaos. There's comfort in knowing that God is looking out for us. If we start to doubt and think that we're alone in a godless universe, then it's terrifying." His words resonated in the pit.

"I think we're hearing our own echoes," Tanya said.

The flare had been burning for over ten minutes. They had only a few minutes left of light. "We need to go," he said. "We can lose our way in the dark and fall into that pit." The flare extinguished sooner than they had anticipated. A sliver of light from the entrance guided their way out. It, too, was getting dimmer by the minute. They stepped out of the crevice as dusk descended on the mountain.

A gravelly voice called down to them. "You the devil's kin?"

Mark looked up to see a grizzled old man pointing a rifle at them. His hair was long and ratted. He wore what looked like a Confederate military sack coat. At his feet was a string of dead squirrels. "Are you the owner?" Mark asked.

"Maybe I am and maybe I ain't," the man replied. "Who are you?"

"I'm a journalist, a journalism student, actually. I'm writing a blog on Americana. You know, all the things that make us American. This place has a lot of history. I wanted to include it into my blog."

"A blog? Sounds like a bunch of horseshit to me."

"And you are . . . ?" Mark asked.

"General Lightning Struck," the old man announced. "So you say you're collecting stories. I know a few tales myself. You want to hear about the gowrow?"

Tanya tugged on Mark's hand to leave, but his curiosity was piqued. The general was touched in the head, but he seemed to be hunting squirrels, not people. "Sure," he said. "We'd love to learn the history of this place."

"Sun's going down soon. We'll need to light a fire," the general said. He pointed to an outcrop, a stone's throw from the cave. "Right there will do. Spread out and find some kindling."

The dead oaks left plenty of kindling lying about. Mark and Tanya gathered some bundles and brought them over to the outcrop. The general had already formed a nest with dry grass and twigs, lit it with a match, and blew on it to fan the flame. He took the bundles from them and arranged them in the form of a teepee around the nest. He skinned and gutted his squirrels and speared them with a sharpened stick to roast over the fire. "That'll do just fine," he said. When the squirrels were cooked through, he tore off some pieces of meat and handed them to his guests.

Mark figured it would be dangerous to refuse the stranger's hospitality. "Thank you," he said and put the piece in his mouth. Tanya did the same.

"If you want to know about the gowrow," the general began, "you've come to the right place. Just keep on eye on the entrance there as I tell you the story."

The crackling fire provided light and warmth. Tanya nuzzled closer to Mark. The general smelled like he hadn't bathed since the Civil War.

"Back in the late 1880s," the general began, "this place was owned by a fella by the name of E. J. Rhodes. Folks were spreading nasty rumors about some dragon living in the cave, so Rhodes figured he had to investigate. The place would be hard to sell if it were harboring some sort of monster. Anyway, he gets himself a rope and an oil lamp and climbs down into the hole. You seen the hole, right?"

"Yes," Tanya replied. "It's about fifty meters in. We threw a rock into it."

The general gripped his sword. "You trying to wake up the gowrow?"

"We just wanted to see how deep the hole is," Mark replied. "We heard it bounce after a couple of seconds. Then we heard what sounded like hiss coming out of the hole."

The general eyed the entrance to the cave.

"Well, E. J. Rhodes, he did like you did, except he used his rope to climb down to a ledge about two hundred feet down. From there the shaft narrowed into a funnel you can only crawl through. All of a sudden he hears this hissing sound coming from out of the dark that scares the hell out of him. Some say he went mad and his hair turned white, but who knows whether it actually did or not. Anyhow, he tells some people about what happened, and a group of them come back to check out his story. This time they bring a rope one thousand feet long. They tie a flat iron to it and drop it in the hole. When it hit two hundred feet, the rope goes taut, and they hear a vicious hissing sound, like some kind of giant lizard might make. Others say it sounded more like *gowrow*. That's where the name comes from. When they pull up the flat iron, it's bent with teeth marks on it. Now what kind of creature can bite hard enough to bend a flat iron? Anyway, they tie a stone to the line and drop it back down the hole. When it hits two hundred feet, something pulls on it, and they again hear this loud hissing sound. When they bring up the rope, it's bitten clean through. Jim, the guide, said he could see the teeth marks on it. At first they thought it was an Indian spirit, but now we know it was a gowrow."

"Has anyone actually seen a gowrow?" Mark asked.

"Hell yeah," the general replied. "It's a dragonlike monster about twenty feet long with enormous tusks. Some say they have short legs with webbed feet, like a duck's, except that the toes have these terrible claws. They're green with thick scales, and their backs are bristled with short horns. They have long tails with sharp grooves that they can swing like a sickle. They'll eat anything they can get their teeth into: goats, deer, calves, and even humans."

"Is there any physical evidence that it exists?" Mark asked.

"Back in 1897 a traveling salesman by the name of William Miller killed a gowrow right on this spot. He went into the cave with a bunch of men when the gowrow had left its lair. They found all kinds of bones in the cave, including human. They waited for the gowrow to return. They felt the ground shake. When it came into range, everyone fired. The gowrow uprooted trees and killed one of the men. It took several volleys to kill it. Miller then shipped the carcass to the Smithsonian, though they deny ever receiving it."

"Was that the end of the gowrow?" Tanya asked.

The old timer laughed. "There ain't just one. That's like saying just because you killed one cougar, you killed them all. Gowrows are all over these parts. A fellow from Missouri even captured one way back when."

"How did he manage that?" Mark asked.

"Pretty clever fellow. He enticed it to eat a wagonload of dried apples. That caused the gowrow's body to swell so much that it couldn't crawl back into its cave. Story goes that he set up a tent and charged folks twenty-five cents to see it. He had a painting of a gowrow devouring a bunch of cotton farmers at the entrance. Before the show could start, the gowrow got loose. People heard gunshots and clanking chains and the tent collapsed. The showman ran out yelling 'run for your lives! The gowrow got loose!' Most folks never did get to see it."

"It could have been a scam," Mark suggested.

"Maybe it was, maybe it wasn't," the general replied. "I heard that at one time there were giant elephants roaming these same woods. If we had giant elephants, then why not gowrows?"

"There were mammoths here at one time," Mark said. "They went extinct ten thousand years ago."

General Lighting shook his head. "The Bible says the earth's only been around for about six thousand. So how can that be?"

Mark figured there was no point in arguing about creationism with a man who believed so firmly in gowrows.

The general sensed his skepticism. "If it ain't a gowrow, then what abomination dwells in that cave?" he asked.

"Well," Mark replied, "it must be called the Devil's Hole for a reason."

* * * *

Seven thousand miles away in the Holy Dormition Monastery of the Russian Orthodox Church, in Pochayiv, Ukraine, Brother Alexiy completed his morning prayers in the Caves Church. He crossed himself three times in the Orthodox tradition and bowed before the silver shrine that held the incorrupt relics of Saint Job. The church smelled of incense and candle wax. The other monks kept their distance. To them he was a heretic who openly defied the authority of the church. Yet the patriarch himself had given strict orders to leave Brother Alexiy alone. He was blessed by the Holy Spirit and had the gift of prophecy.

The Russian Orthodox churches in Ukraine were dying. False prophets from the Kyiv patriarchy were deceiving the faithful. The Ukrainian Catholics were opening new churches in the villages. Even the Poles were reviving the old *kostols*. Brother Alexiy was at least loyal to the Russian Orthodox tradition, beginning with the baptism of Prince Vladimir in Chersonesos, in Crimea, through recognition of the Moscow patriarchy as the third Rome.

Over a hundred pilgrims were waiting by the entrance to the Caves Church to hear him speak. Many had walked over fifty kilometers to hear his message. The beggars who were fixtures in the monastery collected alms with open arms. Their tattered clothes concealed their purses.

Brother Alexiy stepped out into the open air and crossed himself with a sweeping sign of the cross. "In the name of the Father, Son, and Holy Spirit. Brothers and Sisters in Christ, I am humbled by your pilgrimage. I am but a simple monk, a servant of God. He has chosen to give me the gift of sight so that I can show you the path to salvation. The End Time is here. The war in Donbas is but the beginning. Holy Russia is assembling a great army to punish the decadent. It will reunite the Holy Russian Empire and take back Europe before marching on Jerusalem for the fulfillment of Revelations. I see the battle of North and South. I see Armageddon. I see the world enveloped in nuclear war. But fear not. Those of you who follow me will be saved. You will live to witness the Kingdom of Christ on Earth."

The pilgrims ran up to kiss his robe. The braver dared to touch his beard, which extended to his waist. A hunched old *baba* straightened her spine and threw away her cane. An old man rubbed his eyes and claimed that he could see again. Others begged for miracles for their relatives who were too sick to make the journey. Women without head coverings were turned away and directed to the kiosks outside the monastery, where they could purchase scarves. Brother Alexiy laid hands on as many pilgrims as he could before security guards led him away for his safety.

Once in his cubicle, Brother Alexiy took off his monk's robe. He checked his smartphone for new messages and put on a sweat suit. He had the physique of a boxer. He went through the thirty-minute exercise routine that had been drilled in him at the academy. The clergy was one of many tracks available to aspiring FSB officers. It was not as glamorous as the foreign service, but in the end it offered a life as rich as the Vatican. The grueling preparation, in addition to the FSB Academy, included completion of the seminary, several years of monastic life, and mastery of Orthodox mysticism. The gift of prophecy was the Kremlin's idea as were the staged miracles that had become an almost daily occurrence. His supervisors assured him that he was in line to become an archimandrite, if not the next patriarch of Moscow.

He heard a knock on his door.

"Brother Alexiy?"

He donned the robe and opened the door. An acolyte monk stared down at the floor and said, "The abbot asked that I deliver this message. A monk from the Alexander Nevsky Lavra has traveled here to see you. He is waiting for you in the chapel of the beholied icon of Theotokos."

"I shall be there after I complete my prayers."

A visit from the Nevsky Lavra in Saint Petersburg could only mean one thing: the communication could only occur face-to-face. Security was paramount. He waited for a bit longer than necessary, and then proceeded to the tiny chapel that was built to commemorate the four-hundred-year anniversary of the transfer of the wonder-working icon of the Theotokos to the monastery. His visitor was waiting inside. Brother Alexiy shut the door.

"Glory to Jesus Christ," Brother Alexiy said.

"Glory forever," the monk replied. Rather than show deference, the visitor showed his rank. "You've kept me waiting for over half an hour."

"And you are . . . ?"

"I am your superior," the visitor replied. He walked to the small windows of the chapel and looked out to make sure no one was within earshot.

"The password?" Brother Alexiy asked.

The visitor whispered a prayer in Old Slavonic in his ear. Brother Alexiy kissed his hand.

"Ever since Patriarch Bartholomew granted a *tomos* to the Ukrainian Orthodox Church, your influence in Ukraine has been waning."

"I still have a strong following from both branches of the Orthodox Church."

The visitor lit a beeswax candle from the center flame and inserted it into the bed of sand at the base of the stand. He crossed himself in front of the icon of Theotokos. "Nevertheless," he said, "we have a new assignment for you."

"My assignments come from the Almighty."

"The Almighty has taken residence in the Kremlin. We want you to help us infiltrate the American evangelicals. We want you to infiltrate the Christian fellowship they call the Family.

"I thought we already had," Alexiy said.

"Only the periphery. We want to infiltrate the inner circle. We've already laid the groundwork."

"I'm listening."

"We've gained access to the chair of the Senate Foreign Relations Committee. He's the scion of the largest Christian media empire in the United States."

"What makes you think he'll cooperate?"

"Victor Ivanovich has been successful in entrapping him through *kompromat* and credit. His father owns Rich Media Enterprises."

"Ivanovich? You trust the Lord of the Taiga?"

"No one is beyond the reach of the Kremlin."

"Ivanovich is an atheist. He's not reliable. He'll do what's best for himself."

The visitor put his hand on Alexiy's shoulder. "It's in everyone's interest to overturn the Magnitsky Act."

"Tell me more about this senator," Brother Alexiy said.

"He's ambitious but without ability. He's a bird without wings."

"What has he provided us so far?"

"We've gotten him to convince his marquee televangelist, Dr. Mathias Kane, to serve as our spokesman."

"I've heard of Kane," Brother Alexiy replied. "The voice of the Last Awakening. The prophet of the End Time."

"Dr. Kane is organizing a march in Washington on July 4 to promote family values. We've arranged to have you invited not only as a participant but also as a guest speaker. We need you to gain his trust."

"I would need to know more about the man."

The visitor pulled a flash drive out from beneath his robe. "We've prepared a dossier. Everything you need to know about him is here. We've data-mined all of his speeches and prepared a detailed analysis of his views. They're much simpler than our own Orthodox theology. His Achilles' heel is his worldly ambition."

"An American visa?" Brother Alexiy asked.

"We've arranged to have the Americans give you a multiyear visa. We will need to cultivate this relationship over a number of years. If you're successful in gaining their trust, then the Family will give us unfettered access to their levers of power."

Brother Alexiy smiled. This was the opportunity that he was waiting for. With Patriarch Bartholomew granting autocephaly to the Ukrainian Orthodox Church, his future in Ukraine was unpredictable. On the other hand, if he could infiltrate the inner circle of American power, then his advancement was assured. The evangelicals controlled 25 percent of American voters. They believed in the inerrancy of the Bible. If the Russians could convince them that they share a common cause and manipulate them through their beliefs, then they could take America without firing a single shot.

"Are there any potential threats that I should be aware of?" he asked.

"Nothing major," the visitor replied. "Ivanovich tells us he has it under control."

Brother Alexiy gripped his crucifix. "Please elaborate."

"Ivanovich compromised the senator with a *kompromat* using a Ukrainian sculptress as the unwitting bait. The sculptress absconded. Ivanovich's chief of security is looking for her."

"How much does she know?" Brother Alexiy asked.

"Nothing, as far as we know."

"Has she gone to the American authorities?"

"Ivanovich assures us that she has not."

"You don't find that odd?" Brother Alexiy asked. "The woman is exploited in a plot she has no knowledge of, then simply disappears? You may be underestimating her. She can compromise us. I need a dossier on her as well. I also need to see the reports that Ivanovich has been submitting, without any redactions. Who is Ivanovich's chief of security?"

"The Cuban. Dmitri."

Brother Alexiy stroked his long beard and studied the visitor's eyes.

"Do you know the man?" the visitor asked.

"I know him well. He was two years my junior at the academy. His nickname was the chameleon. For all I know, you could be him."

CHAPTER 9

Pawhuska

The Riches' equestrian estate straddled the border between Tennessee and Kentucky. Julian Rich Sr. had bought the estate as a getaway for his wife, who wanted to escape the cigar-filled back rooms of Nashville politics. The Thoroughbreds that the Riches paraded in the winner's circle at the Kentucky Derby and the Preakness Stakes belied the mixed-breed origins of their owners. Eleanor Rich was a past president of the Nashville chapter of the United Daughters of the Confederacy and could trace her ancestry to Caroline Meriwether Goodlett. Julian's forefathers, on the other hand, were mostly common folk who had raised themselves by their bootstraps through luck, hard work, and perfidy.

Julian Rich Sr.'s grandfather was a bootlegger during Prohibition. He distilled whiskey in a cave on the banks of the Clinch River and ran it into Knoxville down the White Lightning Trail. He died in a fiery crash when his Ford Model T Coupe was run off the road by revenuers. The grandmother raised their son Roy during the Great Depression by working as a schoolteacher in Pioneer. At the age of seventeen, Roy killed a man in a bar in Huntsville by smashing him in the head with a cue ball. He claimed the black man had poked him in the ass with a cue stick, and the judge ruled it to be self-defense. Roy enlisted in the marines in 1942 and returned from the Pacific with a bum leg and a Purple Heart.

After the war he opened a bar in Bell Buckle and made most of his money by holding illegal cockfights in the back room. His future wife, Dorothy, taught Sunday school at the local Baptist church. He took her to the Billy Graham revival in Charlotte, where he claimed to be born again. He vowed to give up drinking and take up a respectable occupation if only she'd marry him.

Despite his promise to stay sober, Roy continued drinking and running into trouble with the law. He missed his son's birth due to a weeklong binge and spent the early years of his son's life in and out of prison. Dorothy took up with the local minister, and when Roy was released, he beat his wife into a coma. He died in a hunting accident a few weeks later while out on bail.

Their son Julian was left to fend for himself. He learned as much on the streets as he did in school. His mother never fully recovered from her savage beating, and they lived off her social security disability. He was drafted at age eighteen and deployed to Vietnam, where he was awarded a Bronze Star with a distinction for valor. He rarely spoke of the war. The only other surviving member of his company told the *Christian World* that Julian Rich had been a tunnel rat that slid into underground tunnels in search of the enemy. He was the only one brave enough to lower himself into the unknown without pissing in his pants. He emerged from that spider hole faced with a choice: embrace Christ or forsake Him. He chose to embrace Him, and his life changed for the better.

During his R & R he met his future wife, Eleanor, while she was vacationing with her family at the Hilton Hawaiian Village on Waikiki Beach. Their torrid romance ended with a pregnancy, and he married her when his tour of duty was over.

His father-in-law gave him a job at his Nashville publishing house, and Julian, despite having only finished high school, proved adept at business. He expanded his father-in-law's publishing house into a Christian media empire by branching out into radio, records, and television. When he and Eleanor inherited the company after her father passed, Julian Rich Sr. became the richest man in Tennessee and among the top one hundred richest men in the United States. He rose to the highest ranks of the state's Republican Party. The governor himself once confided that no one could get elected in Tennessee without the endorsement of Julian Rich Sr. He was a man above politics. His allegiance was to his country, and he knew that the best way to serve his country was to serve the Christian political organization called the Fellowship, or as they liked to refer to themselves within, the Family.

When his son was born, Julian Rich Sr. was determined to give him all of the opportunities he never had. But to his bitter disappointment, young Julian proved to be more like his grandfather, Roy, than his dad. He was expelled from private schools for cheating and spent a summer at a rehab boot camp in Florida. The family made a large donation to a new law school and secured him a spot in the freshman class. A female student accused him of sexual assault but dropped the charges after an out-of-court settlement. After graduation, his father arranged a clerkship with a Tennessee circuit court. The judge fired him for his frequent tardiness, and Rich took a job as an associate at the law firm that represented his father's Christian media company.

Julian Jr. was not particularly good at law, so his father encouraged him to pursue a career in politics. Julian Jr. found power to be intoxicating. At the age of twenty-eight, he became one of the youngest state representatives in Tennessee history. Four years later, with the backing of the Republican Party and support of Tennessee's evangelicals, he became the second youngest native son to ever serve in the US Senate by filling a vacant seat.

He married a southern belle from Memphis who was a past president of the Tennessee Federation of Republican Women. She gave birth to their twin girls a year later, and the Riches became a model for southern family values. Rumors of his drinking, spousal abuse, and womanizing were quashed by his father's media empire. Simply labeling them as fake news was enough to convince his evangelical base.

Rich Jr. convinced his father that the real money was in real estate development. Prices were beginning to climb after the crash of 2008, and there was no shortage of interested foreign investors. He dodged the US Senate conflict of interest rules by divesting himself from the family business while in office. Any probes of potential conflicts were quickly stymied by his father's army of lawyers.

Julian Rich Sr. wondered whether his son would ever learn to wipe his own ass. Racehorses were more satisfying to breed: at least they gave you a run for your money. He kept his thumb on the stopwatch as Lucky Lady, his prize filly, came galloping around the turn. He was a ruggedly handsome man in his early seventies who wished that he could live his life all over again. He clocked Lucky Lady at near-record pace despite the sloppy track. She was sweating and snorting through her flared nostrils.

"Good job, Eddie," Rich Sr. said to the jockey. "If she can keep up this pace, she just might win the Preakness." As he started to stroke her neck, the filly suddenly reared and bolted. He turned to see what had spooked her. His son was walking up to the track and arguing with someone on his cell phone. Rich Sr. grabbed the phone from his son's hand and tossed it into the mud.

The son stooped to pick up and wipe off the phone. "I was talking to . . ."

"I don't give a damn who you were talking to," the father replied. "When you come to see me, you talk to me, not to your phone. You startled Lucky Lady. She always seems to get nervous around you."

Rich Jr. couldn't care less about horses. His father bred them because he loved his wife, and she loved the glamour and excitement of horseracing. It was as American a pastime as drinking bourbon.

"Well, get to the point," Julian Sr. said. "You obviously need something."

"Seeing my parents isn't enough?" his son replied.

"I'm too old for bullshit. You're still wearing your suit, which means you haven't stopped in the house to greet your mother and you're not planning on staying. So get to the point."

"I found an investor for our development in Card Sound."

"What's the deal?" his father asked.

"Fifty million in cash for a thirty percent stake, and another fifty million in loans."

"I thought the banks weren't willing to extend credit to us after the bankruptcy of your Diamond Beach fiasco. There's also the lawsuit that the fishermen filed over the environmental impact."

"It's a foreign investor. The bank's in Cyprus."

Rich Sr. spit. "Fucking Russians," he said. "You're dealing with the fucking Russians. You know I want nothing to do with Commies. My daddy and granddaddy would turn over in their graves."

"They're not Commies," his son replied. "They're legitimate businessmen. They're even Christians." Rich Jr. shifted his feet. His Brioni shoes were caked in mud.

"What else aren't you telling me?"

"They gave me an intriguing proposal. They want to help us take our media business global. They're proposing that we promote Dr. Kane's message about the Last Awakening. They say the Russian markets are eager for Christian programming. We ran some numbers. We could triple our television revenue in two years. They also claim they've developed an artificial intelligence program that can help us achieve information dominance on our social media platforms."

Julian Rich Sr. looked at his son with disdain. "What do they have on you?"

"Nothing. This is strictly business."

"It's never strictly business. They're mafia. You get in with them, you can't get out."

"Let's just give it chance," the son pleaded. "You need to have some faith in me. I'm a US senator, goddamn it."

"I've been wiping your ass since you've been born," Julian Sr. replied. "I got you into the right schools, I expunged your record, I paid off your whores, I got you your clerkship, I got you elected, and I bailed you out of your harebrained investments. I got you into the Family. I thought I was helping you become a man, but now I see that I've just been enabling you to be a spoiled brat. Sell the land back to the state, and tell your Russians that they can go to hell."

Julian Rich Jr. felt like a whippersnapper who had just been spanked behind the shed. He decided to pursue the deal regardless of his father's wishes.

* * * *

Mark and Tanya spent the night at the Shady Acre Motel next to Silver Dollar City. The theme park, which mimed an Ozark frontier town, was built near the mouth of the Marble Cave. An Osage legend says that a young hunter was chasing a bear up Roark Mountain. The bear lunged at him and both fell through a sinkhole into what is now called the Cathedral Room of the cave. The other members of the party heard strange sounds emanating from the hole and named it the Devil's Den. They marked trees around the entrance with a danger sign, a sideways V, and never returned.

In 1869 explorers descended into the cave looking for mineral deposits. They found what looked like marble, but in the end the only thing of value ever extracted from the cave was bat guano. The owners changed the name to Marvel Cave and made it a tourist attraction. In recent years they expanded the site to include thrill rides, a stagecoach ride, a steam engine train, and live demonstrations by resident craftspeople, including blacksmiths, potters, glassblowers, and wood-carvers. Mark had debated whether to spend their limited cash for admission and decided that he may never have another opportunity to show Tanya this slice of Americana. The huge model of an ax splitting a log greeted visitors at the entrance.

"Would you like to descend into the Devil's Den?" he asked Tanya.

She laughed. "The Devil's Hole was enough for me. Let's just walk around. I'm curious to see how you Americans amuse yourselves."

"Silver Dollar City is a replica of an Ozark frontier town. Try and imagine yourself as a pioneer in these mountains a hundred and fifty years ago. It's like a time warp. I love to explore these kinds of places. When I was a kid, I used to sneak away with Otto and Mary to an abandoned place called Fort Dells in the Wisconsin Dells. It was a re-creation of a frontier fort. It had places like Frontierland and Indianland.

It was shut down in 1985, so all we saw were creepy remnants of what used to be a vibrant theme park. They're our American version of architectural ruins."

"Like the Land of Oz?" Tanya said.

"Yes, it's a paradox. We search for meaning in places that have no authenticity of their own. The Land of Oz is based on a movie that's based on a play that's based on a novel that's an allegory of American political life. The Marvel Cave used to be the Marble Cave; its only treasure was bat guano. People come here hoping to experience something authentic—a real Indian, a real log cabin, a real white water river. It's American kitsch. They'll buy a souvenir that's made in China and believe that they've experienced the real America."

"But this *is* the real America," Tanya replied. "This is *here* and this is *now*. These kids will remember how they spent the day with their parents exploring Marvel Cave, eating a corn dog, or riding a roller coaster. It's like you and your childhood memories from the Land of Oz and Circus World. Those experiences are more authentic than any artifact from an antique store."

"So one day, when I'm old, I'll recall how I spent the day riding the world's fastest, steepest, and tallest spinning roller coaster?" he asked.

Tanya smiled. "One day you'll recall how you spent a day at Silver Dollar City with *me*. Now let's go and ride this famous roller coaster."

The Time Traveler was all it was hyped up to be—not for its twists and turns, its rickety climbs and spine-tingling plummets, it's screaming spins that pushed the earth into the sky; but for the fact that Tanya squeezed Mark's hand for dear life and laughed like he had never heard her laugh before. It was like a first date when the awkwardness is lost in the fun house, and you spend what little money you have throwing rings at milk bottles, hoping to win an oversize stuffed animal that your date will keep on her bed as a memento of your puppy love. For those few minutes Mark didn't care about the past or the future—he only cared about the present and hoped that it would never end. Mark bought her the key chain picture of them screaming with delight as they plummeted in a free fall with their eyes closed and their hair standing on end.

They spent the rest of the day escaping their troubles. They stepped back in time at Birdle's Cabin and the Wilderness Church. Tanya got soaked on the white water ride on the Lost River of the Ozarks as they plunged into the fake river. They snacked on American delicacies like pork rinds, tater twists, and funnel cake, and listened to bluegrass music at the Pickin' Shed. The blacksmith was more than happy to show Tanya how he hammered the red-hot metal rod into the shape of a horseshoe. They ended the day in Grandfather's Mansion, stumbling on the slanted floors and laughing at their distorted shapes in the fun house mirrors.

As they were leaving Silver Dollar City, Tanya gave Mark a hug. "Thank you," she said. "I'd forgotten what it's like to be an innocent little girl."

Mark was lost in the moment. He didn't know if she was drawing an imaginary line or inviting him to make her a woman again. They had been inseparable for the past two weeks; they had traveled the same roads, slept under the same roofs, and escaped the same dangers. He had seen her clutch her pillow at night and pray in her sleep in a language he didn't understand. He had seen her transform Dana with her art. He had seen her as an angel and as a pagan goddess, naked and wet from the sea spray. He wanted to be one with her, yet he knew that she had suffered unspeakable trauma at the hands of a stranger. Her pain still separated them. He didn't want to hurt her; he wanted to protect and cherish her. He brushed her cheek to make sure she was real. "You're right," he said. "I'll remember this day because I spent it with you."

The drive to Pawhuska took them north through Missouri, then west through the Oklahoma border. All of these lands were once the hunting grounds of the Osage Nation before the white men forced them off their ancestral lands. The wagon trains that rolled west along the Missouri Trail brought settlers, civilization, and disease. The Osage were driven into Kansas in 1825 and relocated to a reservation in northeast Oklahoma in the 1870s. The once great nation was decimated to a few thousand by massacres, disease, and starvation. Through a twist of fate their reservation was sitting on one of the largest petroleum deposits in Oklahoma, and the few thousand Osage who remained became wealthier than their oppressors. Their new life of mansions, chauffeured cars, and white servants lasted only a few decades until they were murdered off and robbed of their wealth by white men during the Reign of Terror.

Tanya gazed out the car window as the mountains turned to hills and the hills turned to plains. She reflected on the genocide that was perpetrated on these lands. The mountains, rivers, and towns still had Native American names, but only the ghosts of their former inhabitants remained. Europeans had replaced the Osage, cattle had replaced the buffalo, and Jesus had replaced the Great Spirit.

"It's getting late," Mark said. "I don't think we'll make it to Pawhuska by nightfall. Let's stop in Joplin. It's famous for its Route 66 murals. I'd like to include them in my blog."

It was still light as the El Camino pulled into the Route 66 Mural Park in Joplin. The former lead-and-zinc-mining capital of the world now boasted an eclectic collection of public murals that depicted a century of progress from its boom days as a turn-of-the-century mining town to its beat days as a stop on Route 66. An upper mural called *Cruisin' into Joplin* pictured a vintage car arriving in Joplin on Route 66 from the west. The lower mural called *The American Ribbon* traced the Mother Road from start to finish. Tanya got out of the car to get a closer look at a 3D mural with a bifurcated red 1964 Corvette that jutted out of the wall and invited viewers to "get their kicks on Route 66."

"A real slice of American pie," Mark quipped.

Teenagers cruised up and down Main Street with their car windows open and music blaring. A few turned on their headlights as dusk crept in from the east.

"If you're up for some more Americana," Mark said, "we can go looking for the Spook Light."

"The Spook Light?"

"It's local lore. Since the 1800s people have claimed to see an orange ball of light that dances from east to west along a stretch of country road called the Devil's Promenade. The Indians first saw it on the Trail of Tears."

"Devils, devils, and more devils. We have a devil following us. You want to look for more?"

"It's only a few miles out of town. If it doesn't appear by midnight, we'll find a motel on Route 66."

Mark and Tanya cut in the queue of Friday night cruisers and drove south down Main Street to Highway 86. After six miles, they turned right on BB Highway until it dead-ended, then turned left on Spooklight Road. The El Camino rambled down the desolate road looking for a good vantage point.

"We should be right in the middle of the Devil's Promenade," Mark said. "I'll pull over and shut the lights."

They were blanketed in total darkness. Mark rolled down the window to let in some fresh air. The din from frogs and insects filled the void. Mark and Tanya stared through the windshield, looking for any faint glimmer of light.

"Why do they call it the Spook Light?" she asked.

"There are several legends. Two involve ghostly lanterns. In one, a decapitated Osage Indian chief is searching for his head. In the other, a miner is searching for his family who were abducted by Indians. The most romantic is the legend of a Quapaw Indian maiden who fell in love with a young brave. He didn't have the dowry to marry her, so they eloped and were pursued by a party of warriors. When they were close to being caught, they joined hands above the Spring River and leaped to their deaths. The Spook Light is the spirit of these young lovers."

Tanya put her head on his shoulder and stared into the darkness. Mark put his arm around her. As the minutes turned to hours, she drifted into a serene sleep. Mark imagined that she was dreaming of riding the Time Traveler, laughing and squeezing his hand like there was no tomorrow. A ray of moonlight peaked through the clouds and illuminated her lissome body. Her golden hair fell over his arm. A button to her blouse had become undone, and he could see the swell of her breast. Her hand rested on his thigh. Mark felt an overwhelming urge to caress her, to stroke her hair, to brush his fingers against her breast, but the plastic Jesus on the dashboard kept a watchful eye. Mark tried to remember what Jesus had said about the love between a man and a woman, but instead, painful memories crept out of his subconscious like evoked demons: his mother standing over him with a crumpled drawing in her hand . . . Mary vomiting on his lap at the drive-in movie . . . Lili telling him he was no better than a missionary in bed. *I'm not worthy of a woman like Tanya.* He squeezed his thigh until it was bruised to suppress his lust.

He stared ahead in hopes of spotting the elusive Spook Light. If he saw the spirits of the Indian lovers he would wake her. But for now he was content to have her rest her head on his shoulder and let her dream. *Here I am on the Mother Road with an angel riding shotgun, heading west to find the Flame of God. Manifest destiny. The men and women of the Bible had lived their lives. It's time for me to live mine.* He closed his eyes. As he dreamed of the road ahead, a flickering ball of orange light hovered over the windshield and then danced west down the Devil's Promenade.

* * * *

The arch that welcomed visitors to Pawhuska read GATEWAY TO THE TALLGRASS PRAIRIE. Reverend Anderson's First Baptist Church was located on the outskirts of town, just a short drive or long walk from the Osage Reservation. The wooden church was built in the 1920s to minister to white people and Native Americans alike. It was larger than the churches in the center of town, but a tornado had recently sheared off the steeple, and the hole in the roof was covered up with a plastic tarp. A ladder and sheets of plywood were leaning against the outside wall. A lone pickup truck was parked in the churchyard, and a notice was plastered on the church door. Mark and Tanya got out of the El Camino to investigate.

"We're closed until we get our occupancy permit, but I'd be obliged if you could climb up and hand me a sheet of plywood."

Still bleary-eyed from their Spook Light vigil, they looked up to see who was shouting down at them. A bare-chested man with a shock of gray hair climbed out from the hole in the roof holding a hammer in his hand. Mark grabbed a sheet of plywood and inched it up over his head while Tanya held the ladder.

"God bless you, stranger," the man said. "Tornado sheared the steeple off last week. Flew halfway across the county, bell and all."

"Reverend Anderson?" Mark asked.

"Why one and the same. And you are?"

"Mark Rider. Mark Riderson, originally. You may have known my father, Dr. Timothy Riderson."

"Tim Riderson from Baraboo? Why sure, I've heard him speak at our conventions many a time. He's a progressive thinker. Now hand me that sheet."

Mark held the plywood as Reverend Anderson nailed it into place. After a few more sheets, they climbed down the ladder for a rest.

"You're not interested to know why we're here?" Mark asked.

"I figured that God sent you to help me."

"What about the other members of your congregation?" Mark asked.

"They got spooked by the tornado. Cody told them that the Great Spirit was angry. Now they're good God-fearing Christians, mind you, but they still keep to their superstitions."

"Cody?"

"Youngest member of the Osage Tribal Council. Good man. We had a recent falling out. He got frustrated over the failure of the Indian protests to stop the Dakota Access Pipeline. He blames all of his troubles on white men, and I just happen to be one of them."

"My father suggested that we talk to you," Mark said. "We're interested in learning more about Dr. Mathias Kane."

Reverend Anderson's face looked as if God had just asked him to sacrifice his only son. "Mathias? Well, it's a long and painful story. We'll talk about Mathias over a glass of the purest spring water you've ever drank in your life. The members of my congregation bring it to me in jugs from a spring on the reservation." He winked at Mark. "They tell me if you drink it rather than liquor, you'll stay potent forever."

* * * *

Reverend Anderson excused himself while he washed up and put on a freshly ironed white shirt. He lived in three rooms of a dilapidated

1920s mansion that once belonged to an Osage chief. The chief, who made a fortune during the oil boom, had helped build the church. He died penniless and bequeathed his home to the church when he died. The other fourteen rooms of the mansion were used as shelter for the homeless or for anyone fleeing persecution, including runaways and battered wives. Reverend Anderson brought out a jug of spring water and invited them to sit at the kitchen table. He brought out a tray of smoked trout and slices of home-baked bread.

"Now what's your interest in Mathias Kane?" he asked.

"I'm studying journalism at Medill in Chicago," Mark said. "I'm doing some investigative work on televangelists and their connections with crooked politicians."

"And the young lady?"

"I'm a sculptress from Ukraine," Tanya replied. "I came to display one of my works, a sculpture commemorating the Heavenly Hundred from our Revolution of Dignity. For some unknown reason, Dr. Kane, whom I've never even met, is calling me the whore of Babylon in his sermons."

"I'm afraid I can't provide any insight," Reverend Anderson replied. "Mathias and I parted ways over a decade ago."

"Why? What happened?" Mark asked.

"Let me start from the beginning," Reverend Anderson replied. "I've known Mathias since he was born. His mother was my cousin, so that makes us kin. His father was a drunk. He kept a bear in a cage and threatened to put young Mathias in it whenever he cried. Old man Kane got killed in a bar fight when Mathias was about six, so the boy grew up without much paternal supervision. He was a miscreant as a child— blew up cats with M-80s, and he once set a freshly oiled street on fire. His mother taught first grade at Cottonwood School, so the townsfolk looked the other way when her boy got in trouble. Then one day he goes off to the Devil's Hole and comes back born again. Once he found Jesus and became a man, he took care of his mom, finished school, and decided he wanted to become a preacher. I was the minister at the First Baptist in Omaha at the time, so his mom asked if I would take him under my wing shortly before she died. Some say she took her own life, but I think she just lost the will to live. I helped him get into the Baptist

Bible College in Springfield, and he came out full of fire and brimstone. He founded his first church in New Hope with thirty members from my own congregation who wanted a more literal interpretation of the Bible."

Reverend Anderson refilled their glasses with Osage Reservation water and took a long drink himself. "Where was I in my story?" he asked.

"Reverend Kane starts his own church," Tanya replied.

"Ah, yes." Reverend Anderson continued. "So Mathias, with the support of his congregants, buys a shuttered movie theater and converts it into a church. They scrubbed the Coca-Cola off the floors and used the theater marquee signs as advertising. Mathias went door-to-door recruiting congregants. He preached against drinking, smoking, card playing, and, ironically, Hollywood movies. He was a charismatic preacher, even at that young age, and a month after his first service, he began a half-hour Sunday broadcast for a local radio station. He bought a printing press and sent out mass mailings for his Sunday service and radio program. He started a phone bank for telephone evangelism—he would literally call you during your dinner to ask if you were ready for the Rapture. But the smartest thing he did was to set up a television camera to tape his Sunday service. He purchased time on TV stations in various parts of the country and set up a direct mail funding operation to defray the cost of production. Soon people were traveling from a hundred miles away to attend the Sunday service. I myself went to more than one. It was like nothing I'd ever seen—he healed the sick and had people talking in tongues. He soon outgrew his movie theater church and moved to Little Rock and ultimately to Nashville."

"You sound proud of your protégé," Mark said. "I thought you said you had a falling out?"

"Mathias was saving more souls in his one-hour broadcasts than I could save in an entire year. He was grateful for my guidance. He called me and asked if I would join his Last Awakening Ministry."

"Did you?" Tanya asked.

"For a while. I was swept up by his enthusiasm. It was infectious. It was the Lord's work, at least in the beginning."

"Why? What happened?" Mark asked.

"The ministry took on a life of its own. Money was pouring in faster than we could spend it. The Riches got involved and turned it into some kind of nonprofit organization, yet profit there was. Fancy cars, private planes, fifty-room mansions."

"Kind of like this place was back in the 1920s," Mark said.

"So Dr. Kane is connected to Senator Rich Jr.?" Tanya asked.

"More to the father than to the son. Rich Sr. is an astute businessman. He made Mathias the star of his Christian media empire."

Reverend Anderson looked at the dilapidated mansion around them. "Good work that ended in greed," he said. "Mathias saw his wealth as a sign that his work was pleasing to God. He felt entitled to his rise to riches. He convinced himself that America needed another Great Awakening, because the End Time was near. He viewed himself as the prophet of the Last Awakening and his wealth as a means to that end."

"So you left his ministry?"

"We became detached from the people we were trying to serve. We were looking into the eyes of television cameras rather than into the eyes of people. I left quietly and decided to minister to those who needed me most."

"You remind me of my father," Mark said.

Reverend Anderson smiled. "I knew God sent you here for a reason."

"You need to rebuild your church," Tanya said. "In my country it's a sacred obligation. You need to get your congregation to help you. I'd like to speak to this Osage councilman who's blocking your efforts."

"Cody Harris," Reverend Anderson said. "Or Running Deer, as he likes to be called. He's a hardheaded young man, so I don't know if you'll have much sway. He walked eight hundred miles from here to Standing Rock to represent his nation in the Dakota Access Pipeline protest. The protests didn't end well. Now he's working on repairing the roundhouse in Hominy about twenty-one miles south of here. I heard it was damaged in the storm as well. If he'll talk to you, ask him if he's seen my steeple."

＊ ＊ ＊ ＊

The drive to Hominy down Highway 99 took them through the heart of the lands of the Osage Nation. Except for the asphalt road, electrical lines, and oil derricks, much of the land was unchanged from a hundred years ago. Bison grazed on tall prairie grass. Clouds winnowed with the wind and disappeared where the earth met the sky. Mark drove below the speed limit, hoping to get a glimpse of America before it was called America. Beat-up pickups driven by Osage Indians in cowboy hats going about their daily business passed them by. A few slowed to view the intruders from Wisconsin before speeding up and belching black smoke from their exhausts.

Mark and Tanya drove through Hominy on their way to the Indian Village on the outskirts of town. They stopped to admire the dozens of colorful Cha' Tullis murals that graced the brick walls of buildings on Main Street. The murals, with names like *Magical Yesterday*, *Crossing Boundaries*, and *Shield of Redwing*, depicted Native American life, history, and culture. The name *Hominy* is derived from "night walker" in Osage, though some claim it's a play on the word *harmony*. Hominy was originally established as a trading post in Indian territory and today embodies the conflict and confluence of Native American and Western cultures. The sculptures of a party of Indians on horseback overlooked the town from a nearby hill.

The roundhouse in the Indian Village had been damaged by the recent storm. Residents were repairing the roof and rehanging the bell that had fallen from the tower during the violent storm.

"Do you know where we might find Cody Harris?" Mark asked one of the volunteers.

"He was here earlier," the man replied. "You might find him at the *New Territory*."

"Where's the *New Territory*?" Tanya asked.

"It's not a place, it's a work of art. You must have seen it from town— the party of Indian riders overlooking the town from the crest of a hilltop. The artist, Cha' Tullis, says they're looking for a place with fresh running water where they can camp and rest. Running Deer usually goes up there this time of day."

Against the sunset, the fifteen silhouettes of Indians on horseback looked haunting, as if they had ridden onto the crest of the hill from another century. As they neared the sculptures, Tanya admired the artistry of the work—each iron sculpture was between sixteen and twenty feet tall with metal feathers that moved in the wind. A lone figure dressed in military fatigues and a Billy Jack hat sat under the statues facing the setting sun. He was chanting with his eyes closed. Mark and Tanya waited to approach him until his chant was finished.

"That's beautiful," Tanya said.

Cody Harris turned around to see who had approached him from the east. He was about Mark's age but with the eyes of an elder.

"It's the 'Song of Sorrow.' Why do you disturb me?"

"I'm a sculptress from Ukraine," Tanya replied. "My name is Tanya. This is my friend Mark. We've come to admire these sculptures."

Cody stood up and looked over the town of Hominy. His name was inscribed on his military fatigues.

"You're a veteran?" Mark asked.

"I was an army cavalry scout in Afghanistan—two tours of duty. I served my country, though I'm not sure it's my country anymore."

"Why?" Tanya asked.

"America has forgotten us. I'm a descendant of the Sky People. We were once a great nation, yet now we're a forgotten people. We were driven from our lands and forced into reservations. When the earth gave us oil, the white men murdered us and swindled it away. When we stand up for what's ours, the government calls our protests illegal and attacks us with armed soldiers, water cannons, and dogs."

"The Dakota Pipeline protests," Mark said. "We followed them in my class."

"I studied political science at Missouri State," Cody said. "I thought we could resolve these conflicts peacefully. I thought we could coexist. Yet these protests have yielded nothing. We're as powerless as our ancestors. Perhaps we were fated to disappear."

"How can you say that?" Tanya asked. "Your history, your art, your language make you who you are."

"An Osage legend says that before the time of the great waters a medicine man proclaimed that the Osage people would live in happy enjoyment of their hunting grounds until an arrow made of human bone pierced the heart of our greatest chief. After many ages a great chief arose who was known for his skill in hunting, his strength in battle, and his beauty. His brother, a young brave, won the heart of a beautiful princess and brought her to his wigwam. They were happy until the chief coveted her and set out to steal her love. Her head was turned by the flatteries of so great a man, and they met many times at night under the shadow of a great oak. One night when the harvest moon was high, the Great Spirit looked down on them. When a hunter passed the great oak the next morning he found an awful curse had fallen on his tribe. The hearts of the guilty lovers were cleft and bound together by an arrow made from human bone. The body of the chief's brother lay by a cliff with a knife in his heart. The next day the paleface riders drove the Osage from their homes into the Indian Territory far from the homes that they loved so well. We continue to suffer for the sins of our forefathers."

Tanya put her hand on Cody's firm shoulder. "These legends define you only if you choose to believe them. In our Christian faith we have the story of Adam and Eve and the original sin. They say we are all sinners just because we're human. I don't believe in inherited guilt. We need to be responsible for our own actions, and not the sins of our forefathers."

Cody looked at Mark. "And you, what do you think?"

"I think that these stories help us make sense of the chaos around us. Why is there death and suffering in the world? Because Adam disobeyed God and took a bite of the forbidden fruit. Why were your people driven from their ancestral lands? Because your chief angered the Great Spirit. It's easier to blame our suffering on the sins of our forefathers than to blame ourselves."

"So you think these are just myths and legends?" Cody asked.

"I think that God speaks to us in the language that we understand. These stories have existential truth. Eve gave Adam the forbidden fruit from the tree of knowledge. Consuming it was man's original sin.

Yet the fruit gave man the knowledge of good and evil. The choice to consume it or not demonstrated our free will. Perhaps this story tells us that we became truly human when we developed the capacity to choose between good and evil."

"And what of my story?" Cody asked.

"It's a story of love and betrayal. The bonds between husband and wife and brother and brother are sacred. When man chooses to break these bonds, the Great Spirit exacts revenge."

"So which God should I believe in?" Cody asked. "Yours or mine?"

"Whichever you choose." Mark replied. "I believe that there's a spiritual side to our existence. I believe that each of us has a soul. I believe that our spirits commune with something greater than us—for me, it's the God of the Bible; for you it's the Great Spirit. I think we each need to find our authentic faith and be true to ourselves. We need to face the reality of our own existence, make a choice of what to believe, and with the help of our faith, live our lives as meaningfully as we can."

The setting sun, when it hit the *New Territory* sculptures, cast long shadows of Indian braves over the town of Hominy. Forty acres of the town were reserved for the Indian Village. The rest was an American town with a public library, a public school, local businesses, and the legacy of an All-Indian professional football team that once beat the New York Giants.

"How do we preserve our beliefs and traditions? How do we preserve our language? How do we keep from being swept away into the American mainstream?" Cody asked.

"I know little of your history," Tanya said, "but I helped make my own. In 2013 my generation rose up in a Revolution of Dignity to stop the assimilation of our country into the Russian world. We chose our own path. We focused on the rights of people that are embodied in your own bill of rights. We discovered our history while fighting for our future."

"Glory to heroes," Cody said.

"So you know our story?" Tanya asked.

"I'm a political scientist. We have much to learn from each other." He offered her his hand. "My Osage name is Running Deer."

Mark could see that Tanya and Cody had forged a bond. She had a way of connecting with people that he did not. He had realized his shortcomings as a preacher in divinity school and decided to be true to himself. He couldn't in good conscience preach things to others that he was not sure of himself. He found true meaning in things that had actually happened, in times and places that had long since passed. He began to search for his own authentic faith in places like the Land of Oz, Circus World, and, now, Route 66.

"There's still the issue of Reverend Anderson's . . ." he began.

"Steeple," Cody cut in. "It landed on our lands during the tornado."

"Do you intend to return it?" Mark asked.

Running Deer laughed. "Yes, of course. More than half of our people are Christians, and many belong to his congregation. We'll help him rebuild his steeple after we rebuild our roundhouse. First things first."

A red bird was perched atop the headdress of the tallest Indian brave as if listening to their conversation. It bobbed its head left, right and then flew off to the west.

CHAPTER 10

Rhyolite

Victor Ivanovich ran the diamonds on his Patriots Super Bowl champions ring across the polished walnut veneer of the dining room table in the Presidential Suite of the Hermitage Hotel. Senator Rich cringed as the ring gouged the table with a ragged *I*. Rich had acquired the ring at a charity auction and given it to Ivanovich as a token of their friendship. Ivanovich in turn had given him an icon of Saint Julian that once hung in a centuries-old church in Novgorod.

Dmitri stood motionless in the doorway. Ivanovich did not ask him to sit down. "How could you let them get away?" he asked Dmitri.

Senator Rich rose from the table and began to pace back and forth across the blue oriental carpet. He glared at Ivanovich. "You said your man was the best. You said it would only be a matter of time."

Dmitri imagined the senator writhing in seizures from a dose of strychnine.

"An actor at a loss for words?" Ivanovich asked.

"I tracked them from Chicago to Rider's family in Baraboo. I know they were there. Then the trail went cold. No cell phones, no logins, no credit cards. They must have dumped the car as well."

"You couldn't extract their location from the family?"

"I considered it, but Rider's parents are prominent members of the community. They're ministers. Their torture and murder would make the national news. I didn't think you'd want that kind of publicity."

Rich stopped pacing. "Torture? Murder? I'm a US senator for Christ's sake . . . I can't be a party to this!"

"But you are a party to this, Julian. You asked me to do whatever needs to be done. Sex and death are opposite sides of the same coin," Ivanovich replied. "You'd better wait in the next room if you don't have the stomach for this."

Senator Rich retreated to the bedroom like a petulant child.

Ivanovich ran his finger over the deep gouge in the table as if to rub it away. "And Turchin?"

"I liquidated him as you instructed," Dmitri replied. "My million euros . . . ?"

"Did he have any last words?"

"He said the Flame of God would exact his revenge."

Ivanovich grimaced and gouged another line in the veneer to form the shape of the cross. "Any witnesses?"

"The rusalka and Rider were at the scene, but I was in disguise. They didn't recognize me." Dmitri failed to mention that he had taunted them at the Creation Museum and at Tootsie's.

"This rusalka is proving to be more trouble than she's worth. You should have killed them when you had the opportunity: a simple bullet to the back of the head. Instead you toy with them like a child pulling wings off a fly."

Dmitri bristled at this disrespect for his artistry. "I take my example from you, Victor Ivanovich. When the Amur tiger killed your godson, did you shoot her from a helicopter with a Kalashnikov? No. You tracked her to her lair on foot and killed her cubs in front of her eyes. You stared into her yellow eyes before you killed her so she would know the pith of revenge. The victim needs to comprehend their fate before they die."

Ivanovich twirled the ring on his finger. "The story becomes more embellished with each telling. Be careful. Your penchant for the dramatic will be your undoing."

Dmitri breathed a sigh of relief knowing that he had deflected Ivanovich's anger. "It's only a matter of time before they surface," Dmitri said. "I've laid a trap for them."

Ivanovich looked up. "Elaborate."

"Rider has a female cousin in Beech Mountain whom he's close to. To our good fortune, one of the underlings at the Internet Research Agency recruited her under the alias of Robert E. Lee to participate in subversive alt-right activities called Saving Dixie. With their permission I took over as her handler. The GRU are orchestrating a demonstration at the Jefferson Davis Memorial in early June, which will likely turn violent. Rider's cousin will be the public face of that demonstration. It's only a matter of time before he surfaces to protect her."

"You're sure you have authorization to pose as her handler? We don't want to be tripping over the Main Directorate."

"I have it from the highest authority," Dmitri assured him.

"You are resourceful," Ivanovich said, "which is why I hired you. Just remember who pays you. I'll have the million euros in your account by tomorrow."

* * * *

Route 66 headed west from the red earth of Oklahoma to the staked plains of the Texas Panhandle. Mark had never traveled the Mother Road before, but to him it was quintessential Americana. Many before him had written about the road, but he needed to drive and experience its quirky attractions, iconic stops, and natural splendors for himself. He figured they could reach the Cadillac Ranch in Amarillo by afternoon and spend the night at the Blue Swallow Motel in Tucumcari. If they left early the following morning, they could be in the Painted Desert by noon and reach Death Valley Junction before midnight. Had he been alone he would have taken a week to make the trip, but Tanya was anxious to reach their destination. They could only stay hidden for so long, and there was no turning back. She had yet to share with whom she planned to rendezvous. Mark rued her lack of trust in him. *Remember what the attorney general had warned: she's just using you.*

Cadillac Ranch was just off the frontage road of I-40. Back in 1974, ten Cadillacs were half-buried nose down in an empty field by hippies from San Francisco as a display of public art. Viewers were encouraged to deface the cars with graffiti and even take pieces as souvenirs. In his search for Americana, Mark had seen scores of car carcasses rusting in junkyards and propped on cinder blocks in front lawns, but most had been forsaken and forgotten by their owners. Cadillac Ranch glorified the end of the road. Lovers inscribed their initials on the rusted chassis to immortalize their love, only to have their hearts and cupid arrows spray-painted over by the next tourist.

"This is fascinating," Tanya said. "It's living art. People proclaim their existence on these dying cars, even if it's just for a fleeting moment in eternity."

A German tourist was writing his name across a car door with a can of spray paint. When he was finished with his inscription, Tanya asked in broken German to borrow his spray can, and he willingly obliged a fellow European. She inscribed her initials on the trunk and handed the can to Mark. He added an MR beneath her TB. Tanya looked at him as if there were something he had omitted. She took the can and added + to couple the two initials.

"We're on this journey together," she said.

Mark smiled. He said little during the two-hour drive from Amarillo to Tucumcari. He was like a moth circling a flame. For the past few weeks they had been inseparable, yet he always kept a respectful distance. She had been violated, and only she knew the depths of her trauma. They were no longer strangers; they were companions and perhaps even friends. Yet he wanted so much more. He hoped that the plus sign she had added was an invitation to draw even closer. He knew that she felt safe in his company, and he dreaded the thought of her recoiling at his touch. *My parents said that everything happens for a reason. It's all part of God's plan. If He wants us to be together, He will let me know. But what if everything is not part of God's plan? What if everything is random, and nothing happens for a reason? If I leave it up to Him then I might lose her.*

The neon sign of the Blue Swallow Motel flashed VACANCY. It

advertised TV and 100 PERCENT REFRIGERATED AIR. The parking lot was nearly full with cars, motorcycles, trucks, and RVs. The license plates hailed from states as far away as Maine. Mark and Tanya parked in the one remaining spot and walked into the office. A purple-haired woman in a Grateful Dead T-shirt lowered her reading glasses to check out her last customers.

"You kids are lucky to get a room. Some couple from California had a go at it, and I had to throw them out. When the sheriff arrived, the husband still had a fork stuck in his forehead. They took him to the hospital and dragged her ass to jail. I just changed the sheets so the room's yours if you want it."

Mark figured that over the last several decades, every room in the motel had a story. He looked at Tanya, and she nodded that it was OK. The woman handed them the register.

"Sign here, name and license plates. Will you be using a credit card?"

"No, we'll pay in cash," Mark replied.

The woman handed them a key attached to a plastic mailer. "Number seventeen, around the side."

The motel room was a throwback to the 1950s. It was air-conditioned as advertised and a vintage television sat atop the dresser. The beds were made, and the room smelled of pine air freshener. Tanya plopped onto the bed by the window. Mark turned on the TV.

He flipped through the channels and stopped when he heard a familiar voice. Dr. Mathias Kane was running a commercial for his Last Awakening Ministry. He announced that he would be delivering the keynote address at the International Christian Media Forum from none other than Sin City in two days' time. Mark flipped to another channel when he saw that Tanya had raised her knees to her chest.

"Sorry," Mark said. "I didn't want to hear him spreading any more lies about you."

"They're not lies," Tanya murmured.

Mark shut off the TV. "What do you mean?"

"He called me a whore. I was . . . a prostitute, before I became a sculptress."

The ardor in Mark's veins turned to ice.

"It wasn't a choice I made."

"I don't understand."

"When I was an infant, my parents put me in an internat. I ran away at the age of fifteen."

"Why?"

"As I was going through puberty, the matron's husband tried to school me in more than just chess." She lowered her eyes. "I had dreams—he took them away from me. I had to survive on the streets any way I could."

"Then . . ." Mark struggled to find the words. "How did you learn to sculpt?"

"Two artists, Toma and Ariadna, saved me from my life on the streets. Ariadna was a Ukrainian American who immigrated to Ukraine after independence. She and Toma fell madly in love and supported each other's creative pursuits. They let me stay in their studio, and I ran their errands. Ariadna taught me how to sculpt and helped me get into the academy. She would speak to me in English when Toma was away—it's a little secret that we shared."

"Your parents never returned for you?"

Tanya forced a bitter smile. "They did come looking for me once I was famous. I told them to go to hell."

Mark thought of hugging her to console her but could not get himself to rise.

Tanya turned her back to him and curled into a fetal position.

His heart wanted to reach out to her, but all he could think of was his mother standing over him clutching his lurid drawing. Tanya's parents had abandoned her, and his wouldn't let him go. Reverend Kane had called her the whore of Babylon. He wondered whether her story of being raped was true or whether it was she who had lured the senator into a trap. *What if she is using me?* He thought. *What if she is colluding with this oligarch to flush out and kill his enemies? What will happen to me when she no longer needs me? Will she toss me away like some used condom? Will some Orthodox priest come to give me his last rites?*

He imagined Tanya sitting on a scarlet beast that had seven heads and ten horns. She was clothed in purple and scarlet, and adorned with gold and jewels and pearls, holding in her hand a golden cup full of abominations and the impurities of her fornication. On her forehead was written Babylon the great, mother of whores and of earth's abominations. He saw that she was drunk with the blood of the saints and the blood of the witnesses to Jesus. *What if she was the figure foretold in Revelations who together with the beast would harbinger the End Time?*

He awoke in a sweat. Tanya was still curled under the covers in her bed. His image of her as Aphrodite rising out of the waves was defaced by the image of the whore of Babylon seated on many waters. And yet, what if her story was true? What if she was an unfortunate innocent forced into a life of sin? Christ had forgiven Mary Magdalene, so why couldn't he forgive Tanya?

The outside temperature had dropped to below fifty during the night. The space heater had kicked in and droned on and off. Mark went out into the parking lot. He got into his El Camino and started the car. *I need to take a drive to clear my head,* he convinced himself. As he started to back up, the glove compartment door popped open. He reached over to close it and saw a small packet carefully wrapped in a piece of tissue paper. When he unraveled the tissue, he found the ticket stubs and key chain viewer from Silver Dollar City. The photo in the viewer captured the magical moment of the two of them on the Time Traveler. *Swallow the chaos,* he decided. He rewrapped the keepsake just as he had found it and turned off the engine.

When he returned to their room, Tanya was sitting up on the edge of her bed.

"I thought you had left me," she said.

"I went out to get some air. I needed some time to think."

She was wearing only a white nightshirt and white socks. She looked vulnerable and dangerous. The springy cotton of her shirt clung to every curve. He sat down next to her and gently put his arm on her shoulder to see if she would recoil. Her hair smelled of lavender. She nuzzled her head onto the crook in his neck.

"I'm sorry about last night," he said. "This had been an emotional roller coaster for me."

"Like the Time Traveler?" she asked.

He felt guilty for doubting her. He recalled how she laughed and screamed and gripped his hand like a child as they twisted, turned, and plummeted into the unknown. He knew he would cherish that memory forever. "Yes, like the Time Traveler," he replied. "We need to get going if we're going to reach Death Valley before nightfall. The road takes us through some of the most beautiful parts of the country. I'd like us to see them by daylight, even if we're just passing through. There's even a place where living trees were turned to stone."

"By the hand of God?" Tanya asked.

"By nature," Mark replied.

The route through the Land of Enchantment transitioned from the flat, dry east of the Great Plains to the sandstone mesas and pine-forested peaks of western New Mexico. If the devil weren't on their heels, they would have stopped to see Inscription Rock, Chaco Canyon, and Santa Fe. By early afternoon they were speeding through the Painted Desert. They were immersed in another world, a surreal landscape of badlands, buttes, and mesas imbued with every hue of nature's palette. They stopped for gas and a quick lunch of Navajo tacos at a trading post along the road. Inside, an old Navajo woman was demonstrating the art of weaving rugs using handspun wool from Navajo-Churro sheep. The trading post peddled jewelry, pottery, kachina dolls, and Navajo rugs. It also served as a convenience store and post office.

Tanya was admiring the handcrafted jewelry made from silver, turquoise, and juniper berries. She was surprised to see that the price of the jewelry fashioned from the berries was on par with the silver and semiprecious stones.

"They're ghost beads," the young Navajo woman behind the counter explained. "They protect you from evil spirits, ghosts, and nightmares. When you wear these beads, the ghost can't get inside you."

"What happens if a ghost inhabits you?" Tanya asked.

"You get the ghost sickness. You become weak, you stop eating, you become depressed, you suffer from terrors."

Tanya thought of the illness that befell Mark in Nashville. "How do these ghost beads protect you?" she asked.

"The juniper berries are collected from the ground after ants have eaten out the insides. They're strung in accordance with the harmony of nature. Because they represent an interconnection between the earth, people, trees, and animals, they can bring peace and protection to the wearer."

"I'll buy two bracelets," she said.

Mark was examining a collection of arrowheads in a corner of the trading post to see if they were made of flint or bone. Tanya came up to him and fastened one of the bracelets around his wrist. She fastened the other around hers.

"Ghost beads," she said. "They'll protect us from the evil spirits that are chasing us. The Navajo woman said they symbolize our oneness with nature. They'll protect us from ghost sickness."

Mark was grateful for the gift. He remembered reading about ghost sickness in his comparative religions class in divinity school. The prehistoric Anasazi had trespassed against nature and were killed off by the wind spirits. Malevolent spirits still inhabit their relics. Disturbing the relics would antagonize the spirits and make the individual vulnerable to ghost sickness. He suspected he had been poisoned in Nashville. But perhaps the poison coursing through his veins was more supernatural than physical. The weakness and anxiety that he was experiencing were consistent with what little he knew of ghost sickness. Perhaps his search for American relics had disturbed the ghosts that inhabited them, and these ghosts were seeking their revenge.

How different, Mark thought, *from what the Bible teaches us.* He recalled Genesis 1:28: "God said unto them, Be fruitful, and multiply, and replenish the earth, and subdue it: and have dominion over the fish of the sea, and over the fowl of the air, and over every living thing that moveth upon the earth." As Tanya had pointed out to him at the Circus Museum, man did indeed multiply and glut the earth with his offspring, but rather than replenish it, he ravaged the earth until it could replenish no more. Diseases emerged out of the deepest jungles, algae choked the oceans and rivers, and heat waves parched the earth. Perhaps God intended that man himself prepare the seven bowls of the wrath of God to begin the Tribulation. The believers would be raptured into the clouds, and the wicked would be left behind to suffer the wrath of God. Man's dominion over nature would end with his own destruction.

"You look perplexed," Tanya said.

"I'm struggling with my faith," Mark replied.

"You don't believe in ghost beads?" Tanya asked. "Perhaps I should have given you a crucifix instead."

Mark smiled. "Now you're making fun of me. I'm just trying to reconcile the things I believed with the things I'm discovering."

"When we dig up the dead," Tanya said, "we're bound to release some ghosts. Are you sure you want to accompany me?"

Tanya made him feel alive. He had thought his purpose in life was delving into the past. Tanya was leading him into the future. "I've never been more sure of anything in my life."

* * * *

They spent the night in the Pahrump Nugget Hotel and Casino. At daybreak they grabbed two black coffees to go at the Golden Harvest Café. Even at this early hour, blue-haired women were working the slots like morning wake-up exercises. The whirr of slot machines was disrupted every few minutes by a red light and siren. The other players would run up to the winner and touch them for luck.

When Mark and Tanya stepped outside, the temperature was already sixty degrees and rising. "We're thirty miles east of Death Valley," Mark said as he started the car. "I think it's time you told me exactly where we're going and who we're going to see."

"We're going to Rhyolite, the Queen City," Tanya replied.

"Rhyolite's a ghost town."

"Turchin said there's a roadside attraction on Highway 374 on the way to Rhyolite called the Death Valley Serpentarium. That's where we'll find the Flame of God."

"The Flame of God? Do you know what he meant?"

"He didn't say. He said we'll know once we're there."

Mark looked at the Rand McNally atlas. "Rhyolite's about an hour north of here. We can drive straight there, but we'll probably get there before it opens. Or we can loop around through Death Valley. I heard that the light in the valley is best in the early morning. It'll only take us a few miles out of our way. We may never get a chance to see it again."

Tanya reflected for a moment. "Yes, of course we can take a detour. In these past few weeks, I've only been thinking about my own quest. I've taken you away from yours. Yes, let's visit Death Valley. The Flame of God will just have to wait."

The temperature climbed as they descended to the lowest point in North America. As the sun peeked over the Funeral Mountains, the shadows receded, revealing the eerie beauty of the scorched basin. They stopped at Zabriskie Point to view the colors of the badlands change from blues and reds to amber and buff. The sun chased the shadows through the nooks and crannies until they vanished like ghosts in the light of day. They drove through Furnace Creek and turned south on Badwater Road toward the Devils Golf Course. The wind had eroded the rock salt into jagged spires. They listened to the pops and pings of the salt crystals bursting in the heat. They continued south until they reached a wooden sign that read BADWATER BASIN 282 FEET/82.5 METERS BELOW SEA LEVEL.

Badwater Basin was an unearthly landscape of salt flats that stretched about five miles across. Mark and Tanya walked onto the honeycombed salt crust. Here and there the white crust collapsed under their weight to reveal the caked mud underneath. Tanya held Mark's hand to steady herself.

Here I am, Mark thought, *in the most forsaken place on Earth, holding hands with a confessed harlot who may be leading us to Armageddon.* Yet he could sense no evil in her. Perhaps he was the one who was evil for judging her. The touch of her hand was more than sensual—it was needy. She was a stranger in a strange land—his land, and she had asked him to be her guide. He looked at the salted waterless earth and recalled Matthew 12:43: "When the unclean spirit is out of a man, he walks through dry places, seeking rest, and finding none."

"You seem lost in your thoughts," Tanya said.

Mark looked into her eyes. They were as pure blue as the sky above them. "This is a good place to reflect," he said. "It's a good place to find yourself."

"Have you discovered who you are?" she asked as she took both his hands in hers.

"I know who I'm not. I'm not a preacher. I don't know enough about life to tell others how to live theirs. I grew up believing that there was only one truth in life, the truth of the Bible. But I wanted to know more. I still believe in the love of Christ, but I also believe that love between people can be just as strong. I sometimes wonder what if there is no heaven or hell, and all we have is ourselves?"

"We would still search for truth, and we would still search for love. Perhaps that's all we can hope for."

The sun scorched the salt flats as it had since the time when nature, or the hand of God, had sculpted this sunken fragment of the earth's crust. The temperature was well over 100 degrees.

"We should get on with our journey," Mark said. "Thanks for letting me show you this face of Americana."

On their way back they took the Artist's Drive loop that snaked through luminous canyons tinted with aprons of metal oxides. It was difficult to imagine that such beauty could be random; it was easier to believe that God had painted the faces of the rock to inspire his children to worship Him. On their way up to Rhyolite, the Mesquite Flat Sand Dunes were visible from the road.

"Are those flowers?" Tanya asked. Scraggly bushes were interspersed among the rolling hundred-foot dunes. Some were blooming with bright-yellow flowers. "I want to see them up close."

Mark pulled over to the side of the road. Tanya ran up a dune to the nearest creosote bush, and Mark followed. She broke off a small branch and brought it to her nose. The orange stamens in the delicate yellow flower exuded pollen. "Smell this," she said. "What does it remind you of?"

The scent was familiar, but Mark couldn't quite place it.

"It smells like rain," she said and then gave him a light kiss on the lips as a reward for giving her this experience.

Life is the journey and not the destination, he reminded himself. His spirit soared as they climbed from the bottom of the basin, over the Grapevine Mountains, and through Daylight Pass on their way to Rhyolite.

* * * *

Rhyolite, the Queen City, was once the largest town in Death Valley, with two churches, an opera, and fifty saloons. The town was born in 1904, when Shorty Harris and E. L. Cross discovered gold in the quartz on Shoshone Hill. During the subsequent gold rush, prospectors staked over two thousand claims, and the town boomed to a population of over five thousand people. By 1911, production at the Montgomery Shoshone Mine slowed, and the population of Rhyolite dwindled to only a few hundred. In 1916, the light and power were finally turned off in the town.

Rhyolite was now a ghost town. Tourists came to view the ruins and snap photos next to the bottle house, train depot, bank, and jail. The Death Valley Serpentarium was located three miles north of Rhyolite on Highway 374. A giant Gila monster in front of a windowless adobe building dared tourists to enter and view the deadly creatures within. Mark and Tanya pulled into the empty parking lot in the late afternoon. The entry door was rigged to sound a rattle that alerted the owner to potential customers who weren't deterred by the ten-dollar admission fee.

"Be with you in a minute," a man called out from behind a curtain of strung beads that separated the foyer from the main attractions.

The foyer was pasted with informational posters of snakes and poisonous lizards. A mechanical cash register rested on a glass counter that displayed souvenirs for sale, including real rattlesnake rattles, shed snake skin, and gag gift bags of "rattler eggs" that would spring a baby rubber snake when opened.

The man who emerged from behind the curtain was tattooed from his neck down to his ankles. He had short-cropped red hair and looked to be about thirty. A silver needle pierced his eyebrow.

"That'll be twenty bucks," he said. "Well worth it. I'm in the middle of milking a diamondback for its venom, so you can see how it's done, no extra charge. Just don't touch anything. They look like they're not moving, but you'll be bit before you know what happened. Hell, I've been bitten a dozen times. I could sell my blood for antivenom if they'd let me. Looks like you're my last customers for the day, so I'll lock up the front door. I don't want some kids barging in during the milking."

Tanya was going to get straight to the point, but Mark stopped her. "Let's see what we're getting into," he whispered.

"You think I don't hear you?" the man asked. "If you got second thoughts, I don't need your money. I make plenty selling the venom. Hell, I can hear every slither, hiss, and rattle. You need to have keen senses to work in a place like this."

"Honey, give the man his twenty dollars," Tanya said.

The man made a display of ringing up the twenty-dollar admission fee on the register. He handed them two tickets, then ripped them as they passed through the beaded string curtain into the world of reptiles. The inside of the one-story building was separated into a series of adjoining rooms. The first had a collection of live lizards that were housed in glass terrariums. Most looked like they were hibernating. The man rapped on their cages to get them to move. He threw some crickets into the cage with a Mexican beaded lizard. The lizard followed the crickets with its rotating eyes and snatched the nearest in a millisecond with its sticky tongue. The man led them past a pen with desert tortoises to his prize possession: a white Gila monster.

"Very rare," he said. "Most are orange and black, but this one's an albino."

A live mouse was frantically trying to climb up a corner of the cage. The orange-and-white lizard waited for it to tire.

"One bite and you'd wish you were dead," the man said. Tanya clung to Mark in fear of accidentally bumping into one of the cages.

An adjoining room housed the venomous snakes in glass vivaria: sidewinders, diamondbacks, Arizona coral snakes, along with nonnative species such as cobras, saw-scaled vipers, and kraits. Each vivarium was labeled with the common and scientific names of the snake. The reptilian smell in the room elicited a primal fear response, as if it were imprinted in one's genetic code.

"Stand back out of striking distance," the man warned. He grabbed a snake hook and pulled an eight-foot diamondback out of its vivarium. Slung over the hook, the snake raised its triangular head. The man carried it onto a white metal table and grabbed it behind the head. With his other hand, he took a glass beaker off the shelf. The beaker was covered with a piece of elastic fastened with a rubber band. The date and species were written on the side with a marker. He brought the beaker up to the snake's mouth, it pierced the rubber with its fangs, and clear liquid venom poured down the insides of the glass.

"Easy as one, two, three if you know what you're doing," he said.

"We're not here to see the snakes," Tanya replied. "Turchin sent us."

The man turned to face them with the snake still in his hand. The fangs in its open mouth were dripping venom.

"Still enough venom in these fangs to kill you," he said. "Who are you? Feds? Russians?"

"I suspect we're like you: pieces in Turchin's final game."

"Is he . . ."

"Dead," Tanya said. "Murdered by one of Ivanovich's men. 'Go to the Death Valley Serpentarium and find the Flame of God' were his last words. He said you'd know what to do."

"Show me some identification," the man demanded. Mark pulled his driver's license out of his wallet and lifted it for the man to read. The snake handler looked at Tanya. "Yours?"

"I don't have any," she said. "Ivanovich has my passport."

"Cell phones?" he asked.

"We realized we were being followed back in Chicago," Mark said. "I destroyed mine before we left. We use cash only. We've stayed off the grid."

The man placed the diamondback back in its containment. "Follow me," he said. He led them to a back room with an electronic lock that opened with an iris scan. The sophistication of the lock was in stark contrast to the seeming disorder of the serpentarium. Mark realized that the reptiles were an elaborate front. Even the man's appearance and oddball personality were part of the charade.

The snake handler flipped on the overhead lights. The fluorescent light gave the room an eerie glow. The secure room was filled with several generations of computers, monitors, and hacking hardware. Within minutes the snake handler had confirmed Mark's identity and accessed his email, phone records, and geo-location history. The hidden camcorder behind the cash register had identified Tanya through facial recognition software. A few minutes more, and he knew more about their situation than they did.

"You're being tracked from Saint Petersburg. They're communicating with someone in the states using advanced encryption. Whomever they're communicating with is currently in Nashville."

"Rich's home state," Mark said.

"Probably someone from Ivanovich's security detail. Why are they after you?"

"I'm a victim of . . ." Tanya stopped herself. "I'm a witness. Senator Rich is colluding with Ivanovich on some business deal involving Christian media. The televangelist Mathias Kane is also involved."

"How was Turchin killed?"

"We were playing chess when an assassin dressed as an Orthodox priest came into the pavilion out of the rain. Turchin told me to run for my life, but not before he told me where to find you. How do I know I can trust you?"

"My internet alias is Uriel." He opened his palm to reveal a tattoo of a flame.

Mark recognized the symbol. "The Flame of God," he said.

Uriel smiled. "Presider over Tartarus. Are you familiar with the dark web?"

"You're a hacker," Mark said.

"I'm one of the good guys. I used to work for the National Security Agency until they crossed some red lines. I went rogue. Turchin contacted me to safeguard some of his files and to only release them in the event of his death."

Uriel pulled a series of encrypted files from the cloud. With a few keystrokes, the ledgers were in full view on his screen: a complete record of Ivanovich's transactions during Turchin's tenure as his accountant. They revealed shell companies, bank accounts, loans, contracts, and silent partners. He crosschecked the files for Julian Rich and came up with several hits. "Rich and Ivanovich are connected through a bank in Cyprus." After several more keystrokes, Uriel let out a cynical laugh. "Looks like the chair of the Senate Foreign Relations Committee is indebted to the Russians up to his ears."

"We need to make this public," Mark said.

"Wait," Uriel said. "Something's not right. We're not the first to access these files. Looks like the feds have had some of them for months."

"The Treasury Department?" Mark asked.

"CIA," Uriel replied.

"They're probably collaborating with the Treasury Department to build a case against Ivanovich," Mark said.

"Or they're protecting the senator, Ivanovich, or both," Uriel speculated.

"But that would be *treason!*" Mark said.

"The deep state has its own agenda," Uriel replied. "For all we know, they want to keep Ivanovich in business. He hasn't been touched by any of the Russia sanctions even though he's in the Kremlin's inner circle. I wouldn't be surprised if he's working both sides."

"How can we find out?" Tanya asked.

Uriel hacked the CIA file on Ivanovich. Most of it had been redacted. Other files were inaccessible.

"There's one name that keeps popping up," Uriel said. "Russ Boyko. He was the CIA station chief in Kyiv awhile back. Looks like he had an active investigation into Ivanovich until he retired from the CIA a year ago."

"How do we find him?" Tanya asked.

Uriel entered a few rapid-fire keystrokes. "He's currently residing on Orcas Island just off the coast of Washington State. Here's his address."

"For your safety, we need to get you out of the middle of this," Tanya said. "Can you give us access to Turchin's files? We'll decide what to do with them when the time comes."

Uriel considered their request. "You're naive," he said, "but that might be your greatest asset. The files are in the cloud. You just need to know where to find them." He scribbled some notes on a piece of paper and handed them to Tanya. "Memorize this," he said.

Tanya studied the paper and handed it back to Uriel.

"You were never here," he said.

"Just one more request," Tanya said, "and we'll leave. We're trying to figure out how Dr. Kane is involved in all of this."

Uriel did a quick search on Kane. "No financial trail yet," he said, "but you can ask him yourself. He's scheduled to speak at the International Christian Media Forum in Las Vegas this weekend. Looks like he's promoting some new app called the Last Awakening. He's also giving the Sunday sermon at the New Beginnings Megachurch."

"The Last Awakening?" Mark asked. "What does the app do?"

"It claims it prepares you for the Rapture. Give me a day or two, and I'll find out what it *really* does," Uriel replied. "Call me from a pay phone. They're in all the casinos."

"Do I use some encrypted number?"

"I'm in the directory: Death Valley Serpentarium. Just say you're on a mission from God. I'll know it's you."

Mark wondered whether this snake handler/hacker was part of God's plan. He had been raised to believe that nothing happens without God's will. Verses from Mark 16:17–18 called out in his head: *"And these signs shall follow them that believe: In my name shall they cast out devils; they shall speak with new tongues; they shall take up serpents."*

CHAPTER 11

Sin City

The WELCOME TO FABULOUS LAS VEGAS sign in the median of Las Vegas Boulevard greeted them as they entered the Strip in Paradise. The red, white, and blue pole sign was shaped like an elongated diamond with a kinetic perimeter of incandescent bulbs. Each letter of *welcome* was imprinted on a silver dollar. Las Vegas was a uniquely American garden of earthly delights, a fantasyland of dancing fountains, pirate galleons, Venetian canals, and pyramids. Americans could see and experience the man-made wonders of the world without a passport. Money was the lifeblood of Vegas, and anyone with a few bucks in their pocket could become a millionaire or, more likely, find themselves at the Greyhound bus terminal wondering what had happened to their last dollar.

"We can have fun, but we don't gamble," Mark advised Tanya.

"I'm not a school girl," she retorted, the neon lights reflecting in her eyes. "I played baccarat in Monte Carlo."

Revelers stumbled across the Strip with plastic cups in hand. Conventioneers paraded with thousand-dollar-a-night escorts. Gambling buses unloaded blue-haired ladies from Kansas. Bachelor partiers tottering across the boulevard gawked at Tanya through the windshield. "You can't afford her!" a shirtless groomsman shouted to Mark.

Mark pulled into Bugsy Siegel's Flamingo Hotel and Casino hoping for a vacancy. The Art Deco hotel was a tropical paradise replete with pools and flamingos. A cancellation for the International Christian Media Forum had opened up a room. Mark signed for a room under the name Jeff Mustang. He explained that his credit card had been stolen and prepaid for three nights in cash. The woman at the desk did not bat a lash and handed him two key cards.

Tanya waited in the white-marble lobby and watched the gamblers amble in and out of the casino: high rollers in Hawaiian shirts, Asians in cowboy hats, grandmothers with "What Happens in Vegas" T-shirts, and conventioneers in Brooks Brothers suits. The logos on the conventioneers' name tags caught her attention. They read ICMF, with the letter *I* formed in the shape of the cross. The conventioneers were an eclectic mix of ministers, gospel choir singers, and Christian media moguls. Several ogled her before being lured into the den of iniquity with its gambling, liquor, and souls that needed to be saved.

Mark and Tanya continued their ruse of being a couple. He was respectful of her personal space, but it was getting more and more difficult. He knew the little things about her. He knew how she liked her steel cut oatmeal in the morning and how she would always sneeze twice when the sun got in her eyes. He knew how she loved to stare out the passenger window at the ever-changing American landscape and then focus her attention on some trivial detail like a predatory bird. He knew how she liked to come out of the bathroom in her towel, comfortable with her body, and comb out the tangles in her long blonde hair.

Their room overlooked the Ferris wheel of the Circus Circus Hotel. As the sun set, the Las Vegas sky turned from red to purple to twilight blue. The dazzling lights of the city emerged like a galaxy of stars. Tanya laid out a red silk dress that Mirana had given her across the bed and went into the shower. When she came out into the bedroom, she was wearing only a towel. She walked over to the window and gazed out at the Ferris wheel as its swinging cars filled with tourists and honeymooners rose and fell. Mark wondered what was going through her head.

He excused himself to take a shower but did not fully close the bathroom door. The steam from the hot water fogged the shower glass. He rubbed an opening in the condensation and peeked out. He watched as she dropped her towel and looked at her reflection in the picture window. He had seen her fully naked only once before, when he had rescued her on Highway 1. She slowly ran her hand over her full figure as if reshaping a sculpture that had been broken. Mark imagined that every eye on the Ferris wheel was watching her as intently as he was. *The goddess of love ruling over the pleasure city.* He imagined that the steam from the shower was the mist rising from the sea and that a goddess had chosen to seduce him, a mere mortal.

He scrubbed the salt of Death Valley off his skin and washed the smell of the serpentarium from his hair. He emerged from the shower and looked at himself in the mirror. His hair still had its boyish locks, but his eyes had aged; he had the soulful eyes of a wanderer who has seen what others have not. Other than his eyes, his youthful features were not yet hardened by his travels. He imagined that she had slipped on the sexy red dress and was sitting on the bed putting on her red lipstick. He planned to sweep her off her feet and dazzle her with Las Vegas by night. He combed his unruly hair and brushed his teeth, and when he came out of the bathroom—she was gone.

He pulled on his khaki slacks and a white linen shirt and rushed down to the lobby to find her. He searched for her in the outdoor tropical oasis with its palm trees, blue-lit pools, and exotic birds. He checked the restaurants and hotel shops. The last place he looked was the casino. He had asked her not to gamble. He wandered into the labyrinth of slots, gaming tables, and bars. The whirrs of the slot machines, rolls of dice, and rattles of balls on roulette wheels created a cacophony of sounds that stimulated the serotonin receptors. The artificial lighting blurred the distinction between day and night. The smells, beyond the women's perfumes and spilled cocktails, were hard to place. If anything, it smelled *lucky*. The palette of the casino was red, green, and black. A cocktail waitress asked him what he would like to drink. At first he thought a light beer, but opted for a Jack Daniels on the rocks.

He spotted Tanya sitting at a ten-dollar blackjack table with four of the Christian Media conventioneers. Her silk red dress was backless. A man in a gold Versace blazer had his arm around her. From her laugh and body language, he could tell that she was flirting. The man's gray hair was tied into a ponytail.

"Queen of spades and the queen of hearts. Lucky ladies!"

Tanya started to split her queens, and the man with the ponytail put his hand on hers to stop her.

"You don't want to do that," he said.

Tanya ignored his advice as if on purpose. "I feel lucky," she said.

The man was amused by her impudence. "Well, let's see just how lucky you are." He slid over a stack of chips. "If you win, you keep the winnings. If you lose, you join me for dinner."

"Hit me," Tanya said.

The dealer dealt her a king and an ace of spades.

"Twenty-one!" the revelers yelled out.

Mark watched as Tanya manipulated—no, *seduced* them. He couldn't help but imagine how she had made a living before becoming an artist. A harlot, his mother had called her. "The whore of Babylon," Reverend Kane had announced over the airwaves. The thought of her flirting with these strangers was becoming unbearable. He downed his whiskey and turned to leave.

"Mark!" she called out. "Over here!"

The conventioneers turned to see what kind of man would attract the attention of a goddess. The man with the ponytail took his arm off her shoulder.

"Mark! Over here! I want you to meet my new friends. They're teaching me how to play blackjack."

The man in the gold Versace blazer wore laceless sneakers and an untucked white shirt to mask his paunch. His ponytail was his trademark. He handed Mark his card. "Rex Meyers."

"Rex is in television," Tanya said. "He produces programs for Christian media stations. He's doing a documentary on Dr. Kane. He said he can get us into the convention and introduce us to some of the stars."

Mark wondered how many other men in the casino Tanya had to hustle before landing on a mark she could use.

"You have to be someone special to have a woman like that," the producer said to Mark. "Let me guess. Professional athlete? Rock star?"

"I'm just a journalism student from Medill," Mark confessed. "I write a blog on Americana to cover my tuition."

"A blog on American history?" the producer asked.

"On what it means to be American."

"Send me the link," the producer said. "Maybe we can turn it into a TV show."

The other men at the table were still wondering what a woman like Tanya was doing with a journalism student who was blogging his way through school.

"Allow me to introduce my colleagues," the producer said. "Reverend Jim Thomas, pastor of the biggest megachurch in Dallas. Dr. Ray Creed, dean at Methodist University. Johnny Heart, lead singer for the Proclaimers."

"My pleasure," Mark said.

Tanya stood up from the blackjack table and put her arm around Mark's waist. "Mark, you should write an entry in your blog about the Christian Media Forum. They're all such interesting people. So *American*. Rex offered to get us in."

"No problem," the producer said. "Just show my card at the gate and tell them to give you some VIP passes. And you," he patted Tanya on her ass, "remember what I said. With those looks and sexy accent, you have the makings of a real star. I'm not talking commercials, I'm talking Hollywood." He handed her a stack of hundred-dollar chips. "Here's a small advance. You never know. This could be your break of a lifetime."

Mark stopped her as they were exiting the casino. "You intended to lose that game so he would take you out to dinner. You were playing him."

Tanya turned her head in a huff. "I didn't realize you knew how to gamble. And why would you care anyway?"

"The end doesn't always justify the means."

"It does when your life is at stake," she said and left to take the nearest elevator back to the room.

* * * *

Hordes of Christian media conventioneers streamed into the Las Vegas Convention Center to attend the morning plenary session called "One Nation Under God." The International Christian Media Forum attracted participants from all forms of media and all corners of the globe. Preachers mingled with Christian rock stars, radio producers with conservative talk show hosts, and Bible salesmen with anyone who would talk to them. The stars of the convention were the multimillionaire televangelists who vied with each other for Nielsen ratings and market share. The exhibit hall featured the latest technologies used to spread the gospel. Reverend Kane's new smartphone app was generating the most buzz—it was being billed as your survival kit for the End Time.

Mark presented Rex Meyers's card to one of the many greeters at the entrance. She escorted them to a booth, where they were handed two VIP passes and convention packets. He took the passes from her reluctantly.

"What's bothering you?" Tanya asked. "This is our chance to learn how Kane fits into the puzzle."

"I asked you not to gamble," he said.

"I wasn't gambling. I saw an opportunity to get us invited into the convention."

"You were manipulating them."

"I was playing the odds. I know what men want." She brushed back her hair. "Why? Are you *jealous*? You never flirt with me."

"I respect you too much," he said. "We're friends."

"Just friends?"

He looked down at his feet. "I care about you. I just want to keep you safe."

"You've been protecting me ever since you picked me up on that highway. Why?"

"I don't know. My life was ordinary. I swallowed the chaos. I found you."

"You like me because I'm not ordinary?" she asked. She lifted his chin and put his hand on her hip. "Is that all? I see how you look at me."

Mark blushed. "I don't mean to spy on you. You're just so open with your body. I don't know how to react. I was taught that every desire is a sin."

She pulled herself closer. "Not all desires are sinful."

A group of ministers walked by, and Mark let go of her hip as if he had been holding a burning bush. "Let's find what we came for," he said. He flipped through the convention program. The morning plenary session featured a keynote address titled "How to Bring Christ into the White House" followed by a panel discussion with current and former ministers to the last three presidents. Every seat in the main auditorium was taken. Mark and Tanya squeezed into a standing-room-only section against the back wall.

The moderator of the plenary session was none other than the Reverend Dr. Mathias Kane. From their vantage point behind the last row, he was not a physically imposing figure. His black hair had a purplish sheen, and his white suit seemed ready to pop its buttons. But when he spoke, the cavernous auditorium resonated with his baritone voice. He had a habit of pausing in the middle of his sentences before delivering the punch line. It was a remarkably effective oratory device. The audience would anticipate what he was about to say, then reward themselves if they guessed right. He had an uncanny ability of making it seem that he was looking only at you, and that if you broke eye contact, he would single you out in front of the gathering on the mount.

"Who are we," he boomed, "if not a Christian nation? Who stands behind the chair in the Oval Office if not . . ."

"God," Mark guessed.

"God!" Kane concluded. He introduced the keynote speaker and took his seat at the table of panel discussants behind the podium.

The White House press secretary discussed the various paths to influence the Oval Office, from formal pronouncements of the Evangelical Council to letters and emails from constituents. She emphasized how the president had selectively increased the representation of Christian media in the White House press corps and reduced the access of the mainstream fake news reporters. She explained the process of how invitations to the White House were issued, and how even a simple preacher from Arkansas could spend the night in the Lincoln Room. She concluded her speech with her personal story of being born again during one of Dr. Kane's prayer breakfast visits to the White House, and the audience rose to give her a standing ovation.

"Let's skip the panel," Mark told Tanya. "I want to check out Kane's new app in the exhibit hall before it gets too crowded." They excused themselves as they squeezed through the standing-room-only crowd and pushed the bar on an exit door. Light streamed into the darkened auditorium. Mark could feel Dr. Kane's eyes on his back as the reverend squinted to see who, out of the thousand attendees, had the gall to sneak out of his plenary.

It felt good to escape the darkness and stuffy air of the auditorium. The multicolored map in their packet guided them to the exhibit hall. Relatively few people were browsing through the hundreds of exhibits at the moment. Most were still at the plenary and would flood the hall during the coffee break. The exhibits were organized by section: written media, radio, television, and digital. The written media section featured Bibles of all sizes, versions, and languages. Mark's prize possession was a leather-bound, King James Version of the Bible that his parents had presented to him when he was accepted into divinity school. It now sat on his bookcase wedged between Plato's *The Republic* and the *Tibetan Book of the Dead*. Tanya picked up a Ukrainian-language version of the Bible published by the Pentecostals who immigrated to the United States in the 1990s seeking religious freedom. She started paging through the book of Revelations.

"Have you read the whole Bible?" he asked.

"No," she replied. "I've listened to the gospel in church, but I've never actually read the Bible."

"It's never too late to start," he said. "Here, let me buy this for you."

The publisher's representative said it was a display copy only and not for sale. Tanya promised to take it back to Ukraine where it could potentially open a whole new market. The prospect of evangelizing Ukraine was too lucrative to pass up, and the representative gave her the display copy without asking for payment.

The next section of the exhibits featured a book fair. Publishers, large and small, displayed scores of books on every imaginable Christian topic. Academic treatises on the Holy Spirit were stacked next to Christian comic books. Biographies of televangelists were stacked next to Easter cookbooks. Authors sat ready to autograph their latest Christian novel. Rotating racks stacked with magazines and periodicals lined the passageways. Mark twirled the stands to find magazines from his youth. His parents had subscribed to only one or two, and here he counted well over a hundred. It seemed that each splinter of Protestantism had two or three of their own publications. The publishers offered special discount rates for subscriptions to anyone with a convention badge.

At the break, the trickle of people turned into a torrent. Mark and Tanya rushed through the radio and television sections to reach digital media before it was flooded with conventioneers. They dodged a radio personality who was ambushing passersby to conduct live interviews. Television screens were playing trailers of upcoming new shows and documentaries, including Rex Meyers's highly anticipated documentary on Dr. Kane. A hologram of Jesus announcing his return marked the entry into the digital media exhibit. *Spreading the word of God through the ages,* Mark thought, *from Guttenberg to Spielberg.* The displays for the digital media products were light years ahead of the foldout tables, newspaper racks, and television monitors of the previous exhibits. They employed the latest innovations in 3D viewers, facial recognition, and artificial intelligence.

Mark had noted that the Rich Media Group logo was branded on a third of the other exhibits. The conglomerate was clearly competing to become the largest player in the multibillion-dollar market. Digital media promised to be the next boom, and all the major competitors, domestic and foreign, were fighting to capture market share. Most had hired celebrities to promote their products. The Rich Media Group had the advantage of an exclusive contract with the Reverend Dr. Mathias Kane. His Last Awakening app was still only available in a beta version, and the official release date was scheduled to coincide with the March for Family Values in Washington.

Forming the backdrop to the *Last Awakening* exhibit was a 650-inch digital screen. The special effects video showed the chosen rising into the clouds while Armageddon raged beneath. Dr. Kane's visage appeared like Elijah and warned the viewers that the End Time was near. The app, he said, would facilitate their Rapture and escape from the Tribulation.

An attractive twenty-some-year-old redhead in a tight white blouse, navy skirt, and red heels manned the Last Awakening exhibit. Her smile revealed a perfect set of teeth that were two shades whiter than snow. Her red-wagon lipstick highlighted her full, wet lips. She reminded Mark of Mary when he was fifteen, and he had looked up from his seat in Sunday school to realize that she had blossomed from a budding young girl into a voluptuous young woman. He often wondered how their lives would have turned out if his mother had not intervened.

Tanya stepped in between him and the saleswoman. "We'd like to learn more about the Last Awakening app."

"It's your stairway to heaven," the saleswoman responded. "Are you ready for the Rapture?" she asked, mimicking her script.

"Do I need to be born again?" Tanya asked.

"Well, of course!" the saleswoman said. "This app is designed for *you*. You're running out of time. The Reverend Dr. Mathias Kane is warning us that the End Time is near. You can suffer through the Tribulation or ascend into the clouds to meet Jesus." She arched her eyebrow at Mark. "Now which of those would you prefer?"

"The Rapture," Mark replied as if he were still in Sunday school.

"Well, then the Last Awakening app will help you get there. What type of phone do you have? Apple? Android?"

"Apple," Mark replied. "But I don't have it with me."

"No problem, I can demo it for you on my phone."

She pulled out her retina-display iPhone. "The nice thing about this app is that you don't have to go through the trouble of entering all of your personal information. The app collects it for you."

"It scrapes your data? From where?" Tanya asked.

"From *everywhere*," the saleswoman replied. "From your Facebook, Twitter, and Instagram accounts." She winked at Mark. "It learns all about you. It listens to you when you talk to it. It even knows how you're feeling. You can control how much you want it to know in the settings. Anyway, the app guides you by developing your own personal salvation plan to reach the Rapture. It anticipates your temptations and pushes Bible verses to keep you from sinning."

"Using algorithms?" Mark asked.

"Not just algorithms, and here's the awesome part. It uses *artificial intelligence*. The passages are specifically targeted to *you*, to help you become a better person. It pushes Bible verses in real time according to *what* you're doing and *where* you are and *how* you're feeling. Let's say you're in Pahrump and pause within a hundred yards of the Mustang Ranch. The app will push Job 36:14. Or let's say you're at the all-you-can-eat buffet at the Rio Hotel. The app figures out that you've been there a bit too long and will push Philippians 3:19. It's like having your own guardian angel."

"Doesn't artificial intelligence violate evangelical principles?" Mark asked.

"On the contrary," the saleswoman replied, anticipating the question. "The Southern Baptist Convention recently affirmed that 'When AI is employed in accordance with God's moral will, it is an example of man's obedience to the divine command to steward creation and to honor Him.' Here, watch this." She clicked on the Last Awakening icon on her cell phone. Nothing happened. "Just wait . . . there it is." A verse from 1 Timothy 6:9 popped up on her phone: "But they that will be rich fall into temptation and a snare, and into many foolish and hurtful lusts, which drown men in destruction and perdition."

"You see," she said. "It *knows* that we're in Las Vegas. You can turn it on when you need it or have it run constantly in the background. Here, you try it."

"What do you want me to do?" Mark asked.

"Ask it to search for something naughty."

Mark spoke to the phone. "Give me a list of the gay bars in Vegas."

A Google search of gay bars in Las Vegas appeared on the screen along with a verse from Leviticus 20:13: "If a man also lies with a man, as he lies with a woman, both of them have committed an abomination: they shall surely be put to death; their blood shall be upon them."

"This isn't for me," Mark said as he tried to hand her back the phone. "It's too intrusive."

A verse from Romans 7:23 popped up on the screen: "But I see another law in my members, warring against the law of my mind, and bringing me into captivity to the law of sin which is in my members."

"You see!" the saleswoman beamed. "It senses your ambivalence! Do you want it to talk to you? In what kind of voice—male, female, celebrity . . . ?"

Mark handed back her phone. "I've seen and heard enough."

"And best of all, it's *free!*" the saleswoman said. "Donations to the Last Awakening Ministry are voluntary. Think of all the souls that can be saved. It's a digital stairway to heaven."

"Or a highway to hell," Mark uttered under his breath.

Mark and Tanya had had enough of the International Christian Media Forum. They walked back to the Flamingo Hotel and called Uriel from a casino phone.

"I'm on a mission from . . ."

"God. I know who you are. I was able to hack into the Rich Media Group computers and download the Last Awakening app. A couple of friends and I spent several hours deciphering the code. It's written in Cyrillic. The Oxford connection is a front. It's Russian spyware—more sophisticated than anything we've seen before. The AI program figures out how to access your other apps. It scrapes data and learns everything about you. I mean *everything*. It even runs facial recognition and voice analysis to measure your emotional state. If you keep it running in the background, it will learn more about you than you know about yourself. It then pushes biblical content to manipulate your behavior. The messaging is controlled by an internet node in Saint Petersburg. It's like getting texts from God, except that God has taken up residence in the Kremlin. Don't download it. *It's a Trojan horse.*"

* * * *

"We need to confront him," Tanya said.

"It's too dangerous," Mark replied. "Dr. Kane is mixed up with Rich and Ivanovich. We have no idea where that killer monk is. He could be masquerading as anyone."

"But what if Dr. Kane is being used?" Tanya said. "What if he doesn't know what he's unleashing on the world? What if Rich doesn't even know? What if they're just useful idiots? What if Ivanovich and the Russians are behind it all?"

"Then we do need to warn him," Mark agreed. "But we need a safer venue. He'll be giving the morning sermon at the New Beginnings church tomorrow. I'm sure it will be televised. If we can get to him in front of the TV cameras, we should be safe."

Tanya looked out the window of their room at the Flamingo Hotel. "We still have today and tonight. I'd like to see and experience Las Vegas. I want to see the fountains at the Bellagio and the moving statues at Caesars Palace. How about you? What would you like to see?"

"I'd like to see the boneyard," Mark replied.

"The boneyard?"

"It's a yard in the Neon Museum where they preserve neon signs from dismantled hotels and casinos. It's an archaeological history of the city."

Tanya laughed. "You and your Americana. I want to first experience Las Vegas as it is today, vibrant and alive. Then you can take me to see its skeletons."

For the next several hours, Tanya was like a child in a toy store. She watched the pirate galleons exchange cannon fire in front of Treasure Island, applauded when the statues came alive at Caesars Palace, marveled at the erupting volcano at the Mirage, and waved at the gondoliers who navigated the canals at the Venetian. She walked past hotels designed as a pyramid, a New York skyscraper, and even an Eiffel Tower.

"I see why most Americans don't have a passport," she said. "You bring the world to them."

"But none of it is *authentic*," Mark said.

"You're wrong. It's authentic *Las Vegas*. You have to experience it to believe it."

The Neon Museum and *Neon Boneyard* occupied six acres on the corner of Las Vegas Boulevard and Bonanza. The visitors' center was the restored and relocated lobby of the La Concha Motel. The seashell-shaped midcentury-modern building was originally located on the Strip next to the Riviera and saved from demolition in 2005. The SILVER SLIPPER sign stood across from the Welcome Center. The *Neon Boneyard* itself encompassed two acres with about 120 signs.

"Now you can tell me all about this place," she said.

"When the historic old motels and casinos get demolished," Mark said, "the coolest signs are donated here. Each of the signs has a story to tell. Many date back to the gangster days, like our Flamingo Hotel. Each is a work of art in its own right. The best way to learn is to take a curated tour."

The skeletons of the neon signs were stacked helter-skelter on either side of a dirt path marked with stones. The signs were relatively well preserved under the hot Nevada sun. One could only imagine how these signs had graced the entrances to hotels and casinos in their own time. The curator led them past signage from the Moulin Rouge Hotel, the Stardust, Caesars Palace, and the Sahara. They viewed the giant fiberglass skull from the Treasure Island Hotel and Casino. Though she had tried to hold his hand throughout the tour, Tanya could see that Mark's attention was focused entirely on these electronic fossils. He was like a child viewing pond water through a microscope. To most people, these were rusting relics from the past. To him, they were a glimpse into a previous age of guys and dolls—a violent, criminal, yet fascinating part of America's past to which most tourists were oblivious.

Mark and Tanya lingered behind the tour to view the sign from the Desert Inn.

"Frank Sinatra had his Las Vegas debut here in 1951," Mark said. "It was quite a place in its day."

Tanya closed her eyes. "I can just imagine the glamour, the lights, the people in their gowns and tuxedos. I can hear the music. I can smell perfume and cigarettes. I can taste the dirty martinis. I feel the electricity in the air."

"Now you're making fun of me."

"No, not at all. I'm trying to share your excitement. If you let your imagination go, it's like an adrenaline rush."

"Yes, that's it!" Mark said. "You project yourself to another time and place, a time when you didn't yet exist. And the world was none the worse for our not being in it."

"What's it like not to exist?"

Mark reflected for a moment. "It's like *nothing*."

"And what do you think it will be like when we die?"

"I pray there's an afterlife, but in truth I don't know. I very much want to believe that our souls will live forever. I don't want all of this to end. I don't want us to end."

Tanya looked up at the Desert Inn sign. "When I first saw you searching for your Americana among the antiques and ruins, I thought you were looking for mortality. I was wrong. You very much want these things to come alive. You're searching for clues to immortality."

* * * *

From afar the New Beginnings Megachurch looked like a giant flying saucer that had landed in the desert to rescue the true believers from the End Time. The main parking lot for the morning service was full, and Mark and Tanya had to take a shuttle bus from the auxiliary lot to the entrance of the building. As they neared the building they were amazed by its sheer size. The capacity was capped at ten thousand, but Mark figured the attendance at well over fifteen thousand. The overflow attendees were jammed into the circular hallways and watched the gospel choirs and warm-up preachers on LED screens. Television cameras covered the service from 360 degrees. Greeters in white shirts and tan pants or skirts welcomed the churchgoers and assured everyone that they would get a glimpse of the Reverend Dr. Mathias Kane.

"We'll never get close enough," Mark said. "It's a madhouse."

Tanya spotted a TV camera that was panning the crowd. "Wave into that camera," she said.

"Why? Do you think your producer friend will spot us?"

"We're an attractive couple. Rex said I had the right stuff for Hollywood."

Within minutes a smiling greeter tugged at Tanya's elbow. "Mr. Meyers informed us that you are VIPs. We have a special section reserved for you near the front. He asked that you stop by in the production control room after the service." He pointed to a fifth-floor window in the back of the hall.

Tanya gave Mark an I-told-you-so smile and followed the greeter as they pushed through the crowd into the main assembly hall. A fifty-person gospel choir was just finishing "Oh Happy Day." Two rows of cushioned seats had been roped off with a velvet cord. Celebrities occupied several of the seats. They were the kind you see on the cover of *People* magazine but need to read the article to discover why they're famous.

Dr. Kane climbed the stairs onto the podium illuminated by a dozen spotlights. He was dressed in an immaculate white suit, white shirt, and white tie. He was clutching a leather Bible. Fifty-foot screens flanked the podium, so all could see his every frown, every glance, and the sweat on his brow. He took a deep breath and began with 2 Timothy 3:1–5:

This know also, that in the last days perilous times shall come. For men shall be lovers of their own selves, covetous, boasters, proud, blasphemers, disobedient to parents, unthankful, unholy; without natural affection, trucebreakers, false accusers, incontinent, fierce, despisers of those who are good; traitors, heady, highminded, lovers of pleasures more than lovers of God; having a form of godliness, but denying the power therof: from such turn away.

His eyes scoured the audience for these unbelievers. "Do you deny the power of God?" he bellowed.

"No!" the thousands replied.

"Are you lovers of pleasure rather than lovers of God?"

"No!"

"Are there scoffers among you?"

"No!"

"Then give up your love of money and your earthly conceits. The Last Days are upon us. I have seen the signs. I have seen the prophecies fulfilled with my own eyes."

Kane always drew his audience from the metaphysical back to the personal. Most had heard the story of his encounter with the beast a hundred times before, yet all wanted to hear it again as if for the first time.

"As many of you know, my daddy was a drunk and a scoffer. Hell, he kept a cage with a live bear and threatened to throw me in it when I was old enough to talk back. When he died in a bar fight, did I pray for him? No. I wished him dead. Did I become a God-fearing child like my mama wanted? No. I was disobedient, brutal, and reckless. My uncle, the preacher, said I was a no-good son of a gun, who was born to be hanged. Then the Lord took mercy on me and on my poor mother. One day I sneaked away to the Devil's Hole to look at a lurid magazine that I stole from a barbershop, and what happened?"

The audience listened without so much as a cough or a sneeze.

"I heard this unearthly sound come out of the hole, like the rumble in the belly of a great beast. It grew louder and louder as if it was calling for me. I was too afraid to run. And then I saw it: the beast of biblical prophecy. A scarlet dragon that had seven heads and ten horns, and upon his horns ten crowns, and upon his heads the name . . ."

The crowd called out the name.

"Blasphemy!" Dr. Kane shouted out. "It was then that I was born again and set out to become a preacher and warn you that the Last Days are at hand. The signs are all around us. Jerusalem is returned to the Jews. We suffer earthquakes and famine and pestilence. Many run to-and-fro, and knowledge is increased. False prophets arise and lead us astray. Scoffers follow their own ungodly passions and cause divisions. For Matthew 24:21–22 writes that 'For then shall be great tribulation, such as was not since the beginning of the world to this time, no, nor shall ever be.'"

Several in the audience began writhing in their seats from imagining the horror of the Tribulation.

"Heed," Dr. Kane said, "the warnings of the three angels. In Revelation

14:6–7 John writes: 'And I saw another angel fly in the midst of heaven, having the everlasting gospel to preach unto them that dwell on the earth, and to every nation, and kindred, and tongue, and people, Saying with a loud voice, Fear God, and give glory to him; for the hour of his judgment is come; and worship Him that made heaven, the earth, and the sea, and fountains of waters.'

"And there followed another angel followed saying: 'Babylon is fallen, is fallen, that great city, because she made all nations drink of the wine of the wrath of her fornication.'

"And the third angel followed them saying with a loud voice, 'If any man worship the beast and his image, and receive his mark in his forehead, or in his hand, the same shall drink of the wine of the wrath of God, which is poured out without mixture into the cup of his indignation; and he shall be tormented with fire and brimstone in the presence of the holy angels, and in the presence of the Lamb: And the smoke of their torment ascendeth up for ever and ever: and they have no rest day nor night, who worship the beast and his image, and whosoever receiveth the mark in his name.'

"Are there any here among you," Dr. Kane shouted out, "with the mark of the beast?"

"No," the masses cried out. The nervous checked their neighbors for the sign of the beast.

"Then fear not the Tribulation. Renounce Satan and be born again." He proceeded to give a timeline of the upcoming End Time, and describe how prior to the Great Tribulation all the dead saints will rise from their graves and all the living members of the church shall be caught up with them to meet Christ in the clouds in the Rapture. After the fulfillment of divine wrath, Christ shall return to rule from the New Jerusalem over the earthly nations for one thousand years. After these one thousand years, Satan will be loosed to deceive the nations, gather the army of the deceived, and take up to battle against the Lord. The battle will end in both the judgment of the wicked and Satan and the entrance into the eternal state of glory by the righteous."

Calls of *amen, hallelujah,* and *praise be the Lord* broke out spontaneously in the audience.

Reverend Kane opened his arms as if to welcome those who wanted to be saved. "Who of you will join me in the Rapture?"

"We will!" thousands of voices cried out.

"I know that many of you believe that you are not worthy," Reverend Kane said. "So I have developed tools to help you. For those of you who embrace technology, I've developed a Last Awakening phone app to bring the Scripture to you, not just on Sundays, but every hour and day of the week. Think of it as your own guardian angel. The app is free, but donations are always welcome to bring the gospel to others. For those of you who prefer to hear the spoken word, you can show support for our church of the Last Awakening by purchasing a Rapture ribbon for a mere ten dollars. These ribbons will help identify those of you who have been born again and are worthy of Rapture. For those of you watching on television, you can download your app on Independence Day or have your ribbon sent to you for just ten dollars plus the cost of shipping and handling."

Greeters went into the aisles, white ribbons in hand, to collect the ten-dollar donations.

The climax of the service was the laying on of hands. "Those of you," Dr. Kane said, "who are suffering in body or spirit, I call upon you to come up to the stage and share your grief so that you can be healed."

Dozens of attendees began pushing into the aisle.

"This is our chance," Tanya said. "I'm going up."

Mark grabbed her wrist to stop her, but she wrested it away. She climbed the stairs to the stage with the rest of the supplicants.

From the control room, Rex Meyers spotted her ascending to Kane. "Focus on that blonde beauty," he instructed his cameramen. As the cameras focused on her face from a dozen angles, Tanya appeared on a million television sets around the country. Reverend Kane saw the cameras focus on this stunning supplicant. He straightened his tie, adjusted his mike, and laid his hands upon her head.

"What troubles you, child?"

She looked up at him in front of the television cameras and said: "Babylon has not fallen because *you* will make all nations drink of the wine of the wrath of her fornication."

Kane took his hands off her head. "You dare to belie John of Revelation?" he asked. "Who are you?"

"You don't recognize me? You called me the whore of Babylon."

Dr. Kane took a step back. "But who are you *really*?"

"I am the second angel. I've come to warn you. Babylon has *not* fallen because you are complicit in her sin. You are the false prophet. Your app is not meant to *save*, its meant to *deceive*. *You* are the one who needs to come out of Babylon." She turned and disappeared into the congregation of bewildered believers.

* * * *

Dmitri received a call on his phone from Gennady.

"I found your rusalka," Gennady said.

"Where?" Dmitri asked.

"On YouTube. You need to see this. The video is going viral." Gennady messaged Dmitri the link.

The YouTube video showed Tanya in Las Vegas face-to-face with the Reverend Dr. Mathias Kane, proclaiming to the world that she was the second angel of Revelation and that he was the false prophet. Dmitri wondered what Turchin could have told her that led her to confront Kane. He needed a plan for damage control. Killing her and her boyfriend was no longer enough. He needed to know what they knew and whom they've told if he had any chance of surviving Ivanovich's wrath.

"When was this video taken?" Dmitri asked.

"About noon today," Gennady replied.

"I need you to locate all known contacts of Bereza and Rider within a day's drive of Las Vegas."

"Already done," Gennady replied. "The rusalka has none. Rider has three potential contacts. The closest is in Nevada City, California."

That evening Dmitri was on flight to Reno. Before leaving, he had poured a few drops of cone snail venom into an atomizer that had been developed at the Kamera laboratory to resemble a three-ounce cologne bottle. The nanotechnology used to aerosolize the conotoxin had the potential to revolutionize pharmaceutical drug delivery systems. He packed his nitrile gloves, air-purifying respirator, and two vials of FAB fragment antivenom. One vial was for him in the event of an accident, and the other for the rusalka so she could trade information for her life. If his plan failed, he always had Dana.

CHAPTER 12

Orcas Island

The El Camino raced north on Highway 95 toward Reno. The air-conditioning had been blowing lukewarm air since Rhyolite. They passed a sign for Yucca Flat that marked the direction to the Nevada National Security Site. Had they had time, Mark would have visited the site where in 1955 the United States conducted Operation Teacup. A fake town known as Survival Town was constructed and populated by mannequins of citizens going about their daily routines. A series of nuclear test explosions turned Survival Town into Doom Town. The site, like Crocodile Lake, offered presages of Armageddon.

Tanya was perusing her Bible. She furrowed her brow.

"How is your Bible reading going?" Mark asked.

"I'm perplexed," she said.

"Why?"

"God in the New Testament is loving and merciful. In the Old Testament, He's *different*."

"In what way?"

"I've only perused some of the books, but He seems to be angry and vengeful. He asks Abraham to sacrifice his son. He sends plagues and devastation. He destroys entire cities with sulfur and fire. He creates a world full of people but reveals Himself only to a chosen few. I can't reconcile the two."

"I've often wondered about that portrayal myself. I've heard it rationalized by biblical scholars—'the fire that burns also provides warmth'—but I agree that it's perplexing."

Tanya paged through the book of Psalms. "There's also great wisdom," she said. "Where can I find more passages that deal with the End Time? That seems to be Reverend Kane's obsession."

"Many places. It's in Matthew, Mark, Luke, and John, especially John. Also Daniel, Timothy . . ."

"Do you believe in the End Time prophecy?"

"I'm a modernist. I don't believe that you need to interpret every word of the Bible literally. Still, I do believe that Christ will come again. I don't know if it will be in our lifetimes, but I see certain parts of the prophecy already being fulfilled."

"The beast crawling out of the Devil's Hole?"

"No, no! Of course not! I mean the things that are happening in our world today. You opened my eyes when we visited the Circus Museum. You said that our burgeoning population is exceeding the ability of the earth to sustain us. You warned it would result in mass migration, famine, and war. So the way I figure, the world leaders have a choice: they can either cooperate to prevent it from happening or try to put their nations first. If they put themselves first, then conflict over what little remains will be inevitable."

"So you see us on the brink of a great tribulation?" Tanya asked.

Mark looked out toward Yucca Flat. "Yes," he said. "If your prediction of a Malthusian catastrophe comes true, then the Tribulation and Armageddon will follow."

Tanya put down her Bible and placed her hand on his knee. "Then which harbinger do I embody for you?" she asked. "The second angel or the whore of Babylon?"

"That would take a convention of biblical scholars to answer."

She pinched him on his knee. "Shut up!"

Mark smiled. "You're Tanya Bereza, a talented sculptress, an amazing woman. You may be as beautiful as an angel, but you're no angel."

"Were you impressed how I quoted Scripture to Kane?"

"It was quite a moment. But millions of people have seen it by now, including Rich and Ivanovich. They know we're somewhere in Nevada. They've probably dispatched their assassin after us."

"We need to stay a step ahead of them," Tanya replied. "We know enough to lock them away. We just need to find someone in your government who's willing to listen to us and look at the evidence."

"Uriel said that someone in the government *did* look at the evidence and chose not to act. We need to find out who's protecting them. Otherwise we'll be labeled as conspiracy theorists. They're probably already covering their tracks."

Mark was pushing the El Camino as fast as it would go. He eyed every car and truck that passed them. The desolate desert landscape added to his anxiety. There was no place to hide.

"We need to get off the main road," he told Tanya. "We're also nearly out of money."

"I still have a couple of hundred dollars from the blackjack table," she said. "That should last us for a few days."

"Orcas Island is at least a twenty-one-hour drive from here, not counting the ferry ride. I think we should take a detour. There's a good friend of my father who lives in Nevada City. It's only about three hours from here."

"Are you sure?" Tanya asked. "Whoever's following us has accessed our phone and computer records. They might anticipate our stopping there."

"My father's friend, George, is an artist. He's completely off the grid. He doesn't use email or social media. He has a landline phone with a blocked phone number. We should be safe. We'll only stop overnight. I'll ask him to lend us some money."

The drive west from Reno to Nevada City took them over the snow-peaked Sierra Range. They exited I-80 at Emigrant Gap and descended into Bear Valley before climbing again through a series of hairpin turns onto Washington Ridge. They caught their last glimpse of the setting sun at Harmony Ridge before descending into the conifer-covered hills of Nevada City.

"This road can become impassable in the winter," Mark said. "George knows the back country, the dirt roads that lead to ghost towns and abandoned gold mines. Once when state troopers closed the road because of a blizzard, he and I bypassed the blockade by taking a three-hour detour over the mountains in his old Mercedes diesel. I remember seeing a mountain lion that crossed our path. I thought that if we got stranded in the blizzard, it would be the end of us."

"You remember it fondly," she said. "I can see that you're very close him."

"He's like an uncle to me. I even have a nickname for him: California George. When I was in college, I spent a couple of my school breaks with him. He was everything my parents weren't. We'd go fly-fishing in Yellowstone, skiing in Tahoe, and hiking in Death Valley. He's open-minded and creative. He's a nonconformist. A bit eccentric, but that's the part of him I find most endearing."

"I can't wait to meet him," Tanya said.

Mark knew the way by heart. He navigated a dozen turns in the darkness. Tanya kept her eyes peeled for mountain lions. The last turn took them down a steep incline into a river valley. They could hear the rushing water of the brook that was bursting its banks from the icy waters of the snowmelt. Tanya could see the outline of George's house in the moonlight. It resembled a small Spanish hacienda. A red Ford pickup loaded with gear was parked next to a Mercedes diesel. The house was dark except for the gray light of a television reflecting from one of the windows. Mark pulled the El Camino up to the pickup. The headlights shone on a burly man with a mustache and overalls who was pointing a shotgun directly at them. He looked like a prospector from an old Western.

"Turn off those damned lights or I'll shoot them out for you," the man ordered. "Come out with your hands up."

Mark shut off the headlights and stepped out of the car. "George, it's me, Mark. Sorry to surprise you."

George stepped up to Mark, shotgun in hand, to make sure it was really him. "Well, I'll be damned." He gave him a hug that nearly snapped his spine. "You're lucky you caught me. I was setting out for Hat Creek in the morning. Who's that riding with you?"

Tanya stepped out of the car when she saw it was safe and offered her hand. "I'm Tanya Bereza. Mark has told me a lot about you."

"Tall tales, I'm sure," George replied. "Come on in. I've got a good episode of *Gunsmoke* on the TV. I've still got some chili in the fridge."

The inside of the hacienda was unlike any place Tanya had ever seen. It was quintessential Americana. One wall in the kitchen displayed a collection of chili pepper bottles from throughout the United States. Outdated surveys of Nevada County's water resources were pinned to the wall. A poster from last year's Gilroy Garlic Festival lay on the floor. A Navajo rug was slung over the couch. Vinyl records from the sixties and seventies were scattered around a turntable. A cathode-tube television was playing *Gunsmoke* in black and white. What caught Tanya's attention the most were the relief sculptures that were hung haphazardly throughout the hacienda.

"I can see," she said to Mark, "that California George shares your passion for Americana."

* * * *

Dmitri arrived at the Reno airport after midnight. He rented the last available car, a Kia Forte, and set the directions on the GPS to the address that Gennady had given him. The drive on I-80 was smooth, but the twists and turns on Highway 20 were treacherous. He arrived at his destination at 3:30 a.m. Three mailboxes marked the entrance to a gravel road that plunged into a ravine. He got out of his car and checked the mailboxes. One of them was the one he was looking for. A dog barked in the distance. Checking each house in the dark in unknown terrain was too risky. He had passed a dozen No Trespassing signs in the last hour. The only people living in these remote parts were people who knew how to take care of themselves. He decided to wait until morning.

Tanya awoke to the sounds of birds chirping. Mark was still asleep in the single bed next to hers. She freshened up in the bathroom and set out to explore the house and its surroundings. George was outside grilling oysters over a manzanita fire. Hundreds of spent shells rested in a pile behind him. A feral cat was licking the shells clean.

"You're up early," George said. "I'm preparing my specialty for breakfast: scrambled eggs and grilled oysters. I was saving these last few oysters for the cats, but you'll do just as well."

"I see your truck is packed. Did we intrude at a bad time?" she asked.

"Hell no. The trout can wait. I'd rather spend the time with Mark and his girl. I'm glad you're with him. That boy spends so much time looking backward that sometimes he gets his head stuck in his ass."

Tanya laughed. "He is curious indeed."

The yard was a sight to behold. Manzanita was creeping in from three sides like the evil queen's thicket in *Sleeping Beauty*. Piles of sand were scattered throughout the yard like giant anthills.

George saw her looking at the piles. "Oh, those? I bring sand up from the river and pan it here rather than on the riverbank.

"You've actually found gold?" Tanya asked.

"A few specks here and there. If you keep at it, it adds up. A fellow once pulled a solid gold nugget out of the river, so there's always hope. The fun is in the panning. Here, I'll show you how to do it." He put the last of the grilled oysters onto a plate and pulled an iron pan from behind one of the piles. He filled it with a helping of sand and some water from a bucket and handed it to Tanya. "Here, just swirl and let the sand fall out of the pan. The gold sinks to the bottom."

Tanya took the pan and with a little practice was panning like a prospector. A fleck of gold shone in the pan. "Look," she called out, "I found some!"

"You got the gold fever," George said. "That's about a nickel's worth of gold."

Dmitri watched the oyster grilling and gold panning from atop the ridge. He focused his binoculars on Mark as he ambled out of the house looking for George and Tanya. Dmitri counted three cars: a Mercedes diesel, a Ford pickup, and an El Camino. He waited to see if anyone else would join them for breakfast. The older man looked to be about sixty but fit enough to be dangerous. He went back into the house and brought out some plates and a pot of coffee. Dmitri counted three cups. They sat around the manzanita fire chatting and having their breakfast. Dmitri regretted that he had never learned how to read lips.

"I saw your reliefs inside the house," Tanya said. "They're really good. I'm a sculptress myself," Tanya said.

"Oh yeah?" George replied.

"I work mostly in metal—welding, brazing, that kind of thing. I'm experimenting with patinas. I want to learn the alchemy of turning base metals into brilliant oxides. What are you currently sculpting?"

"I've moved on from sculpture into another medium—photography. Not the digital kind. I like the old-fashioned methods, photographic plates, chemical developers. I'm finishing up a study on light in darkness. I set up a camera in total darkness in a drift in the abandoned Mother Lode Mine and paint with light. I experiment with different light sources, exposure times, and developers. Carl Jung said, 'One does not become enlightened by imagining figures of light, but by making darkness conscious.' You'd be amazed at the beauty of darkness."

"I'd love to see it," Tanya replied.

"If you want, we can take a ride there after breakfast."

"George, there's one other thing"—Mark butted into the conversation—"that we wanted to ask you. "Could you loan us some money? We're in a jam. It's a long story. We're tracking down a story on Russian collusion, and we've got some dangerous people on our tail. We're almost done, but we need to get to Orcas Island for the final piece of the puzzle."

"Russkies, huh?"

"You're not surprised?" Tanya asked.

"Hell no," George replied. "They've been undermining us for years, stealing the mother lode from right under our noses. It's about time someone had the balls to do something about it." He went back into the house and brought out a test tube. It was filled with gold dust. "Take this into a pawn shop. It's over fifty grams. Make sure they weigh it and don't just eyeball it."

Mark took the test tube and put it in his pocket. "Thanks. I'll pay you back as soon as this is over."

"No need," George said. "Just bring Tanya back and have her pan through the rest of this river bottom."

Tanya laughed. "I'd love to come back. Now I want to see the Mother Lode Mine. You've piqued my interest."

Dmitri watched through his binoculars as they finished their breakfast, put out the fire, and carried their plates into the house. He began his descent to the house on foot. Rather than follow the gravel road, he climbed down through the manzanita and ponderosa pines. When he was halfway down, he saw the three of them getting into the Ford pickup. He retraced his steps up the hill and sneaked into his car just as they were pulling out from the driveway onto to the asphalt road. He sunk in his seat so he wouldn't be seen. When they made the first turn, he started his car and followed.

The Mother Lode Mine was only twenty minutes away, sunk into the hills overlooking Nevada City. It had been abandoned in the late seventies when the EPA fined the mining company for dumping cyanide waste into a runoff stream. The mine had been scavenged for metal, leaving only the wooden skeleton of the building. The entrance to the mine was boarded over with rotted planks. A metal sign with a skull and crossbones dangled from the boards and read DANGER. ABANDONED. MINES ARE DEADLY. DON'T GET TRAPPED. STAY OUT! STAY ALIVE! George put on a hard hat and unwound a wire that was holding one of the larger boards in place. The opening was large enough to squeeze through. The interior was as dark as the Devil's Hole.

"The sign warned to stay out," Mark said as they retreated from the daylight.

"Exactly why I chose it," George replied. "I don't want any tourists with flashlights mucking about my studio. There is one winze, though, where the drift narrows, that we have to watch out for. You can fall right through if you're not careful."

"What's a winze?" Tanya asked.

"It's a vertical shaft that leads to the level below. It's boarded over, but the wood and ladder are rotted through. It's a death trap. I put a foot through it the first time I came through. Just walk behind me and watch where you step."

George's flashlight illuminated the rails that led into the belly of the mine. The floor was uneven and wet from a steady trickle of water that seemed to ooze out of the rock walls. A hundred yards in, the flashlight illuminated a drift to their left. A rusted chicken wire barrier blocked the entrance. George lifted the wire to let Mark and Tanya crawl underneath before entering himself.

"Don't go running ahead or you'll fall through the winze," he warned. "Mark, grab my belt, and Tanya, you grab Mark by whatever."

The drift was narrow enough in some places that they could touch the walls with both hands. George stopped them about fifty yards in. He shone his light on an opening in the floor that looked like the Devil's Hole except that it was boarded over with rotted boards. The beam of the flashlight streamed through a hole in the planks and illuminated the floor about twelve feet below. "Just step around," he said. "Keep touching the wall, and you'll be safe. I set up my gear in a chamber about another thirty yards farther in."

With each step the diameter of the drift narrowed. Other than the beam of the flashlight, they were engulfed in darkness. Mark realized what it was like to be buried alive. His first impulse was to run back to the entrance, but if he panicked, he could easily fall into the winze and break his neck. He clung on to George's belt. Tanya was gripping Mark's shirt. She was sweating and breathing heavily. George pulled them forward until he suddenly stopped. "We're here," he said.

Here could have been anywhere. George probed the interior of the chamber with his flashlight. He rummaged through the gear that was scattered on the floor. He pulled an LED lamp out of a knapsack and flicked it on. The lamp illuminated a small chamber about fifteen feet by fifteen feet wide and six feet high. A yellow seam glistened in the light of the flashlight.

"Gold?" Tanya asked.

"Fool's gold," George replied. "Drove many prospectors mad. They thought they struck the mother lode only to find out it was pyrite. Now watch this." George turned off the LED lamp and turned on a penlight.

He traced patterns in the pyrite vein as if it were a brush. "In total darkness, I can leave the aperture of the camera open for a minute or two while I paint with light." He handed Tanya the penlight. "Would you like to try it?"

Tanya drew a hieroglyphic on the wall by turning the penlight on and off with each stroke. It was as if she were writing in some ancient language that only she and Poseidon understood.

The scrape of wire against rock echoed through the drift.

"Shut the light," Mark whispered to George. "I think we've been followed."

"Could be a ghost," George replied. "Lots of men died in these mines searching for the mother lode. You can see their specters in some of my photographs."

"It's the ghost that's been following us since Williamstown. I'm sure of it."

The single set of approaching footsteps grew louder with each step. The footsteps were slow and calculated. Whoever was there was searching. A tourist would ramble through erratically. These footsteps were probing. They would start and stop.

George pulled something out of his camera bag. "We need to reach the winze before he does," he whispered. "Hang on to me, I know the way by heart. Eighty-five steps."

They were immersed in total darkness. George counted the steps back to the winze.

"What are you doing?" Mark whispered.

"I took out my flash. It will temporarily blind whoever's following us. Remember, if we have to make a run for it, make sure you're touching the side of the drift."

The footsteps drew nearer and then stopped as if the predator were sniffing for its prey. Tanya fingered her ghost beads. They stood motionless in the blackness at the edge of the winze and listened. The only sounds were the dripping of water and the occasional creaking of a wooden support beam. The footsteps resumed. A glimmer of light illuminated the far end of the tunnel. It got brighter with each footstep. George began to softly whistle "Clementine."

What the hell are you doing? Mark thought. *You're leading him straight to us.* But then Mark understood. Now that the predator had heard its prey, it would approach stealthily. George was luring him into a trap. Their stalker shut off his light. The time between each step became longer as the predator navigated the drift in the dark. Mark counted each step. *Another ten . . . maybe five.* It seemed like an eternity. George stopped whistling. They heard the sound of heavy breathing. It wasn't natural. It was as if someone were breathing through a hose with slow, forced exhalations, in and out, and in and out. The breathing seemed so close that they could feel it on their faces.

When George heard the squeak of a rotted plank, he pressed his flash. A hideous specter appeared in the blinding light. A full-face respirator gave it the appearance of a mole. Purple gloves were stretched over its hands. One hand held a phone, and the other a small atomizer.

Mark recognized the eyes. "It's him!" he cried out.

Dmitri lunged toward Mark's voice and plunged into the winze. As he broke through the rotted boards, he dropped his phone and atomizer to keep from crashing through. A splintered board gouged his abdomen but kept him from falling to the level below. He heard his phone hit and bounce on the rock below. He blindly swiped for his prey, but they had slipped past him during his fall. As he clung on to the rotted planks his foot felt the step of a ladder below. He clawed his way out of the winze. He crouched on the wet floor and extracted a large sliver of wood out of his abdomen. Blood trickled down toward his pants. He began groping around for the atomizer bottle and knelt on a wet piece of broken glass— *conotoxin!* He realized with dread that if he didn't make it back to his car in the next eight minutes, he was as good as dead. He staggered toward the exit.

When he emerged from the mouth of the mine, he was seeing double. The path to his car wound through abandoned cyanide pits. He struggled to insert the key into the car door. He bent over and vomited. He pulled up his pant leg and pulled a piece of glass out of his knee. The area around the cut was bright red. He was panting and his heart was skipping like a scratched record. He injected himself with both vials of the antivenom. As he drove out of the Mother Lode Mine, the road began to undulate. He couldn't lift his right foot off the gas and had to use his left foot to brake. The car veered off the road and crashed into a thicket of dogwood.

He awoke in the late afternoon with his head on the steering wheel. His shirt was drenched in dried blood, but his heart rate and breathing had returned to normal. He opened his bag and ripped open a sterile surgical kit. He extracted a large sliver of rotted wood from his wound, doused the skin with Betadine, and stitched the ragged edges together as he had been taught during his training at the FSB Institute. He backed out of the thicket and retraced the route back to the hacienda. The Ford pickup and El Camino were gone. Only the Mercedes diesel remained.

* * * *

"Sorry to bring the devil to your door," Mark said to George. George had just finished switching their license plates.

"Most excitement I've had in a long time. If you can't count on your own, whom can you count on? You sure you don't want me to come along?"

"Thanks, but Tanya and I can handle it from here."

George arched his eyebrow. "I guess this is where we part ways." He gave them a hug. "Follow me until we hit the interstate at Red Bluff. I'm pulling off toward Hat Creek just before Redding. If they're tracking your plates as you say, I'll take them on a wild goose chase. You continue up I-5, and you should make Portland by nightfall. Get back to me when this is all over. Just make sure it's a happy ending."

The drive up to the Pacific Northwest took them through one of the most scenic parts of the country. Mark hated to race by, but they were exposed and vulnerable. Their pursuer had most likely seen the El Camino. Hopefully, he hadn't survived the fall down the winze. He checked the Rand McNally atlas at a rest stop and figured that if they drove straight through, they could reach Anacortes by daybreak and catch one of the morning ferries to Orcas Island.

Tanya read her Bible through most of the drive and fell asleep at nightfall with the book still open on her lap. The blast of the horn from the departing ferry jarred her out of her sleep. She was alone in the car.

The ocean breeze was dispersing the morning mist. She opened the car door and saw Mark walking toward her from the ferry terminal. He was carrying something in his hand.

"We missed the first ferry, but I managed to get tickets for the 7:30 a.m. It gets us into Orcas Island by 8:20 a.m., car and all. I brought us some coffee."

"You drove straight through the night?" she asked.

"Death was over our shoulders."

Tanya recalled how he had offered her coffee that first morning they had met. She was curled up in his car naked, and he was her protector. She took a sip of the hot coffee. "I really need to pee," she said.

"The public restrooms are next to the ticket office. We still have a little time. I'll walk you over."

After a second cup of coffee, a blast of the horn indicated it was time to load the ferry. They lined up their car in the holding area and followed the cars and trucks into the main hold.

"Let's ride up on the deck," Tanya suggested.

The ferry ride to Orcas Island took them through the San Juan Islands. The ocean was calm, and the waves lapped gently across the bow. The waters between the fir-covered islands were a haven for marine mammals: Pacific harbor seals, porpoises, sea lions, and orcas. The air smelled of salt and cedar.

"I really like George," Tanya said. He's so . . . *genuine*. How is it that you became so close? He's so different than your parents."

"My father and George were best friends in high school. From what George tells me, they did some crazy things together. They even traveled around the world together on a high school trip. My father met my mother in divinity school and chose a different path in life. George never gave up on his youthful dreams."

The ocean breeze played with her tangled blonde hair.

Mark put his arm around her. "You never gave up on your dreams either," he said. "I hope you stay forever young."

The ferry off-loaded in Orcas. Mark picked up a tourist map of the island at the ferry dock. The address that Uriel had given was laconic: Russ Boyko, Four Winds Camp Road, Orcas Island. There was no street or postbox number.

The scenic drive took them north around West Sound, past the Turtleback Mountain Preserve, and back south to Deer Harbor before catching Four Winds Camp Road. As they drove down Four Winds Camp Road, horseback riders emerged single file from the woods. All were children except for the lead rider who looked to be about eighteen.

Mark got out of the El Camino and approached the teenager. "Excuse me," he said. "But we're looking for someone who lives along this road. I don't have a street address."

"What's the name?" the boy asked.

"Russ Boyko."

"The skipper? He volunteers at our camp and takes the kids sailing on Tuesdays and Thursdays. I'm pretty sure he lives down on Perseverance Lane, where he moors his boat. It's just about a mile and a half south. Just follow Perseverance Lane and look for his sailboat, the *Ancient Mariner*."

"Thanks!" Mark said.

As they drove south, Mark and Tanya followed the shoreline ridge through the cedars and hemlocks, trying to get a glimpse of a sailboat. After a few turns, they saw it moored in a remote inlet. They pulled their car off the road and looked for a mailbox. They found none. A No Trespassing sign nailed to a tree marked the entrance to a gravel drive that wound down toward the water. The drive jutted into a plateau with a garage, then continued as a walking path to the shore. The final decline was too steep for cars. Hemlocks and ferns obscured what looked to be a barbed wire fence demarcating the property line. Surveillance cameras were hidden in the firs that lined the walkway. Two pit bulls began barking as Mark and Tanya neared a clapboard home that was perched on a ridge overlooking the sound. Wooden stairs with a hewed-lumber railing led down to the shore.

A Chinese American woman opened the door. The two pit bulls came running out in front of her and stopped in front of Mark and Tanya awaiting their next command. "Can I help you?"

"We're not trespassers," Mark said. "My name is Mark Rider, and my friend is Tanya Bereza. We're looking for a Mr. Russ Boyko."

"Well, you found him," a voice said behind them. They turned to see a man in his fifties holding a Winchester rifle.

"Mr. Boyko? We don't mean to intrude. We're here to ask for your help."

"Who sent you?"

"You may not know him," Mark said. "A hacker. He calls himself Uriel."

"Ex-NSA," Boyko replied. "The presider of the dark web. Half the world is looking for him."

"He knew how to find you," Mark said. "He said you could help us."

Boyko looked at his wife. "Any others?"

"The surveillance cameras show only the two of them. They drove in on an El Camino registered to a woman in Baraboo, Wisconsin."

"Let me see your IDs," Boyko said.

Mark handed over his wallet. Boyko looked at the driver's license, Northwestern ID, and auto insurance card.

"Your insurance card says Trans Am. You're driving an El Camino."

"I bartered it from Mrs. Erickson in Baraboo, Wisconsin. I haven't notified my insurance company."

The Winchester rifle was still resting on Boyko's forearm.

"My friend Tanya and I—we're on the run."

"From whom?"

"Victor Ivanovich."

Boyko cocked the Winchester. He looked at Tanya. "Your ID?"

"I escaped from his yacht without any of my things."

"How do I know you're not working for Ivanovich?" Boyko asked.

Mark looked at Tanya. The thought that she might be in collusion with Ivanovich had occurred to him once before, that night at the Blue Swallow Motel in Tucumcari. *Was this whole ordeal a ploy to find and eliminate Ivanovich's enemies? Yet Mirana trusted her. Reya trusted her. Dana and Mary trusted her. Why should he suddenly doubt her?*

"I'll vouch for her," Mark said.

Boyko gave Rider's IDs to his wife. "Check them out." He then turned to Mark and Tanya. "You must have come in on the eight twenty ferry. Hungry?"

"Yes," Tanya replied. "We could also use some freshening up. We've been driving all night."

"Turn around and spread your legs."

Boyko put down his rifle and frisked them, looking for concealed weapons. The two dogs stood on guard. "Sorry, but carelessness can get you killed." Once he was satisfied that they were unarmed, he slung his rifle over his shoulder and let them into the house.

The craftsman house was more spacious than it appeared from the outside. A photo of Russ with Joe Biden stood on the mantel of the fireplace. An open porch overlooked the sound. A high-powered telescope was aimed at the water.

His wife emerged holding her laptop. "They are who they say they are."

Boyko put the Winchester back in its glass case. "You can call me Russ. This is my wife, Kim."

Tanya pointed at the telescope. "Do you check every boat that sails by?"

"Only the ones that come too close," Russ said. "I've been tracking some potential intruders. Would you care to take a look?" He maneuvered the telescope until he spotted his target. "There, about a hundred yards off Victim Island."

Tanya peered through the scope and saw a family of otters swimming on their backs through the blue water.

"They're floating on their backs! So serene, so peaceful."

"Until an orca decides to feed," Russ said.

Kim went into the kitchen to prepare breakfast. At times she would check her laptop as if looking up a recipe. Tanya could smell the coffee, maple syrup, and hotcakes. Kim called Russ over to have a look. He picked up the laptop and showed Tanya a YouTube video of her with over a million hits.

"So you're the second angel, the harbinger of the End Time?"

"Dr. Kane compared me to the whore of Babylon in one of his sermons. I needed to find out why, so I confronted him. We were trying to figure out how he's connected to Ivanovich and Senator Rich."

"Senator Rich? How does he fit into your story?" Russ asked.

"He's the one who raped me."

Russ didn't say a word. Kim took Tanya by the hand. "I'm sorry we're interrogating you," Kim said. "Given our line of work, we can't be too careful."

Mark overheard the last line as he walked out of the bathroom. "Uriel said you were retired."

"You never really retire from this business," Russ said. "I stirred up a lot of trouble for the Russians, especially their criminal bosses. They responded by conjuring up fake news about my running CIA torture prisons for jihadists in Eastern Europe. Now I've got a fatwa issued on my head. Sit down, have some breakfast, and tell me your story."

Tanya began with her travel award from Ivanovich's Institute for Democratic Progress. Ivanovich had promised that her Heavenly Hundred statue would be displayed in the United States capital. She described how she was lured onto the *Kalinka*, drugged, and raped by Senator Julian Rich. Mark rescued her on the Overseas Highway, and together they embarked on their cross-country journey. She told them about Mirana and Reya and their search for Turchin. She described how he was murdered by an assassin who's been tracking them ever since. Turchin's last words sent them to find Uriel. She omitted his location.

"I presume that Uriel gave you access to Ivanovich's financial records."

"Yes," Tanya continued. "But he said that someone from the government had already seen them and chose not to act. That's why we came to you."

Russ took a long sip of black coffee and looked out onto the sound. "Kim and I are the ones who uncovered some of those transactions while I was still the CIA station chief in Kyiv. We relayed them to headquarters at Langley. They decided to bury them."

"But Ivanovich is conspiring with Senator Rich, the chair of the Foreign Relations Committee. Some say he may be the next vice president. Isn't that treason?" Mark asked.

"Who do you think has the power to protect him?"

"The president?" Tanya guessed.

"The people who actually run this country, the people *behind* the president," Russ replied. "Years ago, when I was still a graduate student on a FLAS scholarship at the University of Illinois, I got approached by a recruiter from the CIA. We developed a good rapport. He asked me what my main reason was for considering a career in the CIA. I answered that it was because I'm a patriot. 'Wrong,' he replied. 'It's because you want to know how the world *really* works.'"

"What have you learned?" Mark asked.

"Money and power—that's how the world works. The rich get richer and the poor get poorer."

"We need to change that system," Tanya said.

"The system corrupts people faster than we can reform it."

"I can't believe you've lost your faith in a rule-based world order," Mark said. "We've had relative peace for much of the last century."

"It's only a rules-based world order if everyone plays by the same rules. The problem is the rules have changed. The Russians even spelled it out for us in the Gerasimov doctrine."

"The Gerasimov doctrine?"

"Back in 2013, General Valery Gerasimov, chief of Russia's general staff, published an essay on the future of war in the journal the *Military-Industrial Courier*. He wrote that 'The very rules of war have changed. The role of nonmilitary means of achieving political and strategic goals has grown, and in many cases they have exceeded the power of weapons in their effectiveness.' We've seen their hybrid war in action: the cyberattack on Estonia in 2007, the little green men in Crimea in 2014, the interference in our own elections in 2016. When we challenge them, the response is always the same: lie, deny, and escalate."

"That's unethical," Mark said.

"Don't be naive," Russ replied. "There's nothing ethical about war. We've been engaged in hybrid warfare ourselves for years. We just don't admit it. When they challenge us, we also deny it."

"I believe that truth will overcome power," Tanya said.

"I believed that too," Russ replied. "But now we live in a post-truth world. Fake news, social engineering, psychographic targeting, fracking . . ."

"*Fracking?*" Tanya asked.

"It's a type of psychological manipulation used to make us lose faith in our own system of government. The Russians are especially good at it. They study our society and identify the fault lines—race, religion, immigration, gay marriage, Confederate war heroes—then they frack the divisions by injecting a toxic slurry of fake news, hate speech, and inflammatory diatribe on both sides of the issues. Half the time you have Russian trolls arguing with other Russian trolls hoping to sucker us in while we stare at our screens and think that America is going to hell. Once they have a foothold on an issue, they become your online peers and infiltrate the grassroots organizations that promote those issues. Khrushchev boasted that 'we will take America without firing a shot. We do not have to invade the US. We will destroy you from within.'"

"Ukraine has been the testing ground for this societal fracking," Tanya said. "They divide us by language, religion, East and West. They pit brother against brother in the war in the East."

Mark thought about his cousin Dana and her new friend Robert E. Lee. "So you think all this controversy about Confederate war heroes is fabricated?" he asked.

"It's a real hot-button issue," Russ replied. "But think about whom it draws in—neo-Nazis, KKK, antifa. You flood social media with hate speech on both sides of the issues, and the next thing you know the crazies are incited to violence."

"So how do we stop them?"

"With truth," Tanya said. "We need to expose the lies, the conspiracies, the methods of manipulation."

Russ studied the wind blowing over the sound. "Would you like to go for a sail? It'll be safer to talk on the open water."

Mark wondered for a moment if the deep state was planning to drown them.

"We'd love to," Tanya said.

The wooden house, despite its barbed wire, surveillance cameras, and pit bulls, seemed vulnerable. The only way someone could get to them on the sailboat would be by another boat, and she was confident that Russ had anticipated and prepared for that scenario.

Russ and Kim were experienced sailors. He captained the boat, and she took the role of first mate, though she seemed equally capable of handling the boat by herself.

"Are you also—" Tanya began to ask.

"CIA? I'm a securities analyst by training—University of Chicago. I investigate money laundering. I retired from the company the same time Russ did, after we got restationed to Budapest. We had hit a nerve in Kyiv, and they wanted us out of the way. They reduced our security clearance. They let us retire gracefully with full pensions. Except that when we complained about the Russians spreading fake news stories about Russ's running torture prisons, the company told us that we're on our own. That's when we moved to Orcas Island."

The wind and salt air made Russ look older than he was. He was fit and ruggedly handsome. The truth that he had been seeking, rather than having freed him, hung like an albatross around his neck. He raised the sail and Kim trimmed the sheets as they rounded Victim Island before heading out into the open water of the sound. Mark and Tanya sat in the stern and waited for Russ to open up. A pod of orcas came perilously close to the boat.

"The truth is rarely what you think it is," Russ said. "It was after the Maidan Revolution, and our job was to help the newly formed Ukrainian government cut the strings of Russian influence. We were working to identify the levers of power: the bribes, the blackmail, and the secret deals that Russia was using to undermine the Ukrainian democracy. Many of our leads ran back to Ivanovich. To all appearances, he was a legitimate businessman with interests in the Ukrainian energy, metals, and telecommunications sectors. He had several shadow businesses, among them arms sales, mostly in the occupied territories. After the signing of the Budapest Memorandum, Ukraine thought it had sufficient security guarantees from Russia, the United States, and the UK, and started systematically dismantling its military. Ivanovich purchased warehouses full of these weapons from corrupt generals and resold them to warlords in Asia and Africa. He then expanded his operation into mercenary armies. He would not only sell you the weapons but also provide you with a private army so you could deny you invaded your neighbor."

"Little green men," Tanya said. "Why did the CIA choose to protect him?"

"Because we're one of his customers," Russ replied. "There are over fifty armed conflicts in the world today. We have Special Forces operating all over the world. Sometimes our Navy SEALs aren't enough. That's when we contract with Ivanovich and his mercenaries."

"How does Senator Rich fit in?" Mark asked.

The wind shifted, and Russ changed tack. The boom swept across the stern as the sail went listless, and then it caught the wind. Kim trimmed the sails.

"Rich is the chair of the Senate Foreign Relations Committee, so he must have been briefed on Ivanovich's clandestine operations, at least those that were in our own security interest. The CIA labeled him an asset. At the same time, Ivanovich worked to improve his public persona. He hired top Washington law firms and PR specialists to protect his interests and burnish his image. One of his consultants is a former deputy director of the FBI. He became a philanthropist, one of the largest donors to the Clinton Foundation. He set up his own nongovernmental organizations to seemingly promote democracy. He and Rich would meet socially at Davos, the Yalta Conference, embassy parties. Once Ivanovich befriended him, he began to propose seemingly legitimate business deals. He would guarantee Russian buyers for Rich's real estate investments. Ivanovich would take his ill-gotten gains and launder them through offshore accounts. These foreign banks bankrolled Rich's investments with Russian money."

"But senators need to file financial disclosures," Mark said. "How could this get past the Senate Ethics Committee?"

"Rich Enterprises is a privately held company with Rich Sr. as the principal. The son used to manage the real estate holdings. When the son entered politics, he purportedly divested himself of any control—that is until his father dies and he inherits everything."

As they rounded Crane Island, the pod of orcas gave chase to some harbor seals. One of the seals tried to scramble onto the boat before he was snatched in midair by an orca. The splash of the killer whale on their starboard side drenched them. Tanya tightened her life vest and clung to Mark. "Will an orca ever jump onto the boat?"

"It's been known to happen," Russ said.

"But what is Ivanovich's end game?" Mark asked. "Money? Power? Or do you think he works for Russian intelligence?"

"He's above that. He's Russian mafia—*vor v zakone*. The intelligence services contract his services. There are only a few people in the Kremlin that he's beholden to, and he's doing their bidding. I tried to get him on the Magnitsky list, and that's when they revoked my security clearance."

"I guess what you're telling us is that if we expose Ivanovich's and Rich's financial dealings, the US government won't support us."

"Or worse," Russ said. "They'll try and protect their interests. Let's get back to your Dr. Kane. What I don't understand is why, if you're on the run from Ivanovich's assassins, did you choose to confront him in public?"

"Because *he* went public with his lies about me and my country, so I had to expose him publicly," Tanya said. "More importantly, I wanted to *warn* him about what he was getting himself into. He couldn't harm us with a million people watching," Tanya said.

"Warn him about what?" Russ asked.

"When I was on the *Kalinka*, I overheard Rich and Ivanovich discussing some new venture about saving souls. We learned that Dr. Kane, who is one of Rich's marquee televangelists, is promoting an upcoming app called the Last Awakening. Uriel hacked into the beta version. It's an artificial intelligence program that learns everything about you, especially your sins, and manipulates your behavior by pushing verses from the Bible. Uriel traced it to a hub in Saint Petersburg."

"Social engineering through Scripture?" Russ asked. "Well, I'll be damned. So this isn't just about having Rich in their pocket. The Russians are using Rich's media empire to infiltrate the American evangelical movement. It's twenty-five percent of our electorate. They've already tried to infiltrate the National Rifle Association. But controlling the evangelicals through the Bible? It's diabolical but ingenious. So that's why you called Kane a false prophet."

"We wanted to warn him that he's being manipulated," Tanya said. "We thought that if he knew the truth, he wouldn't sign on to their scheme."

"So you think he's just one of the Kremlin's useful idiots?" Russ asked.

"I'd bet on it," Mark said. "From what we've learned about him, he's too much of a patriot to betray his own country willingly. He's just blinded by ambition."

"I'll pass what you told me to my few remaining friends at the CIA. I can't guarantee that they'll act on it. I don't see what more the two of you can do without getting yourselves killed."

"There may be another way," his wife suggested. "Tell them about Roman."

"Who's Roman?" Tanya asked.

Russ didn't answer.

"A photographer," Kim replied. "He came to us while Russ was still station chief in Kyiv. He knew that we were investigating Ivanovich. He said he had an incredible story and a video to back it up. He asked for asylum."

"What kind of story?" Tanya asked.

"Do you know how Ivanovich earned his nickname, Sayan?" Russ asked.

"No."

"In Siberian legend, Sayan was a mythical warrior whom the ancient gods made the Lord of the Taiga. Ivanovich was given that nickname by the Russian criminal clans. He earned it when he claimed that he had single-handedly tracked down and slayed an Amur tiger that had killed his godson. The young man, Oleg Sklyarov, had asked his godfather to take him on a tiger hunt for his twenty-first birthday. The tiger is a critically endangered species, so the hunt required a special permit from the provincial governor. According to Ivanovich, his godson set out from the camp on his own one morning before the others were awake, apparently to prove his manhood. He was ambushed by the tiger, killed, and devoured. When Ivanovich awoke, he followed the bloody trail to the tiger's lair, slaughtered her cubs in front of her eyes, then shot and skinned her. He presented the head and skin to his *kum* to show that he had avenged his godson's death."

"A *kum*?" Mark asked.

"When you ask someone to be a godparent to your child, they become your *kum*," Tanya said. "It's a sacred bond."

"So what was Roman's role?" Mark asked.

"Roman was a wildlife photographer that the local governor had assigned to the party to film the hunt for a local television station. According to Roman, Ivanovich's version of events was a blatant lie. The two had been drinking until the early hours of the morning. Roman could hear them from his tent toasting to wives, mistresses, and the motherland. At daybreak, they *both* set out for the hunt. An overnight blizzard had buried their camp in a foot of snow. It was still snowing heavily in the morning with limited visibility. Ivanovich was stone sober. His godson staggered behind him. Roman followed them unnoticed and filmed them from afar with his telephoto lens to get a true-life video of the hunt. The tiger picked up the hunters' scent and circled around them. Young Sklyarov was straggling about thirty meters behind Ivanovich. The tiger crept up from behind and pounced on the boy before he could fire a shot."

"What did Ivanovich do?" Tanya asked.

"*Nothing.* When the tiger charged and mauled his godson, Ivanovich never fired his rifle. It was gruesome. You can hear young Sklyarov screaming to his godfather for help on the video."

"But why would Ivanovich want his godson dead?" Tanya asked.

"That's still a mystery," Russ said.

"Why didn't the photographer go public with the story?" Mark asked.

"He didn't know who else was in on it. He was afraid to trust his own people. Ivanovich would have killed him had he known there was a video, and Sklyarov would have killed him for not doing more to save his son, so he brought it to us instead."

The sailboat cut through the waves with no one saying a word. Finally, Tanya asked the inevitable. "Why didn't *you* act on this information?"

Russ changed tack to clear the shoal of Victim Island. "We tried, but Langley told us it was an internal Russian affair. The *kum* is now the deputy minister of the interior. We would have been accused of fabricating the information. Whom else could we have shown it to?"

"Sklyarov," Tanya said.

"We didn't have that kind of authority. It would have been a Russian mafia bloodbath."

"Do you still have the video?" Tanya asked.

"No," Russ replied. "He played it for me on his laptop but wouldn't give me a copy. When he learned that Langley wouldn't act on the information, he became paranoid and refused to share it."

"So you don't know if it's genuine?" Mark asked. "It could have been a fake."

"Perhaps," Russ replied, "but I doubt it. Once you've seen it, you can't unsee it."

"If Ivanovich killed his godson, he had to have a motive," Tanya said. "Is there any way you can look into this now?"

"I no longer have that kind of clearance," Russ replied. "I'll deny I said this, but you might want to ask your friend Uriel to see if he can dig up the dead."

An orca burst out of the waves with a seal in its jaws. As it fell back into the water, the waves rocked the boat.

Tanya was unfazed by the violence. "Where is Roman now?" she asked.

"I managed to get him asylum—on religious grounds. He became a Pentecostal."

Tanya stood up and grasped the helm. "You need to tell me where to find him. More than just our lives are at stake. Rich, Ivanovich, and Kane are leading us to Armageddon."

Russ hesitated.

"You'll find him in Cooke City, outside Yellowstone," Kim said. "He's a wildlife photographer."

"If he helps us, can you protect him?" Tanya asked.

Russ looked at her with the weight of the albatross still around his neck. "The only way any of us will be safe is if the Russians take care of Ivanovich themselves. Our own government failed us."

"Is that why you're hiding here on Orcas Island?" Mark said.

"Orcas Island is the end of my own personal journey," Russ replied. "From what I see, it's just the continuation of yours."

"During the Maidan," Tanya said, "we used to say alone we are only a drop; together we make an ocean."

"Well then, I hope you're right," Russ said.

"About what?" Tanya asked.

"That truth will overcome power."

CHAPTER 13

Cooke City

The drive over the Continental Divide left Mark exhausted. Thunderstorms had followed them through most of Idaho and the Bitterroot Range into Montana. As the clouds dispersed and the mountains gave way to prairie, Mark could see why this was called Big Sky Country. An endless blue canopy stretched from horizon to horizon. Mark had read that there were over one thousand Minuteman missiles scattered across the state. For a moment he imagined that the pristine sky was marred by the contrails of missiles rising from their silos toward Armageddon.

He looked at Tanya as she rested her head on his shoulder and banished the thought. She had kept him alert through the twists and turns of the high mountain passages as the rain turned to sleet and then to rain again. She had told him of her childhood in the orphanage, her abuse by her chess tutor, her life on the street, and her miraculous salvation through art. She sang songs that she had learned while on the Maidan, and he shared songs by Woody Guthrie and Bob Dylan. She let herself fall asleep only after they had descended into the relative safety of the high prairie.

Mark had hoped to visit the dinosaur collection at the Museum of the Rockies in Bozeman for his blog, but he decided not to wake Tanya. He would surprise her with some local color instead. He followed Highway 89 south along the Yellowstone River and veered off on Highway 540 toward Pray. Highway 540, which runs parallel to 89, was the road less traveled and passed through the historic heart of Paradise Valley. He opened his window to breathe in the fresh air and slowed down until he could hear the buzzing of insects and the chirping of birds in the tall prairie grass. He looked twice at a blur of brown in a dogwood thicket that could have been a grizzly with her cubs.

Tanya raised her head from his shoulder and stretched her arms. She looked at the beauty around her. "Where are we?" she asked.

"Paradise Valley," Mark replied. "We're taking a little detour before heading into Yellowstone and Cooke City. We're almost there."

A few miles down the road, a wooden sign with the C in the shape of a wagon wheel pointed to their destination: Chico Hot Springs Resort—2 miles.

The Chico Hot Springs Resort and Day Spa lay at the edge of the Gallatin National Forest at the foot of the Absaroka Range. Mark had first heard of the hot springs from California George, who raved about the medicinal value of soaking in its hot mineral baths. George would stop in for a rejuvenating dip every Labor Day after his annual fly-fishing excursion to Yellowstone. The original Chico Warm Springs Hotel had been built in 1900, and the historic Main Lodge was still standing. Mark was eager to soak in the hot springs and write about the experience in his Americana blog.

"We'll just stop in and soak for an hour or two," Mark said, "then see if any cabins opened up at Mammoth."

"What do people customarily wear . . . to soak?" Tanya asked.

"Bathing suits. Did Mirana pack one of hers for you in your bag?"

"No."

"I'm sure you can wear some shorts and a T-shirt. In America people wear just about anything anywhere."

The open-air mineral spring pool was filled with bathers of all ages, shapes, and sizes. Many had come in from far and wide to spend Memorial Day weekend in Paradise Valley. Tanya emerged from the women's locker room wearing a Saint Laurent Mariner tee over a pair of cutoff jean shorts. Every hot-blooded man in the pool gave her a glance.

Mark waved to her from a corner of the pool. Tanya eased into the welcoming water. Her T-shirt when wet was nothing short of revealing. Mark remembered that morning when she had emerged from the Atlantic wearing nothing but the rivulets of salt water that dripped down her body from her wet, golden hair.

"The water's really hot," she said.

"Ninety-seven degrees," Mark replied. He closed his eyes and let the healing mineral water do its work. He reflected on the past few weeks. They had traveled thousands of miles from sea to shining sea. They had seen mountains and valleys and deserts. They had seen America unfold before their eyes. They deserved this brief escape to this Last Best Place. He opened his eyes to see if Tanya was as relaxed as he was and saw that she was gone. He looked around the pool. Perhaps she had waded to the other side. She was not in any of the lounge chairs on the perimeter.

The outdoor pool was connected to an indoor bar. Mark spotted her talking to three cowboys who had cornered her against the bar. They were fully dressed, and she was in a wet T-shirt and cut-offs that barely covered her bottom. He climbed out of the pool to intervene, but after watching them for a moment realized that she had them wrapped around her little finger. They were clearly flirting, yet she knew how to keep them at bay with a playful push, a smile, or a tilt of the head. In her world, they were greenhorns. Tanya saw Mark looking at them and waved back. She told her beaus something that made them stop, scratch their heads, and tip their cowboy hats to him. She emerged from the bar carrying two cold beers.

"What was that all about?" Mark asked. "Were those cowboys bothering you?"

"They were just being friendly," Tanya said. "I wanted to surprise you with a cold beer, and they asked if they could buy me a round. I told them they could buy me two."

"Why did they tip their hats to me?"

Tanya laughed. "I told them you were a rodeo cowboy, a celebrity, and that you were here with me incognito. I said you didn't want to be recognized. They then began to guess who you were. A couple of other boys at the bar swore they knew you."

"Why a rodeo celebrity?" Mark asked with a grin.

"Because you're so . . . *American.*"

Mark looked back at the cowboys, outstretched his index finger, and clenched his fist. They raised their beers in salute.

"What did you just signal to them?" Tanya asked.

"I rated you a ten and they concurred."

Tanya and Mark eased back into the hot mineral spring and sipped their cold beers. The shocks on the El Camino had seen their day, and for the last several hundred miles the two had felt every bump in the road. The hot mineral spring washed away the aches and pains and rejuvenated them. When the skin on their fingertips began to pucker, they knew it was time to go.

Cooke City was less than one hundred miles away, and the ride would take them through one of the most beautiful national parks in the country. Tanya would see America the way she used to be, unspoiled, resplendent in her natural beauty. This was the America that Mark longed for. This was the America he wanted her to see.

They headed south toward Gardiner and stopped for bison burgers at the Corral, a roadside stand. It was still early in the season, and the traffic to the North Entrance of Yellowstone was light. They entered the park through the Roosevelt Arch. The seven-day pass that Mark purchased from the ranger was more than they needed, but he hoped to spend a few extra days after their stop in Cooke City to explore the area.

As they crossed the 45th Parallel Bridge Tanya called out, "Look!"

Mark looked up through the windshield to see a herd of mountain goats on the side of a cliff. The Boiling River gurgled beneath. Intrepid bathers were braving the confluence of waters, where the hot springs flow into the cold Gardiner River.

As they entered Mammoth Hot Springs, Tanya marveled at the terraced travertine formations that were carved out of the limestone by the hot springs. Elk grazed on the lawn of the historic Mammoth Hot Springs Hotel. The hotel had opened for the season only a few weeks before and still had vacancies. The masses of summer tourists would flood the park once school was out. Mark and Tanya rented a frontier cabin with two queen beds, a shower, sink, and toilet.

"Let's view the hot springs before it gets dark," Tanya said.

Tanya ran ahead on the boardwalk to the Minerva Terrace like a schoolgirl on a class field trip. Underground water heated by a volcanic heat source rose through fissures in the rock and cascaded down the terraces in a series of steaming waterfalls. As the hot water bubbled up through the limestone, it dissolved calcium carbonate and deposited it as a white crust on the surface of the terrace. The white waterways were carved into a backdrop of auburn hills. Thermophiles colored the pools orange, brown, and green. Mark caught up with Tanya to make sure she wouldn't stray off the boardwalk. He had heard stories of tourists ignoring the warning signs, wandering into forbidden areas, and breaking through the crust into scalding hot water.

"It's beautiful," Tanya said. "I've only seen something like this once before at Pamukkale in Turkey. I went swimming in Cleopatra's Pool."

Mark couldn't imagine anything more exotic. *Or erotic.* He imagined her bathing in the champagne water of Cleopatra's Pool. In his imagination he always associated her body with water: emerging from the sea, coming out of the shower, bathing in a hot spring.

Tanya held his hand as they traversed the cascading falls of Minerva Terrace. She pointed out the mounds and fissures sculpted by the boiling water. "It's like a living sculpture," she said.

When he looked at the surreal landscape, he saw Sodom and Gomorrah scorched by eternal fire. He yearned to succumb to temptation. His passion for her was breaking through his mores like a geyser heated by molten magma.

* * * *

Mark's passion erupted in a wet dream. As he lay in his own bed, he listened to the gentle sounds of her breathing and searched for words to convey his feelings. He was falling in love, yet he was afraid to ask her if she shared his feelings. She was single-mindedly focused on her quest, yet she had held his hand when they strolled down the yellow brick road, rode the Time Traveler, walked across the salt flats of the Badwater Basin, and listened to the water as it cascaded down Minerva Terrace. She had kissed him when they smelled rain in the creosote bush in the desert. He had shared more of himself with her than with any other woman, yet he feared that his lust would debase their relationship. He viewed her as a goddess and he as a mere mortal.

When he awoke, Tanya was singing in the shower. She came out of the bathroom fully dressed and ready to go. "You were talking in your sleep," she said.

Mark blushed not knowing which of his fantasies he might have revealed in his dream state.

"What did I say?"

Tanya put her hands across her heart. "Let me see if I can remember some of the words . . . How beautiful you are with such delights. Your navel is like a round goblet. Your breasts are like clusters of grapes, your breath like apricots."

Mark turned red as a beet. "The *Song of Solomon* . . . I was reciting the *Song of Solomon* in my sleep. It's right there in the Bible."

"Oh yes," Tanya said. "And you called me a Shulamite."

The walls of the cabin seemed to be closing in. Mark got out of bed, grabbed his clothes, and retreated to the bathroom. When he emerged, she gave him a light kiss on the lips.

"Wine in my navel? Hmm."

"I confess. You bring out the poet in me." He put his arms around her. "Once we find Roman, maybe we can take some time to explore Yellowstone at our own pace. I want us to experience Old Faithful, the Grand Canyon of the Yellowstone, and the Hayden Valley. Let's finally have some time for *ourselves*."

The drive from Mammoth Hot Springs to Cooke City took them through the Blacktail Deer Plateau to Tower Junction, then through the Lamar Valley up into the Absaroka Range to Silver Gate and Cooke City. The two-lane road was fairly empty this early in the morning except where cars congregated for wildlife sightings. Several cars jammed into an overlook of the Lamar River to view a herd of American bison. A few miles down the road, a group of wolf watchers had pulled off the road and set up their cameras to watch the pack of wolves that was following the bison. Tanya thought she spotted a grizzly with her cubs crossing Soda Butte Creek. As the road climbed toward Silver Gate, the sagebrush steppe gave way to conifer forests. Occasional breaks in the lodgepole pines offered glimpses of the Beartooth Mountains beyond.

After exiting the Northeast Entrance to the park, they stopped at the Silver Gate General Store for coffee and huckleberry ice cream. The historic mining community was now just a hamlet of log cabins that offered visitors a respite from the crowds that jammed the park during peak season. The Beartooth Highway opened in late May, and visitors were just beginning to trickle into the park from Red Lodge through Beartooth Pass, called the most beautiful drive in America.

Cooke City was a high mountain town that was a sister village to Silver Gate. Mark figured that in a town with a population of 150, someone like Roman wouldn't be hard to find. Everyone knew everyone else's business. The only question was how they would take to strangers. The Cooke City slogan "where adventure meets inspiration" seemed prescient.

They pulled over at the Stop the Car Trading Post to ask questions. Rather than get straight to the point, Tanya strolled through the gift shop examining the handcrafted jewelry, keepsakes, souvenirs, and especially the local photographs. The wildlife action photos were stunning: wolves bringing down a bison, a grizzly gorging on an elk, an eagle with a red trout circling over Yellowstone Lake.

"These are amazing," Tanya said to the shopkeeper. "Who's the photographer?"

"Local fellow," the shopkeeper replied. "Are you interested in buying one?"

"Are they signed?" Tanya asked.

The shopkeeper pulled the photograph of the wolves off the wall and examined the front and the back. "Can't say that they are."

"How do I know that they're not just stock reproductions?" Tanya asked.

"They're one of a kind," the shopkeeper replied and hung the photograph back on the wall. "If you don't believe me, you can go ask him yourself."

"Where can I find this photographer?" she asked.

"Two blocks down on Main Street, the red building, just above the bakery. So do you want this photograph or not?"

"Not just yet," Tanya replied. "First I want to track down this photographer and ask him if his photos are really one of a kind."

The El Camino was at home in Cooke City. No one gave them a second glance. The entry to the apartment above the bakery was in the back. Mark and Tanya climbed up the rickety outdoor stairs and knocked on the door. A young black-haired woman opened the door. From her looks and accent, Tanya guessed that she was Roma.

"Sorry for disturbing you," Mark said, "but we're looking for a photographer by the name of Roman."

The woman eyed them suspiciously. "Who sent you?" she asked.

"We were admiring the wildlife photographs at the Stop the Car Trading Post, and we were hoping to have them signed by the photographer. The shopkeeper sent us here."

"How did you know his name was Roman?" the woman asked.

Mark cut in. "My friend is a famous photographer in California. You may have heard of him. He goes by the alias California George. He's familiar with Roman's work and suggested that we pick up one of his pieces. He says they'll be worth a lot of money one day."

The woman took out her cell phone and made a call. No one picked up. "Damned cell service in Yellowstone."

"So he's currently in the park?" Tanya asked.

"He's obsessed with capturing a photo of an eagle with a snake in its claws. For the past several days he's camping out somewhere by the Yellowstone Falls. If you see him, tell him to call Ivona. Tell him I'm getting restless. One day he'll come home, and I won't be here waiting for him."

"We will," Tanya said. "We'll tell him you miss him."

The Yellowstone River flows northward from Yellowstone Lake and drops through the upper and lower falls into the Grand Canyon of the

Yellowstone. Mark and Tanya returned to the park through the Lamar Valley and headed south into the caldera. Tanya studied the visitor's map and decided that the best place to begin their search for Roman was at Artist Point. The overlook was on the south rim of the Grand Canyon and gave a panoramic view of the falls.

"There are dozens of trails that lead from here," Mark said. "Several are day-long hikes. How do you propose that we find him?"

"He'll probably come back here for provisions, but that could be days. There are hikers going up and down these trails every day. I suggest we ask them if they've seen anyone who looks like a professional wildlife photographer."

The afternoon passed without any leads. Toward evening, a fit couple with backpacks and walking sticks was coming into Canyon Village from the direction of Inspiration Point. They had seen a young man with camera gear and a pup tent perched just above the Yellowstone River.

"How far down the trail?" Tanya asked.

"Toward the bottom of the canyon, near the Seven Mile Hole. It's about a five-mile-long, fourteen-hundred-foot descent to the bottom of the canyon, and then you have to make your way back up. It's a full day of strenuous hiking. There's no way you can do it in the dark."

"Then we'll wait for daybreak," Tanya said to Mark. "We need to wait here in case he returns tonight. We can take turns on watch. I'll take the first watch."

Mark knew there was no point in protesting now that they were so close to finding the last piece of the puzzle. He lay down in the bed of the El Camino and covered himself with a blanket. When he awoke, it was sunrise. Tanya had decided to take the entire watch herself. He found her sitting against a gnarled dead tree near Inspiration Point. She had convinced an early morning hiker to lend her a spare canteen. She had broken a branch off the dead tree and snapped off the smaller branches so she could use the branch as a walking stick.

"Have you been up all night?" Mark asked. "It must have dropped into the forties during the night. You should have woken me."

"I couldn't sleep," she said. "I'd check Canyon Lodge every hour or so thinking he might come in."

He sat down next to her and rubbed her arms. She was shivering, and he could feel the gooseflesh on her skin. The sun was just beginning to light up the upper rim of the canyon.

"Let's go," she said. "It's light enough to see the trail." She was wearing a sweatshirt over a pair of shorts and T-shirt. Mirana's sneakers were designed to walk the sidewalks of Wynwood rather than hike down to the Seven Mile Hole, but they would have to do. He was wearing shorts, a windbreaker, and leather sneakers. He fashioned another walking stick out of the deadwood and they set off down the trail.

The trail initially took them along the rim of the canyon, through forests and active thermal zones, before descending into the canyon. Throughout much of their trek they could see the blue Yellowstone River carve its way through the yellow canyon. Here and there the yellow stone was stained with red from pockets of iron ore. The climb down was tricky, but the ascent would be grueling. Halfway down, Tanya took off her sweatshirt and wrapped it around her waist. Her T-shirt was wet with sweat.

As they neared the bottom of the canyon in the early afternoon, Tanya spotted a yellow pup tent tucked in a clearing that overlooked the river. She turned to Mark. "You need to wait here for me. If you accompany me, we might spook him. He won't fear a lone woman."

"I'm not letting you confront him alone," Mark objected. "He knows he's a marked man. There's no telling how he might react."

"I'll talk to him in his native tongue. Trust me, he's as frightened as we are. I know how to get through to him."

Mark reluctantly took a seat on a stump. He broke off a tall blade of grass and used the stem to poke at his teeth. He looked around and noticed a several-day-old pile of bear scat. Tanya disappeared over the ridge.

Tanya scampered down the trail until she reached the one-man pup tent. A duffel bag hung on a rope from a tree out of the reach of bears. She followed a path of trampled grass down toward the river. She spotted a camera on a tripod with a telephoto lens the size of a small cannon aimed at a cliff across the river. As she walked up to the camera, a voice called out from behind her.

"Don't touch that!"

She turned around to see a man in his early thirties with a week-old beard. He was dressed in hunter's camouflage that blended into the landscape. He eyed her and saw that the only potential weapon she was carrying was a makeshift walking stick.

"It's a pretty far hike from the rim to the river. Are you alone?"

"My boyfriend decided to take a break. He's somewhere behind that ridge. What are you aiming your camera at?"

"There's an eagle's nest on the other side. I'm photographing the mother as she brings food to her young."

"That's quite a camera. Are you a professional photographer?"

"It pays the rent. You can view my work in Cooke City."

A bald eagle circled in the updrafts from the canyon, eyeing the shadows in the rapids. The photographer began snapping. It dove down from above, swooped a trout in its talons, and flew it up to its nest.

"Here, take a look," he said.

The eagle dropped the still flapping fish into its nest of hungry young.

"It's a majestic bird," Tanya said.

"The messenger of the gods," the photographer replied.

"Does it ever feed snakes to its young?" Tanya asked.

Roman took a step back. "Who are you?"

"My name is Tanya Bereza. I'm a sculptress."

"Are you here to kill me?"

Tanya switched from English to Russian. "I'm on the run, just like you. We share a common enemy."

"How on earth did you find me?" Roman asked.

"Russ and Kim. They said they helped you get asylum."

Roman scanned the ridge for any sign of her companion. "What do you want from me?"

"I need your help to put an end to the running. We need to destroy Ivanovich before he destroys us."

"What makes you think he'll come after me?"

"I saw his assassin murder Turchin with my own eyes."

The disarming innocence in Tanya's eyes was gone.

"You led him to him?"

"I . . ."

Roman looked at her as if she'd signed his death warrant. "What makes you think you can do something that the CIA couldn't?"

"Because we're not beholden to anyone," Tanya said. "I know you went to them with evidence, and they buried it."

"So why dig it up now?"

"Because I want to show it to the one person who can exact revenge."

"Sklyarov," Roman said beneath his breath as if afraid to utter the name. Roman walked over to his camera and looked through the viewfinder. "Look," he said. The NIKKOR telephoto lens revealed the eagle ripping apart the fish with her beak and talons. "See how she grips her prey. She uses her talons to kill."

"And we'll use our wits," Tanya said. "Why didn't you go to Sklyarov first?"

Roman smirked. "What do you know of Sklyarov?" he asked.

"I know he's now the deputy minister of the interior."

"He's a cold-blooded killer," Roman said. "He was a colonel during the Second Chechnya War. His nom de guerre was Beria. If a family refused to give up a partisan, he would have the whole family killed—women, children, grandparents, and even distant cousins. His atrocities were too numerous to count. He would be tried as a war criminal if he weren't under the protection of the Kremlin."

"He'll see from your video that it was Ivanovich who murdered his son."

"Once he sees the video, his rage will know no bounds. He'll think we were in on the cover-up. It will be the death of us all."

"It could also be our salvation. I'm running for my life. You're hiding in the wilderness. There's only one way to end this. *You* be the eagle that subdues the serpent."

A sulfurous steam hissed out of a fumarole on the opposite bank of the river followed by a several-second tremor. Rocks careened down the cliff face into the depths of the canyon. Tanya held on to Roman for support.

"It happens at least once a day," he said. "Did you know we're standing on top of a super volcano? The magma below us is stirring. Some say it will erupt in our lifetimes. Others say it will be in a thousand years. If it erupts, this whole caldera will spew magma and hot gasses and spread ash over a thousand miles."

"An apocalypse," Tanya said.

Roman watched through his lens until the eagle took off to hunt more prey for its young.

"You won't say how you got the video or where you found me?"

"On my life."

Roman capped the lens of the camera and collapsed the tripod. He crawled into his tent, brought out his backpack, and secured the camera to his pack with bungee cords. "We'd better start our climb back up if we want to make it back to the rim before nightfall."

Tanya found Mark where she had left him. "Meet Roman," she said. Mark offered his hand, but Roman only nodded.

"Make sure you keep up," Roman said. "It gets more dangerous as it gets darker."

The climb up the canyon took twice as long as the climb down. Roman led the way with Tanya in the middle and Mark in the rear. Mark and Tanya had drunk all of their water before reaching the bottom and had to rely on the sips of Yellowstone River water that Roman would offer from his canteen. The afternoon sun began to scorch. Even in May the rays refracted off the cliffs and burned exposed skin. Mark began to see faces in the cliffs: crags became wrinkles and the hollows became eyes. His heart was pounding in his chest. As they climbed, Mark kept his eyes trained on Tanya's fit legs and buttocks and didn't ask to stop or rest. They reached the rim an hour after sunset. The last hour had been a flat walk along the rim, and they were able to navigate the trail by moonlight.

They walked into the Canyon Lodge and plopped down exhausted onto a sofa in the lobby. Mark went to the bar and brought back a tray with three glasses of ice water and some pretzels. He ripped open the bag for all to share. When Roman went to the bathroom, Mark said: "He doesn't talk much, does he?"

"Give him some space," Tanya said. "He's ambivalent about his decision to help us. It's like his elusive photo of the eagle with the snake in its talons—it's an inner struggle between wisdom and passion, morality and vengeance."

When Roman returned from the bathroom, he seemed resigned to his fate. He had the look of a martyr who wasn't entirely convinced that there is an afterlife.

"Where are you staying?" Roman asked.

"Mammoth Hot Springs Hotel," Tanya replied. "Cabin number 83."

"I'll meet you there in the morning," Roman said. He grabbed his backpack and went out into the dark.

* * * *

That night Mark and Tanya still slept in their separate beds at their cabin at Mammoth. There was no way to know if Roman would show up in the morning or if he would bolt. They may have led him to his doom like they did with Turchin. If the assassin had tracked them, he would most likely dispatch Roman first and then come after them.

Tanya tossed and turned and cried out in her sleep as if she were being chased by a shape-shifting boogeyman. At one point he shook her to wake her out of her nightmare. The cabin was cold, but she was hot and sweating. She muttered some words in Ukrainian, then turned and covered her head with the blanket.

He slept in spurts. He couldn't tell if he dozed for minutes or hours. He was afraid to close his eyes and let the boogeyman crawl out of his subconscious like a horrific mole.

Dawn couldn't come fast enough. Mark got out of bed at first light, washed his face in the sink, and walked over to the main building to bring back some coffee. There was no sign of Roman. The night chill was still in the air. The only other early risers in the Mammoth Hotel lobby were hikers and backpackers. One of them was filling up his thermos with black coffee.

"Where are you headed?" Mark asked as he waited behind him.

"My friends and I are hiking to Undine Falls. You?"

"We did Seven Mile Hole yesterday. If we do go out again, we'd be looking for something easier, just for the day. Any recommendations?"

"Try Slough Creek," the hiker replied. "Loads of wildflowers in the creek meadows. Spring came early this year. The ranger said we might even get into the low sixties by midafternoon. You'll see mule deer and bison. Keep an eye out, though—it's prime wolf territory. You might also run across a grizzly, so I'd recommend you carry your bear spray and some bells."

"Where can I find some?"

The hiker finished filling his thermos and looked at Mark's shoes. "You're new to the trails?" he asked.

"I've done a lot of traveling, but I'm not a seasoned hiker," Mark confessed.

"You can rent or buy some bear spray at Canyon Village. But hey, I'm near the end of my stay. You can have mine. My fellow hikers will still have theirs. Let me show you how to use it."

The hiker pulled a can of spray out of his belt holster and demonstrated the technique. "If a bear charges you, don't run. Stand your ground and spray from forty feet away." He reached into his backpack and pulled out some bells. "Tie these around your shoe laces when you're on the trail. You don't want to surprise a bear, and this way he'll know you're coming. Look out for fresh tracks and grizzly bear scat."

"How do I recognize grizzly bear scat?" Mark asked.

"It's the one with the bells in it."

Both men broke out laughing. "Just pulling your leg," the hiker said. "Have a great hike. If you don't use the spray, give it to somebody else."

Mark returned to the cabin with two cups of coffee, a pair of bells, and a holster armed with bear spray. Roman was sitting on the bed talking with Tanya. She was in her nightshirt. Her bare legs dangled over the side of the bed. She was clutching something in her fist.

"I'm surprised you came," Mark said.

Roman got up off the bed. "I'm tired of hiding. I put my life, and *yours*, in the hands of your avenging angel." He brushed past Mark on his way out the door.

Mark looked at Tanya. She was smiling from ear to ear. She opened her clenched fist to reveal a flash drive. "I got it," she said. "Roman came through."

Mark thought of saying it could be a ruse but he decided not to. There was more than hope in her eyes—there was joy.

"Even if it shows what Russ said it shows, we still don't have a motive," Mark said. "I think we should call Uriel."

Tanya dressed in front of him without answering. The hot coffee took away the chill. As they walked from the cabin to the main building, he could no longer see his breath in the air. Elk were grazing on the lawn. The sunrise hikers had hit the trails, and tourists were just making their way to the Mammoth Hotel dining room for breakfast. Mark dialed the Death Valley number and loaded the phone with quarters.

"Death Valley Serpentarium."

"I'm on a mission from God."

"I'm listening."

"We found Russ Boyko and his wife on Orcas Island. He gave us a lead on a photographer who accompanied Ivanovich on a tiger hunt, where his godson, Oleg Sklyarov, was killed. The photographer claims that Ivanovich planned his godson's death. He gave us a video that apparently proves it."

"Have you viewed the video?" Uriel asked.

"Not yet. We don't have access to a computer."

"It could be fake," Uriel said. "You'd be surprised what you can do with deepfake technology today. I could make it look like *you* killed him."

"That's why we need a motive. I was hoping you could help."

"His godson, you say?"

"Oleg Sklyarov."

"Give me a couple of days. I'll see what I can find out."

"Please deposit another three dollars and seventy-five cents," said the operator. Mark hung up the pay phone. "Uriel says he's on it."

Tanya let out a big sigh of relief. "We're going to help Roman's eagle catch its snake."

Mark liked the sound of the *we*.

Tanya put her arms around him and gave him a lingering kiss on the lips. "Thank you. Thank you for saving me. Now tell me what you're planning to do with those bells."

* * * *

Spring had awoken the Lamar Valley. The bison had finished calving, and the newborns were grazing on the tender prairie grasses surrounded by a circle of females. Mark and Tanya had heeded the hiker's advice and set out on the Slough Creek Trail. The trail was an old wagon road that followed a stream valley into a series of meadows. Pockets of snow still clung to the crevices. The towering peaks of Sugarloaf and Cutoff Mountains provided the backdrop to the lush meadows and spruce forests. The Memorial Day tourists had gone home, and Mark and Tanya had the trail to themselves.

They reached the first meadow in the early afternoon. A rocky outcrop on the other side of the creek promised spectacular views of the meadows.

"Let's wade to the other side," Tanya said. "We'll be able to see the whole valley from there."

"Are you sure?" Mark asked. "It could be dangerous."

"Are you afraid?"

"No!"

"Good. Then swallow the chaos," she said. "We may never have this chance again."

"We'll need to find a shallow place to cross," Mark said. The water in the fast-moving creek was roiling and churning from the snowmelt. "Take off your shoes and hold my hand."

The banks were muddy and their feet sunk to their ankles. A crook in the creek seemed like the best place to cross. The stones on the creek bed were slippery, and the creek was deeper and faster than it looked. The water swirled above their knees. Tanya teetered, feigned a slip, and pulled Mark into the creek alongside her. The current swept them for several yards before they found their footing. They emerged soaking wet.

"The water's freezing!" Mark exclaimed.

Tanya was laughing.

"What's so funny?" he asked.

"In my country there's a legend about water nymphs. We call them *rusalky*. They lure young men into the water with their beauty and drown them."

"We need to dry out these clothes." He helped her climb the grassy bank on the other side of the creek and scale the rocky outcrop. He stripped down to his shorts and laid his wet clothes and holster against a boulder to dry. The rock was warm from the afternoon sun.

Tanya watched his modesty with amusement. When he was finished undressing, she removed her wet blouse. She undid her bra and wiggled out of her wet shorts and panties.

He watched as she unfolded her clothes and laid them next to his on the boulder. His reaction was rock hard.

She stood over him and said: "I thought you didn't find me attractive."

"You're the most beautiful woman I've ever seen."

"Then why have you treated me like a sister for these past several weeks?"

Mark struggled to answer. "I . . . because of what happened . . . I thought you needed your distance. I wanted to respect you."

"Is it because you think of me as a harlot?"

Mark knelt up and took both her hands. "I think of you as a goddess, an angel."

"A rusalka?"

"You're not luring me to my death. I freely chose to follow you. I would follow you to the ends of the earth."

She looked like she did the morning he had first laid eyes on her. Rivulets of water ran down the curves of her body from her wet blonde hair. But her eyes, rather than wild, were serene, as if she had forgotten the past and cared only for the present. She lowered him to the soft spring grass. She knelt astride him and gave him an inviting open-mouth kiss . . .

Mark tensed, unsure if he could please her.

Tanya smiled. "Love me as if I were your first."

They lay in this place that time forgot like Adam and Eve before the fall. They were unashamed of their nakedness. Tanya caressed him in ways he had never been caressed before. He waited to enter her. He reveled in every curve and valley of her body. Her nipples were like grapes, her lips like apricots, and her navel tasted of wine. She was the goddess of love, and he a mere mortal, but he wanted her to be of this earth, of this place. He wanted her to love him like she'd loved no man before. When she was near ecstasy he entered her and plunged into paradise. Their union was like this place, beautiful, savage, and natural. They came together with the force of a geyser then lay still and caressed, waiting for the geyser to erupt again.

As they lay in the grass under the open sky, he said, "I would have tasted it with you."

"What?" she asked as she turned and lay on top of him.

"The forbidden fruit from the tree of knowledge of good and evil. If you offered me a bite, I would not have refused you."

"Hmmm," she purred. "You would have given up the Garden of Eden for me?"

"Body and soul."

"This world that we're condemned to live in can be a beautiful place," she said. "There's death and suffering, but there's also love, beauty, and art."

"I've wanted to ask you, what's the significance of the trident on your shoulder. You drew it in the mine. Is it a symbol of Poseidon?"

"It's a *tryzub*. It's the symbol of my country."

The sun that had illuminated their union was now low in the sky.

"Our clothes should be dry enough to wear," Mark said. "We'd better start heading back."

As they dressed, Tanya spotted a herd of mule deer in the marshland, grazing on the spring grasses. Suddenly they picked up their heads and turned up their ears. In seconds they scattered and bounded across the creek. She looked to see what had frightened them. A lean grizzly emerged from a thicket below them. It gave chase at incredible speed but stopped after fifty yards. It stood up on its hind legs to its seven-foot height and sniffed. The wind was blowing from behind them.

Mark and Tanya crouched to avoid being seen. "I think it's caught our scent," Mark said. "We need to back away slowly." The top of the rocky outcrop was covered with a thicket of conifers. As they ducked into the thicket, the bear bounded toward them. Mark figured it would take the bear at least thirty seconds to cover the distance between them and climb the outcrop to their location. He reached into his holster and pulled out the can of bear spray. He undid the safety clip. "We'll escape down the other side," he said. "Watch our backs."

As they dodged through the pine branches, the bells in Mark's laces tinkled. He stooped down and ripped them off his shoes. The backside of the outcrop was steeper than the way they had ascended. They listened for huffing, growling, or breaking branches behind them but heard nothing.

"Maybe it stopped," Tanya said.

"Or maybe it's stalking us. If it charges us, whatever you do, don't run."

They sidestepped down the back of the outcrop, trying to avoid loose stones that might reveal their location. Ten feet of marsh separated them from the creek.

"I don't see or hear it," Tanya said.

They slogged through the boggy ground to the bank of the creek— still no signs of the predator. They eased knee-deep into the swirling water.

Suddenly Tanya screamed. The grizzly rose out of grass behind them. Its ears were erect and forward. It lurched toward the creek with its head down.

Mark aimed at the charging bear and discharged the spray toward its head in a several-second burst. The bear kept charging. When it entered the creek, he sprayed again, hitting it in the eyes. The blinded bear rose and flailed. It dove its head into the water.

"Run!" Mark yelled.

They crossed the creek as fast as the slippery stones and rushing water would allow. The bear was diving, roaring, and diving again. They climbed up the bank and slogged through the mud until they could run on firmer ground. Mark looked behind them every few seconds to see if the bear was giving chase. They ran into a hiker who was returning from the second meadow.

"Head back to the trailhead," Mark warned. "A grizzly attacked us about a quarter mile back. I hit it with some spray, but it dove into the creek and may have washed it off."

"You're lucky to be alive," the hiker said. "When we get back, make sure you report the attack to one of the rangers."

They parted with the hiker at the trailhead and trekked back to Mammoth Springs. Tanya was still hyperventilating.

"Try and take slow, deep breaths," Mark said. "The danger's over."

"For now," she said. "For now."

* * * *

That evening Tanya crawled into Mark's bed, put her arms around him, and refused to let go. He felt the rhythm of her heart as it slowed into a steady, even beat. He felt her breaths as she nuzzled closer. Tonight, for her, he would make this bed the safest place in the world—no bears, no boogeymen, no oligarchs or senators.

As she slept he planned how best to dispel their demons. His classroom knowledge and skills in investigative reporting would be put to the test. He would delve into Turchin's files, cross-check his facts, and publish an exposé that would be picked up by every newspaper, radio, and television station in the land. The news would go viral, and an army of reporters would descend on Rich and Ivanovich before they would have time to react. He would also send it to the attorney general in Nashville together with the link to Turchin's hidden files.

Tanya woke him with a gentle kiss on the lips. The panes on the windows lightened from black to gray. Birds were chirping with the first light. He tried to rise, but Tanya pulled him back.

"Just a little longer," she said. "I feel so safe here."

He hugged her tighter and refrained from running his hand over her bare body. For now she just wanted to be held. He knew her well enough to know when she wanted to make love.

"We'll have a big American breakfast at the hotel dining room: eggs, bacon, hash brown potatoes, a stack of pancakes, and your choice of toast."

"Rye," she said.

"Today let's see Old Faithful and the Norris Geyser Basin," he suggested. "Tomorrow we can see Yellowstone Lake. I think we've done our share of backcountry hiking. Let's just be ordinary tourists and see the sights from the safety of our car."

"I still want to hike," she said. "We need to confront our fears, not hide from them."

"Well, if we survived an American grizzly attack, we can survive a Russian bear."

The tall ceilings and windows of the dining room offered views of the surrounding hills and the elk grazing on the manicured lawns. Tanya took her eggs sunny-side up, and he asked for his over easy. He poured huckleberry syrup over their stacks of pancakes until it ran down the sides and onto their bacon and hash browns. The coffee tasted especially rich that morning. A couple sitting next to them had finished eating and left a copy of the *Bozeman Daily Chronicle* on the table. Without his phone and computer, Mark had lost touch with the news. He grabbed the paper and perused the headlines.

A headline on page three caught his attention: "Alt-Left and Alt-Right Set to Clash at Jefferson Davis Monument." The article detailed how liberals were demanding to demolish the monument to Jefferson Davis, the president of the Confederacy, which serves as a memorial of his birthplace at a Kentucky State Park. Threats and counterthreats were circulating on the airwaves and on social media. The governor had ordered the national guard to protect the monument in case of a riot. The confrontation was set for June 3, Jefferson Davis's birthday.

"You look concerned," Tanya said.

"I'm worried about Dana. She's into all this radical Confederate nonsense. The paper says that antifa is threatening to tear down the Jefferson Davis Monument on June 3. The press is predicting a bloodbath. I just want to be sure that Dana isn't somehow involved."

"Then call her," Tanya said.

After breakfast they changed a few dollar bills to again use the pay phone. Dana picked up after two rings.

"Dana, it's me, Mark. I'm just calling to see how you are."

"Never better," Dana said. "Where are you? I've been trying to reach you for weeks, and you never get back to me."

"I'm sorry," Mark said. "I've been traveling for my Americana blog, and I lost my phone. I'm calling from a public phone."

Mark heard someone whisper to Dana in the background. "From where?"

"Who's talking to you?" Mark asked.

"My friend, Robert E. Lee."

The chill in Mark's blood was colder than Slough Creek.

"Where are you?"

"Fairview, Kentucky. Some liberal assholes want to tear down the Jefferson Davis Monument. We're not going to let them."

"Let me speak to your friend . . . Robert E. Lee."

Dana handed him the phone.

"Mark Rider," Robert E. Lee said in a Carolina drawl. "Dana's been worried to death about you. She thought you ran off with some Ukrainian nymph and forgot about her."

"If you so much as . . ."

"I feel like I'm a friend of the family. She's told me all about her aunt and uncle and cousins in Baraboo. You live in Chicago, right? In the Ukrainian neighborhood."

Mark knew the voice all too well. He had heard it in Wynwood, in Williamstown, and in Nashville. Even with its local accents, it was still the same taunting tone.

"What do you want?"

"To meet you. I'll keep Dana under my protection. How is our nymph, or what did the good reverend call her, the whore of Babylon? Is she there with you?"

Mark didn't answer.

"I know you're a fan of Americana," Robert E. Lee said. "There's nothing more American than defending our Confederate heroes. Blood and soil! Come down to Fairview and bring your lady friend. You'll be front and center at the rally, right next to Dana. We're expecting you. Be here in the next three days or you'll miss all of the action." Robert E. Lee hung up the phone.

The color had gone out of Mark's face.

"What is it?" Tanya asked.

"He's got Dana. I need to get to Fairview, Kentucky."

"What does he want?" Tanya asked.

"He wants you."

CHAPTER 14

Fairview

Reverend Kane flew into Tennessee's Portland Municipal Airport
at 7:00 a.m. on Rich Sr.'s Gulfstream. Kane had received a call
from Rich at the ungodly hour of 3:00 a.m. that had awoken
him in his suite at the Trump International Hotel in Washington, DC.
Kane had spent the past several days working the Hill in support of his
upcoming March for Family Values that was scheduled for Independence
Day. Several of the legislators whom he approached had tried to excuse
themselves to spend time with their families on the nation's holiday.
Kane reminded them, in no uncertain terms, that the Lord and the
voters would know who supported family values and who didn't. Kane
suspected that Rich Sr. had been drinking when he made the call. He
had not asked Kane to come—he had summoned him.

A limo with tinted windows had driven him to Dulles, where Rich's
plane had been fueled and waiting. Dawn was just breaking over the
Highland Rim as they landed on the mile-long runway. Rich's limo
drove up to the tarmac and whisked Kane through the tobacco fields to

Rich's equestrian estate. The buzzing of insects, croaking of frogs, and neighing of horses calmed the soul. Kane stepped out of the limo into a pile of horse manure and then scraped it off the bottom of his shoe onto the bumper of the limo. The morning dew soaked his suede shoes. The chauffeur escorted him to the main building and knocked on the door. The butler let him in, inspected the sorry state of Kane's shoes, and offered him some slippers.

"Mr. Rich is in the breakfast room. He will see you now."

Rich had begun his breakfast without waiting for Kane. His near empty plate was smeared with the remnants of egg yolks and grits. He was chomping on a slice of applewood-smoked bacon.

"Sit down, Mathias," he commanded Kane. He snapped at his servant, "Julie, bring the reverend some breakfast and get me another cup of coffee."

Kane pretended to be unfazed by the rudeness. He said grace before biting into his first biscuit. He waited for his coffee, added cream and sugar with aplomb, and only then responded to his host.

"What's this all about?" he asked Rich.

Rich signaled to a servant to bring over the iPad and play the YouTube video for his guest. The video showed a beautiful blonde confronting Kane at the New Beginnings Megachurch in Las Vegas. "I am the second angel," she said. "I've come to warn you. Babylon has not fallen because you are complicit in her sin. You are the false prophet. Your app is not meant to save, it's meant to deceive. You are the one who needs to come out of Babylon."

"As you well know," Rich said, "this clip has gone viral—over three million views. At first it boosted your ratings, but now they've fallen off by twenty percent. Your rival televangelists are claiming that this woman *is* the second angel and that God had sent her to expose you. They quote Matthew: 'And many false prophets shall rise, and shall deceive many.' The March for Family Values is one month away. The innermost members of the Family are concerned. They're thinking you may not be our man. Several of your rivals have volunteered to lead in your stead."

Kane started to speak and nearly choked on his biscuit. "I've been set up," he said, "by none other than your own son."

Rich motioned for the servants to leave the room. "Explain," he said.

"Your son and a business partner of his, a Russian by the name of Victor Ivanovich, met me at the Oak Bar in Nashville several weeks ago. I had no idea this Russian was coming to the meeting. He tried to convince me to join forces with the Russian Orthodox Church. He said that only by working together could we Christians defeat the wickedness in the world."

"You say this Ivanovich is my son's *business* partner. How do you know?"

"I'm only guessing. They were both trying to convince me to expand my televangelism into international markets, especially the Russian-speaking market."

"It's not your business to expand," Rich said. "If you check the fine points of your contract, you'll see that I own you."

Kane loosened his collar. "I thought that your son was speaking for you. I couldn't imagine he hadn't consulted you."

"He came to me with some harebrained proposal a few weeks ago. I forbade it. I told him his fucking Russians could go to hell." Rich stood up and walked over to the window. His prize stallion had come home to stud. Despite winning the Belmont Stakes two years ago, the stallion had not sired any potential winners. He had considered bringing in mares from different corners of the globe but decided to stay American. "Tell me about this woman," he asked Kane.

"She's some Ukrainian sculptress that Ivanovich brought over to America to display one of her pieces. He said they had a falling out, and she started spreading lies about him. He asked me to shame her, so I called her the whore of Babylon in one of my sermons. She must have heard it, and she sought me out."

"She accused your new app of *deceiving* rather than saving. What did she mean by that? We own your intellectual property. That makes it my app and my liability."

"Your son and Ivanovich proposed it. It's a killer app. It uses artificial intelligence to push Bible verses in real time depending on who you are, where you're at, and what you're doing. We're anticipating a million downloads in the first week. It's free, but it's constantly soliciting donations."

"When's it set for release?"

"We're planning to coincide the release date with the March for Family Values. That way we'll get the most press coverage."

"Independence Day," Rich said. "Send me your current beta version of the software. I'll have my friends at the NSA check it out. And this woman . . ."

"The whore of Babylon?"

"The whore of Babylon or the second angel, it doesn't matter. You need to get her to publicly recant her accusation. Cast out her demons, or whatever it is that you do."

"I understand. There's one more thing," Kane said.

Rich looked at him with disdain.

"Ivanovich asked me to invite one of their Orthodox monks to our March for Family Values as a sign of solidarity. We've already decided to make the march interdenominational. I can disinvite him at a moment's notice. Just say the word."

Rich walked over to Kane and put his hands on the reverend's shoulders. "Keep your friends close and your enemies closer. Invite this monk. Bring him to Washington. Tell him you'll extend a follow-up invitation for the National Prayer Breakfast. We need to figure out what these Russians really want. Once he's on American soil, I'll have the FBI over him like flies on shit."

"What about your son?"

"My daddy and granddaddy would turn over in their graves if they thought we were conspiring with the Russians. If he betrays the Family, then he's no son of mine."

* * * *

The El Camino sped east along the Buffalo Bill Cody Scenic Byway toward Cody. Their route to the Jefferson Davis Monument State Park in Fairview, Kentucky, would first take them through Wyoming and into the Black Hills of South Dakota, past Mount Rushmore and the

Crazy Horse Memorial. The full drive to Fairview would take twenty-two hours, and they needed to devise a plan. By capturing Dana, Dmitri had turned the game in his favor.

"We can't rush into this," Tanya said. "We need to control the clock. I wonder what Turchin would have done?"

"I think we should call Mary Lou Jackson," Mark said. "She said she could help us."

"She doesn't have jurisdiction in Kentucky," Tanya said. "Even if she did, she's after Senator Rich. Ivanovich is the one holding your cousin."

"Then let's call the Kentucky state police."

"And tell them what? That you suspect your cousin's Nazi boyfriend is a Russian mafia hit man?"

Tanya pondered every move and countermove as they sped toward the Black Hills. None of the tactics was without risk. She kept returning to Turchin's game with Mechnikoff. She played every permutation a hundred times in her head. There was no way to win. The most she could hope for was a draw.

Mark had wanted to drive straight through to Fairview, but Tanya insisted that they needed to control the pace. Ivanovich had moved his piece. It was now their move, and Dana's life depended on it. Billboards for Mount Rushmore were counting down the miles to the national memorial.

"We need to step back and think creatively," Tanya said. "Perhaps your past presidents can inspire us."

Mount Rushmore was iconic Americana, and Mark could hardly disagree.

The majestic figures of George Washington, Thomas Jefferson, Theodore Roosevelt, and Abraham Lincoln, carved into the granite face of Mount Rushmore, faced southeast over the land stolen from the Lakota. The Treaty of Fort Laramie had granted the Black Hills to the Lakota in perpetuity, but once the white men discovered gold, the land was seized from them in the Great Sioux War of 1876. Over two million visitors walked the Avenue of Flags each year to view the faces of the presidents. Ponderosa pines flanked the stone pillars that displayed the flags of each state, one district, three territories, and two commonwealths. Tanya stopped to look at the flags of the states they had traveled through.

"Why are you taking such an interest in the state flags?" Mark asked.

"I'm looking at what inspired the artists who created them. The flags are as different as the lands we've traveled through."

"They each have their own story," Mark said.

"What's this one?"

"New Mexico. It's the sacred sun sign of the Zia tribe, a Native American Pueblo community from the Four Corners region. The Zia sun sign represents the four cardinal directions, the four seasons of the year, and the four phases of life. It's one of the most admired flags in our country."

"Fascinating. Why did they sacrifice their individuality to form a union?"

"That's the great thing about the United States: they didn't have to. Our states evolved from colonies that were very different from each other. The framers of the Constitution envisioned that state governments, and not the national government, are the main units of government for citizens on a day-to-day basis. We're all Americans, but we're also proud Floridians, Texans, and New Mexicans."

The Avenue of Flags led to the Grand View Terrace, which offered unobstructed views of Mount Rushmore. Tanya approached one of the rangers and asked, "Why did the sculptor choose these four presidents?"

"What state are you from?" the ranger asked with a welcoming smile.

"I'm visiting," she said, "from Ukraine."

"We get visitors here from all over the world. I can't say we've had many from Ukraine."

"The four presidents?" Tanya asked again.

"The sculptures were carved under the direction of Gutzon Borglum and his son Lincoln and completed in 1941," the ranger explained. "They tell the story of the birth, growth, development, and preservation of the United States. George Washington, understandably, holds the most prominent place. He was our first president and the father of our nation. Thomas Jefferson was the primary author of the Declaration of Independence that inspires democracies around the world. He purchased the Louisiana Territory that doubled the size of our country. So Borglum chose him to represent growth. Theodore Roosevelt presided over the rapid economic growth of our country in the early twentieth century. He was instrumental in the construction of the Panama Canal that linked east and west. He broke up large corporate monopolies and worked to ensure the rights of the workingman. Borglum chose him to represent development. And Abraham Lincoln, that's a pretty obvious choice as well. He preserved the Union and abolished slavery. Borglum chose him to represent preservation."

"Can you tell me more about the sculptor?" Tanya asked.

"Gutzon Borglum was an interesting fellow," the ranger said. "He was born in Idaho in 1867 to an immigrant family from Denmark. He took to art early, studied in Europe, and had one of his sculptures acquired by New York's Metropolitan Museum of Art. In 1915 he signed on with the United Daughters of the Confederacy to carve a memorial on Stone Mountain in Georgia to the heroes of the Confederacy—Jefferson Davis, Robert E. Lee, and Stonewall Jackson. For a while he even aligned himself with the Klan. He was fired from the memorial project and chased out of the state. He was nearly sixty when he took on Mount Rushmore. He died in 1941, and his son Lincoln finished it a year later."

Tanya was still wearing her ghost beads. "And what of the Native Americans who once lived here."

"The ghost dancers? If you take the Presidential Trail to the left," the ranger pointed, "you'll come to the Lakota, Nakota, and Dakota Heritage Village, where you can explore the history of the American Indian tribes who once lived here. You can see teepees and all sorts of memorabilia."

"I have a better idea," Mark said. "We still have an hour or two of daylight. Let's go see Crazy Horse."

They took a right turn out of the national park, headed west on 244, and turned south on US 16 toward Custer. The largest sculpture in the world loomed in the distance. The face of Crazy Horse seated on an unfinished horse was carved out of the top of Thunderhead Mountain. His hand was outstretched over the horse's head, pointing to his ancestral lands. Even from this distance, the enormity of the project was astonishing.

Dusk was creeping into the Black Hills. Mark pulled the El Camino to the side of the road and stepped out with Tanya to view the mountain monument.

"It's breathtaking," Tanya said.

"Legend says that when a cavalry officer asked Chief Crazy Horse where his lands were now, Crazy Horse replied, 'My lands are where my dead lie buried.' His hand points over the sacred lands of the Lakota."

"Then it belongs here," Tanya said. "I know it's late, but let's drive in for a closer look. I want to learn more about the sculptor."

More cars were exiting the Crazy Horse Mountain Memorial than coming in. The complex included a welcome center, Indian museum, cultural center, and the sculptor's home and workshop. A viewing veranda next to the Laughing Water Restaurant offered the best views at this late hour.

"Getting a good spot for the laser show?" a young attendant asked Tanya. "It should be starting in about thirty minutes." The girl looked to be about eighteen. The name on her badge read Winona.

"We need to get to Custer to find a room for the night," Mark replied. "We can only stay for a little while. Winona—that's a beautiful name. I see from your badge that you work here."

"I'm a sophomore at Black Hills State. I'm working here for the summer. It's my first week."

"Can you tell us a little bit about the monument?"

The girl beamed. "I can tell you *a lot*. I'm part Lakota Sioux, part German, and part Irish. My uncle and cousins work on the mountain."

"Who came up with idea?" Tanya asked. "We were just at Mount Rushmore. This project seems to be the antithesis."

"About sixty years ago," Winona said, "Chief Henry Standing Bear was looking for someone to carve Crazy Horse. You know that Crazy Horse beat Custer at Little Bighorn. He was one of the last Sioux who never signed a treaty, never left the Plains, never learned English, and never lived on a reservation."

"Who was the sculptor?" Tanya asked.

"Korczak Ziolowski. He was born in Boston to Polish immigrants and came here in 1939 to work on Mount Rushmore. He got into an argument with Borglum's son and quit after just a few weeks. One of his sculptures had won an award at the World's Fair in New York so Chief Henry Standing Bear invited him to work on the Crazy Horse Monument. He died in 1982, but his family continued the project."

"It's an enormous undertaking," Tanya said. "I know, I'm a sculptress."

"Perhaps you might want to join the project," Winona said.

"It's noble, but I have battles to win in my own country."

The setting sun imbued the majestic figure of Crazy Horse in shades of auburn, yellow, and red.

"'A very great vision is needed, and the man who has it must follow it as the eagle seeks the deepest blue of the sky,'" Winona said.

"Whom are you quoting?" Tanya asked.

"Crazy Horse."

* * * *

They left Custer for the Badlands at daybreak.

"Did our presidents and Crazy Horse inspire you?" Mark asked.

"Each in their own way."

"What did you learn?"

"I learned that we need to put our faith in ourselves."

The first stop on their eighteen-hour drive across the Great Plains was to Wall, South Dakota, to get some ice water for themselves and a flash drive to copy Roman's video. Wall Drug Store was a cornucopia of Americana kitsch: collectible brass ornaments from all fifty states, wall-mounted jackalopes, Black Hills honey, fool's gold, and assorted sundries. They bought a sixteen-gigabyte flash drive and an Indian necklace of a turquoise pendant looped through a leather cord. Tanya replaced the pendant with Roman's flash drive and hung it around her neck. She stuck the duplicate drive in her pocket.

"I need to access a computer," she said to the woman behind the counter. "Do you mind if I use yours?"

"There's a public computer at the Wall Community Library just a few blocks away," the saleswoman replied.

The small stone building looked more like a frontier trading post than a library. The one public room had the welcoming comfort of ink-smudged oaken tables surrounded by racks of worn, hardcover books. A single computer sat on the oaken table ready to take the user on a magic carpet ride to the far corners of the earth. Tanya plugged in the flash drives. Roman's drive had a single MP4 file. She opened it with Video Player and turned up the volume.

The five-minute video was shot with the eye of a wildlife photographer whose skill lies in capturing nature's life-and-death struggles without being seen. Young Sklyarov staggered in the knee-deep snow, apparently drunk. The camera panned to Ivanovich who was leading thirty yards ahead. Snow devils danced in the wind. Ivanovich turned, knelt, and looked through the scope of his rifle.

Tanya turned up the volume on the video.

The wind howled. The camera panned back to Sklyarov. Just as it came into focus, the crouching tiger pounced on her unsuspecting prey. Sklyarov collapsed beneath the weight of the four-hundred-pound beast. He kept screaming "*Vitya, spasi menya!*," "Victor, save me!" He didn't stop screaming until the tiger ripped out his throat. His blood stained the fresh snow. The cry for help echoed through the library. The camera panned back to Ivanovich. He stood up without firing his rifle and slowly backed away. Tanya turned down the volume as she saw the librarian approaching to reprimand them. The last several seconds showed the tiger dragging Sklyarov's still-twitching body into a thicket of birches.

Tanya closed the file as the librarian walked up to the screen. "You're creating a disturbance," the librarian admonished them. "If you're going to be playing violent video games, then I'm going to have to ask you to leave."

"I'm sorry," Tanya said. "I should have used the headphones. I just need to copy a file that I was working on." She dragged Roman's file onto the flash drive that they had purchased at Wall Drug. "Almost done. Let me just double-check to make sure." She opened the copied file and saw Sklyarov staggering in the snow. "Finished." She ejected the flash drives and slipped the original with its leather cord around her neck. She handed the copy to Mark.

"Hold on to this," she said. "It's your life insurance."

Mark hesitated before putting out his hand.

"You look like you're having second thoughts," Tanya said.

Mark took the drive. He felt like a spike had been driven through his hand. "I'm feeling queasy. I need to use the bathroom."

"Good idea. It's a long drive ahead. You first."

Mark ducked into the bathroom, knelt over the bowl, and kept vomiting until all he could bring up was bile. When Tanya took her turn in the bathroom, he escaped into the open air, but even Main Street seemed threatening. He climbed into the safety of his El Camino and locked the doors. He tried to clear his mind, but the gruesome scene of the tiger dragging the twitching body kept pouncing back into his head. *What have I gotten myself into? The taiga is on the other side of the world. 'Don't get entrapped in a Russian mafia war,' the attorney general had warned. It's not my war, it's theirs.* He felt a desperate need to call her. He started the car.

The rumbling engine rattled the plastic Jesus on the dashboard. Mark looked at himself in the rearview mirror. He didn't look like a hero. He looked like a martyr who was about to recant his faith. He searched for a Bible verse on courage but none popped into his head. He recalled how he and Mary had braved the mysteries of the creek on his parents' farm, how he had found the courage to quit divinity school and choose his own path in life, how he had stopped to pick up a naked runaway on the Overseas Highway. *'We have to put our faith in ourselves,' Tanya had said. I have to find the courage within me. I've failed everyone else in my life. I'm not going to fail her and Dana as well.* He turned the key and shut off the engine.

Tanya tried the car door and found it locked. She knocked on the window. Mark leaned over and pulled up the lock post.

"Why did you lock the door?" she asked.

"I was being cautious."

"Are you sure you're not having second thoughts?"

He braved a smile. "No, not all. I was just learning to put my faith in myself. I'll share the video with Uriel," Mark said. "He'll know what to do."

Her eyes brightened. "One move at a time. We need to think ahead. We need to think how Turchin would have played our position."

For the rest of the journey, Tanya stared out the windshield as if in a trance. The drive through the Great Plains took them through cities and towns whose names commemorated those from whom the land was taken—Sioux Falls, Sioux City, and Omaha. They reached Paducah, Kentucky, on the bank of the Ohio River, by nightfall. From Paducah, it was only a ninety-mile drive to the Jefferson Davis Monument State Historic Site in Fairview. They stopped in Doe's Eat Place for a bite before looking for a motel for the night. The waitress brought them steak and tamales.

"You folks here to see the National Quilt Museum?" the waitress asked. "Do you know that UNESCO designated us as the world's seventh City of Crafts and Folk Art? We also won the Great American Main Street Award back in 2010. Heck, we got all sorts of creative endeavors going on—arts, crafts, performing artists, writers . . ."

"We're just passing through," Mark said.

"Well I hope you're not headed to the demonstration at the Jefferson Davis Memorial. Looks like it's going to get ugly. We've had all kinds of radicals coming through—alt-right, Klansmen, antifa—just itching for a fight. You folks look like you're more the creative type." The waitress saw that her customers didn't want to chat and moved on to her next table.

Tanya hadn't touched her meal. She was scribbling something on a napkin that looked like chess notation. "Of course!"

"What is it?" Mark asked.

"I figured it out!"

"What?"

"How Turchin beat Mechnikoff! He sacrificed his *queen*. Hubris begets the fall. He lured Mechnikoff into thinking that he had captured his queen through his superior play, when in fact it was the ultimate ploy. Once Mechnikoff takes the queen, Turchin completes the checkmate with a pawn and a knight. How long would it take you to go through Ivanovich's financial records, including his dealings with Rich, and write an exposé for the press?"

"I don't know—a few weeks perhaps, if I got Professor Johnson to help me and maybe recruit a few students."

"Could you have it ready before the Fourth of July?"

"Yes, probably, why?"

Tanya reached across the table and gripped both of his hands. "Hear me out. It's in Ivanovich's interest to keep me alive, at least for the time being. My sculpture of the Heavenly Hundred is scheduled to arrive in Washington the first of week of July. If I'm not there to claim it, the Ukrainian embassy will come looking for me. If I'm missing, there will be an investigation. I'll convince him that my loyalty can be bought. I'll go with him to the embassy willingly. That way there will be no questions raised about my disappearance. In the meantime, we work on exposing him."

"It may work in the short term, but what happens after your unveiling? As long as we're alive, we'll remain a threat to him."

"Not if Sklyarov gets him first."

"It's too risky. Too many things can go wrong between now and July 4."

"I'm the one who brought this devil to your family's door. It's my responsibility to cast him out. I don't see another way, do you?"

Mark didn't respond.

"One of my heroes, Vasyl Stus, was a Ukrainian dissident poet who died in the Gulag. Rather than abandon his principles, he said 'Until my death, I will stand for the defense of truth from lies, honest people from murderers, and Jesus Christ from the devil.' Mark, we need to confront the devil *now*."

It was one thing to run from the devil; another to run toward him. Mark didn't have a better plan. When he quit divinity school and changed his name, his father had hugged him for what he thought was the last time and said: "Resist the devil, and he will flee from you."

"I marvel at your courage," he said.

"The truth is, I'm terrified," Tanya confessed. She looked as vulnerable as the day she had first come into his life. "Toma and Ariadna saved me from a life on the streets. I owe it to them . . . no, I owe it to myself to confront my fears. I *need* to be brave. I need you to be my knight."

"Then we'll confront him together," Mark said.

"Like we confronted the gowrow?"

Mark smiled. "Yes, just like we confronted the gowrow and Kane and the ghost in the mine—*together*. What's our next step?"

"We'll call Dana in the morning and set up a meeting."

"Why not call her now?"

"Because this boogeyman will track down our location and come looking for us. We need to set the venue. It needs to be in a public place in broad daylight where he can't take the risk of harming us."

"The Jefferson Davis Memorial," Mark said. "We'll meet him at the rally."

They spent the night at a Red Roof Inn. Mark chained the door even though he knew it would offer little resistance if they were discovered before their rendezvous. He closed his eyes and imagined he was dropping a stone into the Devil's Hole. He dreamed he heard a hissing sound emanate from the hole. As he ran for the exit, the beast of Revelation crawled out of the hole and out of the mouth of the cave. He awoke in a cold sweat. A sliver of daylight peeked through the drapes. Tanya was already up. She handed him the motel phone. He dialed Dana's number from memory.

"Dana, it's me, Mark."

"I'm so glad you're here! Robert promised you would come. Are you close? We can meet for breakfast."

"We're about an hour away. Let's meet at the foot of the Jefferson Davis Memorial at noon."

"OK, but be prepared to be frisked by the state police. They're all over the park trying to separate the right and the left. Our patriots are guarding the monument."

"Love you. See you at noon."

Mark turned on the television. The Jefferson Davis Monument rally was on every local and national news channel. An alliance of civil rights, political, and religious organizations calling themselves America for All had obtained a permit to stage a protest rally at the monument. Their stated goal was to urge the county and the governor to demolish the obelisk that marked the birthplace of Jefferson Davis.

A coalition of far-right groups, including neo-Nazis, KKKs, and self-proclaimed state militias, assembled under the banner Preserve Our Heritage, had preemptively occupied the state park on June 1. They seized the obelisk and museum building, and formed a defensive perimeter around the site that was growing larger by the hour. The state police had decided not to disperse the counterprotestors in fear of provoking a riot. So far the only skirmishes were over control of the public bathrooms, but the liberal Kentucky gun laws threatened to turn the demonstration into a firefight.

The America for All protestors were hunkered in the covered pavilions scattered throughout the park. Reporters estimated the current number of protestors and counterprotestors to be twice the size of Charlottesville. The governor was threatening to call in the national guard if the violence escalated.

Mark and Tanya checked out of their motel after listening to the morning news. A light drizzle fell out of the gray sky. Insects had splattered the windshield during their thousand-mile trek through the Great Plains, and the worn wipers smeared their guts across the windshield in symmetric arches. Mark promised himself that one day he would return to this part of the country to see the giant Superman statue across the Ohio River in Metropolis, Illinois, with the words "Truth—Justice—the American Way" inscribed at its base.

The Jefferson Davis Memorial State Park was ninety miles from Paducah, and the traffic got heavier the closer they got. Cars, pickups, and motorcycles jammed the road leading into the nineteen-acre state park. Amish horse-drawn buggies trotted through the traffic oblivious to the politics of the day. Squad cars with flashing lights were stationed at the intersections, directing traffic to the parking lots and fields. Mark parked the El Camino close to the exit in case they needed to make a quick getaway.

The imposing 350-foot-high obelisk was visible from the highway. A cordon of police separated the circle of defenders from the agitators who would tear it down. As the ragged circle expanded with new arrivals, the gaps in the police cordon grew wider and wider. The America for All demonstrators tested the defensive perimeter by throwing bottles, taunts, and slurs. Riot police were huddled in pockets around the park, waiting for orders to move in if necessary. Reporters and their cameramen filmed the clashes and interviewed anyone who might give them a provocative sound bite for the evening news.

Mark and Tanya navigated their way through the America for All protestors toward the obelisk. The drizzle had worsened into a steady rain. The protestors were a rainbow coalition that included a spectrum of America from left-leaning community organizers to ordinary folk and university students. Many carried signs that read AGAINST WHITE SUPREMACY, NO TO RACISM, and MY GRANDPA FOUGHT NAZIS SO I WOULDN'T HAVE TO. Others were masked and carried makeshift shields with the symbol of the Iron Front.

Jeers of *racists* and *fascists* resonated behind them as Mark and Tanya dashed across the cordon to the Preserve our Heritage side. As they crossed the cordon, Mark thought of Luke 12:53: "For from now on in one house there will be five divided, three against two and two against three. They will be divided, father against son and son against father, mother against daughter and daughter against mother . . ."

They were welcomed on the monument side of the cordon as patriotic white Americans. The defenders were predominantly white males waving Confederate, Black Cross, and KKK flags. They were shouting profanities against African Americans, gays, and Jews. Mark took Tanya by the hand and zigzagged through the madding crowd toward the obelisk.

Dana was waiting at the top of the flight of stone stairs that led into the entrance of the obelisk. Her hair was buzzed, and she was wearing a black T-shirt with an SS lightning bolt blazed across her chest. A small backpack was strapped to her back. The young man next to her was clean-cut and fit. He wore a white polo shirt and khaki pants.

When Dana saw Mark and Tanya at the foot of the stairs, she smiled and ran down to greet them. She gave them each a big hug. Robert E. Lee waited at the top of the stairs.

"Where have you been?" she asked. "Gallivanting across the country with Tanya? I haven't seen an entry in your Americana blog since you left Beech Mountain."

Mark looked up at Robert E. Lee. He was watching them with a smirk on his face.

"I don't know why you wanted to meet here," Dana said. "We're in the eye of the storm. We could have met at a local bar in Fairview. Anyway, it doesn't matter. Come up and meet my friend Robert."

As they climbed the stairs, Dmitri extended his hand, but Mark didn't shake it. Dmitri came up to Tanya and kissed her three times on the cheeks. She stood as still as a statue.

"Robert! You see a pretty woman, and the first thing you do is kiss her," Dana laughed. "Robert hasn't let me out of his sight in the past week."

"My bad," Dmitri said in a Carolina drawl. "Let's step in here out of the ruckus so we can talk."

The Jefferson Davis Monument was the tallest unreinforced concrete structure in the world. The entrance led into a cramped portico where one could ascend to the observation room in a creaky elevator or climb a seemingly endless flight of stairs. Despite the mayhem outside, the portico was as quiet as a tomb.

Mark and Tanya faced Dmitri and Dana. Dmitri put his hands around Tanya's neck. She didn't blink.

"Rusalka," he said in Russian.

Dana looked at him with alarm.

"This is between us, so I'll speak in our native tongue."

Dana jerked away from him. "Robert! What the hell are you doing? Speak in English for God's sake."

"His name isn't Robert," Mark said. "He's not who you think he is."

Dana ran into Mark's arms. He retreated with her into a dark corner of the portico.

"You've been a bad girl," Dmitri continued in Russian. "What did our dear reverend call you—the whore of Babylon?"

"What does Ivanovich want?" Tanya asked.

"Isn't it obvious? He wants you."

"Tell him we have something to trade," Tanya said. "Tell him we saw the Flame of God."

Dmitri smiled. "Turchin's last words." He eased his grip on her neck.

"You can tell him yourself."

Tanya knew that Dmitri had fallen for her ploy. "What will he do if I choose not to go with you?"

Dmitri's smiled disappeared. Tanya saw the soulless eyes of the Orthodox priest in Lincoln Park.

"If you choose not to come, I will start by killing your friend and his silly little cousin."

"What makes you think I care about these Americans?" she asked.

"Rusalka, I've been watching you for these past several weeks. You nurse him back to health, you hold his hand, you share the same bed. You make sculptures for his family. Personally, I don't understand why you would care for these people. Look outside. They're at each other's throats like wild dogs."

"You incite them," Tanya said.

"We simply unleash them," Dmitri replied.

Tanya looked at Dana as she huddled in Mark's arms. Despite her butch appearance, she was as fragile as a girl on her first date.

"I'll come with you," Tanya said. "But first let me say goodbye to my friends. I may never see them again."

"Have Dana come over to me first," he said in his low country drawl. "Don't worry, I won't harm her."

Mark hesitated, but Dana stepped forward and switched places with Tanya. "That's my brave girl," Dmitri said. He put his arm around Dana and slid his hand into her backpack.

Tanya went over to Mark in the corner and hugged him.

"Are you sure you want to go through with this?" he asked.

"Yes," Tanya whispered in his ear. "The queen sacrifice. I'm counting on you to be my knight. Come for me on Independence Day."

"I will. I promise."

"What did she whisper to you?" Dmitri demanded.

"She said the game is over," Mark replied.

Dmitri pushed Dana to the floor and grabbed Tanya by the wrist. He pulled her down the stairs into the flurry of Confederate flags. Mark helped Dana off the floor and waited with her inside the portico until Tanya and her captor were out of sight. Dana was sobbing uncontrollably.

"He said he *loved* me. He said we would reclaim the South together."

"We need to leave," Mark said. "I'll explain on the way home."

The steady rain had turned to a downpour. The flags that had flown so proudly were drenched and clung to their poles. Defenders crowded up the obelisk stairs and into the portico to escape the rain.

Mark walked Dana to his car oblivious to the storm. On their way out they passed a commemorative plaque that read "Jefferson Davis's salute to Kentucky: 'Kentucky, my own, my native land. God grant that peace and plenty may ever run throughout your borders.'"

* * * *

Tanya and Dmitri were the only two passengers aboard a chartered jet that lifted from Hopkinsville-Christian County Airport at eight o'clock in the evening. The plane had been delayed on the tarmac for two hours waiting for the storm to pass. Tanya looked out the window at the land that she had come to know so well during her trek through America. The setting sun basked the white leather interior of the plane in a reddish hue. Tanya sat across from her captor.

"Dmitri," she said. "That is your name, Dmitri?"

"How did you know?" he asked.

"I remember you from the *Kalinka*. You brought me aboard Ivanovich's yacht in the launch."

"What else to you remember about me?"

"Nothing," Tanya replied. "That's the only time we'd ever met before today."

Dmitri smirked. "The chess pavilion?"

"I didn't see you at the chess pavilion. I saw an old Orthodox priest play a game of chess with Turchin. I wonder what ever happened to the chess master."

"I'm afraid he died of natural causes," Dmitri replied. "He was cremated shortly thereafter."

"So you see, other than the *Kalinka* and the Jefferson Davis Monument, we had never met before."

"What's your point?"

"I've seen how Ivanovich treats you. He doesn't appreciate you. You're a performance artist. You had that girl believing you were a homegrown neo-Nazi."

"An American patriot," he corrected her.

"You need to be recognized for your talent."

"And what is it that you think you can do for me?"

"I said I have something to trade," Tanya said. "I said it was for Ivanovich. It's not. It's for you."

Dmitri sat up in his cushioned chair and looked into her eyes. "I'm listening."

"The Flame of God gave me access to Ivanovich's financial files. But the Americans already have those. He gave me something much more valuable."

"What might that be?"

Tanya pulled the leather necklace with the flash drive pendant off her neck. She handed it to Dmitri. "See for yourself."

Dmitri took out his laptop and plugged it into the USB port. His Kaspersky antivirus program scanned it for viruses, malware, and worms. When he was satisfied that it was clean, he clicked open the MP4 file.

Tanya watched him as the video reflected in his eyes. His face stayed expressionless, as if he were reading a script to see if he would take the role. At one point he paused the video, reversed it, and played it again. When it was over he closed his laptop.

"I presume you have a copy," he said.

"The next move is yours," she said, "if you have the courage to play it. Otherwise you can forfeit and tempt fate with your boss."

"What do you want in return?"

"My life and the lives of my friends."

"I'll consider your offer."

Before he could react, Tanya grabbed his shirt and ripped open the buttons. His chest was marked with the tattoo of a bull, the mark of a hit man. Fresh stitches zigzagged across the gash in his abdomen. He recoiled from her touch.

"I've known men like you," she said. "Intimately. You live and die by a code. Honor the code."

He took her hands off his shirt and fastened the few buttons that remained. He looked out the window at the patchwork of lights below.

"Where are we heading?" she asked.

Dmitri leaned back into his chair. "Washington, DC."

* * * *

The drive from Fairview to Beech Mountain would take over seven hours. Mark stayed within the speed limit.

"I can't believe I was so stupid," Dana said. "The first time a boy pays attention to me, I sell out my family and my friends. Are you going to tell me who he really is?"

"All I know is that he's a Russian who works for an oligarch. You don't need to know his name. He had us all fooled, me more than anyone. He taunted me in multiple disguises. In Miami he was first a Marlin's fan and then a Cuban gardener. In Williamstown he was a Bible salesman. In Nashville he was a Predators fan. In Chicago he was an Orthodox priest."

"Christ," Dana said. "What do these Russians want from us?"

"I can't tell you everything that I know or how I know it. Tanya got mixed in with them, and I ran into her just by chance. They came after us, and we've been running from them ever since. I just regret that I led them to you."

"But I met Robert E. Lee on social media months ago," Dana said.

"You met someone who claimed to be Robert E. Lee," Mark said. "I think this Russian hit man took over his identity."

"But why? Why am *I* so important?"

"You're one of hundreds," Mark said. "The Russians are fracking us. They look for the fault lines in our society and inject propaganda to amplify them. They try and pit us against each other. When you started browsing the white supremacist websites, they probably latched on to you. They post divisive messages on both sides of an issue and then their bots amplify them until they go viral. I just didn't think that they would infiltrate us with provocateurs on our own soil."

"Why didn't you go to our government?" Dana asked.

"Because powerful people in our government are conspiring with the Russians for their own gain."

"So whom can you trust?" she asked.

"Trust yourself," Mark replied. "I remember my young cousin who once questioned everything and thought for herself. Somewhere along the way, I don't know if it was my uncle's death or my aunt's drinking, she lost her way. You need to find your way home. I heard of an underground railroad that helps people like you get their lives back. Think about it."

Dana opened her backpack and pulled out her daddy's Redhawk pistol. She waved it through the air in the shape of a swastika.

"What the hell are you doing? Put that away!" Mark yelled.

"You said to put my trust in myself. That's what I'm doing."

"I can't believe you brought that gun to the protest."

"Robert E. Lee, or whoever he is, told me to bring it. He said I might need to defend myself against the leftists."

The realization hit Mark like a collision with a ten-point buck. The gun was Robert E. Lee's plan B. If he couldn't convince Tanya to accompany him, he would have murdered them all . . . some bizarre murder-suicide plot pinned on his cousin Dana. The Russians would have fabricated some bullshit manifesto and plastered it on her Facebook page.

"I'm sorry I let you down," Mark said. "I broke away from my family to find myself, and I lost you. I'll help you get through this. We'll start by getting you back into school. You need to start going to church again."

The blue grass and rolling hills of Kentucky rose into the Smokies. Night had fallen, but Mark was determined to drive his cousin home without stopping. *Protect your family,* Tanya had said. *We're being attacked by an invisible enemy through the airwaves, through Wi-Fi, and through social media. We're being brainwashed with fake news and alternative facts. Our leaders, rather than protect us, conspire with those who want to destroy us. Perhaps Reverend Kane is right. Perhaps the End Time is here.*

CHAPTER 15

Washington, DC

The white-marble obelisk of the Washington Monument illuminated the night sky. The global beacon for democracy, hope, and justice towered over the concrete obelisk in Kentucky. As the charter flight made a wide circle around the protected airspace, Tanya gazed at the illuminated Capitol and Lincoln Memorial. For her this was the last bastion in the fight against kleptocracy, cynicism, and the rule of power. During the February nights on the Maidan, when the barricades burned and government snipers massacred the Heavenly Hundred, Tanya and her compatriots had put their faith in the West. Now the same cancer of corruption that was consuming her country had metastasized to Washington.

A private limo transported them from Reagan Airport to the Royal Suite at the Four Seasons Hotel in Georgetown. A closed-circuit security system and bulletproof glass guarded the suite and its wing of adjacent bedrooms. Swarovski crystal fixtures glittered in the foyer ceiling like stars.

Ivanovich was waiting for them on the private terrace that overlooked M street. Dmitri seated Tanya on one of the cushioned terrace chairs and stood behind her. Ivanovich flicked the ash off his cigarette without so much as looking at him. Dmitri retreated inside the suite to give his boss and his captive their privacy. Ivanovich sat down across from her and put his hands on her knees.

"Rusalka, rusalka, the trouble that you've caused me."

"Your senator raped me," Tanya said.

"I know. I have the video."

Tanya clenched her fist. She looked around the terrace for anything that she could use as a weapon.

"Don't be foolish," Ivanovich said. "Dmitri is right outside the door. If I wanted you dead, we wouldn't be having this conversation."

"Then what is it that you want?"

"I want *everything*. I want to know where you've been, who you've talked to."

Tanya decided to tell him what he already knew and nothing more.

"I was drugged. I was hallucinating. All I could think of was to run."

"To *swim*," Ivanovich corrected her. "That was quite a feat—a mile through shark-infested waters."

"I flagged down a car. An American student, Mark Rider, he . . . helped me."

"Go on."

"Can I have a cigarette?" Tanya asked. She didn't smoke, but the request made him release his grip on her knees. Ivanovich lifted a Treasurer cigarette from his sterling case and lit it for her with his DuPont Ligne lighter. Tanya made a pretense of inhaling. The smoke burned her vocal chords.

"You were saying?"

Tanya coughed. "I have a friend in Miami, Mirana, an artist."

She took another draw of her cigarette. So far, Ivanovich seemed satisfied with her story.

"Mirana put us up at her place on Indian Creek. She then introduced us to her friend Reya."

"Ah, yes, Reya. How is . . . she?"

"You know Reya?" Tanya asked.

"I know *of* her. She's a madam who caters to peculiar tastes. What information did she give you?"

"She told us where to find Turchin."

Ivanovich inhaled his cigarette with deep satisfaction and exhaled a sequence of perfectly shaped smoke rings. He again put his hands on Tanya's knees and leaned forward.

She could smell the nicotine on his breath.

"The truth will set you free," he said. "What did Turchin tell you?"

Tanya took a chance. "He told me how to access your financial records on the internet."

"And what did you do with this information?"

"Nothing."

"Does your friend Rider know how to access these files?"

"No, I didn't want to put him or his family in jeopardy."

Ivanovich pulled back from her face. He studied her eyes to see if she was lying. "I believe you," he said. "Where have you been these past several weeks?"

"Mark is a . . ." She was going to say journalist but stopped. "Mark is a writer. He's writing a blog on Americana. I journeyed with him across the country as he collected material for his blog."

"Fascinating. Where exactly?"

"We visited Williamstown, Nashville, Chicago, Baraboo. While we were driving to Chicago I heard Reverend Kane single me out on the radio. He called me the whore of Babylon. I needed to know why. I convinced Mark to take me to Las Vegas so I could confront him."

"I know. I watched the video. You said you were the second angel. You called him a false prophet. Why would you say something like that?"

Tanya's cigarette had burned down to her fingers. She dropped it, and Ivanovich snuffed it out with his shoe. He took her hand and kissed her singed fingers. Tanya let him do what he pleased.

"The second angel?" he asked again.

"Mark told me to say those things. He was a divinity student. He disagrees with Kane's message of the End Time."

"I see," Ivanovich said. "Continue."

"From Las Vegas we sought out Mark's friend in Nevada City. He took us with him up to Hat Creek. We camped out there until Mark called his cousin. I knew then that I had nowhere to run."

"Your friend Rider called his cousin from a public phone in Yellowstone."

Tanya hesitated before replying. "We were taking the scenic road back east—for his blog on Americana."

"You did well, my rusalka, to come back to me. I intend you no harm. For political reasons, I need for you to make your peace with Senator Rich. We'll tell him you took an antianxiety pill that evening that made you hallucinate. They understand these sorts of things in America. After your sculpture arrives, we'll make a point of meeting with him in public, so he doesn't think that you bear him ill will."

"What am I to do until then?" she asked.

"You'll be my guest, of course."

"Your prisoner?"

Ivanovich laughed. "No, no. You're free to wander about the city. Dmitri will escort you at all times. After your perilous adventure, I wouldn't want anything to happen to you in Washington."

"I understand," Tanya said.

"I'll be back in a moment. You must be starving. I'll order up some champagne and crab cakes."

Ivanovich stepped back into the suite and closed the terrace door. Dmitri was waiting in the kitchen.

"What do you want me to do with her?" he asked.

"We'll indulge her for now. No access to phones or computers. You can take her outside, but stay with her at all times. I need to parade her in public to not arouse any suspicion."

"And then?"

"We'll send her back to the gutter from where she came. Addict her to heroin, make her a junkie, and then put her to work on the street with the rest of them."

"What about Rider?"

"Tell Gennady to keep him under surveillance. We'll find out soon enough how much he knows."

* * * *

Mark sat at a table in the corner at Buddy Guy's Legends with his back to the wall. He admired the memorabilia on the walls—records, photos, and guitars of blues icons, from Bo Diddley, Koko Taylor, and Buddy Guy to Eric Clapton, David Bowie, and the Rolling Stones. It was quintessential Americana. The blues bar, at the crossroad of Wabash and Balboa, was a frequent haunt of Bo Johnson's. A young black musician was performing an innovative version of Big Bill Broonzy's "Key to the Highway." Mark hoped that Professor Johnson had seen the note he had stuck on the guitar in his office that morning that read "Urgent. Need your help. Buddy Guy's at noon. MR."

Professor Bo Johnson walked into the bar and spotted Mark in the corner. The manager greeted him with a smile and a handshake.

"Professor Johnson," Mark began.

"No titles. In here everyone knows me as just Bo."

"Bo, I need your help."

"I can see that. You look like hell." Mark had driven from Beech Mountain straight through the night.

"I've been on the road."

"You haven't been home?" Bo asked.

"No. I'm afraid I'm being followed."

"So you haven't read your mail?"

"No, it's still at the post office. Why?"

"Some anonymous donor paid your tuition in full," Bo said. "You should check your student loan. They may have paid that off as well. The Rich Media Group contacted the school. They want to offer you a paid internship."

"They're trying to buy my silence."

"So as I see it," Bo said, "you again find yourself at a crossroads. You can take the money and hope that they never come after you, or you can turn down their money and make sure that they do. It's not your fight, so I'll understand whatever choice you make."

"It *is* my fight. If I don't stop them, then who will?"

"So you don't want to sell your soul to the devil?" Bo asked.

"I have a sweet woman to save me."

Bo nodded in agreement. "How is she?" he asked.

"She's alive, for now." Mark leaned over the table so no one else could hear. "We tracked down our source. We have information that can put Rich and Ivanovich in jail."

A waitress came up and offered Mark a menu. "The usual, Bo?" she asked.

"A gumbo and catfish po'boy. My young friend here will have the same."

Bo watched the young musician's fingers make his guitar cry. He looked about nineteen but played as if he'd been born with a guitar in his hand.

"The boy's good," Bo said. "I had him figured for jazz rap, but he respects his roots. Reminds me of myself when I was a kid."

Mark needed a beer. "Can I get you a cold one?" he asked.

"I gave up drinking," Bo said. "If I have one, I'll have to have fifty. Now tell me more about this evidence that you claim you have."

"Our source gave us access to Ivanovich's financial records. I downloaded them onto a flash drive at the Harold Washington Library this morning. There are hundreds of accounts. I need help going through them. I need advice on how to make them public. I know they're watching me, so it has to be done discreetly. I need to do all of this in the next three weeks."

Bo took a long drink of his ice water. "Have you thought about going to the FBI?"

"I don't know whom to trust. I met with the CIA station chief who was investigating Ivanovich. The CIA shut down his investigation."

"Looks like this oligarch has powerful friends," Bo said. "What if he comes after you first?"

"For Tanya's sake, I need to take that risk." He put his hand in his pocket to make sure the flash drive was still there. "I have . . . insurance, if he tries to come after me."

"Life insurance?" Bo asked. "Sorry, bad joke. I assume there's more that you're not telling me. Here's my advice. First, if you think they're monitoring your communications, then let them. Use your phone, use your email, and keep your same passwords. If you know they're listening to you, then you can control the flow of information. Don't turn down the bribe, at least for now."

"If I play along, then how can I complete this investigation?" Mark asked.

"For the next three weeks you'll need to lead a double life. Go home and be yourself. Let them see what you want them to see. In the meantime, at Medill we'll put together a team of faculty and students. I'll get some colleagues from the business school and law school. I know a couple of students who are looking to do an independent study. If the evidence looks compelling, we'll talk to my friend at the *Tribune*. I'll tell them this is *your* story, but they can have the exclusive. Once we give it to them, they'll fact check it. If it's as compelling as you say, they'll publish it."

"It's all coming to a head on July 4: the March for Family Values, the release of the Last Awakening app, the unveiling of Tanya's statue . . . I need to be in Washington, DC, when the story breaks. I need to get Tanya away from them before they retaliate."

"I'll tell my friend at the Trib to leak the story to the major news outlets just before midnight on July 3. Have a plan in place and prepare for a media firestorm."

Mark looked at his watch. It was 10:00 a.m. in Rhyolite. "I'll be right back," Mark said. "I need to make a call."

"Here, you can use my phone," Bo offered.

"I think they might be monitoring your phone as well."

Bo called over his friend, the manager. "Ray, my friend Mark needs to make a call. Can he use your house phone?

"No problem," Ray replied. He led him to a phone by the kitchen. The aroma of Louisiana gumbo and the crackle of frying catfish filled the air. Mark dialed the number he knew by heart.

"Death Valley Serpentarium."

"I'm on a mission from God."

"You joined the Blues Brothers?" Uriel quipped. "I see you're calling from Buddy Guy's."

"I convinced my professor Bo Johnson to help me go through Turchin's files. Have you been able to find out anything more about

Ivanovich and his godson?"

"I asked my hacker friends in Russia to do a little digging. The autopsy report confirmed that young Sklyarov was drunk. The alcohol level in the vitreous humor was sky-high, so no one challenged Ivanovich's version of events: he testified that his godson couldn't hold his vodka and wandered off to hunt on his own. But there were loose ends. The local authorities didn't get to the scene until the next day. By then, the blizzard had covered the tracks. The local police chief who handled the investigation got a short-lived position in one of Ivanovich's companies—he died of a heart attack a few months later at the age of forty. The locals who accompanied Ivanovich and his godson on the tiger hunt—a guide, a cook, and the photographer—simply disappeared. No one's heard from them since."

"Roman," Mark said.

"Looks like he's the only one who got away."

"But why would Ivanovich kill his godson? What was the motive?"

"Greed. Several years ago Ivanovich was the CEO of the third largest oil and gas company in Siberia. The Kremlin raided it, put Sklyarov on the board of directors, and demanded the usual fifty percent take of the company. The ironic thing is that Sklyarov and Ivanovich were *kumy*: in Russia you keep your rivals close by asking them to be godparents to your children. Sklyarov asked Ivanovich to hire his son as comptroller. It wasn't pure nepotism; the boy had credentials. He'd completed a master's in economics at Moscow State University and had been working for a western hedge fund in Moscow. Ivanovich was stealing from his own company through asset transfers. He would sell off the Siberian gas fields to other companies for pennies on the dollar presumably to raise capital for exploration and drilling. Turns out he *owned* those companies, so he was basically selling to himself and stealing from the Kremlin. The Kremlin thought they were getting half his company when in reality they were getting half of the shell of a company. I suspect that young Sklyarov figured it out. When Ivanovich couldn't bribe him, he had to take him out."

"What happened to the company?"

"It's been bought and sold a dozen times by intermediaries from

Adygeya to Komi to Tatarstan. It has more shells than a matryoshka doll. As they say in Russia, without vodka you can't figure it out."

"You're a godsend," Mark said.

"I'm the Flame of God," Uriel replied, "and I'm counting on you to exact His vengeance."

* * * *

Two Orthodox monks strolled around the Ellipse between the Washington Monument and the White House. July 1 was predicted to be the hottest day of the year to date, and they were sweating beneath their black robes. Brother Alexiy was the taller of the two men. Dmitri purchased two bottles of ice water from a street vendor and gave one to Alexiy. They sat down on a bench in the shade. Demonstrators from around the country had begun to arrive in Washington, DC, for the July 4 March for Family Values, and many spent the days before the event touring the nation's capital. They reminded Dmitri of the troves of visitors he had seen at the Ark Encounter and Creation Museum.

"You asked to see me," Dmitri said. "It's been a long time since our days at the academy."

"Too long, my friend, too long." Alexiy took hold of Dmitri's hand, one cleric to another. Alexiy's robes smelled of incense and beeswax.

"When this assignment is over," Dmitri began, "perhaps we can rekindle the flame we had at the academy. It takes a real man to put me . . ."

Alexiy cut him off. "The Americans are on to our scheme."

Dmitri feigned surprise, like a child who watches an ant burn under a magnifying glass. "What? But how?"

"The second angel. Ivanovich's attempt at *kompromat* has compromised us instead."

Alexiy's statement confirmed Tanya hadn't been bluffing. Ivanovich's plan was unraveling. It was only a matter of time before the Kremlin decided to clean up the loose ends. "How can you be sure?" he asked.

"The signs are everywhere. The cleric that was assigned to accompany me in the March for Family Values is an FBI agent. I've been taken off the list of speakers. Most troubling to my superiors, the Last Awakening app that is scheduled for release in three days has been modified."

"In what way?" Dmitri asked.

"The AI code we inserted has been deleted. It's useless to us. It's now just another one of many Bible apps, and not a good one at that."

A child ran up to Alexiy and tugged on his beard to see if it was real. The child's mother caught him, apologized, and yanked him away.

Given Tanya's warning and Alexiy's revelation, Dmitri knew that Ivanovich was near the end of his days. "There's more you should know," he told Alexiy.

"Speak."

"Tanya Bereza is our captive. She confided in me that the collusion between Ivanovich and Senator Rich is on the verge of being exposed."

"Then you may need to find yourself another employer," Alexiy said.

"She also showed me a video."

"The *kompromat* from the *Kalinka*?"

"No. Something even more valuable. It's a video of Ivanovich and his godson on that ill-fated tiger hunt."

"*Beria's* son?"

Dmitri acknowledged the fact by not answering.

"What does it show?" Alexiy asked.

"You'll need to view it for yourself." Dmitri wore the necklace and flash drive on his neck as if it were the finger bone of a saint. He took the sacred relic off his neck and entrusted it to his brother monk.

"As my friend, no, as my brother, I beg you to intervene on my behalf. Tell Beria it was I who discovered Ivanovich's treachery and brought it to him. Tell him my allegiance is to our code, not to my employer who betrayed it."

A long gold crucifix on a gold chain dangled from Alexiy's neck. He removed it and replaced it with Dmitri's relic. He placed the Orthodox cross in Dmitri's hand, cupped his hand over his, and said: "Always the chameleon. Fear not. We are brothers. We can turn this to our advantage. It appears that Ivanovich has betrayed us all. I'll make a call to Beria from the embassy. He'll tell us what to do."

* * * *

Through all of June the Medill investigative team pored through every transaction in Turchin's files. They cataloged, corroborated, and peeled back layer after layer of shell corporations. As a carryover from the old bureaucratic Soviet system, Turchin kept meticulous records. Every ruble was accounted for. The financial documents revealed the usual Russian oligarch MO: asset stripping, dilutions, transfer pricing, and embezzlement. Where it hit home were his deals with American partners: businessmen, CIA middlemen, and politicians.

Ivanovich was funneling money to both Republicans and Democrats. He did not discriminate by political party. The common denominator appeared to be the candidate's willingness to repeal the Magnitsky Act. The money to the political campaigns was funneled through intermediaries—gun rights groups, cultural associations, and advocacy groups.

Senator Rich was also entangled with Ivanovich in several speculative real estate investments. When Rich's investments were close to bankruptcy, Ivanovich and his buddies bailed them out, mostly in the form of unsecured loans from a bank in Cyprus. The Little Card Sound development was the most recent.

With Professor Johnson's help, Mark prepared a series of exposés, each more sensational than the one that preceded it.

Mark was in Washington for the release of his first exposé. His article "Russian Black Cash Finances Florida Development" went to press in the late evening on July 3. The article was set to appear in the business section of the *Chicago Tribune* on Independence Day. The only reference to Senator Rich was in the last paragraph, which few people ever read. It simply stated that the property was one of several included in a blind trust that Senator Julian Rich Jr. had established once he took office. The *Tribune* gave credit for the article to Mark Rider and a team of investigative journalists from Northwestern University's Medill School of Journalism. CNN had included a brief reference to the breaking news article on its eleventh-hour news program.

Mark hardly slept that night despite being put up at a luxury suite at the Ritz-Carlton in Georgetown. Every hotel room in Washington, DC, was booked for the March for Family Values. Uriel had hacked into the hotel computer and canceled a reverend from North Carolina who was still arguing with the front desk when Mark checked in as a new Platinum Elite member. Uriel had hacked into the smartphone of Senator Rich's chief of staff and told Mark to sit tight until further word.

The blue display on the bedside alarm clock advanced the time minute by minute. Whenever Mark closed his eyes he saw a human mole in a creepy drift or felt an unseen presence lick the back of his neck. His sweat soaked into the bedsheets. His stomach burned. At 4:41 a.m. he knelt over the toilet and gripped the porcelain bowl. He steeled himself and overcame the urge to vomit. The streaming water in the shower purged the demons from his head. He put on a clean white shirt, pressed gray slacks, and a red tie. He donned the blue blazer that he last wore at his convocation. It still had the Wheaton pin that Mary had given him as a graduation gift.

The hotel phone rang at 6:35 a.m. He took a deep breath and picked up the phone.

"We got them," Uriel said. "Rich's chief of staff has him scheduled for a breakfast meeting at Seasons restaurant at 7:00 a.m. Ivanovich is staying in the Royal Suite. I hacked into the hotel computers, and he's reserved three tables at Seasons for the same time. This is your chance."

"Any bites on my article?" Mark asked.

"The paper hit the stands forty-five minutes ago. I'd say we should alert the major news networks at seven."

"That's cutting it close," Mark said. "I need to confront them before the press arrives."

"It's 6:45 a.m. your time. The Four Seasons is four blocks away. I'll give you fifteen minutes, and then I'll send out a Twitter blast."

"I'm ready," Mark said. "Blast it in ten."

Ten minutes later every news service in Washington, DC, received the same tweet: "Senator Rich now meeting with Russian black-cash financier at Seasons restaurant in Georgetown." The origin of the tweet appeared to be the White House.

* * * *

Breakfast at the Seasons restaurant was rated among the best in the capital. Ivanovich reserved three tables: one for himself and his two guests; one for the senator's retinue; and one for Dmitri. In the high-power environment of Washington, DC, a breakfast meeting between a senator, philanthropist, and their staffs was nothing out of the ordinary. Senator Rich made his entrance after his security detail had checked out the room. They stood out by the seemingly inconspicuous cords that snaked from their collars to their ears. The senator was dressed for the March for Family Values. He wore an impeccable navy suit with an American flag pin, white shirt, and red tie. Ivanovich was dressed in Armani jeans, a linen shirt, and Brioni loafers. Tanya was dressed to kill. Ivanovich had decked her out in a red Versace dress and a string of Mikimoto pearls that plunged into her décolletage.

"Julian, have a seat," Ivanovich offered without standing up. Tanya offered her hand.

Senator Rich kissed her hand and inhaled the scent of the Jo Malone lime, basil, and mandarin cologne that she had dabbed on her wrists. The perfume reminded him of their tryst in the Keys. "It's a pleasure to see you . . . again," he said.

"The pleasure is all mine, Senator," Tanya replied.

Ivanovich had preordered a bottle of Dom Perignon White Gold that was chilling in an ice bucket by the table. He signaled to their waiter, who poured three flutes of the champagne.

"A toast," Ivanovich began, "to clear up a past misunderstanding." He motioned to Tanya to recite the apology that they had rehearsed together.

"Senator Rich . . . Julian, I want to apologize for my rudeness the last time we met. The alcohol interacted with a medication that I take for my nerves. I wasn't myself."

The senator placed his hand on her wrist. "No need to apologize. I've been known for a few benders myself," he joked. "Let's put it behind us and start anew." They clinked glasses and toasted to a new beginning.

The waiter began with the lady in red. "Madam?"

"I'll have a green apple juice, roasted pineapple crepes, and a black coffee." The senator ordered a Georgetown Benedict with a side of hash browns. After perusing the menu for an extra minute, Ivanovich settled on the Wagyu steak and eggs.

"Please bring us a dozen bluepoints on the half shell," the senator added. "It's good for the libido."

"Immediately, sir," the waiter replied.

Senator Rich watched as Tanya dabbed the oysters with the vinaigrette and expertly slurped them from their shells. She felt a foot climb up her high heel to her ankle and inch up the back of her calf. Senator Rich smiled when she did not withdraw. For now, she let him do as he pleased. The senator continued talking without the slightest hint of his intrusion as he caressed the back of her calves.

Dmitri had selected the tables the night before with a view toward security and privacy. His solo table provided a vantage point of the entry. He assessed every patron as they waited for the maître d' to find their reservation and lead them to their table. The phone in his pocket began to buzz. Only a handful of people knew his number, and each was a call he had to take. He got up from his table and took the call in the men's room.

"Chameleon."

Dmitri didn't recognize the phone number, but he recognized the voice. "I'm listening."

"Beria has seen the film. He says he understands how remorse could drive a man to take his own life."

Dmitri's phone buzzed with another incoming call. Before he could hit hold, Alexiy had hung up.

"Gennady," Dmitri said, recognizing the number.

"Your rusalka betrayed us. An article appeared in the business section of the *Chicago Tribune* this morning. It's about the Little Card Sound development. The reporter who wrote it is none other than Mark Rider."

"I see," Dmitri said.

"The news stations are picking up the story. You need to get Ivanovich as far away from Rich as you can."

"Contact the captain of the *Kalinka*," Dmitri said, "and tell him to sail to Tavernier. Have the pilot ready the plane to fly us from Dulles to Tavernaero Park Airport in an hour. We set sail for international waters as soon as we land."

He called up to a member of Ivanovich's security detail who was stationed in the Royal Suite. "Vlodya." Then he said in Russian, "Victor Ivanovich will be bringing a guest upstairs, and he requires complete privacy. Turn off the security cameras as you leave the suite."

Before he returned to his table, Dmitri pulled a pen out of the inside pocket of his suit. He held it over the washbasin and clicked. A small drop of clear fluid, indistinguishable from water, fell into the drain. He looked in the bathroom mirror and congratulated himself on anticipating the denouement. When he returned to the restaurant, he casually walked over to Ivanovich's table and whispered something in his ear. As Ivanovich listened, Dmitri clicked the button on the pen and released a drop into his flute that dissolved instantly among the effervescent bubbles.

"Finish your champagne," Dmitri said. "We need to leave soon."

"What is it?" Rich asked.

"A minor security issue," Ivanovich replied. "I'm afraid that Ms. Bereza and I will need to leave a little sooner than expected."

Tanya felt a shudder crawl up her spine. Rich's shoe was still rubbing the back of her leg. Her lacquered nails traced the string of pearls into her décolletage as Rich's eyes followed. "About my sculpture . . . ?" she asked.

"Business before pleasure," Rich said. "Victor tells me that your sculpture is currently held up in customs." He summoned his chief of staff from the adjacent table. "Virginia, can you see to it that Ms. Bereza's sculpture is released from customs? Also, call the park service and tell them we would like it displayed in Meridian Park from now until Labor Day."

"I'll get right on it," she said.

When she returned to her table, Rich's press secretary was frantically scrolling through the messages on his cell phone. "You're not going to believe this."

"What is it?" Virginia asked.

"This meeting . . . I mean right *here* and *now*, is all over the wires. We need to get him the hell out of here."

The chief of staff grabbed the phone and read the messages herself. Words like *collusion, scandal,* and *conspiracy* screamed on the screen.

Dmitri was the first to spot Mark Rider. He was standing at the entrance as the maître d' checked for his reservation.

"Ah, here it is," the maître d' said. "I see you're sitting at Mr. Ivanovich's table."

With his red tie and blue blazer, Mark looked like he belonged in the Seasons. The maître d' led him directly to Ivanovich's table.

"I'm sorry, sir," the maître d' said to Ivanovich, but your secretary must have added Mr. Rider's name to your reservation at the last minute. Allow me to pull up a chair and an extra place setting."

Rich's bodyguards began to rise from the adjoining table, but Ivanovich waved them off. Dmitri did not rise. He watched to see whether the play would follow the script that he had imagined.

Tanya pulled her leg away from Rich's probing shoe.

"So you're the infamous Americana blogger," Ivanovich said. "You have a lot of balls walking in like this."

Mark looked at Tanya. She was no longer the girl in the El Camino with the "Got a Truck?" T-shirt and windswept hair. She looked like she had stepped off the cover of *Vogue*. Tanya smiled, knowing that her queen sacrifice had worked. Without saying a word, Mark took out his phone and handed it to Ivanovich. The screen displayed a PDF of his article with the headline: "Russian Black Cash Finances Florida Development."

As Ivanovich was scanning the article, Rich's chief of staff went up to the table and whispered something in the senator's ear. The senator turned as pale as the white tablecloth.

"I'm afraid something's come up," he said as he rose from the table. "It was nice meeting you Mr. . ."

"Rider. Mark Rider."

The maître d' was arguing with someone at the door. The intruder was holding a microphone and was accompanied by a cameraman.

Rich's bodyguards escorted the senator toward the kitchen exit.

"Senator Rich!" the reporter with the microphone called out. "Would you care to comment on the story in today's *Chicago Tribune*?"

The other patrons in the restaurant turned to see what the commotion was all about. The cameraman shoved past the maître d' and continued to film the senator's humiliating escape. Rich's press secretary blocked their pursuit.

"The senator was having a meeting with the director of the Institute for Democratic Progress regarding an upcoming cultural exhibit. We'll issue a statement shortly."

Ivanovich had finished scanning the article on Rider's phone. He took a last sip of champagne, looked Rider in the eye, and slashed a finger across his throat.

Mark leaned across the table. "Do you read the Bible, Mr. Ivanovich?"

Ivanovich lifted his hand to his head as if the room were beginning to spin. He dropped Mark's phone onto the table.

Mark quoted Job 12:22: "He reveals the deep things of darkness and brings utter darkness into the light."

Dmitri went up to the table and helped Ivanovich out of his chair. Ivanovich was having a difficult time maintaining his balance. He pointed at Tanya. "Bring her with us," he ordered.

Dmitri made a pretense of trying to force her out of her chair but placed something in her hand instead. "I'll return for her," Dmitri said. "Right now I need to help you back to your room."

As they were leaving the restaurant, the reporter tried to stick her microphone in Ivanovich's face, but Dmitri waved her away. "Mr. Ivanovich has taken ill and will not be granting any interviews today," Dmitri said without a hint of accent. He handed her Ivanovich's business card. "Please feel free to check again tomorrow morning."

The reporter and cameraman rushed to the back exit of the hotel hoping to get a video of Senator Rich escaping in his limo. They paid no attention to the young man in the blue blazer and woman in the red dress who calmly walked out of the lobby and disappeared into the throng of pedestrians on Pennsylvania Avenue.

Dmitri steadied Ivanovich as the elevator rose to the Royal Suite. He plopped Ivanovich onto the king bed and pulled a silk belt off a robe in the bathroom. He tied the belt into a noose and fastened it to the chandelier in the dining room. He tested to see if it would hold his weight. As Ivanovich groaned on the bed, Dmitri wrote a brief suicide note on the hotel stationary in Ivanovich's handwriting: "The guilt over my godson's death has been too great to bear." He lifted Ivanovich into a standing position on a chair, tightened the noose around his neck, and waited for the marine worm toxin to wear off.

Ivanovich opened his eyes to realize that he was standing on a chair held up by the tension of a noose around his neck. Dmitri sat across from him with his foot on the chair. Ivanovich put his hands around the noose but Dmitri teetered the chair forcing him to put his hands down.

"Dmitri! What the hell are you doing?"

Dmitri savored the moment. "I worshiped you," he said. "Mighty Sayan, the Lord of the Taiga. I revered you. But to you, I was nothing more than an attack dog that eats your scraps. What was it that you did when your godson pleaded with you '*Vitya, spasi menya!*' as the tiger ripped out his throat?"

Ivanovich's face turned white.

"*Nothing!*" Dmitri continued. "I realize now that I am more of a man than you ever were."

Ivanovich raised his hands to his neck, but Dmitri again teetered the chair.

"I'll make you rich beyond your wildest dreams—ten million, a hundred million . . ."

Dmitri did not take his foot off the chair. "What good is a fortune to a dead man?"

He stood up with his foot still on the chair and hit the red record button on his phone.

Ivanovich's last words were as panicked as his godson's. He ripped open the buttons on his shirt to reveal his tattoos. "*Vor v zakone* will avenge me," he threatened.

Dmitri rocked the chair. "Your treachery has been exposed. Your thieves-in-law have sanctioned your fate. Oh, and one last thing . . . Beria says he'll see you in hell."

Dmitri kicked the chair and recorded Ivanovich's gasps, kicks, and convulsions as his face turned purple and his eyes bulged out of his head. When he stopped moving, Dmitri turned, stopped the recording, and removed the Patek Philippe Sky Moon Tourbillon watch from Ivanovich's dead wrist.

* * * *

Senator Rich ordered the driver to take him directly to Dulles. He texted his pilot and told him to ready the plane for an immediate flight to Portland, Tennessee. When he arrived in Portland, a bulletproof limo with a police escort picked him up on the tarmac and drove him to his father's estate. He arrived shortly before noon. Julian Rich Sr. was in the living room watching the March for Family Values on television.

"Dad . . ."

Julian Rich Sr. motioned for him to sit down. Reverend Kane was in the middle of his keynote sermon to the multitude that had assembled for the March for Family Values. He was holding his Bible and reading from Second Peter 2:1–3:

But there were false prophets also among the people, even as there shall be false teachers among you, who privily shall bring in damnable heresies, even denying the Lord that bought them, and bring upon themselves swift destruction. And many shall follow their pernicious ways; by reason of whom the way of truth shall be evil spoken of.

"The second angel came to me." He paused to let his viewers guess his next words. "And warned me that the End Time is upon us."

"Dad, I need your help."

"I know all about it," Julian Rich Sr. replied. "I warned you. Stay away from the fucking Russians. And what did you do? You conducted real estate deals with Russian oligarchs behind my back. You compromised Reverend Kane by inviting an FSB operative to his March for Family Values. You conspired to replace the word of God with Russian spyware. Artificial intelligence? It's Russian intelligence! You sought to deceive those who trust us. You betrayed the Family. You sold your soul to the devil."

"I . . . I was being blackmailed. I had a fling with a Ukrainian whore on Ivanovich's yacht in the Keys. He filmed me, that bastard. I'm going to order him deported."

"You won't need to," his father said. "Ivanovich hung himself in his hotel room this morning."

"This morning? I was just with him a few hours ago." Senator Rich had the panicked realization that the Russians were cleaning up their mess. "I need more protection," he said feebly.

Julian Rich Sr. flipped through the news channels. They were airing clips of his son escaping from the Seasons restaurant, a staggering Ivanovich declining an interview, and the police cordoning off the Royal Suite at the Four Seasons Hotel as a potential crime scene. The news channels were scrambling to outdo themselves by interviewing former FBI directors, ethics lawyers, and federal prosecutors. A Fox News reporter flashed a presidential tweet on the screen that praised Senator Rich as a "good man caught up in a witch hunt." A second tweet a short time later claimed that the two had never actually met in private. Senator Rich's press secretary appeared on camera saying that the senator had left Washington to spend the holiday with his family.

"This will blow over," Julian assured his dad. "By tomorrow it will be old news. We can blame Kane. We'll say he put me up to this. We'll say he ensnared me in a Russian plot for his own ambition. I'll have my PR firm advise us on next steps. We'll say *he's* the false prophet."

"You'll do no such thing," Rich Sr. stated. "Kane is a man of God. He's a red-blooded American patriot. He's a member of the Family. He trusted you."

"Colluding with the Russians was *his* idea."

Rich Sr. looked into his son's lying eyes. "Kane told me about your meeting at the Oak Bar in Nashville."

Julian rubbed his temple. His artery was pounding. He looked at a photo on the fireplace mantel of Rich Sr. standing with the Reverends Billy Graham and Mathias Kane on the White House lawn. "Then I can repent," he offered. "I can be born again. I'm sure I can still retain my base. We'll blame the media. We'll say it's all fake news."

"There's only one next step you're going to take," Julian Rich Sr. said. "You're going to resign from the Senate."

"I . . . I can't resign! God chose me to be elected. I have a mandate from heaven."

"*I* chose you to be elected. The Family gave you your mandate. That mandate has now been revoked. I've already called the attorney general of the United States. He's going to hold off on a formal investigation, citing issues with your mental health."

"But I'm perfectly sane."

"Money laundering, campaign fraud, tax evasion, conspiracy against the United States, treason . . . do you want to hear more?" Rich Sr. shook his head. "You have your grandfather's genes."

Senator Rich looked like a boy who would never live up to his father's expectations. "Even if I resign," he said, "Mary Lou Jackson will come after me on state charges."

"No, she won't," his father said.

"Why not?"

"Because I've already offered her my endorsement."

CHAPTER 16

Cape May

The *Kalinka* sailed through the deep blue water of the Gulf Stream on her way from Tavernier to Nevis. Flying fish followed in her wake. Dmitri breathed easier once the yacht had crossed into international waters. He sat on the sun deck, opened a bottle of Ivanovich's Belver Bears Belvedere Vodka, and poured himself a hundred grams. He turned the hand on his Sky Moon watch ahead one hour to Nevis time. He messaged the encrypted video of Ivanovich's last gasp to Alexiy and waited.

Ivanovich's suicide had gone according to plan. Dmitri set the security cameras to replay a loop of Ivanovich leaving and entering his suite alone that had been taken three days earlier. He made sure that Ivanovich wore the same jeans, linen shirt, and Brioni loafers. Given his days on the stage, Dmitri had a sixth sense for drama. He suspected that Beria would exact his revenge to coincide with the March for Family Values. He had left the suicide note on the dining room table and pressed the "Do Not Disturb" button on the entry door. He had locked the door from the inside and escaped through the terrace by climbing down the outside of the building to a window he had opened in the suite below. Vlodya discovered Ivanovich's body at noon. By then, Dmitri was already aboard the *Kalinka*, entering international waters.

It was in no one's interest to investigate Ivanovich's death any further, he figured. By handing Tanya the *kompromat* video, he had made Senator Rich the primary suspect in any murder investigation. Given Rich's clout and the CIA's clandestine dealings with Ivanovich, an official ruling of suicide was convenient for everyone.

The satellite phone rang as the *Kalinka* was rounding the east coast of Cuba.

"Chameleon, you did well."

"Did you intercede on my behalf?" Dmitri asked.

"Beria's son can finally rest in peace, now that his murderer is dead. Beria respects those who honor the code. He wishes to induct you into the *vor v zakone* himself."

Dmitri shuddered. *That could be an offer to get a bullet in the back of the head*, he thought. But there was no point in refusing the deputy minister of the interior. He could only hope that Beria's gratitude was sincere.

"What shall I do with the *Kalinka*?" he asked Alexiy.

"Whatever you want. The yacht is yours."

"But I can't afford to maintain her."

"Have you checked your bank accounts?"

Dmitri quickly logged into his bank account in Nevis. His net worth had increased by several orders of magnitude. "How is that even possible?" he asked.

"In his 'revised' will, Ivanovich had named you as his sole beneficiary. The revisions were witnessed by two signatories and validated by a judge in Moscow. You are now the thirty-second richest man in Russia."

"But didn't Ivanovich have family? I thought he had a son and a daughter."

"Not anymore."

"I see." Dmitri admired the intricate carvings and astronomical functions on his dead man's watch. *Better on my wrist than buried*, he thought. "Ivanovich always reached higher than his grasp," Dmitri said. "He often boasted that he was among the top five richest men in Russia."

"He was. His estate needed to pay some outstanding debts when he died."

Dmitri looked out at the squall that was approaching from the east. "My gratitude is beyond words."

"Chameleon, listen carefully. The *vor v zakone* rewards loyalty. Beria owns you. His wishes are absolute. Do you understand?"

"Completely," Dmitri said and poured himself another hundred grams of vodka. *The thirty-second richest man in Russia*, he thought. *I still have a ways to go.*

* * * *

The Heavenly Hundred sculpture was unveiled on a muggy, dog-day morning next to the cascading fountain on Meridian Hill. The kinetic sculpture of a hundred doves ascending to heaven came to life with each breath of wind and shimmered in the rising sun. The setting was idyllic, except for the graffiti and vandalism that marred the historic park that overlooked the capital. The reporters at the unveiling outnumbered the attendees. They were eager to interview the mysterious Ukrainian sculptress about the rumors of a sexual assault that were spreading through Washington like wildfire. The Ukrainian embassy had downplayed the event so as not to provoke a political confrontation with the chair of the Senate Foreign Relations Committee. Senator Rich had been unavailable for comment since taking a leave of absence for health reasons.

Tanya stepped up to the rack of microphones wearing an embroidered Ukrainian shirt and an amber necklace. "I want to thank the American chapter of the International Association of Art for inviting me to display my sculpture in your nation's capital. I created this work to commemorate the fifth anniversary of the Revolution of Dignity.

"For over seventy years my country suffered under the totalitarianism of the Soviet Union, a system that robbed us of our values, our religion, and our dignity. Stalin starved millions to death during the Holodomor. Our best and our brightest—our teachers, our musicians, our poets—

were summarily executed during his reign of terror. Families were uprooted from their ancestral homes and shipped by cattle cars to Siberia. Those who spoke out against the terror were sent to the Gulag from where few ever returned.

"When the Soviet Union collapsed and we declared our independence, we thought that the evil had died. But the evil lived on. The elites simply changed their names. The communists became democrats. The party chieftains became oligarchs. We became not a democracy but a kleptocracy. In the winter of 2013 and 2014, I stood with my brothers and sisters on the Maidan to confront this evil through the Revolution of Dignity."

She pointed to the sculpture and the cameras followed. "Over a hundred of those who stood with me on the Maidan made the ultimate sacrifice. Government snipers gunned down men, women, and adolescents. Some were abducted and tortured to death. Others simply disappeared. Each dove ascending to heaven represents a hero who died defending our right to live in a country that respects the rights and dignity of every human being.

"We fought not just for ourselves—we fought for you. We fought for democracy and the rule of law. We continue to fight in the trenches in Donbas, in the waters of the Kerch Strait, and on the global airwaves. This same evil that has invaded my country now threatens yours. Don't be the good men who do nothing. Don't turn a blind eye to our plight, because when the last Ukrainian soldier dies, this evil will come for you."

After a few seconds of perfunctory applause, the reporters launched their questions:

"Ms. Bereza, is it true that you intend to press charges against Senator Rich regarding your allegation of rape?"

"Dr. Kane called you the whore of Babylon. What's your reaction?"

"The Russian stations are showing a video of you at the Jefferson Davis rally. Are you really a neo-Nazi as they claim?"

"When you say the same evil is threatening America, what evil are you referring to?"

Tanya chose to answer only the last question. "The rule of power rather than the rule of law."

The Ukrainian ambassador stepped up to the microphone. "I'm afraid that Ms. Bereza has another engagement, and she won't be able to take any more questions at this time." As Tanya stepped away from the podium, the ambassador's security detail kept the press at bay. The reporters raised their cameras over their heads and kept bombarding her with questions. Frustrated, they turned their cameras on the ambassador.

"Mr. Ambassador, Senator Rich's spokesman claims that Ms. Bereza is being funded by the Democrats to discredit him. Can you confirm or deny that allegation?"

Mark took the opportunity to whisk Tanya away to his car, which was parked by the Dante statue on Fifteenth Street. The beat-up El Camino greeted them like an old hound. Tanya sat down in the passenger seat, took off her embroidered Ukrainian shirt, and pulled on the "Got a Truck?" T-shirt that she snatched from Jeff Mustang at Tootsies.

Mark looked in the side mirror. The gaggle of reporters had spotted them and started running toward their car. He pulled out of his parking space and stepped on the accelerator. A few of the reporters chased them on foot before being weighed down by their cameras.

"Your speech was inspiring," he said.

Tanya put her face in her hands. She began to cry. "All they wanted to know is whether I was still a whore."

"They wanted to know whether you were going to press charges."

"Of course I am! *You're* the one who tried to convince me that America is a country with the rule of law."

"What I'm trying to say . . . what I'm trying to do is to prepare you for the legal battle ahead. Senator Rich will hire the best lawyers. Their strategy will be to accuse the victim. They'll make you out to be—"

"A whore?"

"They'll dig through your past to uncover anything they can use against you. They'll say you seduced him. They'll say it was consensual. They'll say it's your word against his. You declined to be medically examined after it happened. You could have gone to the police, and you didn't. You're now coming out three months after the incident without any concrete evidence."

"I have proof," she said.

"What kind of proof?"

"I have the video."

"Of Ivanovich and his godson?"

"I have the video of Rich raping me. Ivanovich filmed us as a *kompromat*. Would you care to view it?"

Mark blew through a red light and swerved to avoid the cross traffic. He slowed to just below the speed limit. "No, of course not. How did you get the video?"

"Dmitri gave it to me at the Seasons restaurant."

Mark realized that Dmitri had *allowed* him to approach Ivanovich and the senator. He had anticipated Mark's bravado. It was all a part of Dmitri's script.

"This assassin . . ."

"Dmitri," Tanya replied.

"He's been one move ahead of us this whole time."

"You're wrong," Tanya said. "We made him believe he was winning. It's Turchin's ploy."

Mark wondered what role he had really played in this match: knight or pawn? He knew in his heart that he had put his faith in himself and rescued her. He changed the conversation back to her art. "Your sculpture is very powerful. It captures the heroism more than any essay ever could. Your remarks about your sculpture and the Revolution of Dignity came from the heart."

"Do you think they heard me?"

"I don't know. We'll see. They recorded your speech, but what they actually televise will be up to the editors. Public radio may air it in its entirety. The other stations may play only selected sound bites. I wouldn't be surprised if the major networks invite pundits to debate the pros and cons of the points that you raised. In their attempts to appear unbiased, they'll distort the truth. Up is down, and down is up. People won't know what to believe."

"They'll *defend* the slaughter of innocents?"

"They'll say it's a matter of perspective. Those in power want to persuade us that there's no such thing as absolute truth. 'Truth is not truth,' they'll say. In the end the public doesn't know what to believe."

"Are people really that uninformed?"

"The problem," Mark replied, "is that people will create their own narrative based on their beliefs rather than facts. They believe that *my* truth is just as valid as *your* truth. They depend on preachers and pundits to explain events to them in simple terms that conform to their own worldview."

"What side do you take?" Tanya asked.

Mark thought for a moment before answering. "I don't take sides. I went into journalism to find the truth and report it as best I can. When I came to the realization that I couldn't serve people by preaching, I decided to serve them by opening their eyes to the world as it really is."

"As it really is or how you'd like it to be?"

"A little bit of both. Come, let me show you."

"Where are we going?"

"America's front yard."

* * * *

Mark and Tanya stood in the south chamber of the Lincoln Memorial like eighth graders on a class field trip and read the Gettysburg Address, which was inscribed on the wall. The final words of the address were "that these dead shall not have died in vain—that this nation, under God, shall have a new birth of freedom—and that government of the people, by the people, for the people, shall not perish from the earth."

"'That these dead shall not have died in vain.'" Tanya repeated the written words out loud. "I can see why your heroes gave their lives to preserve your United States. They gave their lives to defend 'a government of the people, by the people, for the people.'"

"We often take their sacrifice for granted," Mark said. "Hundreds of thousands of her sons and daughters died to defend this place we call America."

"America isn't just a place. It's a set of ideals that you aspire to live by."

"We shall be as a city upon a hill, the eyes of all people are upon us."

"A city upon a hill . . . that's a beautiful metaphor. Who said that?" Tanya asked.

"Jesus. It's from the parable of salt and light in His Sermon on the Mount. 'You are the light of the world. A city that is set on a hill cannot be hidden.' John Winthrop repeated the phrase in his sermon aboard the *Arbella*, as the Puritans were nearing the coast of New England."

"Do any of your politicians still uphold these ideals?"

"A few. I especially respected our late senator John McCain. His dying words to our country were: 'We are citizens of the world's greatest republic, a nation of ideals, not blood and soil.'"

"Wise words. Don't forsake your ideals. The world still looks to you for inspiration."

The neoclassical design of the Lincoln Memorial resembled the Parthenon. It seemed fitting that a memorial to the man who defended democracy should be modeled after its birthplace. From atop the stairs, the National Mall stretched as far as the eye could see. The Reflecting Pool mirrored the Washington Monument. The white dome of the Capitol Building shone in the distance. Thousands of visitors from near and far, many with tourist maps in hand, explored the monuments, memorials, and places where American history had been made. Lovers strolled hand in hand along the elm-lined promenades. Locals picnicked, played kickball, and threw Frisbees on the grass. Unlike the March for Family Values the week before, today the mall was alive with people of all colors celebrating diversity, rather than protesting against it.

Tanya held Mark's hand as they walked through Constitution Gardens toward the Vietnam Memorial. The black granite cut into the earth like an unhealed wound. Mark searched for two names among the over fifty-eight thousand that were etched into the Memorial Wall. Friends and relatives were rubbing the names of the fallen onto pieces of paper with graphite pencils.

"George told me about two of his friends who died in Vietnam. They were in the same high school class with him and my dad. My father rarely talked about the war, but George couldn't forget it."

"Did either of them fight in the war?" she asked.

"No. My father got a student deferment by going to divinity school."

"And George?"

"He got lucky. He had a high lottery number, and the war ended before he was called up. The closest they both came to violence was getting beat up by the police at the Democratic National Convention back in '68. He said the war touched everyone who grew up in that era, whether they were sent to Vietnam or not."

"Your father was a *hippie*?"

"He was a pacifist. You know, make love, not war. He found peace in Christ, and he and George went their separate ways. Many of the vinyl records at George's place actually belonged to my father."

Mark located the two names in the directory, touched their names on the wall, and said a silent prayer for each.

"One day," Tanya said, "we will honor our own heroes with a memorial like this. It will climb up Institutska Street, where many of them were killed, to a museum of the Revolution of Dignity atop a hill—a museum not just for ourselves, but for all who struggle to be free of tyranny." She put her hand to the wall and closed her eyes as if to absorb its enduring power.

Mark reflected again on the high price of freedom. He prayed that one day freedom would be attained through the power of words rather than the shedding of blood. "I want to show you our Charters of Freedom. In those documents our founders first inscribed the ideals that make us who we are. There's a sculpture garden along the way that I thought you might want to visit as well."

Before heading to the garden, they bought some hot dogs and Cokes at a food truck on Fourteenth Street. Tanya reached for the ketchup, but Mark insisted she try the yellow mustard instead. As they were enjoying their all-American meal, a peddler tried to sell them an overstock T-shirt from the March on Family Values that was made in China.

"I think it was the March *for* Family Values," Mark corrected him, but the man did not seem to have a command of English.

The National Sculpture Garden was a welcome oasis from the hustle and bustle of the mall. As they strolled through the six-acre garden, Tanya admired each of its seventeen sculptures. She was familiar with many of the sculptors and told Mark about their lives, their art, and her interpretation of their work.

"This mosaic by Chagall is called *Orpheus*. You see Orpheus charming animals with his lute, accompanied by the Three Graces, and the winged stallion Pegasus. My favorite scene is over here, in the left-hand corner. Do you see the people crossing water under a blazing sun? I see them as immigrants trying to reach America."

"Like Mirana," Mark said.

"Yes, just like Mirana."

The other sculpture that captured her imagination was *Puellae* by Magdalena Abakanowicz—thirty bronze figures standing rigidly posed among the trees.

"This work reminds me of the nameless silhouettes in the park in my home town of Ternopil. Her work depicts children who froze to death as they were being transported in cattle cars from Poland to Germany during the war. The figures in Ternopil depict the victims of sex trafficking. The oppressed need asylum. They need America to keep her doors open."

From the sculpture garden they crossed the street to the National Archives. The Declaration of Independence, Bill of Rights, and Constitution were displayed under glass in the perimeter of the Rotunda. The Faulkner murals that graced the curved walls depicted scenes from the presentation of the Declaration of Independence and the Constitution. Mark had searched for the origins of Americana in the far corners of the country, but it was all here, inscribed on several pages of parchment, in the heart of the nation's capital.

They pored over as much of the sacred texts as the eager crowds would allow. Mark explained the historical significance of each. "The Declaration of Independence, written in 1776, announced our break with Britain and the ideals on which our country was founded: 'that all men are created equal, that they are endowed by their Creator with certain unalienable Rights, that among these are Life, Liberty, and the pursuit of Happiness.' And here, the Bill of Rights protects freedom of speech, press, religion, and assembly." He was as excited showing her these documents as he was when his parents had first shown him the amazing life-size posters at the Circus World Museum. "Come and see the Constitution. 'We the people . . .'"

"Your founders acknowledge the Creator," Tanya said, "but these sacred words are the words of man."

Mark had never felt prouder to be an American. "We still have another hour or so before the museums close. Are there any other places in the mall that you'd like to see? We have some great dinosaurs in the Museum of Natural History. We have the Lunar Module at the National Air and Space Museum."

"There is one museum I would very much like to see," Tanya said.

They walked across the mall to the National Museum of the American Indian. The curvilinear limestone structure resembled rock formations carved by wind and water over thousands of years. In her trek through America, Tanya had seen what most Americans had forgotten: the pervasive heritage of the Native Americans. Rivers, mountains, cities, and states had Native American names. She had seen the land of the Osage, the Navajo, and the Sioux. She had seen their art. Their ghost beads had protected her. Their plight had reminded her of the injustices suffered by her own people. Like Ukraine, America belonged first and foremost to the people who had lived there for thousands of years, rather than the invaders who trace their lineage over a handful of generations.

One of the exhibits was entitled *Our Universes: Traditional Knowledge Shapes our World*. It focused on native cosmologies related to the creation and the order of the universe.

"I see that you're still wearing your ghost beads," Mark said.

"And yours?" she asked.

He regretted that he had taken them off once the danger was over. "They're in the glove compartment of the El Camino. Right next to your Ukrainian-language Bible."

"Your search for Americana needs to begin before the Declaration of Independence. It needs to begin here."

"The Native American saga? It's a tragic part of our history."

"You're justifiably proud to be Americans. But you also need humility. You are not the first nation on this land. Since the United States was founded, you have been, and you will always be, a nation of immigrants. You fled persecution and economic hardship in your home countries.

With your Declaration of Independence, your Bill of Rights, and your Constitution, your Founding Fathers created a country 'of the people' and 'for the people' rather than a country governed by the rule of power. You preached that all men are created equal, yet you held slaves. You stole and killed under the banner of Manifest Destiny. You forced indigenous peoples out of their ancestral lands and onto reservations."

"But we brought them the word of God. We saved their souls."

"Perhaps. But from what I experienced in the Black Hills, their spirits seem content to be with those of their ancestors rather than in the gates of heaven. You said that God speaks to different peoples in their own languages. Perhaps they listen to the spirits of the earth and speak the language of nature. Do you really think our Creator would turn away entire tribes of men, women, and children because they'd never heard the words of the Bible?"

* * * *

Tanya was waiting for Mark at the entrance to the Ukrainian embassy in Georgetown. At dawn on Saturday morning, the city was just beginning to stir.

The embassy was housed in a red brick building known as the Forrest-Marbury House. General Uriah Forrest had commissioned the house in 1788. His guests had included his former commander, George Washington, and a room at the embassy was still known as the George Washington Room. The ambassador had insisted that Tanya stay at the embassy as his guest while the State Department worked through her visa extension. She was scheduled to testify before the Senate Ethics Committee, and he thought it best to keep her out of the limelight until the hearings were over.

The El Camino pulled up to the entrance on M Street, and Tanya hopped in. She was as ebullient as a high school girl who sneaked out of her parents' house to rendezvous with her boyfriend.

"How did you manage to elude the ambassador?" Mark asked.

"He left for a meeting in New York. We have the whole weekend to ourselves. Where are we going?"

"Where everyone goes to escape the City of Magnificent Intentions on a hot summer weekend. We're heading to the Jersey Shore. We're going to hit the beach, walk the boardwalk, eat some crabs, and relax at a B and B."

She leaned over and gave him a kiss. "Relax? I don't think so."

Mark smiled and gunned the accelerator on the El Camino. *Don't be ordinary. Swallow the chaos.*

Their route took them around Chesapeake Bay and across the Delaware River into the Garden State. Delsea Drive wound through the forgotten towns, roadside fruit stands, and historic diners of rural New Jersey. As they neared the Jersey Shore, the wooded farmlands opened into expansive saltwater marshes. The smell of the ocean filled the air. Billboards for motels, restaurants, and boardwalk attractions welcomed visitors to the beach. The old slogan "Wildwoods: the Vacation Heart of South New Jersey" had been replaced with "Wildwood: as Wild as You Want to Be."

"You're going to love Wildwood," Mark said. "It's a blast from the past. It's real Americana."

"As real as Nashville?" she asked.

"Some say it's the birthplace of rock and roll. Bill Haley & His Comets performed 'Rock Around the Clock,' the first rock and roll record, there on Memorial Day weekend in 1954 at the HofBrau Hotel. There are over two hundred motels, most of them built during the doo-wop era of the 1950s and 1960s. Kind of like the Las Vegas architecture that we saw in the neon graveyard."

"You've restarted your blog?"

"Yes. I bought myself a new laptop and a new phone. Uriel helped me load some software that will alert me of any Russian hacks."

"So he'll have access to your computer?"

"Better the Flame of God than the devil."

"I think I'll go back to hand writing letters," she said.

They pulled into the parking lot of a surf shop, which was jammed with weekenders. Tanya tried on several bathing suits.

"How do you like this one?" she asked.

In her yellow polka-dot bikini, Tanya looked like she just stepped out of a 1950s Wildwood postcard.

"You look stunning. Maybe get a cover-up to match."

She completed her beach outfit with a throwaway pair of sunglasses, flip-flops, and a knitted white cover-up. Mark picked up a cooler, sunscreen, two blue-striped beach towels, and two "Life's a Beach" plastic tumblers. They stopped in a supermarket and filled the cooler with ice, a bottle of rosé wine, a couple of cherry lime La Croixs, and Jersey farm-stand peaches.

Tanya had swum with sharks in the Keys and sailed with killer whales in the Pacific Northwest, but the Wildwood beaches were unlike any she'd ever seen. Doo-wop motels lined Ocean Avenue. They were filled to capacity with families, students, and weekenders like themselves. Throngs of carefree beachgoers had already claimed their spots on the expansive beach. Teenage boys were throwing Frisbees and hopping over sunbathing girls who seemed oblivious to their antics. Fathers sucked in their stomachs, and mothers lifted their sunhats as Mark and Tanya hopscotched through the maze of beach towels and umbrellas. The smell of sunscreen and horseshoe crabs filled the air. Waves rolled in from the ocean, crested, crashed, and spilled onto the shore in churns of white surf.

Mark and Tanya claimed a rectangle of sand and spread out their beach towels.

She lay facedown on the towel and asked, "Can you put suntan lotion on me?"

He dabbed the Coppertone onto her shoulders, back, and thighs. He could feel her hamstrings tighten as he massaged the lotion into her supple white skin.

"Do you want me to do the front?" he asked.

"I can handle that myself," she laughed, "but let me repay the favor."

He lay down on the towel and felt the warmth of the sand on his face. The gentle strokes of her lotion-filled hands on his neck, back, and thighs made him stiffen. He sat up, opened the cooler to distract her attention, and poured the chilled rosé into the insulated beach tumblers. They each took a long sip.

"Can you hand me a peach?" she asked. She took a big bite of the juicy white peach.

"Delicious," she said and offered it to him.

The forbidden fruit, he thought. He took a bite.

As beautiful as she was on land, Tanya was a rusalka in the water. "The ocean's calling!" she said. "Let's ride the waves."

They ran into the surf like children and dove under the first big wave. She emerged with her wet, golden hair flowing over her shoulders. She looked like she did the first day he had laid eyes on her. Her eyes that were once wild and afraid were now playful and alluring.

Bathers of all ages were frolicking in the surf. The adults would passively let the waves bob them up and down, while the teenagers and children would body surf them to shore. Tanya and Mark waded out to chest-deep water and waited for the right size waves. When one rolled in, they would paddle atop the crest and let the force of the breaking wave carry them to shore. Tanya had an uncanny ability to feel the rhythm of the waves and time her launch. Mark was constantly missing the crest. She held him by the hand.

"Wait . . . wait . . . now!" she called out.

Mark kicked up his feet. He felt the wave lift him, crest beneath his chest, and break into churning foam as it hurtled him toward shore. He finished in knee-deep water, but the receding rip current upended him backward, and he toppled underwater. He felt the sand bottom with his hands and lifted his head to catch a breath just as another wave crashed over his head. Salt water gushed up his nose. When he emerged, Tanya was standing next to him laughing.

"What's so funny?" he asked. "I almost drowned!"

The force of the crashing waves had pulled his trunks halfway down his butt. He quickly pulled them up only to realize that the pockets were full of sand.

"You're going to keep at it, until you learn to body surf," she said. She grabbed him by the hand and waded back into the chest-deep water. They rode wave after wave after wave, until he was able to body surf as well as any of the kids that were shooting past him like flying fish. A single propeller plane flew overhead pulling a banner that read "Christine, will you marry me?"

At four o'clock, many of the beachgoers began to fold their umbrellas and shake out their beach towels so they could return to their doo-wop motel rooms, shower, and secure a table for dinner at one of the popular seafood restaurants. Mark and Tanya opted to first explore the boardwalk. She donned her white knit cover-up, and he pulled on a T-shirt.

The boardwalk was quintessential Americana. It stretched for thirty-eight blocks between the beach and the boroughs. They hopped on a sightseeing tram that rumbled past souvenir shops, arcades, and eateries painted in pastel pinks, blues, and greens. Iconic signs for Coca-Cola, Marlboro, and Dairy Queen made it seem like they had entered a time warp into the last century. They passed by the white Boardwalk Chapel, with a sign that quoted John 14:6: JESUS SAID TO HIM, "I AM THE WAY, AND THE TRUTH, AND THE LIFE." Countless eateries tempted the passerby with American delicacies, like New York pizza, Philly ballpark hot dogs, and fried Oreos. The smell of fresh french fries filled the air.

"Ready for some cheap thrills?" Mark asked.

They hopped off the tram by Mariner's Pier. The three amusement piers were jammed with a hundred rides, including a Ferris wheel, roller coasters, water parks, and fun houses. Many of the visitors, like Mark and Tanya, were still in their bathing suits. Tanya wanted to take a ride on the Giant Wheel. They climbed into an open gondola that elevated them fifteen stories above the boardwalk. From this vantage point she could see the whole of the barrier island. After several rotations, the Ferris wheel came to a halt with them near the apex.

"Do you see that lighthouse all the way south?" Mark asked. "That's Cape May. That's where we'll be staying tonight."

When their gondola reached the apex, Tanya leaned over and gave him a kiss on the lips. "How's that for a cheap thrill?"

Mark could taste the ocean on her lips. He felt as if they had risen to Rapture. If this was all there was to life, then it was enough. For this moment, on top of the world, there was no other place he would rather be.

When they descended to the pier, they hopped on the tram and rumbled back through the pleasure island of thrill rides, body-piercing parlors, old-time photo studios, and fudge and taffy shops. American flags waved in the sea breeze.

They got off by the blue WILDWOODS sign and walked back to the car holding hands.

"I'm a big fan of local color," Mark said. "Tonight we're having local fare. I made a reservation at the Crab House at Two Mile Landing. It's on our way to Cape May."

Mark stood watch outside the car as Tanya wriggled out of her bikini and pulled on a pair of cut-offs and a blouse. He slipped on a pair of shorts over his swimming trunks. The short drive south down Ocean Drive took them past Diamond Beach to the turnoff for Two Mile Landing. They passed the concrete shell of a beachfront condo development that was now home to hundreds of gulls. The sign of Rich Enterprises had blown off during Hurricane Sandy.

"That's the subject of the next article in my series," he said as he pointed to the abandoned ocean shore development. "It's one of the reasons I chose Cape May for our weekend getaway. My article went to press this morning. Public land gone private through corruption— it's another one of Senator Rich's fiascoes." By Sunday afternoon, the abandoned development would be teeming with reporters.

Mark had reserved a waterfront table to watch the sunset. The outdoor table was covered in brown paper and featured views of the water and the tidal marshes of Thorofare Island. The waitress gave them each a plastic bib. Mark ordered two 7 C's American pale ales and all-you-can-eat blue crabs that were locally caught and steamed. After their first beer, the waitress brought them a pail stuffed with a dozen crabs and sides of fries and corn on the cob.

"The crabs look delicious," Tanya said. "But how do I eat them?"

Tanya may have been an internationally acclaimed sculptress and fluent in four languages, but Mark was the expert on local fare. He was happy to demonstrate his knowledge.

"Watch me. First you crack off the legs like so. Then the claws." He turned the crab over. "Now you pull up this apron, and then crack off the shell. You scoop out the yucky green stuff and then you can either crack it in half or, better yet, cut these sections off with your knife to reveal the meat inside. Then you just pluck it out and eat it."

Tanya grabbed a steamed crab and after a few cracks and squirts was picking out the succulent meat within.

"Eating crabs is as much about the experience, as it is about the food," he said.

"We can eat as many as we want?" she asked.

"It's an American tradition. We have all-you-can-eat hot dogs, all-you-can-eat pancakes . . ."

"Everything in excess," Tanya said.

He thought of telling her the story of the first all-you-can-eat Buckaroo Buffet at the El Rancho Hotel in Vegas but decided to eat another crab instead.

The protected water between the barrier islands reflected the sky as the spectrum changed from yellow to red to violet. A cacophony emanated from the tidal marshes. Mark paid the check once the sun had set and only the afterglow remained.

The short drive down Ocean Drive over Bennett Creek and Skunk Sound took them into Cape May and its Victorian past. Mark had reserved a grand suite in a B and B in the historic heart of Cape May. Wooden stairs led to their corner bedroom, sitting room, and bath. The antique oak bed was covered with a fluffy white duvet. The Paris green wallpaper, high ceiling, and oval mirrors made it seem like they had stepped into the Victorian era. The sumptuous bathroom had a claw-foot tub, rain shower, and pedestal sink. Tanya opened the window in the bedroom to let in the ocean breeze. She lay down spread-eagle on the bed.

"You first," she said.

"Undress?" he asked.

"No," she laughed. "Shower and wash off the salt. After you're done, I'm going to take a long, hot bath."

Mark took his pajama bottoms out of his overnight bag and stepped into the bathroom. It took a few minutes for the water from the showerhead to run hot. He washed the salt off his body and scrubbed the sand out of his hair. The luxuriant body wash smelled of lemon and coconut. After brushing his teeth, he looked through the bottles of complimentary toiletries to see if there was anything he could use. He decided on the mint mouthwash and hand cream. He donned the terry cloth bathrobe, fastened the belt, and opened the bathroom door.

Tanya was sitting on the bed waiting her turn. She stood up and loosened the belt on his robe.

"That's better," she said. "Relax. Write your blog. I'll be awhile."

Mark turned off the lights except for a Tiffany lamp on the nightstand. Its multicolored stained glass provided just enough light to read. He heard her draw the water into the bath. He opened his laptop and tried to jot down notes about Wildwood. He imagined Tanya adding bath salts to the water, easing in, and soaking like Cleopatra. He thought of her combing her hands through her wet, lathered hair. His heart rate quickened as he thought of her running the sponge over her breasts, stomach, and thighs. He wondered if she was thinking of him as much as he was fantasizing about her. After what seemed like an hour, he heard the stopper open and the water swirl down the drain. He imagined her drying herself with the luxuriant Turkish towels and tying one around her hair as she put on her lipstick. He heard the whirr of the hair drier. When he looked down at the screen of his laptop, he realized that he hadn't written a single word. He thought of turning off the light, but he wanted to first lust with his eyes.

Tanya emerged from the bathroom wearing nothing at all. If he had been a sculptor, he couldn't imagine a more perfect body. His image of her as Aphrodite was seared in his retinas. He felt embarrassed at still being in his robe. He took it off and began to pull down his pajama pants.

"Wait," she said. "I'll do that."

He lay back on the bed and tensed, not knowing what to expect.

She turned off the light and sat on the side of the bed. The bedroom was bathed in moonlight. "Close your eyes," she said.

"But I want to look at you," he said.

"In time. First, I want you to relax. Desire begins in the imagination. I want you to dream. I can be whomever you want me to be."

"Anyone?" he asked.

"Yes," she purred "but you have to share your fantasy. Tell me about your first love."

Mark took a deep breath. He released memories that had been suppressed for a decade. "I imagine I'm eighteen, and I'm in my parents' car with the first girl that I had a crush on."

"At the drive-in theater," Tanya whispered.

Her recognition made him tense, but she put her finger on his lips before he could protest.

"We're in your parents' car," she said. "I've never done anything like this before. You're the first boy I've ever been with."

Behind the safety of his clenched eyelids, he broke his taboos. He imagined that he was with Mary at the Winnebago Drive-In in the Dells. She was wearing red-cherry lipstick, a tube top, and a dress that came up just above her knees. He put his hand on her knee, and she put her hand on his. As he braved to move his hand up her thigh, her legs first closed and then opened. She pulled down her tube top and put his other hand on her breast. He could hear her breathing. As he pulled down her panties, he could feel her wetness. She gave him a deep French kiss and put her head in his lap. At that moment he climaxed prematurely. He tried to open his eyes, but Tanya would not let him.

"Not yet," she said.

"I feel like a school boy."

Tanya gave him another open-mouth kiss. "You needed to free yourself of that fantasy," she said. "I want to hear another."

She put his hand on her thigh and waited.

He could feel her supple muscles tense and release under her soft skin. After a few minutes he began to inch his fingers up her thigh.

She could feel his heart accelerating. "I am a woman of infinite variety. Who do you want me to be?" she asked. "I can be Shulamite, the country girl, or I can be the Queen of Sheba . . ."

"I've often fantasized what it must have been like to be of *this* world— to lust without guilt, to make love without sin." His heart was pounding.

"I know whom you desire," she purred. "I can be your harlot. I can make you drunk with the wine of my immorality."

With that one biblical verse, she plunged him into the deep pit of desire. She was skilled in the art of love. For the next hour and a half, he imagined that he was among the wicked who were destined to suffer the wrath of God. He imagined that Slough Creek began to boil, that the Yellowstone caldera erupted, and they were incinerated in lava and ash. He succumbed to the pleasures of the flesh in ways he could not have imagined. In the end he lay sweaty, scratched, and exhausted, yet he never climaxed. Tanya lay next to him as spent as if she lay with the worst of sinners.

As she lay sleeping, his mother's words rang in his head: *"Then when lust has conceived, it gives birth to sin; and when sin is accomplished, it brings forth death."* But when he looked at Tanya in the moonlight, she was as alive and vibrant as the first day he had laid eyes on her. She was not a sinner. She was true to herself and purer than he. Perhaps his mother and the men she quoted from the Bible were wrong. Perhaps one did not have to choose between the world of man and the kingdom of God to be saved.

The cry of songbirds came moments before the dawn. The window that had let in the ocean breezes now let in the warmth of the sun as it rose over the ocean and saltwater marshes and beckoned all to enjoy a new day. The first rays of the sun illuminated Tanya's heavenly body.

She was the second angel, and not the harlot of Revelation. He followed the lines of her body from her cascading hair to her high cheekbones to her lips now without the gloss that had been spread over his body by a thousand kisses. He followed the line of her chin to her soft neck that plunged between her full, young breasts. The concave of her stomach rose to her hips and fell to her thighs, knees, and toes.

He leaned down and kissed the bottoms of her feet. She did not awaken. He kissed her toes and ankles and came up to her knees. Still she did not awaken. When she finally stirred, she pulled him in like an incoming tide. He was lost at sea. Her rocking felt like the rhythm of the waves, constant but unpredictable, giving, pulling, and giving again. He tasted the sea and saw her as she was that morning in April with the rivulets of seawater splashing down from her hair onto the red hood of his car. She was as innocent and as vulnerable as he remembered her. She welcomed him in, and it was he who gave of himself rather than she. He kissed her lips and lifted himself with his arms as he thrust into her with all his might. He watched her face as she rolled her eyes and arched her back as they came together in ecstasy.

He buried his face between her neck and breasts as he finally withdrew.

"You were wonderful," she said. "Who were you imagining making love to?"

"You," he said. "I was making love to you."

* * * *

The B and B breakfast featured freshly squeezed juices; locally picked berries; banana-pecan stuffed French toast; johnnycakes with poached eggs and roasted tomatoes; apple, sausage, cheddar quiche; freshly baked scones and Danish; Jersey Shore coffee; and assorted teas. Mark and Tanya feasted at a table for two that was set with a white tablecloth, silverware, and antique china. A few other late risers were finishing their coffee and tea in the Victorian-era parlor. A couple at an adjacent table had left a copy of the *Cape May County Herald*. The headlines on the front page read "Local Politicians Implicated in Diamond Beach Development."

Mark took the paper and scanned the story.

"The local Sunday paper has picked up on my second exposé that was published in the *Tribune* yesterday. Folks here have been trying to raze Rich's unfinished development on Diamond Beach. I didn't have this in my story, but the local paper claims that the zoning board was paid off by Rich and his partners."

"Ivanovich?" Tanya asked.

"Russian money laundered through banks in Cyprus and Estonia. A couple of the investors were going to be put on the Magnitsky list, so they pulled out before their assets were frozen."

"What's your next exposé about?" Tanya asked.

"About how Russian money was being funneled into American political campaigns on both sides of the aisle, Republican and Democrat. It's going to make a lot of people open their eyes. Several of the politicians are household names. The Russians' goal was to support candidates who were most likely to overturn the Magnitsky Act. Some of the money was funneled through businesses and organizations affiliated with Senator Rich, though he was only one of many."

"It's great investigative reporting," Tanya said. "I hope you win the Pulitzer Prize."

"I wouldn't have uncovered any of this without you. I'm definitely giving you credit."

"What will you write about me?"

"I'll write about how a courageous Ukrainian woman helped to expose a conspiracy to infiltrate and control our religious right."

"Whatever you write about me," she said, "make it real. No fake news. Show me as I am, both good and bad."

He began to protest, but she put her finger over his lips the way she had last night.

"Will you write about *us*?" she asked.

"Our story will remain our story. Perhaps one day I'll write a novel. That way I can make you as beautiful as you really are."

Tanya took a sip of her tea. "I want to go to church," she said. "The couple next to us was talking about a United Methodist church just a few blocks away."

Mark realized that he hadn't been to church since they had confronted Dr. Kane at the megachurch in Las Vegas.

"Yes, of course," he said. "Let's get dressed and go. It will do our souls some good."

The visitors' church was a simple white wooden church that had served the community of Cape May since the mid-1800s. During the tourist season the minister welcomed visitors who flocked to the oldest seashore resort in the United States. The church was filled with worshipers as diverse as the visitors who flocked to the Jersey Shore from small towns and big cities along the eastern seaboard. In her reading of the gospel and subsequent sermon, the minister focused on the Beatitudes in Matthew:

Blessed are the poor in spirit:
for theirs is the kingdom of heaven.
Blessed are they that mourn:

for they shall be comforted.
Blessed are the meek:
for they shall inherit the earth.
Blessed are they which do hunger and thirst for righteousness:
for they shall be filled . . .

As they were leaving the church after the service, Tanya said, "'Blessed are they which do hunger and thirst for righteousness.' Do you believe that Christ really said those words?"

"I do," Mark replied.

"But I thought you questioned the veracity of the Bible."

Mark pondered his response as they strolled through the historic district of Cape May toward Beach Avenue.

"I believe," he said, "that the words in the Bible are *inspired* by God. This was a debate that we had had countless times in divinity school. In the King James translation of the Bible, 2 Timothy 3:16, it is written 'All Scripture is given by inspiration of God, and is profitable for doctrine, for reproof, for correction, for instruction in righteousness.' That passage was incorrectly translated from Hebrew. The correct translation is: 'All *God-breathed* Scripture is profitable for doctrine, for reproof, for correction, for instruction in righteousness.' I take that to mean the words spoken by Christ are God-breathed Scripture, and I take them to be God's words. Men wrote other parts of the Bible. They are sacred texts that contain great wisdom and bring us closer to God. They may be true, or they may be allegorical. They are still words to live by."

"You seem ready to be born again."

Mark took her hand and brought it up to his face. Their hands still held the scent of rapture from the night before. "I love this world too much," he said.

"I believe you can love this world, experience all her beauty and wonders, and still go to heaven," Tanya replied.

"I'm not sure my parents would agree. In their eyes I fall far short of the glory of God."

"You're wrong. Your parents would be proud of you."

"For what?" he asked.

Tanya stopped walking and looked into his doubting eyes. "For seeking the truth in your own way, for protecting their way of life . . . for protecting me."

He kissed her hand. "I'm proud of you too."

"For exposing the collusion?"

"For much more than that . . . for believing in your power to change things for the better, for believing in me. Have you ever wondered if perhaps you were always part of God's plan? Maybe you really *are* the second angel."

Tanya laughed. "After last night you still think of me as an angel?"

They strolled down the Beach Avenue promenade, hand in hand, past Victorian cottages and mid-1900s seaside motels. The sun rose higher in the clear blue sky. Families and couples were carrying umbrellas, beach towels, and boogie boards to spend their Sunday on the beach.

"I'm glad you got to see historic Cape May," Mark said. "It's a real slice of Americana. People have been coming here to enjoy the sand and sea since the 1700s."

"It's beautiful, but for me, America is much more than just these places," Tanya said. "You've shown me wonders I couldn't imagine—the Blue Ridge Mountains, Death Valley, the San Juan Islands, Yellowstone . . . but they were here before we arrived, and they'll be here long after we're gone. And America isn't just the folklore, the colorful legends, the art, the music, and your city upon a hill. You've been searching for America in abandoned theme parks, junkyards, and haunted highways. For me, the beauty of America is in her people—dreamers from all parts of the world believing in your Constitution and believing in the freedom to pursue their own American Dream. America is great because of people like you and people like Mirana, Reya, the king of Beech Mountain, Professor Bo, Uriel, California George, Running Deer . . . that's who I'll remember when I think of America."

"So you'll be leaving," Mark said.

"America is beautiful, but I love my country as much as you love yours. I'll stay to testify at the hearings, but then I need to go home."

"Will I ever see you again?"

Tanya put her arms around him and gave him a loving kiss. "Of course," she said. "You've only shown me thirty of your fifty-two states. But first you need to visit me in Kyiv. I have an exhibit of my sculptures scheduled to be displayed in the Arsenal next April."

"I don't have a passport."

"Then get one. It's a big, beautiful world out there. There's so much to see and do. So much you can write about."

"I don't know, maybe."

"You *must* come," she insisted. "I'm already planning a very special sculpture for my exhibit. One that really captures the spirit of America."

"What is it?"

"Come and see." Tanya took off her shoes and ran across the warm sand toward the surf. When she reached the cool, wet sand she said: "Turn around and close your eyes. I'll tell you when I'm finished."

Mark turned around and faced the historic buildings of Cape May. He shut his eyes as instructed and thought about her vision of America: a Cuban-born graffiti artist, a queen in a garden of earthly delights, a surfer king of Beech Mountain, a Delta Blues journalism professor, a snake-handling hacker, a photographer of light in the darkness, an Osage leader chanting the "Song of Sorrow." He thought about his own blog on Americana, about Tanya's vision of America, and about how an extraordinary woman from a faraway land had opened his eyes to his own country. "No one can be a prophet in their own land," Jesus had said.

He took in a deep breath of the salt air. In his mind's eye he saw a curious boy dig up artifacts in a creek bed on his parents' farm, a hot-blooded teenager put his hand on his sweetheart's knee at the Winnebago Drive-In theater, a divinity student choose to pursue the mundane rather than the divine. He saw a young journalist in an El Camino enter a crossroad in the heart of the country with Jesus on his dashboard and a sweet woman at his side.

"You can turn around."

Tanya was kneeling in the wet sand with the blue Atlantic behind her. The surf was lapping at her feet. She had molded a sand sculpture with her bare hands. "What do you think?" she asked laughing.

"My El Camino."

"*Our* El Camino! When we come back from Kyiv, you're going to show me the rest of America. There is one place, though, that I want to return to."

"Where's that?" he asked.

"Yellowstone—the Eden on the Slough Creek trail where we first made love. That will forever be *our* piece of Americana."

ACKNOWLEDGEMENTS

Amerikana is a novel about America – her people, her places, and her ideals. It is a political thriller about how Russia could influence American politics by infiltrating the religious heart of our country. From a literary perspective, *Amerikana* is a novel about a journalist's search for what it truly means to be American. The idea of exploring the authentic in American life was inspired by my son Nicholas, who holds a doctorate in cultural tourism, and who is always opening my eyes to the historical markers, roadside attractions, "World Famous" restaurants, and folklore that give our communities their local color. The underlying themes of political corruption, the rule of law, and fake news were inspired by my son Alex, who after practicing law decided to study public policy and embark on a career in global conflict resolution. I am grateful to my wife, Christine, for her love and support over the three years that it took me to write this novel. I have dedicated *Amerikana* to my parents, Dmytro and Natalia, for showing me through their example the vital roles that immigrants have played in building our great country.

I am grateful to my friend and colleague, Professor John Serio, the Honorary Editor of the *Wallace Stevens Journal*, who was the first person to read and edit my novel. My effort to capture the local color of the places that the protagonists visit was inspired by our discussions about his dissertation on "The Poetics of Place in the Poetry of Wallace Stevens." Each chapter of *Amerikana* unfolds in a new location, and I hope that for my readers, these places become as much a part of the experience as the characters and the story. I want to thank my professional editor, Karen Brown, and the editorial team at Kirkus for their insightful edits. I also want to thank Alan Pranke for the cover design and interior layout. His artistic depiction of threatening shadows encroaching upon an iconic Evangelical church captures the essence of the novel.

I am grateful to my friends and colleagues who inspired key elements of the story and who helped bring the characters to life. Zorian Sperkacz first opened my eyes to the pervasive influence of Christian fundamentalism in American politics. Dr. Stevan Weine alerted me of the very real attempts by the Russian government to radicalize American youth. I am grateful to Livia Krzeminski who reviewed my manuscript with an author's eye. Annie Rasiak and Marilyn Hudson helped to make the story real by providing insights into Evangelical thinking and American culture. I am grateful to many others for assisting me with specific parts of the story: George Strutynsky, a photographer who actually had an exhibit on light in the darkness of an abandoned mine; Natalka Ivaschenko, who was a chess champion in Ukraine; Dr. Eugene Kovalsky, an avid sailor; and my global health colleague, Dr. Andrew Dykens, for sharing his childhood memories about the Spook Light. In my story Dmitri, the chameleon, is an assassin who has a penchant for poisons. I am grateful to my fellow medical toxicologists in the Toxikon Consortium for fostering my lifelong fascination with poisons.

Caught in the Current

(Langdon Street Press, 2013)

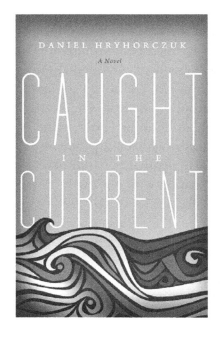

Caught in the Current takes the reader on a magical mystery tour of Eastern and Western Europe during the summer of 1970, a tumultuous period of free love, equal rights demonstrations, and Vietnam antiwar protests in America, but an equally revolutionary period in Alec's life. Raised in Chicago as Ukrainian, Alec is caught between identities--is he American or Ukrainian? His personal beliefs are pushed to the limit as he undertakes a risky mission to learn about political dissidents in Soviet-dominated Ukraine. Detained, interrogated, and finally deported from the Soviet Union, Alec seeks refuge in earthquake-ravaged Banja Luka where he begins to see the world from a different perspective. Questioning himself and his values, Alec finally finds his anchor in Stefi, his girlfriend from Chicago, who helps him discover his true identity.

Myth and Madness

(North Loop Books, 2016; Clio Publishing, 2018 [Ukrainian translation])

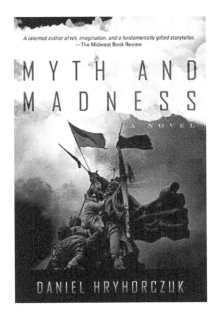

During Ukraine's Revolution of Dignity in the winter of 2013-14, Dr. Natalka Slovyanka, a beautiful young psychiatrist from Donbas, tries to cure her mysterious patient of his "philosophical intoxication." Raised by a Molfar, Telesyk is a storyteller who hears voices in the wind. His mind drifts between the immuring reality of the psikhushka and an imaginary world inhabited by witches, nymphs and dragons. He engages the other patients in a fairy tale of the quest for a horse that eats burning embers and drinks fire, a myth that parallels Ukraine's search for its identity. Both patient and therapist embark on their own quests—Telesyk, to free himself from the prison of his mind and Natalka, to escape the dark secrets of her past. Natalka struggles to free him of his delusions until she discovers that his world is real, and that dragons are deceivers who disguise themselves in the world of men. As different as East and West, they realize that they must unite to slay the family of dragons that are threatening their existence. *Myth and Madness* blends magical realism with historical events on the Maidan to tell the modern day fairy tale of a nation's quest for its identity.